Praise for Cheryl Grey Bostrom

A thoughtful, insightful story of second chances, forgiveness, and how to let go of the wounds of the past while still cherishing the years that shaped us. Beautifully told.

SUSAN MEISSNER, *USA Today* bestselling author of *Only the Beautiful*, on *What the River Keeps*

Cheryl Bostrom's gorgeous, lyrical writing invites readers on a poignant journey of exploration and restoration. With captivating characters and haunting prose, *What the River Keeps* unravels a destructive web of family secrets. Only the exposure of truth, the breaking down of dams, has the power to heal and restore life. A riveting story.

MELANIE DOBSON, award-winning author of *The Wings of Poppy Pendleton*

Cheryl Grey Bostrom has a writing voice unlike anyone else. When you see the world through the eyes of her stories, you see a beauty and depth few authors can achieve. *What the River Keeps* is a deliberate and thoughtful portrait of a young woman searching for truth and for herself, perfect for fans of authors such as Erin Bartels and Leif Enger.

KATIE POWNER, Christy Award–winning author of *When the Road Comes Around*

Rich, moving, and deep, *What the River Keeps* invites you into the stunning, shadowed woods and waters of the Pacific Northwest by an author who knows it well. This is a finely crafted, timeless novel that will be read and revered a hundred years from now.

    LAURA FRANTZ, Christy Award–winning author of *The Indigo Heiress*

Told through the beckoning beauty of the natural world, *What the River Keeps* paints a vivid portrait of two broken lives desperate for air and forgiveness. Cheryl Grey Bostrom treks their turbulent journey from entrapments of regret, fear, and self-doubt to freedom found in truth and grace. A rich and compelling story blending the patient strength of friendship and love—beautifully, lyrically written.

    CATHY GOHLKE, Christy Hall of Fame author of *This Promised Land*

Bostrom's novel reveals the full freedom we have in Christ while blanketing the story in the beauty of nature. This book is both heart-wrenching and heart-warming, with deep and true characters who will stay with you long after the last page.

    CHRISTINA SUZANN NELSON, Christy Award–winning author of *What Happens Next*, on *What the River Keeps*

Cheryl Bostrom's unique characters in *What the River Keeps* will take you on a fascinating journey through a beautiful location and deep into the human psyche. Don't miss this stirring, redemptive story that will make you take a long look at the strongholds in your own life.

    KAREN BARNETT, award-winning author of *When Stone Wings Fly*

Leaning on Air is a gem. . . . A poignant and authentic characterization of the power of love and of the land, and the capacity each has for restoration.

    BOOKTRIB

Leaning on Air . . . [is] a book about the power of unconditional love to heal us as people and partners, to plant the seed of faith in our hearts, and to resurrect hope within us. And it's as gorgeous as the landscape in which it is set.

    KELLY FLANAGAN, award-winning author of *The Unhiding of Elijah Campbell*

Bostrom's prose is propulsive and detailed. . . . A true page-turner all the way to the end. An engrossing tale of survival and redemption in the Pacific Northwest.

    KIRKUS REVIEWS on *Sugar Birds*

Suspenseful. Lyrical. Redemptive. Bostrom's voice reminds me of Delia Owens' *Where the Crawdads Sing* and Annie Dillard's *Pilgrim at Tinker Creek*.

    TARYN R. HUTCHISON, award-winning author of *Three Colors of Courage*, on *Sugar Birds*

What the River Keeps

WHAT THE RIVER KEEPS

CHERYL GREY BOSTROM

Tyndale House Publishers
Carol Stream, Illinois

Visit Cheryl Grey Bostrom online at cherylbostrom.com.

Tyndale and Tyndale's quill logo are registered trademarks of Tyndale House Ministries.

What the River Keeps

Copyright © 2025 by Cheryl Grey Bostrom. All rights reserved.

Cover photograph of mountains copyright © Elisabeth Ansley / Trevillion Images. All rights reserved.

Cover photograph of river copyright © Carolin Drößiger/Wirestock/Adobe Stock. All rights reserved.

Interior photograph of trees by river copyright © Dillon Kydd/Unsplash.com. All rights reserved.

Author photo by Amy Vande Voort, Copyright © 2021. All rights reserved.

Map copyright © Emma VandeVoort Nydam. All rights reserved.

Cover designed by Eva M. Winters

Edited by Sarah Mason Rische

Published in association with the literary agency of Books & Such Literary Management, 52 Mission Circle, Suite 122, PMB 170, Santa Rosa, CA 95409.

Unless otherwise indicated, all Scripture quotations are taken from the Holy Bible, *New Living Translation*, copyright © 1996, 2004, 2015 by Tyndale House Foundation. Used by permission of Tyndale House Publishers, Carol Stream, Illinois 60188. All rights reserved.

Scripture quotations marked NIV are taken from the Holy Bible, *New International Version*,® *NIV*.® Copyright © 1973, 1978, 1984, 2011 by Biblica, Inc.® Used by permission. All rights reserved worldwide.

What the River Keeps is a work of fiction. Where real people, events, establishments, organizations, or locales appear, they are used fictitiously. All other elements of the novel are drawn from the author's imagination.

For information about special discounts for bulk purchases, please contact Tyndale House Publishers at csresponse@tyndale.com, or call 1-855-277-9400.

Library of Congress Cataloging-in-Publication Data

A catalog record for this book is available from the Library of Congress.

ISBN 978-1-4964-8158-0

Printed in the United States of America

31	30	29	28	27	26	25
7	6	5	4	3	2	1

*For bighearted Beau,
with more love than
continents of longhorns*

Everything that is hidden will eventually be brought into the open, and every secret will be brought to light.
—MARK 4:22, NLT

For our struggle is not against flesh and blood . . .
—EPHESIANS 6:12, NIV

I will give you back what you lost . . .
—JOEL 2:25, NLT

And you will know the truth, and the truth will set you free.
—JOHN 8:32, NLT

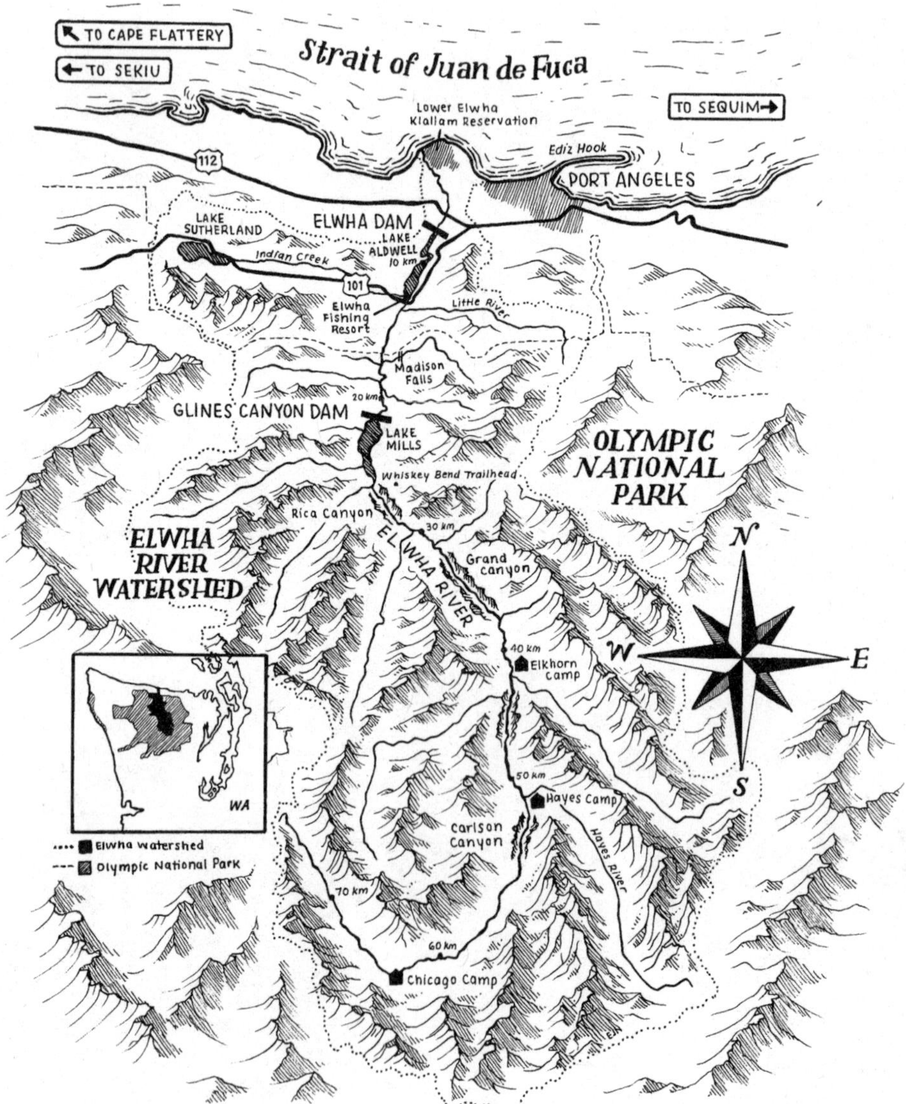

TO CAPE FLATTERY
TO SEKIU
Strait of Juan de Fuca
TO SEQUIM
Lower Elwha Klallam Reservation
Ediz Hook
PORT ANGELES
112
LAKE SUTHERLAND
ELWHA DAM
LAKE ALDWELL
10 km
Indian Creek
101
Elwha Fishing Resort
Little River
Madison Falls
20 km
GLINES CANYON DAM
LAKE MILLS
Whiskey Bend Trailhead
OLYMPIC NATIONAL PARK
Rica Canyon
30 km
ELWHA RIVER
ELWHA RIVER WATERSHED
Grand Canyon
N
W
E
S
40 km
Elkhorn Camp
50 km
Hayes Camp
Hayes River
Carlson Canyon
70 km
60 km
Chicago Camp
WA
Elwha watershed
Olympic National Park

PROLOGUE

HILDY

FISH

**ELWHA RIVER VALLEY, WASHINGTON STATE
1985**

On her tenth birthday, Hildy Nybo was casting a spinner under the Elwha River bridge when a streak of silver broke the surface. She whistled softly and pointed as the fish flicked its tail and disappeared into the pool's shaded depths.

Upstream, her father glanced, then threaded a night crawler onto a hook's shank. "I saw him." He raised his brow, aimed the hook toward the river like a dare.

The fingertips working Hildy's reel stalled, and she eyed the water, rapt. "They hush me, Daddy. Every fish I see."

"I noticed," he said. "Why, you think?"

She gazed into the water, considering. "It's like . . . like if I'm talking, I'll miss their music. It's like they're all little banjos, and somebody's strumming happiness on 'em."

She didn't notice her dad approach until he palmed her blonde head. Then he lifted his chin toward the forested foothills rimming their family's fishing resort, where the river entered sapphire Lake Aldwell. "Could be you're hearing his riffs."

"*Whose* riffs?"

"Your Banjo-Strummer. The Fish-Maker, Tree-Maker. Same, same." Dad shrugged, then thrust the tip of his rod toward his workshop like a band conductor's baton. "The music's in heartwood and burls for me, but maybe you'll hear him best through fish."

Hildy bobbed her line to her dad's words, sending concentric circles from the thin filament into the current. Would she? She'd love nothing more.

At bedtime, Hildy mentioned to her mother how she thought she met God through fish.

"That imagination of yours," Momma said. "If you know what's good for you, Hildy Rose, you won't mention *that* notion to a living soul." Violet fingered Hildy's braid with busy fingers, then crouched to eye level as she tucked the blankets. "Stick to facts, daughter. No more fiction. If you spread that God-fish story around the playground . . ."

Hildy read *hopeless* in the wag of her mother's head.

She bit her lip, squeezed her eyebrows together. "But Dad said—"

"He's pretending with you, as usual. Indulging that fantasy world of yours. You're ten now, Hildy. Old enough to give it up. You can't live on fairy tales."

Violet turned off the bedside lamp, but her voice found Hildy in the dark. "You don't want classmates to shun you again, do you, honey?"

No, I don't. Hildy curled toward the wall. Pulled the blankets to her chin.

"Let her be, Vi." Her dad's voice came from the hall. Seconds later, his hand touched Hildy's shoulder, and she rolled toward him. His lips pressed her forehead before he stroked it. "Those banjos you told me about today? Keep listening, sweetheart. That mind of yours is a gift."

She nodded. Closed her eyes against confusion.

A gift? She couldn't imagine how. Her ideas made kids avoid her and, worse, made Momma unhappy, something she didn't want, ever. If not for Momma . . . well, what would she do without her mother telling her which thoughts were right, or what to say or keep secret?

This time, Momma knew that if Hildy mentioned God and salmon in the same breath at school, *everyone* would call her Fish Girl—not just a few. Peers would mumble about her more than when she'd brought those trout gills for show-and-tell or wrote that report on the stabilizing properties of dorsal fins.

Even so, warmed by kindness at their next Sunday meeting, Hildy almost, *almost* told the group that Scripture verses reached her heart best when she thought about fish. The Lord on that cross? How better to illustrate than with iridescent salmon returning upstream, dying for their spawn? She raised her hand, nearly bursting with awe over her epiphany until, from across the circle, her mother caught her eye.

Violet pinched her lips and twitched a *no*. Instantly, a dark form Hildy sometimes saw around their house climbed her mother's back and draped her like a heavy shawl. Hildy dropped her raised hand to her lap and cowered, scarcely breathing until it slid away.

She had to tell Momma. Outside, while Dad went for the car and her sister talked to friends, Hildy whispered to her.

Her mother crouched nose to nose. "Stop, Hildy. I mean it. Make-believe is one thing when you're little, but at ten? *Ten?* One more wacked word to *anyone* about that creepy shadow and I'll..."

Dad pulled the car to the curb, so Momma didn't finish, but Hildy saw her eyes. On the ride home, the girl made two vows. First, she would never again mention this *thing* no one else could see. Second, she would keep the Fish-Maker to herself, too.

1

HILDY

UNDERGROUND

SEATTLE. 1999

Even if *not* wedged under her bed, Hildy wouldn't have answered the door. Instead, she shrank as the clapper struck the metal bell outside her basement apartment. One clang. Two. Loud enough to alert the too-close residents of her Seattle neighborhood that someone stood in the concrete well at the foot of her stairs, bugging her.

Again.

Mouselike, she peeked from beneath the bed rail, studying the window well closest to the door. Unlikely whoever was ringing would crouch and peer through the slatted blinds, but one never knew.

Something thunked the door. Footsteps scuffed a quick ascent. A truck rumbled and departed.

UPS. *Why* couldn't they deliver a package without ringing? They had to know she wouldn't answer. She never answered. Bad enough that she lived smack in the sightline of all those houses, their windows full of eyes. But a knock or ring at her door? A trespass.

She exhaled and wiggled deeper into the cramped space, where she extracted her latest stone from a row of rocks beneath her headboard. The diameter of a driveway cobble, it size-matched hundreds more crowding the space under her sofa and along her baseboards. Pebbles, both polished and rough, overflowed from galvanized buckets in three corners of her living space. Large or small, she'd assigned a number and a memory to each.

She smiled at this new one—river-smoothed chert, formed in the magic concoction of silica and sediment and time. When this stone had called to her from shore, she'd answered, tucked it in her pack, and returned to count coho smolt heading to sea.

Squirming free of the narrow slot, she opened her bedside notebook, confirmed the rock's black Sharpie ID on its underside, and jotted more details about the day she found it. Then she squinted into the empty stairwell through the door's wide-angle peephole and slid the chain from its hasp. Quickly she toed the package inside, relocked the deadbolt and chain, and opened a small box of bagged powders.

"Grit for the tumbler, Butterness."

Sun through a tilted blind lit the cage on the table, where a canary chirped, cocked his head, and flapped to a higher perch. Hildy bent to the thin metal bars and pursed him a squeaky kiss as an older diary entry came to her—recorded on a brilliant afternoon the previous May. She lingered over favorite details: how she'd spotted the bird from the aviary's newest batch of fledglings, his bright yellow body, black crown and wings indistinguishable from the plumage of a native willow goldfinch. How she'd told herself he was *marked to be free*, then had brought him home.

Butterness eyed her, dropped to his cage floor, and pecked stray seeds.

She carried the open box to her cluttered table and brushed aside a robin's nest to make room. A tag protruding from the nest prompted her, and she pulled a different notebook, found the nest's number, and read the corresponding entry: *Thurs. Oct 22, 1998. 3:00 p.m. Scattered clouds, no rain. Eating PBJ. Left UW Fisheries Bldg for car in south lot past crimson sunset maple. Tree 70 percent denuded after 30 MPH morning wind. Exposed American Robin's nest within reach.*

She'd loosened the empty nest from a crotch in that maple and brought it here, to the table, exactly five months after she'd chosen her bird. She nodded, reviewing other hours that day, recorded before and after this entry. She remembered them all.

In the bathroom, she snipped open a small packet from the UPS box and scooped a tablespoon of gray grit into a pitcher-sized rubber barrel filled with small stones—twenty-one of them—from her three-week stint on the Nisqually River. She spritzed the rocks and grit with water from a spray bottle, seated the pliable barrel and its lid in the rock tumbler's metal frame, checked the screws anchoring the polisher to a plywood base, and plugged it in.

The motor hummed. The platform vibrated. Butterness, his throat feathers fluffed and trembling, sang accompaniment. She swayed to his rolling trills and bursts, imbibing their froth like a dessert.

When he finished, she plucked a piece of romaine from the fridge, rinsed and clipped it to the cage. The canary sidled toward the leaf and nibbled ruffles into the edge. "My little singer," Hildy said, then squeaked him another chirpy kiss. She jotted bird and song and lettuce into her notebook before she spat on a dried sauce drip on the tiled floor and rubbed it with a stockinged toe. She closed the book and grinned. "I won't write *that*," she said.

She could, though, and no one would know. With the exception of her sister, Tess, for the last two of her five years in this apartment, she had allowed no one inside, choosing instead to live alone below the small, hip-roofed main floor where silver-haired Mrs. Kraft padded softly and, evenings, played her harp. Hildy poked rent checks through the slot in the old woman's door and made no requests. In return, Mrs. Kraft, equally reclusive, never rang Hildy's bell.

But what if she did ring it someday? Hildy appraised her living quarters as Mrs. Kraft might. The woman's eyes would first land on beautiful Butterness, piping from his cage. If the woman were to come on a day like today, she'd likely watch the bird bathe in a slant of sunlight wending through a narrow south well. She'd surely appreciate Hildy's handcrafted bed and desk, too—there, under the west window, where Hildy could see sky above the well's concrete lip whenever she looked up.

Aagh. Hands at her nape, Hildy wadded her waist-length hair, blonde and kinked from the braid she only unleashed here, in her sanctuary, where no one could see. *Who am I kidding?* If Mrs. Kraft responded to the shelves and ledges and walls and floor like Tess did, the old woman would probably evict her.

On Tess's recent spring visit from Sekiu, she'd eyed Hildy's rocks and garage sale finds, then plucked a spiral bound notebook from dozens on a long shelf. She frowned at an entry.

"Stop it, Tessie." Hildy snatched the book. Re-wedged it into the sequence of diaries.

Tess balled her fists. "Do you need to write *everything* down?"

Hildy covered her ears, her mood gone to iron. "You know I do. You can burn them when I die, but don't try to stop me."

"Fine, fine. But all this *stuff*?" Frustration rode Tess's sigh. "Where did my sweet, funny sister go? Why are you living like this?"

"Like what?"

"C'mon, Hildy. This amped-up hermit thing? All this junk? It's like a yard sale on steroids in here." She batted Hildy's undergrad honor cords and the UW master's hood hanging between a child's fishing pole and a kazoo. "No, it's a doggoned *museum*. Ever since your boyfriend . . ."

"He has nothing to do with it." She'd only begun adding physical specimens to her diaries' detailed accounts two Novembers ago—long months after she and Cole split. He was the least of her worries.

"Well, something or somebody does."

Hildy's anxiety surged. Tess's reaction clinched her growing resolve to refuse her sister's visits, too. If Tess—who had grown up with her, for heaven's sake—couldn't grasp why she needed her records and keepsakes to jog her memory and keep her reality accurate, how could anyone else?

Only at work could she leave all that behind. At hatcheries or on Pacific Northwest rivers, when the wonder of fish eclipsed everything dark.

⁂

Though Hildy had spotted the old man in his yard on her undergrad visits to the Pipers Creek watershed, on the day she actually met him, she was wading a tributary of the Seattle stream, clipping DNA samples from spawned-out salmon. He stood on the low bank, his bunchgrass hair sparse and white, his shotgun a seesaw plank over one arm. She blushed and straightened. Sputtered about the fish count, stream health.

He listened, nodding, then asked her name. Frowned at her reply. "Every time you come around, I swear you're my Dee," he said. "My girl come home, thirty years younger." He doddered ten feet up-trail toward his yard before he turned back to her. "Can I show you?"

From midstream, Hildy eyed the man and the neglected bungalow thirty feet past him. Considered the gun.

The man chuckled, tapped the weapon's carved stock. "Aw. Don't mind this old relic." He jerked his chin toward a run-down trailer park next door. "I bark at the dopers when they sneak over here, but I don't bite."

Relic. The gun or him?

He leaned the weapon against a tree. "Ain't loaded, anyway. No need. One look at these double barrels and them miscreants hightail it back to their tuna cans."

Creek water curled around her boots. She locked her knees, didn't move.

He looked at her curiously, then held a finger aloft. "Forgetting my manners." He tapped his chest and shuffled sideways. "Name's Everett. You wait. I'll get my pictures."

Wearing loneliness, she thought, then waded to shore, stood on tiptoes, and peeked over the cutbank after him. Inside a mullioned window, he pulled a book from a shelf.

Hildy climbed the slope as he carried the album to a pair of lawn chairs and wiped the seats with his sleeve. "You have time to set?" he asked.

She surprised herself by sitting.

He flipped pages and tapped snapshots of two girls, as blonde and slight as she was. "Both gone east," he said. "Both grandmothers now."

He pointed at the taller of the two teens straddling a log at a lake somewhere. "My Dee. In the Carolinas for thirty years now. Waynesville. Great Smokies—with a raft of kids and grandchildren. Says she'll drag me out there, if she has to."

The girl looked more like Hildy's sister than Tess ever could. "Think you'll go?"

Everett rocked, his gaze on the photo. "Feels good to be wanted like that. Never mattered to me before my Margaret passed last year. Dee's fixed up a little apartment for me in an old chicken coop. At first I balked—get it?"

At the pun, his grin framed cracked, brown teeth. Her mouth bent like a canoe.

"Looks right nice inside, though. Last month she sent me pictures and a ticket to Asheville."

Hildy scanned his treed, unkept yard, the weary home. She could practically hear the house crying to her. "You want a renter? Better than leaving it empty."

His eyes narrowed, traced her face. "Took me two dates to know my Margaret was the one. Got that good sort of feeling about you, too, Miss Hildy. The way you nurse that creek? Talk to those fish and birds? I'd be glad to know you're here, tending. You can send the checks to my Dee for putting up with me."

A month later, she took Everett to the airport, installed a driveway gate, and moved from her basement apartment on Seattle's Capitol Hill to the nine-hundred-square-foot bungalow. Despite her protests, Tess made the four-hour drive from Sekiu to see the place. "You're nuts," she said, after she assessed the run-down yard and dilapidated trailers next door. The house's stuffed, decrepit rooms.

But Hildy loved the place. Filtered by trees, east and south light streamed through age-worn wooden windows, brightening worn plank floors and shiplap ceilings like those in their cabins back home. Here she had an extra bedroom and storage and salmon in the creek swimming right past all those messy trailers to spawn in her backyard tributary. Her own paradise, at the end of the road.

Even before the trailer park sold, she cleaned flower beds. And while the developers bulldozed and smoothed the vacated land next door, she replaced the bungalow's rotted boards and painted everything, tapping into years of working alongside her dad at their family's lakefront fishing resort. Before builders framed the first house on that old trailer ground, she screened the property line with laurel and cedars, red osier dogwoods and firs, and she tended them with fertilizer and care. One at a time—and in the order of their acquisition—she placed her numbered stones around her gardens.

When she finished, the transformed cottage crouched hidden on a soft fescue lawn in a creek-side haven where, as before, she lived alone. *By necessity,* she reasoned. *No one* could begin to understand that keeping her records and memorizing her days demanded her full concentration—and every square inch on her walls.

For more than ten years she gathered deliveries from the coded box beside the gate only she passed through. Filled her diaries with detailed accounts of her activities and her rooms with mementos linked to those entries. As she worked the gamut of regional rivers and taught about them, she interacted with her colleagues and students and family only when required, living only for aging Butterness—and for fish and their watery world.

Until, on February 23, 2010, her ringtone chimed from one of the few numbers she chose to answer.

2

HILDY

PHONE

SEATTLE, 2010

Hildy's phone sounded as she riffled through mail at her locked gate. She turned away from the feeble sun, read the screen, and answered Everett's daughter on the second ring.

"How y'all doin', Miss Hildy?" Seattle-born Dee's voice, turned Carolina Southern by her years away.

"Hey, Dee." Hildy tucked the mail under her arm, curious. *Another rent increase?*

"Mournful sorry news for you, darlin'. You got a wall to lean on?"

"I'm at the mailbox. Here. I'll sit." Hildy lowered herself to a porch step, the phone pressed to her ear. "What kind of sorry?"

"We lost our daddy. Found him in my garden stone-cold dead, a week ago Monday, his hand fulla curly kale."

Hildy clicked to speaker, set the phone on the stair. Leaned her head to her hands. "I'm so sorry, Dee. So sorry."

"Yeah, well, we're all countin' our blessins here, you bein' among 'em. If not for you, he'd a never moved here. A ten-year bonus a lovin' him up—you gave us that, Miss Hildy."

Hildy's eyes roved her secluded winter grounds—the frosty lawn, the skeletal, dormant alders and maples, the dark, heavy-boughed conifers along the soft-spoken creek that lulled her to sleep at night. "More than a fair trade, Dee. This place . . ."

"Yeah, darlin'. A-a-about that." Dee's stammer surprised her. "After the funeral, we held a little business meetin' with the powers that be, and majority rules, ya know. And the majority a Daddy's heirs want to sell your place before this droopy housing market crashes like an old drunk. That little acreage you're sittin' on is development property, ya know?"

Oh, Hildy knew—all too well. The property's value had outrun her qualifications to buy the home years prior. "I see." Nervously, her deft fingers removed bobby pins and uncoiled her braid. "How long until you want me out?" She pulled the band and stripped her hair's weave.

"No hurry, darlin'. We'd like to list it come May, after the market wakes up from its winter snooze out there—if it rouses at all this year."

An hour after Dee's call, Hildy plucked an empty soda can from the creek and reentered the house. Where would she ever find a place like this in Seattle's sprawl? If she wanted to maintain her positions as both adjunct professor *and* US Geological Survey biologist, she'd have to live within commuting distance of the University of Washington's School of Aquatic and Fishery Sciences *and* her USGS office at the Western Fisheries Research Center. But how? A rental as private as this one between Lake Washington and the U? Rare as gold in a gutter.

"We'll be sardines again, Butterness. Trapped in a little box." Pensive, she studied the bird. "I guess you already are. Here, baby." She secured the doors, closed the window blinds against collisions with glass, and opened the bird's cage. The canary lit at the opening, cheeped, and flew a swaggy path to a floor lamp finial, a window ledge, a bucket of rocks. While Hildy stood at the counter, the bird hopped flat-footed on the table and pecked at spilled millet, a hummingbird's nest, fir cones, feathers, and pebbles. Fluttering into the forest of hangings hooked and nailed and pinned to Hildy's walls, he perched on an antique adze near the ceiling and sang.

Later, she refilled his seed, freshened his water. He watched her from the cuff of a logger's caulk boot hanging from a peg, and when she set a slice of apple on his cage floor, he flitted to it through his open door. "We'll figure this out, little bird." She was latching him safely inside when her phone rang again. Her sister, Tess.

"Forty-five degrees, Hildy. Pouring rain. Violet's in a ratty nightgown, on her knees. Paddling that old skiff with one oar as if it were a kayak."

"You're at the resort now?" Hildy struggled to hear past wind on the other end. *Third time this month.*

"I'm on her porch. Looking right at her. I yelled, but she's ignoring me. What am I supposed to do, lasso her?"

Hildy sighed. Their confused, bedraggled mother, tooling around on the Lake Aldwell reservoir as if it were summer. "Whistle to her. Tell her she's cold and wet. Say you have hot chocolate. She'll come in."

"We can't leave her alone anymore, Hildy. I called Dave Cloud."

"You called Dave Cloud." A slow burn spread to Hildy's ears.

"You know, at the Lower Elwha Tribe. He said—"

"I know Dave Cloud. Since *when* is my job your business?"

"A fish whiz like you? You could work there in a heartbeat. Besides, I need you. Mom needs you."

"I can't just quit my j—"

"Look, sister. Unlike me, you're single. You're childless. You rent. Dave said that the NOAA, USGS, and half a dozen other agencies are sending teams up the river to count those fish and document habitat before the wrecking ball smashes the first dam next year."

"They'll use excavators, Tess. Hydraulic hammers."

"Whatever. He's hiring. Don't you want a front-row seat when those dams come down? When those salmon start snooping around their old spawning grounds? One more summer before our lake's drained and gone. Don't you want to be here?"

Be *there*? On the *Elwha*? At the jump in her chest, Hildy pressed two fingers to her carotid artery. "Where's Mom now?"

"Lying over the stern. Paddling with her hands."

"Tessie. Get her inside before she goes hypothermic."

"I can't keep doing this, Hildy. Driving here, not knowing what I'll find. Not like I can just drop everything and skip in from Sekiu. You know my man. Soon as March tenth hits, Bingo'll be chasing blackmouths and I'll be up to my elbows in winter Chinooks and sloshed fishermen. We have eleven groups booked in the next six weeks, sister of mine. *Eleven.* I can't ask June and Otis to look after Mom every second."

Hildy sighed. *Steamroller Tess.* Arguing was pointless. "I know. See if she'll come home with you until I can get there." *In a straitjacket, maybe.*

"But I can't—"

"Just until Friday. Three days. If I leave work early, I should get to the resort by one thirty. Is Otis working the store this weekend?"

"Yeah, but—"

"Meet me Friday. One thirty, at the store."

"If you—"

"Friday." Hildy donned her parka and slipped the phone into a pocket. Last time, Tess had railed on for twenty minutes before she came up for air. Hildy buckled her waist pack and stepped outside, where she scuffed a muddy stripe along her rutted driveway, then bent to pluck a piece of granite—sharp, black-specked. A hemlock cone drew her, too, small and waterlogged. She added her finds to two nut-size stones already inside her pack: jasper, agate. Both rough.

Dusk was settling when Hildy hung her coat on a hook, emptied her pack, and carefully arranged the new stones like boats on wavy burls in the walnut desk her dad had crafted and buffed. Four more stones, in addition to yesterday's quartz and Monday's muddy carnelian. She had rinsed the red rock clean until its color soothed her, looked like candy.

With a paper towel, she squeezed moisture from the tiny cone, then sat at her table and held it to the bars of her canary's cage. "For our little Scampers, Butterness. Think she'll like it?" The bird raised feathers at his crown and hopped to a higher perch. She swept birdseed the canary had strewn on the table into her palm, opened a kitchen cupboard, and settled the seed and cone in a pile beside a fluffy nest of grasses, moss, and shredded napkins. At a gap in the cupboard's rear panel, mouse whiskers twitched toward hairless rodent pups.

For the third time that day, her buzzing phone lit. Annoyed, Hildy closed the cupboard and checked the screen. *Dave Cloud. Calling me?* She liked the man. Truly she did. And she'd enjoyed shadowing the biologist during her internship on the Elwha River early in her training. But for him to reach out to her now? What had Tess told him? She considered voicemail, but her thumb refused.

"Nybo here."

"Hildy, Hildy. Too long, old friend."

The voice she remembered warmed her. "Hey, Dave."

"We've got teams arriving every week now, from every agency you can name. Your old backyard's about to host the most spectacular renewal in US river history. Ever think of coming back for it?"

"Not really." A relative term, *really*. Of course she'd thought about it. She'd *drooled* over the prospect of working that river again. But how could she risk it?

"Yeah, I imagine you're pretty dug-in over there. I heard they fast-tracked you into a lead spot at the research center after you published in *Science*. Pretty impressive rise to stardom. You're what? Thirty-five?"

"Thirty-four." Anybody but Dave and she'd have fled the accolades, hung up. She hadn't achieved to be flattered or recognized. "I love the work, Dave. The fish. You've known that forever."

"And you love our Olympic National Park and our trapped Elwha. I can still hear you upriver, midstream in your waders, talking about those stalled plans to set the river free. And, if I dare say so, I recall you hate the city."

He remembered things. Remembered her. He couldn't see her smile. "Right on all counts, Dave."

"So maybe you'll consider coming home? I'm looking for a seasoned biologist and you're my first choice, Hildy, hands down. A staff position, not a grant temp, so you can see this thing all the way through. You'd be lead project biologist for the Lower Elwha Klallam Tribe. For the next year and a half, we'll gather final baseline data for the entire river's ecosystem—while it's still being strangled by those dams. Got some great teams coming in to track fish and river health through the dismantling. Have you crossed paths with Bryce Dixon from the NOAA? Liz Nocero at the UW?"

"I've worked with Liz. Met Bryce at the World Fisheries Congress." *Where he wouldn't leave me alone.*

"Top-drawer scientists, both of them. Dennis Hopson will be here from Fish and Wildlife, too."

She liked Dennis. Kind, smart. Quiet.

Dave paused.

Hildy waited.

"You still with me?" he said.

"I'm listening."

"Good. No, *great*. If you stick around after the reservoirs go, I'll have you coordinate the revegetation work. You can help oversee multiagency teams working on fish recovery, too. Create a model for other rivers slated for parole. I can already see more of your fabulous papers spreading the news."

"I don't get it, Dave. You've waited most of your career for this—and those are your jobs. Now you're bowing out?"

"I want to share them with you, Hildy. *Share* them." She heard him tap his keyboard, multitasking, as usual. "I'll be sixty-seven in October. I've bumped my retirement until the first dam's gone, but Linda's not doing well. We'd like to travel a little while she still can. See the grandkids in New Mexico."

She'd heard. *Parkinson's*. "Sorry about your wife." He was pouring water now. Fixing coffee, probably.

"Yeah." He cleared his throat.

"The job sounds like a plum, Dave, but—"

"Just think about it, will you? As long as you tell me either way by the first of March."

"Okay. Get yourself a Plan B, though. I'm not guaranteeing anything."

"I'll email you the official job specs. And if you happen to be in town, stop by the reservation. I've got a raft of data in my office that'll get your blood pumping. Our river's going to be beautiful, Hildy. Magnificent. Soon as they pull her tourniquets . . ."

She listened soberly. Magnificent or not, she'd have to return to the peninsula . . . *live* there again . . . to see it.

"I'll be in touch." Hildy croaked a goodbye through her tightening throat, slipped outside, and sat shoeless on her icy stoop until stars emerged, and her pulse slowed.

Dave's call was timely, at any rate. She pictured herself and Butterness kicked from Everett's bungalow to a curb, with no prospects for a decent permanent address. Another urban apartment would strangle her.

She knew she was qualified for the position he offered, despite the rumblings about her. Ten years post master's, she'd leapfrogged older, more credentialed candidates for her Seattle teaching and research positions—skipping steps, some thought. Not paying her dues. Colleagues would likely contest her assignment to a pivotal role in the largest river restoration in US history. A river that ran past the Elwha Fishing Resort and spilled into Lake Aldwell at Cabin 7, where Violet had delivered Hildy into the midwife's waiting hands. A river she'd spent her childhood exploring.

If she took the job, she'd have to return to her heartbreak's ground zero for more than a visit. To the birthplace of her great sadness—and her fears, where shadows ran amok. To Port Angeles, and maybe to stay at the resort itself, where she'd lost her father and almost lost her mind.

If not for college and her cramped apartment—well, despite their constraints, those locations and a decade here in Everett's bungalow had saved her. Nowhere in Seattle had her belongings disappeared.

Her eyes swept the yard. Out here, and inside the front door behind her, all her keepsakes remained exactly where she put them. The bungalow's rooms and her diaries held records of every single day since her freshman year at the UW, with nothing forgotten, nothing lost.

Only after leaving the Olympic Peninsula had she begun to compensate for her forgetfulness in earnest, to believe that maybe, just maybe, her mind wouldn't always *betray* her, as Violet had put it, with amnesia or conjured memories. Hard-won, that progress. A return to the Elwha could risk it all.

If she did go home, would her mental faculties cooperate? Could she keep track of things?

Maybe, if she hedged her bets and brought *everything* from this place to her new one. Once there, she'd have to maintain and guard her inventory—each imported piece a bulwark against those earlier losses. Losses that plagued her still.

Chill penetrated her socks when she left the porch. Mid-lawn, she buffed her upper arms against the cold and studied her sleeping yard. Moonlight washed the meandering path, the curved flowerbeds and rectangular garden—and the softball-size rocks rimming them like a necklace. She assessed them with satisfaction. *So many rocks.*

Too many to take. Best to leave these outdoor stones, gathered from every river she'd visited since her basement studio days. Remarkable rocks, exactly where she'd situated them, with every stone accounted for and mossed soft with the green beauty she considered proof of their permanence.

3

HILDY

MEETING

OLYMPIC PENINSULA, 2010

On an outside deck, Hildy braced against February wind as the MV *Spokane* pulled away from the Edmonds ferry terminal and crossed Puget Sound's heavy chop. Through a brief strip of open sky, rocky peaks bunched over the Olympic Peninsula like a fleet, their snowy crags like sun-dazzled sails above a sea of low-running clouds. Her memory ran the steep terrain of the peninsula's dense forests and mountainous, untamed interior, its weather unpredictable and dark tempered. *This place will swallow me,* she thought. *Like it did Dad.*

Shivering, she tracked the ship's arc toward the Kingston landing. Then she retreated inside for coffee, returned to her car on the dank bottom deck, and slouched in her driver's seat until the dock ramp clanked to the deck. When the ship spit her to shore, she sped toward the sunny Dungeness Valley, where she stopped in the little town of Sequim for a sandwich—and to gather her thoughts and resolve.

The bright respite was brief. Another seventeen miles west and she passed through the larger town of Port Angeles, where the sky had clotted to pewter. Seven miles more, and charcoal clouds roiled.

She fought to breathe.

At the Lake Aldwell overlook, she climbed from her SUV, raised arms into the wind, and filled and refilled her lungs until she calmed. She squinted into the churning sky, then scanned the steely water below. Peekaboo views of waterfront cabins told her the rustic campground and square-dance hall, the dinghies and gas pumps and store still hid in the treed foothills along the shore, their firs gone somber in the winter murk.

In one of those buildings was her mother, monitored by Tess, she hoped. June would be working the noon crowd at the store's lunch counter, flipping burgers—if anyone showed on this bone-chilling day. It had once been Violet's job, before dementia had crept like a weasel into her brain, stealing eggs of memory, reason, and the wherewithal to tie her shoes.

Rain spattered her. Hildy exhaled, swiped away drops, and returned to her Yukon, where she braced for her descent into the valley. Her fingers itched to write, to protect her mind with records of her every move. Moments later, she dug in her bag for a notebook and pen.

12:55 p.m. Pulled into Elwha overlook in a squall. Drove 45 mph downhill to the curve. Stopped beside Tess's Suburban at store. Saw Otis leaning on red truck at gas pumps. Left car running, heater on high for Butterness.

"Welcome home, missy. They're waitin' for ya." Otis pushed himself from the wood-slatted sides of a pickup's bed and arched his back.

"Hey, Otis." Only eight months since she'd seen him, but his pain had clearly grown worse. The handyman pulled a gas nozzle from the truck and flipped the rusty pump's lever. He took cash from the driver and waved her inside with a gnarled hand.

She paused at the door. "You joining us?" Violet's best move, hiring him and June after Hildy's dad disappeared. Back then he'd been an immediate ground peg for the flapping tent of her. Not ten years older than her mother, but an instant grandfather.

"Nah. You gals talk. I'll tune an ear from the cooler."

She returned the man's smile and slipped into the store. The door's jangle alerted Tess, who lumbered toward her between the shelves, bumping toilet paper and Doritos. The corners of her sister's mouth drooped into jowls as she wrapped Hildy in heavy arms and squeezed. "She's bad, Hildy. Real bad."

Hildy scanned the little market and lunch counter, then peered past a folded accordion door to private quarters in the back of the store. Otis and June's space now. "Where is she?"

"Taking a nap in her cabin. I made sure she was asleep before I left her, but no telling how long she'll stay down. Wakes up and roams every couple of hours. All day, all night long." Tess rubbed her eyes. "I swear, I'm newborn-baby tired. We'd better talk before she gets up—and before I crash for a snooze myself."

Hildy spun a standing rack of fishing lures. No question her sister was weary. "Can't the doctor give her something?"

Tess wagged her head. "Not that easy. She—"

"Thought I heard you, missy!"

Hildy brightened as a short, weathered woman emerged from the kitchen drying her hands.

June rounded the lunch counter, tossed the towel over a plaid-cottoned shoulder, and cupped Hildy's cheeks. "Smooth trip over?"

Hildy nodded and leaned into her. *My Junie.* The sight of the woman roused images she'd tried to forget: of returning home from a school trip at age sixteen not to her mother or father, but to June from their tiny church. To Junie, who had taken Hildy's face in her hands then, too, only that time to tell her that her beloved dad was missing. And while bereft Violet took to her bed and others roamed the backcountry searching, she had fed Hildy food more substantial than grief.

Straight-armed, June held Hildy's shoulders, absorbing her as if she were sunshine. "I've missed you, sweets. Near killed me to rush away last summer, but leave it to our independent Lisa to have that baby on July fourth. If you hadn't helped Otis . . ." She gave Hildy's biceps a quick squeeze. "With your momma under the weather and all those campers, he couldn't have managed."

"Happy to, Junie. You know that."

The towel fell from June's shoulder. "Guessin' it's hard for you to come back so soon, girl, but it's good you're here while we sort this out." Her voice was gruff—a remnant of her smoking days. "We need someone around here who knows fish, seein's how your momma's tryin' to be one herself. She goes finnin' on her belly the second we're not lookin'. I think she's forgettin' what oars are." She glanced at the back door. "Can you stay?"

Hildy shrugged and picked up the cloth.

"Why don't you girls move her into the store with us? Our kids're only here once a year, 'n their sprouts prefer them sleepin' bags and cabins more'n their granny's fussy sheets and clean floors and front door janglin' mornin' to night."

Hildy shook her head. "No, Junie. No."

"Aw, Vi can have my sewin' room upstairs. We'll leave our bedroom door open. If she comes paddin' down in the night, we'll hear her, us sleepin' like feathers nowadays. I can keep her busy round here."

Tess's lips rattled an exhale. "She's a slippery one and you know it, June. You've got enough to do without chasing her. Besides, all that rowing? She's strong as a moose. What'll you do the first time she bucks you?"

Hildy fingered a pack of elk hair caddis. Once fishermen discovered the brand, her dad had ordered the flies in bulk. "She's right, June. Mom'd be a full-time job for both you and Otis." *Already is.*

Hildy's next words roped her, and the concession in them crushed her voice to a quiet the others craned to hear. "I can watch her for now. I took some vacation days. Staying until we figure something out for her, find someone. Assemble a team or something."

Tess plucked a Nutty Buddy from the freezer, peeled the wrapper, and bit. Peanut crumbles bopped from pendulous breasts to a thick roll at her midsection. "The cost of help . . . How, Hildy? She's only sixty. No Medicare for years yet, and she burned through Dad's life insurance years ago."

"Otis talked her into a long-term care policy." At the sound of his name, the man looked up from a crate of bottled water, his arthritis-wracked spine a crooked *S*. Hildy smiled at him gratefully. "Mom's concussion history? Those headaches? He thought it wise."

"She *qualified*?"

Hildy nodded. "Yeah, four years ago. Passed the exam without a hitch back then."

"No way she's stayed current on *those* premiums." Tess caught a drip with her tongue. "Even early in this mess, she could hardly buy groceries. Her desk is a boar's nest. I dug through it, but never saw a single bill for a policy like that."

Hildy looked away. "Mom named me as a contact, so the company wrote me before it lapsed. I've covered the payment the last two years."

Tess lunged into a one-armed hug, the cone suspended. Hildy didn't say that the money was less for their mother than for herself. The prospect of *ever* caring for Violet sank her. Made her quiver.

And now here she was.

Otis stowed lager in the cooler. "Good thing you did, Hildy girl. Your momma's losin' it fast. Last week I called to her from Cabin 5 and she looked at me like I was from Mars. 'Hey, Violet,' I says. 'Violet?' she says, like she doesn't know her own name."

As if on cue, the cowbell hanging from the back door clanked, and their mother entered, disheveled from sleep.

"Here, Mom." Tess rounded a shelf of sundries, intercepted Violet at the apartment pass-through, and straightened the woman's crumpled dress.

A rear bell now, too, Hildy thought. Under her breath: "She always walk right in?"

June leaned to Hildy's ear. "Pops in every couple hours or so. Forgets she doesn't still live here."

Violet stood at the pass-through, her eyes darting. June crossed to her and took her hand. "Hello, dear. Want a cuppa tea?"

Her mother shuffled to a cupboard for two mugs and fiddled with dials on the stove. June filled the kettle and redirected her. "Sit, Vi. I've got it."

Violet fumbled to a chair. Bent to her untied laces.

Behind her, June whispered, "I unplugged her stove this mornin'. Burner was red as a poker with nothin' on it, and she was sittin' on her porch in that wintry blast, not ten minutes after Tess left for supplies. No coat, door wide open as if it was May."

In the store, Otis closed the cooler and flattened empty boxes. "I'll leave you ladies to your sippin'," he called. He zipped his jacket, caught June's blown kiss, and hauled the cardboard to a green utility vehicle outside.

The women turned their attention to Violet, whose eyes now lit with recognition. "Well, well, my Hildy Rose. Tea for her, too, June Bug? I made snickerdoodles, just this morning. Your favorite." She stood, stretched an arm toward Hildy, and bumped thick fingers along her braid. "We used to call that a milkmaid braid. Against your fair skin? So pretty. My pretty girl."

Tess shot Hildy a look.

"Mom." Hildy stepped to the oval mirror behind the table and checked the plait where her mother had touched it. Wrapping her head like a crown, the white-gold braid held tight, to Hildy's relief.

"My angel." Violet beamed at her younger daughter.

There are two of us, Mother. Hildy scrambled for a distraction. "Those cookies, Mom. Where?"

June banked her head toward a sealed package of gingersnaps on the counter. Hildy eased to her feet and pulled scissors from a wooden block. Her cheeks burned. Nothing new, her mother's selective attention, but still.

"Well, these look tasty. Thanks, Mom." Her hands low over the plastic, Hildy snipped, extracted, then plated the wafers as if fresh from the oven.

Violet dunked a cookie in tea and bit, oblivious. Talked with her mouth full, her fat white teeth speckled with crumbs. "How long can you stay? I made up your bed. Those flannel sheets you like."

As if expecting me. As if everything were all right.

Tess raised her brows, her mouth crooked. Hildy nodded, eyes on her sister, then on June, who lifted and lowered her shoulders. "Oh, a few days," Hildy said. "I have some people to see over at that new hatchery. For when they drop the dams."

"The dams. Oh. Yes." Violet licked a finger, pressed it to cookie bits on the table. "That'll be years yet, though."

"No, Mom." Tess's voice swelled. "*Next* year. Twenty eleven. After next year, no more dams. No lakes. No more resort. Or rowing."

Violet tossed her head, and frosty hair flew into a shoulder-length cloud. Crepe arms peeked from the bell sleeves of her paisley muslin shift—a California hippie dress, too summery for this day and faded now. Six months into grad school, Hildy had splurged on it for Mom's birthday.

"Oh, phooey. They've been threatening to blow up those dams since you girls were little."

"Not just threatening, Mom. They have *plans. Soon.*" Tess thumped her mug on the wood. "They're about to pull the plug on your la-la land."

June raised her hand. "Not worth it, Tessie. Your blood pressure."

Tess cracked her knuckles. "I gotta go."

June tapped the cookie plate. "Here, girls." Violet took another and dunked it beside the abandoned one floating in her cup.

Tess stood and checked her watch. Frowned at her mother and turned to Hildy. "Call me."

Hildy followed her sister outside. Tess propped a foot on her rig's running board. "Mom drives me—"

"Hildy?" The store's door shuddered in Violet's wake. "You're not leaving, are you, honey?"

"Go easy on her, Tess." Hildy's throat constricted, and she swallowed hard.

"You'll see what she's doing. Call me," Tess said again.

4

HILDY

LAUNDRY

HILDY TURNED TO VIOLET as Tess's rig rolled onto the deserted highway toward tiny Sekiu and her sister's other life an hour west. Wind flapped Violet's hair behind her like a flag and pressed the muslin dress into her curves.

"C'mon, Momma. Let's get you home." Hildy hooked her arm in Violet's, blinked into the storm, then steered her mother past the gas pumps. Violet lunged ahead to the last in a row of weathered cabins.

"Hold tight, Mom. Gotta get my stuff." Her mother gripped the jamb while Hildy sprinted to her vehicle, backed to the cabin's door, and opened the hatch to her canary's cage, its quilted cover snapped tight against drafts. "Back in a jiff, little guy." She grabbed her small suitcase, closed the car, and stepped past her mother into the tidy living room.

Her lungs tightened at the sight of familiar furnishings crafted by her father and, to her surprise, still lustrous. The live-edge table and four chairs from that big-leaf maple across the river. The wooden arms of the tan, coarse-weave love seat—and the rocking chair beside it—shaped from alder in her dad's shop. She noticed furry nubs in a vase of willow catkins on the table—pussy willows, fresh cut, like those she used to pet.

In the small corner kitchen, the compact fridge, three-burner stove, enamel sink, and stacked washer and dryer gleamed white. Uncluttered counters shone clean below open shelves of glassware, cereal bowls, and mugs, their handles all aimed left. Four of everything, straight as soldiers. Her eyes roved to a pieced lap quilt hanging above the love seat, then through a west window to the heavy skies and the lake's tin-colored chop.

She lowered her suitcase by the door, but at the click of her mother's tongue, she lifted it again, her skin prickling. Maybe Cabin 6, right next door, her usual lodging on the rare occasions she visited, would be better than here. She and her mother hadn't slept under the same roof—where Mom dogged her, picked up *anything* she left out of place—since Hildy had left for college.

C'mon, she told herself. *That was then.* Her mother needed a caretaker around the clock now. And until they could hire live-in help, Hildy was it.

Clouds broke in the wind and a mote-free sunbeam stretched to the dustless plank floor, prompting Hildy's urge to lotion herself against her skin's errant flakes. Instead, she stroked a stone in her pocket she knew was granite and pictured its riot of black spots. If she could, she'd release the rock as a Dalmatian puppy to frolic through the cabin and track the floor with river mud, shaking dog hair and dander into her mother's sterile beams. Wagging a happy tail.

Violet reached for the suitcase.

"I've got it, Mom." Her jaw tight, Hildy swung the bag out of reach and crossed—*stomped*—to a closed room. Feet away, another door stood open to her mother's polished maple bed, its wedding-ring quilt smooth and tucked.

Smiling, Violet hoisted a laundry basket instead.

Hildy sighed. Her inability to keep house like this didn't warrant distancing herself from her well-meaning mother. Though Violet never said so, Hildy knew she hurt her mom with every rebuff. Wasn't Hildy's clutter—not to mention the scattered, undependable brain that caused it—disappointment enough? Though the truth embarrassed her, Hildy had to admit that apart from how she presented herself in public, she could never come close to her mother's standards for cleanliness and order.

Only in Hildy's studies and her meticulous data collection and analyses did she begin to approach her mother's fastidious ways. At least her tidiness away from home allowed her to hold a job. Two, actually.

And, just as she had earned grades that lied, that told others she was not only smart but competent, now she worked at her occupation with such attentiveness that no one had guessed her secret. For a while, she hoped, no one would discover that, like her mother, she was already losing her mind.

A frigid gust met her when she opened her bedroom, and her irritation flared again. Her bird would freeze in here. Lowering her bag, she gulped the fresh, cold air, then closed the window, upped the bedroom wall heater's thermostat, and opened the door wider for the flood of heat from the living room.

She returned to the SUV for Butterness, set his cage on the dresser, and waited to uncover him until the room warmed. Hand to the heater, she crouched close to his perch, whispering, "A couple more minutes, little love, and you'll be warm as toast."

More rocks rattled in a pocket when she tossed her parka onto the bed. One by one she extracted them and lined them up in a serpentine course along the window ledge her dad had cut to fit snug in the frame—before he stained the fir deep red and painted the shiplap walls the color of cream. Her tension abated as she laced twigs and a feather from her chest pocket into the stream of pebbles. *Like fish in a river,* she thought. *Free to swim away.*

She turned from the ledge to find Violet in her doorway, staring blankly toward the window. "Mom. A little privacy please," Hildy said, and swung the door closed.

Upending her bag, she strewed its few contents across the duvet. Toothbrush and paste. Chapstick and lotion. Leggings and a tee for sleep. Undies. Two changes of clothes in colors she loved: moss, pecan, alpenglow, buttermilk. "Your brand," Tess had claimed years before. "Can always see you coming."

She dropped underclothes and nightwear into one drawer, then hung outer garments in the three-foot closet. Settled enough, she closed the bedroom door behind her and crossed to the bathroom, where she lathered to her elbows with rosemary soap from Violet's homemade stockpile, inhaling the scent like a sedative before she picked up a hand towel folded beside the little sink. Surprised, she sniffed the cloth, then patted a pair of bath towels stacked on another open shelf. Like the hand towel, they were *wet.*

On a hunch, she walked past Violet to a kitchen drawer, where she found washcloths, folded but damp. Oven mitts in the next drawer smelled of mold. She reached into her mother's basket and squeezed the contents. "Mom." She patted a rolled pair of socks to her mother's cheek as if it were a powder puff. "You feel that?"

Violet wiped the sheen stamped below an eye and stared at the balled fabric in Hildy's hand. "More laundry. I swear, Hildy, you go through stockings as fast as—"

"They were in here, Mom." She held the socks over the wicker basket. "With all the other wet ones you're rolling."

Her mother snatched the socks as Hildy let go. "Don't throw your dirty things there, daughter. I just washed them."

This was worse than she thought. "Mom. These socks." She pointed to the bathroom, the kitchen. "Those towels. You didn't *dry* them."

"Nonsense." Fear ran Violet's face, then slipped from view.

"They're wet, Mom, and you didn't even notice. You can't go on pretending about this anymore."

"Pretending?" Violet had gone blank again.

"Oh, Mom." Hildy's eyes welled. "You're pretending . . . that you're not forgetful. That you can live alone. That you aren't scaring us all out of our minds with your rowing and random walks and , , , and . . . You're pretending *everything*, Mom. And you can't anymore. We can't. For your own safety, you need someone with you twenty-four seven."

"Absolutely not. You're making a mountain out of all your little rocks."

The wit—and sarcasm—sideswiped her. "I mean it, Mom. We're getting you help, and you need to *cooperate*."

Violet continued folding as if Hildy hadn't spoken. *Face facts, Hildy.* Trustworthy cognition had left Violet months earlier. She'd forget their conversation in minutes.

Rapid, early-onset dementia, the doctor had told Tess. From that college head injury, he surmised, when a crew teammate's oar cracked her skull. Though the diagnosis had alerted them, both she and her sister had been pretending, too, thinking they had *time*. Now they had to catch up to the reality of their mother's condition. Violet alone here, even with June and Otis nearby? Unplugging the stove wouldn't keep her from injury—or worse.

Riddled with dread, Hildy knelt beside the laundry basket. "Mom, I'll stay—and we'll get someone to be here when I'm at work, so you won't be alone. Or maybe you can visit June when I'm gone."

"Why June? Can't Tess stay home from school?" Violet's eyes clouded.

"Tess has a husband and grown boys and clients to look after. Their season's starting and all of them will be working it."

"What do you mean, 'their season'?"

"Sport fishing for Bingo, Mom. Fast Tide Charters, remember? And their boys' trollers. You remember Tess married Bingo, right?"

Violet looked over Hildy's shoulder at a framed photo. "Of course I remember. Those are their little boys. I babysit."

"You used to. For Rudy, Joel. They're nineteen and twenty now, working their own boats out of Sekiu."

Violet stared at her. Spit bubbles formed at the corners of her mouth.

"So I'll keep you company, Mom."

Violet nodded. "We can go rowing."

"Sure, Mom."

Rowing? Violet's thing, not hers. Hildy was caving again. She *hated* the sport. A familiar tug-of-war began in her, stretching her between the compassion she longed to extend to her mother and a resistance to physical or emotional nearness to her. A conflict fueled by a vague darkness she couldn't name tore at her, infusing the chronic longing she felt for her mother's affection with yet another surge of anxiety. Unresolved confusion returned in a flood.

The physicians she'd seen after she left home had been no help at all. No physical cause for her agitation, they'd said, just as they'd said meds could take the edge off Hildy's turmoil. Of course she'd refused. No matter how much doctors reassured her, she wouldn't risk altering the keenly functioning part of her brain—the only part of her worth *anything*—just to feel calmer.

Eventually, every professional had suggested she see a therapist. But if pleading with God hadn't helped, why would spilling her weirdness to a human counselor do anything but make her feel worse? No, as long as she was sharp enough to do her job, she'd endure the anxiety and, by recording her days, would guard against any more memory lapses. She'd hide all this, just as she had for most of her life.

"Rowing. I'd like that, honey. I'll fix us a lunch," Violet said.

5

HILDY

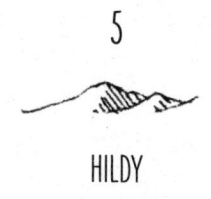

WRECK

MIDNIGHT. HILDY AWOKE SHIVERING, and her first thought was of Butterness. She cranked the heat higher, gripped the bedding, and scrolled tighter into the flannel sheets and comforter.

And caught a whiff of cold lake air.

Adrenaline juiced her as she tossed blankets, leapt from her bed, and burst from her room to Violet's empty one.

"Mom?" Shrill with fear, her cry spilled through the gaping front door, bounced cross-lake, and returned as an echo, unanswered. She fumbled into boots, snagged her coat from the hook, and raced outside. "Mom! Violet!" Her shout clouded in the stillness, and she shuddered from this snap freeze, the eerie quiet after the storm's bluster, and her rising panic.

"Mother!" She hurried to the dock, but the boats were tied, the water flat, the reflected stars uninterrupted by oar or splash.

Hildy's call again pierced the air, and she broke into a run. Her boots crunched gravel. Her lungs heaved.

Shrieking now, she was halfway to the store when lights flicked on in June's kitchen, then flooded the porch. Otis, tousled with sleep, appeared on the landing—buttoning, scuffing into boots, suspenders draped at his hips.

"She's gone!" Hildy gasped.

June appeared behind him and tugged his jacket hood over his head. He stuffed arms into sleeves and thumped three wooden stairs toward Hildy. "You check the dock?"

"Yeah. Not there." She rounded the building as lights from the store's gable and gas pumps invaded the moonless dark and spilled onto the road. Only then did Hildy spot Violet, barefoot on the highway centerline, thirty feet from the Elwha River Bridge.

Hildy screamed her mother's name. To her left, headlights angled downhill toward the highway's turn to the river, the road's icy glaze a sheen in their path.

"Mom!" she screamed again and stumbled onto the slick pavement. She caught Violet's arm and jerked her mother toward her. The truck's high beams trapped them both in the instant before the driver swerved.

The sharp downhill curve, the jerk of a wrist at the truck's steering wheel, a week of rain frozen fast in a quick turn of weather. A skid, its force centrifugal on a sickening, icy arc into the oncoming lane. Hildy clung to Violet in horror as the truck skated, then slammed broadside into a concrete abutment at the bridge.

A split-second eternity. As if deciding, the rig, its bed heavy with a slide-in camper and a pair of canoes, paused, teetered on the bridge rail, then flipped toward the river below. Still clinging to Violet, Hildy tracked the truck's descent by the grind and crunch of metal on rocks, the splash and sizzle of river on engine. Otis, his twisted back bent like a spy's, passed her at a run and skittered down the bank and out of sight.

June hurried to the highway's shoulder and claimed Violet with one hand. Her other pressed a phone to her ear. Chilled and shaking, Hildy's mother studied her hands as if they were new. *Like an infant,* Hildy thought. *With no idea what just happened.*

June waved the phone at Hildy. "Nine one one. On their way. You help Otis." Wobbly Violet leaned as June turned her toward the store.

Hildy hurried to the bridge and peered over the riverbank for the steep route Otis had taken to the truck twenty-five feet below, now roof-down in the water. A front tire spun, and its chrome spokes blinked at the ice-disk moon. On the downstream side of the cab, the dark shape that was Otis stood knee-deep in the inky river, hammering the partially submerged passenger window. With a club? A rock? She couldn't tell.

The river's current pummeled bridge pilings beyond outlines in the gloom: vehicle, boulders, man. Had the truck landed mere feet to the north, the entire rig would have sunk in the hole where her dad caught that twenty-inch bull trout. She focused on the truck's dark hulk until her eyes adjusted, then bent to tie her boots.

Then she dropped the laces and stared.

A black shimmer of motion was rising through the underside of the truck. Steam from the engine? Gas fumes?

No. Too far behind the engine, this emission came through the floorboards of the upended cab. Rather than actually seeing it, Hildy *perceived* it as a heat wave, or a mirage in summer air. It was vaguely conical, without definite edges. Dimensional, but transparent, a distortion in the darkness. As if alive, the sensation rose three feet above the truck and hovered for a few seconds before it lifted overhead and loitered. A chilling membrane against the black sky and icy stars, it seemed to scrape the air before it dropped and dissolved in the river.

She'd seen this one before.

No sooner had the shadow disintegrated than she felt a second, larger asymmetry rise from the underbelly of the cab. Like the first, this impression hovered, but unlike the other, it seemed sharp, fragmented. Uglier. Like a dangerous cloud of broken glass, it sped erratically away from the truck, upriver. Hildy sensed it shrinking into the timbered foothills.

"Otis," she called.

He was already climbing toward her. "Cab's half full a water. I broke the window with a rock, but with that door caved in, no way to get it open or to reach that seatbelt release. Other door's pinned against a slab. You got a knife on ya?"

"No."

"Mine's in my truck." He rubbed hands on his thighs and expelled a breath. "Only one guy in there with his face underwater, what's left of it. His head's—I couldn't find no pulse."

"June called nine one one."

"Won't help. The man's gone." He reached a hand.

Hildy pulled him onto the highway's shoulder. She scuffed feet on the pavement, testing the icy road. "He had shadows, Otis. I saw them leave."

He wiped his forehead and nodded. "Them? How many?"

"Two this time."

Otis lunged into a crooked-backed trot beside her, and they hurried toward his pickup beside the shop. He gulped air every few words. "Only one . . . soul in that . . . truck. How many . . . death wrecks you seen on . . . this nasty corner . . . anyway?"

"Too many. And too many of those ghastly shadows." Her

vocal pitch climbed. "I told you, I'm wacked." Mom had already decided as much, when Hildy was ten.

Otis stopped abruptly, squared to face her, and shook his head, his breath a frozen mist. "Ain't a crime to glimpse the unseen. Could even be a help." He touched her cheek, glanced back toward the river, limped on.

Last July, she'd shown Otis her brain scan, but he refused to let her off the hook. Instead, he'd pressed a red area on the image with his thumb—one of the lit-up hotspots dotting her lobes. "Could be inherited, I s'pose, but anxiety's tricky, missy." He set the report on the table and stroked an ear. "Some get it from soakin' up toxins or eatin' poorly. Others are livin' wrong, or they've been hurt or scared so bad their brains are just plain jumpy. A whole lot more have lie-makers hanging around, messin' with 'em."

"What do you mean, *lie-makers*?"

"Hellhounds, accusers, fearmongers. Dark spirits. Like them shadows you see leaving the deceased. They prowl the earth, ya know. Lookin' for chances."

He cocked his head and studied her for too long. She squirmed under his gaze, until she reminded herself that this was Otis looking at her. Wise old Otis, who loved her.

"So what's my reason, Otis?"

"A combo, prob'ly, and whether the chicken or egg came first don't really matter."

"That's no help."

"You was frettin' at Sunday meetin's long before your dad disappeared, so it didn't start with that. All that doctorin' you done? Except for them red spots in that scan, your body checks out fine. All things considered, I'd say a lie-maker's been workin' you for a good long while. Get it gone and I'd wager that brain a yours'll settle down in no time."

The man resumed his trot on the highway's gravel shoulder, and Hildy stared after him. How would she remember this, write it all down? *Awoke to cold. Door open, Mom gone. Ran outside, checked lake—smooth water, boats tied. Otis—suspenders, coat. Mom in road. Truck—swerved, hit bridge, then river. Shadows escaped. Otis . . .*

He was twenty feet out when she jogged to catch up.

His shout made plumes in the frigid air. "You want to get free a those chains a yours? All that anxiety?"

Here we go again. "You know I do."

"Then—"

"Stop, Otis. You've told me fifty times." Maybe not fifty, but while Fourth of July campers had settled into the resort's quiet hours, he'd repeated himself so often she could hear him in her sleep: *Do some diggin'. Find the lie.*

Was he right?

"I care about ya, girl."

"I know, but it's not that easy."

He skipped, his stride contorted. Arched his back and winced. "Ya don't have to do it alone."

She couldn't think about that right now. "Mom can't stay here, Otis. Young and strong as she is, there's no telling what she'll do."

He didn't seem to hear. A siren wailed in the distance as he heaved open the passenger door of his old Ford and read his watch. "That was quick. Trooper musta been nearby. You go look after your momma. Nothing you can do now, anyway. Gonna be a hard, ugly scene out here. You don't need another one a those."

He dug in the glove box, extracted a utility knife. "I recognize that truck, Hildy. Belongs to that uncle of yours that Vi wouldn't talk to. She hid in the back whenever he came to the store."

Her uncle? She and Tess had glimpsed him a time or two, but Mom squirreled them out of sight. Tess had pushed for a reason, but Mom wouldn't say why. She could hardly recall what he looked like.

When Hildy stumbled into June's kitchen, blank-eyed Violet sat hunched at the table, rotating her balled hands, her hair loose and snarled, her tea steaming, untouched. June draped a parka over the woman's shoulders and poured another mug from the kettle. Hildy wrapped her fingers around the warm earthenware. Outside, more sirens wailed, nearer now.

Hildy stood at the apartment's folding door and watched through store windows as a caravan of lights descended the grade. A patrol car, then two emergency rigs passed the state gravel yard at the curve, pulled in past the gas pumps, and crowded the patrol car at the bridge. Beacons flung nets of red and blue light over grocery shelves, forest, and Hildy's clothes as EMTs jumped from trucks and hurried down the riverbank. A trooper laid flares in the road. A second officer talked with Otis, who pointed him toward the pumps. Toward Hildy. When the officer knocked at the store's front door, she admitted him, described the crash, and led him into the apartment to Violet.

The man seated himself across from June, who rested quiet hands on Violet's nervous ones. He lowered his flat-brimmed hat to the table and leaned toward Hildy's mother, asking, coaxing. Gentle with Violet's nonsensical replies, his voice hummed low.

June can handle this. Hildy crossed into the empty store and leaned against the counter. Tapped knuckles to her sternum to soothe her racing pulse. Waited.

Too long later, chairs scootched on the apartment linoleum. The officer, louder now, wrapped up, said goodbye. He touched his hat when he passed her and crossed the highway to the riverbank.

Fidgety, Violet got to her feet at Hildy's return to the kitchen.

"C'mon, Mom. Time for bed." Hildy threaded her mother's arms into a parka, zipped her own, and pecked June's cheek before she herded Violet toward Cabin 7.

June hugged herself against the cold and called from the stoop. "Try to sleep some."

Fat chance. At three a.m., with the deadbolt set and duct-taped against escape, Hildy lay wide-eyed and alert as Violet's soft palate rattled with sleep. When fumbling at the lock roused her at three thirty, she directed her mother back to bed. And at four twenty, when she apprehended Violet with a leg through an open bedroom window, she clutched her mother to her and cried. Violet wouldn't release her, so until she slept again, Hildy lay stiff on the bed with her mother's arms around her and wished she could return the embrace.

6

HILDY

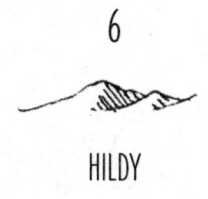

U-HAUL

JUNE KNOCKED AT EIGHT A.M. with coffee. While her mother slept on, Hildy—showered, dressed, and braided—stripped heavy gray tape from Cabin 7's door and let her in. June waved a list. Hildy read it wearily.

"I took the liberty." June ran a finger down the paper. "These three have space. If you want to look, I'll stay with her."

The bed creaked. Violet appeared at her door, her smile bright. "Well, June, Hildy. You drink all that coffee, or is there a splash for me?"

"Of course, Vi. Always enough for you." June rose, poured, and locked eyes with Hildy.

"Running errands, Mom. Back in a bit." Hildy tucked the list in a chest pocket and grabbed her keys, phone, jacket. *Enough craziness.* She wished her voice held tenderness, but exhaustion and her inner drummings had stolen every shred.

Four hours later, she called the store.

"Elwha Fishin' Resort. Hold on, please." The old cash register dinged, and she heard Otis count change for a customer. "Thanks for waitin'. Best flies and burgers, right here."

She could picture him, tugging the cord, the old black phone to his ear.

"How's she doing now, Otis? Still with us?"

"Right as rain. She an' Junie brought me lunch an' we laughed like old times."

"So what do we do now? I found a place for her. They can take her today. But if she's acting normal—I can't bear another night like that, Otis. None of us can, Mom included. If she stays here, it's only a matter of time until something else awful."

"What place?"

"Hillview."

"Good. Good. Let Junie an' me bring her. May take a bit of talkin', but after goin' through all that with Junie's momma, we're pros, ya know. You mind the store, and we'll call ya from Hillview when she's settled. You can take her things later."

"Okay. You sure?"

"I'm sure. She'll think she's at the Hearst Castle, crowned queen."

A fairy tale. The simple image, the help from him and June, the relief she felt—they broke and spilled her pent-up guilt, sorrow, anger. Sleep-deprived and caffeine-jittery, Hildy sobbed into her phone—and only patient Otis heard.

At five o'clock, Hildy stood in the Hillview lobby and glanced at her watch. Dinner aromas wafted from the adjacent meal hall.

A food cart rolled into the memory-care wing as Otis and June approached. Fatigue preceded them.

"My turn, I guess." Hildy watched the heavy door close behind the cart. Winced as the lock clicked.

June shrugged into the jacket Otis held for her. "Give her a few days, Hildy girl. I wouldn't rock the boat right now."

Hildy frowned. "She okay?"

"Is now," June said. "But her brain was scrambled as eggs by the time we got her here. Took a while to calm her down."

"She was so lucid this morning."

Otis propped a hand under his wife's elbow. "Comes and goes like that. You'll be glad to know we left her pluckin' a Go Fish card from the floor nurse's hand, butter-clam happy."

"I should've—"

"No. No shoulds." June steered Hildy through the exit to her Yukon. "You can help me collect her things. May as well get that done now, too."

Inside Cabin 7, June quickly scanned the rooms. "She won't need much from here, spare as your momma likes things. A few changes of clothes. That wall quilt, maybe. Never was much for memorabilia, our Vi." June took a long look at Hildy, who hung back. "I'm happy to gather, if you'd rather not."

Hildy looked at her hands, certain that touching her mother's things would scald her. "Go ahead." This final packing already felt like death, only without a body—or the bleak, departing vapors Otis called dark spirits. What June didn't pack, Tess could take. Hildy wanted none of it.

June nodded, quickly filling the laundry basket her foot scuffed cross-floor between cupboards and drawers. Hildy watched her choose from the closet.

"See anything else?" June asked. Hildy shook her head and carried the belongings to June's truck.

Mom's holdings, reduced to a wicker basket. And Violet unable to pack a single item herself, much less lay to rest a resort that would die as the dams came down. No question now, June, Otis, and Tess needed Hildy here.

But for how long? The USGS would grant her a leave, but she'd need more than six months to make it through this last summer season, then to close the resort and sell the rowboats, store fixtures, tools. The equipment and cabin furnishings. To say goodbye to June and Otis, who would have to move on.

And she sure wouldn't want to be living here counting aluminum oars with a job on hold in Seattle. Not when her training could plant her smack in the middle of the Elwha River's rewilding.

Yes, she had to come home. Even if shadows badgered her. Even if she misplaced everything she owned and lost her mind, to boot.

At six o'clock the next morning, she texted Everett's daughter Dee. **House all yours April 15.** At nine she called Dave Cloud. "I'm in," she said. "I'll be there the first Monday in May." She could hear him smiling. At ten and ten thirty she emailed two resignation letters, first to her boss at the USGS, then to the UW.

With forty-seven days to button up her life in Seattle, pack her belongings, and load the U-Haul, she snatched her diary, knotted her boots, and headed upstream to sit on a rock and write everything, *everything* down.

On April 14, the twenty-foot truck she'd rented lumbered to a stop outside Cabin 2. Hildy grabbed her hat and jumped from the cab, absorbing the citron green of understory leaves unfurling on the ten-foot riverbank. Raising her arms, she gulped a lungful of honeyed air—the scent of cottonwoods in the fresh heat of early spring.

Over a deep pool in the river, a nylon rope swing dangled from one of those trees—a replacement of the sisal one her dad had hung thirty years earlier—close enough to reach from her log cabin's porch. Her insides warmed. How good to live here, in Cabin 2, near the happy swing on the river, instead of on the reservoir where, a hundred yards to the north—in front of her mother's Cabin 7—Lake Aldwell incarcerated the Elwha. Beautiful, that water, but a prison, nonetheless.

Her mother, however, could never get enough of the lake. When Violet relinquished the store's apartment to Otis and June, she had chosen to live in Cabin 7, her and Dad's original home, precisely because of the lake views and the little house's proximity to the resort's ten rental rowboats. Her mom loved that vista—the trees climbing foothills, the wild, unpopulated shoreline, the aqua and indigo in the lake itself. A day rarely passed that Violet hadn't rowed the reservoir—a five-mile round trip, end to end. "Record pace!" or "Clear to the dam!" she'd cry, though both Tess and Hildy knew their mother's oar would have tapped the log boom guarding those spillways, not the concrete itself.

Oh, the worry each time her mom set out! The fright! Old feelings flooded Hildy, hot as if new: her helplessness at age five, alone and tearful on the dock as Violet's boat shrank downlake and vanished around the bend.

Worst was her terror when her mother rowed after dark. When the UTV fired up for Violet's ten p.m. campground check, Hildy would creep from her blankets to the window and watch the gravel lane for her mother's return, praying to hear her parents' muffled voices, with Violet safe in their bed.

But if too many minutes elapsed with no sound of the returning vehicle, no click of the downstairs latch, and no footfalls on the floor below, she knew Mom would be rowing the dark lake alone. Without houses or roads or any lights along the shoreline, who would see her mother's boat when it flipped or foundered? Who would hear her momma's cries besides night birds or hungry beasts or all those dark, silent trees in the steep foothill amphitheater? Night after night, Hildy lay haunted, imagining the fear in her mother's eyes as the lake bed rose like an animal and swallowed her whole.

After Mom's late-night rows, Dad's rumbly tone and her mother's high-pitched one would rouse her. *War,* she'd tell herself, though she couldn't make out their words. *Why the lake, Momma? Over us?*

Hildy blinked hard and wrenched her thoughts to a summer afternoon when she was nine. Her months-old pup had barked from Mom's returning boat and leapt from the bow when Hildy, giddy with relief, slapped her thighs at the dock. Violet had been flush-faced and jubilant, her sweaty caress of Hildy's cheek and her "Hi there, honey," a balm.

Breathe, she told herself. At least here in Cabin 2 she wouldn't have to look at the reservoir. During the weeks she'd sorted, packed, and closed up Everett's bungalow, she'd dreaded living near its shore, already eager for the dams' turbines to go silent and the draining of Lakes Aldwell and Mills to begin. She seated her cap over her braid and turned her thoughts to the river running free, to how she'd feel like flying when it did.

June emerged from the store and called to her. "The place is all scrubbed and ready for you." Her dark hair was shorter now, a bob, gray-streaked, and she held a key that swung on a leather strap like a metronome, keeping playful time to her footfalls before she dropped it in Hildy's open palm. "Here you go, girl. The key to a new life, in your own cabin, not your momma's."

Hildy's smile faded. "How is she?" She and her sister depended on June's weekly updates on their mother. Tess, cooking for hungry fishermen, had visited the facility only once since Violet moved there. Hildy, busy with packing, not at all. *Soon,* she'd told herself in Seattle, taping another box closed.

"Same. No more of that agitation, thankfully, though she fiddles with those locked doors most days. Causes a ruckus sometimes wanderin' into others' rooms. Still knows me now and then. Don't get that look again, Hildy. She hasn't mentioned your name. I've seen her clear-minded once, and then she only asked about the resort operations, and if those workers had opened the dam's floodgates after all that rain. I hate to say it, sweets, but I doubt she recalls her daughters anymore."

Tears stung Hildy's eyes, but for her own sake, not her mother's. It seemed that Violet remained worry-free—even when losing her mind. Anxiety, useless as ever, was Hildy's department. She seated the key in the lock and swung the door inward.

June stayed by the truck. "You check the place out. Soon's you raise that truck's big old door, Otis and I'll be here in a flash to help you unload. Like they say. Many hands—"

"—make light work." Hildy finished the phrase, and it cheered her. June had first said it by the gas pumps all those years ago, when the search parties had gone home and Hildy forgot how to fill a fuel tank. She'd repeated the expression through Hildy's high school years, whenever Hildy was too scrambled or forlorn or friendless to clean a cabin or stock a shelf in the store. Chatty June always sniffed her out, lightened her work and her heartache.

Hildy turned from her to the well-tended old cabin, smaller than her Seattle bungalow and one bedroom short. Inside, shadows from window grilles crosshatched on the cabin's plank floor, the red fir grainy and worn. She lowered a wooden blind, pleased. *So many windows for a cabin this size. So many ledges.*

And apart from that single photo behind the door, a feast of empty walls. She lifted the antique frame from a nail and studied the sepia image of her paternal grandparents, still young, the half-built store behind them.

She ran a finger along stripes of chinking between logs. Swiped the flat of her hand down her dad's shiplap on the interior walls where she would place her freestanding bookcases. She would build more shelves too—like those she'd attached to her Seattle bungalow.

Light slanted through the square window in the gable—where its mullions formed a simple cross. A reminder. How had she never noticed it, passing by all those years, or cleaning the cabin after campers departed? Years when only her secret faith kept her upright.

She liked the ceiling, too: its ten-foot vault lined with more shiplap, the tight, creamy backdrop between pole beams perfect for items suited to hooks. The flat top of the tiny woodstove, stained by the pots and kettles of winter fishermen before her dad ran power to the cabins—it could serve as a summer shelf.

She stepped off dimensions of the combined kitchen and living room, the bath, and the bedroom, considering crannies where the old logs joined. Her keepsakes would crowd the place a little, but they and their stories would all be with her—visual memories, defying her childhood's lost ones. She needed them more than ever here.

Especially here.

The time would go fast—two years in this cabin, max. As the dams fell and reservoirs emptied, the Elwha Fishing Resort would die, too—and with it the life Hildy's family had known for almost seventy years.

Tess had heard the gossip. Having acquired both of the dams, their reservoirs, and adjacent property, the Department of the Interior had begun accepting private bids to excavate the resort's gas tanks, raze the store, and bulldoze every cabin and shed. After the lakes drained, the DOI would relegate not only their business, but her family's presence on river to history.

The demolition clock also ticked for Otis and June, who had promised to stay through the resort's final days before they moved—to Chelan, perhaps. Or Boyer, Pond Oreille, or Coeur d'Alene. A waterfront campground somewhere in the Pacific Northwest. Anywhere.

With so much happening, Hildy had shirked enough, left too much responsibility to others. This last full resort season, closing the business . . . It all would rest on her shoulders now, plain and simple.

Her dad would want her here.

But even Dad wasn't the reason she'd come home. Something else beckoned her, though she couldn't say *what*.

A hundred feet away, June hauled a trash bag to the dumpster and looked toward the cabin. Hildy waved from a window before she walked to the U-Haul, unlocked the rolling metal door, and shook her arms like a sprinter in blocks. Otis appeared at her shoulder, pulled the ramp from the truck's underbelly, and lowered it to the ground. Hands on hips, he assessed the truck's contents, whistling low.

"I hope there's air in those boxes, missy. Your cabin'll fall in the river if they're full."

They carted the wooden table and chairs first, to the sunny south window. Then the love seat and Hildy's walnut desk. When she and Otis packed her bed frame inside, he steered it toward the bedroom.

"Let's put it out here, Otis, under that beam. We'll stack the other stuff in the bedroom until I can go through it."

She neglected to say that she'd already gone through everything back at Everett's. If she had room for the items in these boxes, she'd unpack them. If not, they'd be perfectly happy stored, as long as they were close by.

Late in the day, Otis bungeed the hand truck inside the emptied U-Haul. Boxes lined the cabin walls and filled Hildy's only bedroom, floor to ceiling.

"You've got your work cut out for you." June yanked the cord and the truck's rolling door clattered shut. She brushed hands on jeans, pressed two fingers to her lips and blew Hildy a kiss. "Let me know what I can haul to Goodwill."

Hildy nodded, mentally cataloguing June's gesture until she could write it down. June's love was like her dad's, given without expectation or theft. Nourishment she'd display on logs above her bed, if she could.

7

HILDY

DECOR

AT FIRST LIGHT, HILDY AWOKE in her new cabin to the steady drum of rain. She rolled over in her fresh sheets, strained toward her table, and pulled a lightweight cover from Butterness's cage. "Rise 'n shine, lovie." The bird shook feathers, sidestepped to a cuttlebone at the end of a perch, and preened. "I'll let you out soon as I hang stuff."

She slid into slippers. After she punched the coffee maker, she tore a cinnamon roll from the tray June had left on her counter and pulled a jar of applesauce from the stocked refrigerator, smiling at a week's worth of favorites. Then, shivering, she turned to the bird. "Chilly in here, little guy. You okay?" With nothing to hide—yet—she raised a blind and read the thermometer clipped to the canary's cage. "Sixty-five degrees. No wonder you're puffed." She turned a dial on the wall heater and donned a fleece. "I brought your favorite landing spots," she said. "Mine, too."

Within the hour, the contents of several boxes lay strewn across the floor and she'd lowered the blind again, twisting the slats half closed. She flattened cardboard, stacked it on the porch, and located her hammer. Then, while the canary sang to her humming, she hung treasures on the log and shiplap walls and along the beam at the peak of the little cabin.

By the time she'd used a pack of one hundred hooks, she'd located another hundred—and her tub of nails—and had sliced the tape on seven more moving boxes, from which she extracted items tenderly, matching their numbers to those in notebooks she assembled on a freestanding bookcase. Mouthing their stories.

She hung the vintage woodworking tools first, imagining her dad's hands on hers, teaching her. "Remember this one, Mr. B?" She raised a tenon saw to the bird, then hung it between two other specialty saws—*sash*, *dovetail*, Dad called them. "What would we do without yard sales?"

Two weeks before Hildy's high school graduation, she'd been helping her overwhelmed sister in Sekiu when Violet sold Dad's tools at her own sale. Hildy discovered the empty workbench and shrieked.

"Oh, honey. It's for your college," her mother had said, then handed her the proceeds.

She hung the drawknife, chisels, mallets, and planes, their wooden handles smooth with use and age. Plumb line, auger, square, all from yard or garage or estate sales, each purchase noted in her records. Other tools she suspended from the multicolored vinyl clothesline she'd cut from the roll in the shop and attached at a diagonal between her perpendicular living room walls.

Over a fat nail, leather caulk boots dangled from tied laces, the spikes on their soles still shiny. Her dad's boots, saved from his logging days in the woods. She must have been four when she climbed into them and clomped across the woodshop. Laughing, Dad had lifted her and pointed at the spike holes in the old plank floor.

She'd found the boots years later, deep beneath his workbench, missed in Violet's purge.

When she stopped to eat, Hildy sat on her haunches, satisfied with her progress. How good to have her things—and the stories and feelings she attached to them—here, in plain sight.

Their comfort fueled her, and she added birds' nests to the collection of tools. Eighty-three, at last count, all tokens from her fishery work. Nests of robins, of course, and of hummingbirds, knit with spider's silk and lichen. The mossy homes of Pacific wrens and sparrows, juncos and grosbeaks, finches, thrushes, and kinglets. Nests of warblers and jays, knocked loose in early autumn storms. Of towhees, pine siskins, and cedar waxwings—all built by birds that warmed her heart almost like fish did, and all as illegal to possess as were the feathers and stones she brought home from parks she worked.

Another reason to hide her home from prying eyes.

Unfolding a doll's metal high chair, she reattached the legs and hoisted the toy. "I ever tell you about my high chair, little bird? It was just like this one, only white, with blue flowers, not red. How could I lose something this size?" But she *had* lost it, and though she'd replayed the day forwards and backwards, she couldn't recall how. Mom had frowned when she cried about it.

By two p.m., Hildy had hung duplicates of other missing toys—all replacements, the originals' whereabouts unknown. She spun a wheel on an old steel skate and rolled its mate across the floor—their design identical to the pair she'd tightened to her shoes at Erickson Playfield. While Dad watched from a bench, she and Tess had skated smooth tennis courts, rough sidewalks. She'd bought this substitute pair, complete with that funny key, at a farm sale near the Marblemount Fish Hatchery.

Late afternoon, the rain quit. Hildy assessed the bedroom—still three-quarters full—and carried one more box to the living room. Surely she could find places somewhere for these little items. She opened the lid to more small rocks, all polished in the tumbler. The otter skull and two Mason jars of feathers in fanned bouquets. Pencil-size driftwood from estuaries, fall alder leaves melted to lace, dried kelp bulbs and starfish, freshwater clamshells and conifer cones.

She had positioned the last of them in the few remaining crannies when she spotted June through a slat in the blind, walking the lane. Headed her way. Seeing the room as June would, the growing warmth and safety she'd felt since morning shriveled.

She met the woman on the porch.

June grinned at her from the grass. "No trace of you all day, girl. Came to see if you got lost in there. Or buried. Gettin' settled?"

Hildy crossed her arms. Uncrossed them. Crossed them again. Knew her brows crouched. "I am." She smiled wanly.

June's smile faded. "Do I get a tour?"

No way she could hide her treasures—or her need—from June. Prohibiting her visits would be impossible. "Just you. Only you, Junie. And only this once."

June laid a hand on her arm. "Hildy. It's me you're talkin' to."

The swung door was her reply. When June entered, Hildy closed it between them and walked to her Yukon, where she pressed her cheek and palms to the hood.

Five minutes passed. Ten. Hildy closed her eyes against the anxiety coursing through her, then stretched each exhale as an antidote to panic. She almost climbed in her rig and drove off. Would have, if not for Butterness and her keys on the table.

When June touched her back, she flinched. "That cabin's a big old stove, darlin', with stories still cookin' inside. I remember you tellin' me a few of them."

"You do?"

"I can't begin to know what they all mean, but I trust those memories will make sense to you once they're baked. Some will even be beautiful."

"They will?"

"When the time's right. Smart of you not to open that oven too soon, or to any old passerby."

Hildy eased herself upright from the hood, her eyes averted.

"No shame in what you're savin', sweet pea. And I'll bet you remember more than you think you do. That brain of yours is part of the beautiful."

8

HILDY

RENTER

JUNE'S VISIT EXHAUSTED HILDY. For distance's sake, that evening she took an old pair of walkie-talkies off a hook, fitted them with batteries, and took a handset to June, who beeped Hildy six times in an hour simply to giggle through static. The next day, however, June's call held purpose. "Somebody here to see you," she said. "She wants to rent Cabin 1. Over."

Hildy pushed back from her table and the clutter of resort paperwork Tess had handed off to her. "Does she realize it's only twelve by sixteen? No shower? Closest to the highway?" Cabin 1 typically rented last, and never by request.

"A business proposition," June said. "She's sittin' at the lunch counter. You got time to talk to her?" The transceiver beeped twice. "Over." She giggled again.

"Roger that. Be right there."

At the front door's jangle, a lean woman in jeans, a white tee, and a linen blazer spun toward Hildy on a lunch counter stool. Mid-forties, Hildy guessed, and queenly. Without threat, the woman's hazel eyes searched Hildy's. Lines at her mouth deepened with her closed-lip smile. She pulled brunette hair over one shoulder and stretched a hand. "Miranda . . . Rimmer. My maiden name." Her resonant voice filled the empty store like a woodwind. "Your mother babysat my little brother and me."

"Really?" Hildy didn't try to mask her surprise. Far as Hildy knew, her mom had refused to watch *any* children besides her own until Tess's boys were born—and then only in a pinch.

"Just a couple of times, right after our family moved here. Your mother was the only person my mom knew to call when they first arrived. She'd known her when they were kids."

"Oh?"

"My grandparents summered on the Sol Duc, next place upriver from your grandparents' property. Mom was a few years older than Violet, but being next door, they played together every vacation until . . . until they didn't."

"Pretty out there."

"Yes. Mom had fond memories of the peninsula. She'd always wanted to live around here, so when a teaching job opened up in Joyce, Dad jumped on it. We moved from Seattle into Grammie and Gramps's summer home when Luke—my brother—was a baby. Our grandparents visited on holidays, then joined us after Gramps retired from Boeing."

"I don't remember you."

"Before your time. I remember Mom calling Violet a newlywed when we came here. Later, when I asked your mom what *newly wet* meant, she wouldn't stop giggling. She seemed happy. Kind. Laughed when I spun on these stools. Very different from your grandfather, if I may say so."

"You knew my grandfather?" Hildy was riveted now. On the few occasions she saw him, the man had seemed downright menacing. *Mean.* Neither she nor Tess would come within ten feet of him.

"We were acquainted with him, but that's a story for another day." She pressed an open hand to her chest. "So sorry to hear about your mom."

Hildy shrugged.

"For now, I'm here on business. June said I should chat with you about my idea."

"Something about Cabin 1?"

"Yes. I'm wondering if you'd consider renting it to me, longer term. For a ceramics studio. A new venture for me, but I know business. I'm a nutritionist by trade, but I owned a successful health food store in Bremerton until my husband left me for a . . . a young nurse at his medical clinic." Disdain crossed her face, then was gone. "I sold my shop after we divorced, then got out of Dodge."

It's still hard for her.

"I've been living out at Lake Sutherland in our . . . now *my* summer place, throwing clay pots on the wheel. And at the wall now and then, whenever I think too much about him—with her."

She waved a hand. "But I digress. Truth is, I have more product than I know what to do with. Thought if I set up a little shop with a kiln and potter's wheel here on the 101, right next door to your store, tourists might stop by and clear some of my inventory. Maybe take a lesson or two. I expect more traffic when the dams come down, given all the publicity. I can design and make themed work for all that. Souvenirs. Take my mind off the crud of the past two years."

Hildy walked to the window and gauged Cabin 1's proximity to her own. Fifty feet apart and with trees between, Cabin 1's blank north wall faced her cabin's south windows. Better Miranda next door—with business hours—than a series of noisy fishermen and campers twenty-four-seven.

"You do know that in a couple of years this whole resort will be gone, right?"

"I'm well aware. With all that's happened to my family in the last five years . . . yes, I understand transience."

Five years? Did something else . . . ? She shook off the question. No business of hers. "That could work, Miranda. May I think about it? Get back to you?"

"Certainly." Miranda scribbled a number on a napkin. "I'll pay you the going rate plus whatever fees—you'll be fairly compensated."

"I'm not concerned about that." Miranda Rimmer roused none of Hildy's overactive suspicions. She liked the woman.

"Good." Miranda smiled warmly. "Thank you. I'll look forward to your call."

⛰

Over dinner, Otis endorsed Miranda's proposal. June pledged to try the potter's mud. During dessert, the three talked rents. After Hildy slept on the idea, had coffee, and let Butterness explore their new home, she called Miranda and said yes.

On Wednesday, April 21, 2010—four days after they met—Hildy's tenant arrived in spattered clothes, claimed the key from June, and painted the interior of Cabin 1 robin's-egg blue. Hildy stopped for a look after lunch, then documented the activity in detail. Three pebbles from the riverbank commemorated the day.

Thursday, a week into Hildy's new life, a plumber carried a toilet and utility sink into the studio. An electrician upgraded the wiring.

Friday morning, a freight truck arrived with the kiln. Her cheeks rosy, Miranda clapped as two men dollied the oven inside. "Come see!" she called to Hildy, who watched from Cabin 2's stair.

Half an hour later, the women were crouching at the open kiln door when a black pickup with a bed-width galvanized toolbox drove in. A contractor's truck, with a metal frame above the box and a ladder strapped on top.

Miranda towed Hildy outside and hugged the dark-haired driver. Hildy stiffened, then tried to slip away, but Miranda held the man's arm with one hand and caught her with the other. "Hildy! Meet my baby brother, Luke. He's going to build my *shelves*."

Shyly, Hildy worked her gaze from the man's boots to his jeans, his black tee, his ears—then gave a quick nod. A grin split his close-trimmed beard—thick as the curls from under his cap.

"Hi there, Hildy." He stepped toward her and extended a hand. "You made my sister pretty happy with this place."

Hildy nodded again. Looked at his palm and shook it. Noted callouses and warmth she'd record in her diary.

"Glad it meets her needs." Hildy poked hands in her pockets and fingered the stones there. *Clear eyes like his sister's.* Arms tight to her sides, she mustered a smile. "I'll let you get to work," she said, and didn't breathe again until she reached Cabin 2 and locked herself inside.

9

LUKE

MEASURES

MIRANDA WATCHED HILDY'S RETREAT, then leaned to her brother's ear. "She's skittish, right? Don't take her personally. I wondered if I had a spider on my nose the first time we talked."

Luke's gaze stalled on Hildy's cabin door. "Whoa. No offense, Mirsy, but is there a more beautiful woman on the face of God's green earth than the one who just walked in that cabin?"

Mouth ajar, Miranda stared at her brother. "Five years, Luke. In all that time, this is the first I'm aware of that you've noticed another woman."

"Yeah, well." He inclined his head toward Cabin 2. "I can't believe it either, but consider the inspiration."

Had that initial glimpse of his Eden, swinging her feet from the dock all those years ago, caught him by surprise like this?

Miranda wadded a delivery strap and tossed it in a bin. "You know what I mean."

Luke turned away, sideswiped by the remembered image of his slight, red-haired wife, her face agleam with water-bounced sunshine. He shut his eyes and saw her years later—corralling strewn fishing poles on that same dock. He saw their girls, too, plain as day—Quinn, just six, and Lucy, not yet four—swinging bullheads from thin lines. As if it were yesterday.

He felt Miranda's hand at his neck. A hand that had fed him after he found them, when he couldn't eat on his own. When he could hardly breathe.

"Not for me to say, little brother, but I can ask. Think it's time?" She eyed him toeing the ground. "C'mon, Luke. No guilt. You're not unfaithful if you return to life."

"Just surprised at my reaction is all. I don't want to forget her." He pulled a tape measure from his belt and ducked into the studio.

Miranda followed. "You'll never forget her, sweetie. Your heart's big enough for a past and a future. Love's not either-or, you know."

"Getting ahead of yourself again, aren't you, Mirs? I show a passing whiff of interest and you're already hooking us up. You even know the first thing about that woman?"

"Only what June told me. Apparently, she's a fisheries biologist. Just took a job on the Elwha. Grew up at the resort. Last name's Nybo."

"Nybo. Like the guy who owned this place? The one who disappeared twenty years ago?"

"Yes. He was Hildy's father."

"I knew him. Worked for him."

"I thought so. But I bet you didn't know this." Miranda ducked toward him. "Her mom, Violet, is Ulysses Diller's *daughter*."

"No kidding. That old griz had *kids*?"

"Two. Violet and an older brother, who died in that bridge crash last winter. He was a chip off Ulysses's old block, June said."

Miranda nudged him with an elbow. "Makes you want to know more, doesn't it?"

"Makes me pity Violet—or want to give her a medal for living with him. Ulysses was a piece of work."

"I know. Says a lot about Violet that his nastiness didn't rub off on her. She seems— *seemed*—his polar opposite. Accommodating. Nice as pie. She's in a lockdown unit now, though. Dementia. Too bad." She snagged the hooked tip of his tape and ran it along the wall. "I'm thinking a display shelf here?"

He nodded. Jotted measurements from two walls as his thoughts floated again to his two little girls, his wife. From the moment he'd met his Eden, every woman had paled next to her. Even after five years, none had come close to attracting him, though he hadn't been looking, anyway. Memories had demanded his attention.

But this Hildy? Something about the woman struck him like a hammer. Or a feather, more like it—and it wasn't just her smooth-skinned beauty.

At the click of a button, the tape retracted, and he clipped it to his belt. "That's all I need for now, Mirs. I've got some nice birch in the shop. You good with that?"

"Sure. You leaving already? Got time for a coffee at the sto—?"

"Getting outta here."

"I upset you. I'm sorry." Miranda moved toward him, but Luke raised a hand.

"I'm okay. Like I said, I'm just surprised. Best if I head home, get my bearings."

Her face fell. "If you need someone with skin, I have good ears."

"You always did. Let's see . . . Friday today . . . Will you be here Tuesday? Bring some of those mugs—or whatever else you're displaying. I'll have shelves."

He forced a smile and lifted two fingers at Miranda from the steering wheel as he turned the truck up the Elwha Valley grade toward Port Angeles. His composure held while the cabins retreated, but at the Lake Aldwell overlook, he pulled off the highway and buried his face in his hands.

Feet away, a Subaru parked at a slant. The driver lowered a window and raised her binoculars toward the valley.

Crowded, Luke blinked until his tears stopped. His vision cleared in seconds, but his mind didn't. He backed out slowly and reentered the highway, oblivious to everything but the road until it carried him into the hillside town seven miles east. Only when he descended Lincoln Street toward the strait did he scan the sky and salt water, gray and sullen at the foot of the slope.

He glanced past an oceangoing freighter to Ediz Hook—the alluvial arm that guarded Port Angeles harbor from the unpredictable Strait of Juan de Fuca. *Puerto de Los Angeles,* he mouthed absently. *Port of the Angels.*

"To the early Spaniards, maybe," he said aloud, picturing his wife in the adjacent seat. "Those angels didn't help you or the girls, baby."

Self-reproach, mostly absent for the last year now, reared ugly in him as he remembered. He knew the judgment well, a complication of the grief that lived in him as a steady companion. He'd learned to refuse the accusation most of the time, once he had allowed forgiveness to reach him. But unbidden, the old tape could still bludgeon him.

Like it was doing now.

The memory always began with that April day—a day much like this one. At the marina in Sekiu, he'd fired the twin Cummins diesels on the *Safe Seas,* the commercial salmon troller where he and Eden and the girls lived in space scarcely big enough for two. Where they filled the hold with line-caught fish, and where Eden homeschooled their young daughters. That last time, while his wife had herded the girls from the Sekiu dock to the gangway, he'd untied lines, returned to the wheelhouse, and watched them climb in the truck before he set out.

Hours of smooth water later, he spotted the truck in the parking lot at the Port Angeles Boat Haven. His wife and daughters waited at his berth in that marina, holding hands. The girls had hopped and high-fived at the slip when he docked.

He thought of other years, how they'd moored here each time he took this trip. How, on each visit to Port Angeles, Eden welcomed the break from tiny Sekiu, enjoying the larger town's bustle, the easy access to shopping and high school friends and swimming lessons for Quinn and Lucy.

He scarcely remembered their rote drive to Fairchild Airport or their routine goodbye that afternoon. Only snippets came to him: Eden's fingers twining his hair. The smell of her neck. How he'd kissed the girls' crowns while their arms wrapped his waist and thigh. "Back in a week and a half," he'd said. "Have fun."

He'd climbed on the prop plane to Seattle eagerly, then boarded the 737 for Hawaii. At thirty thousand feet, he reviewed his route through Oahu and Maui. A packed ten days had followed, during which he renewed every contract for his small fleet's hook-caught wild salmon. He'd added new clients for his IQF—individual quick frozen—fish, too. King salmon: *Chinook*— cold-water beauties for which those high-end restaurateurs paid top dollar.

Elated, he'd called Eden after he checked in for his return flight. His wife laughed. "See you tomorrow with bells on, love," she'd said, then handed the phone to Lucy. "Daddy, I gots starfishes."

He'd texted his wife on the quick Seattle layover. Hadn't thought to look for a reply.

The remembering landed in Luke's chest, which heaved as he pulled to the shoulder at the top of the Morse Creek hill. He hadn't noticed his drive through the rest of Port Angeles.

Stop, he told himself. *Enough torture.* But the memory was alive again in its thousandth replay. Ten thousandth. He gulped air and returned to it.

He'd landed at the little airport at midnight, expecting to see Eden at the wheel of their crew cab and his sleepy, pajama-clad daughters buckled into the back seat. He recalled his confusion when the truck hadn't showed, when his call went to voicemail.

The recollection dizzied him, left him breathless. He surfaced and noted the whizzing cars. Felt the protective numbness advance.

Hang in there, he told himself. *See it through.* Running from the memory in those early years had only heated his loss, then spread it in a thick film across his days and nights. The agony had so disabled him that he'd sold their vessel and his other two boats, along with all those contracts, to Bingo Brink in Sekiu. The right decision, in retrospect. Even the smell of his farm tractor's diesel could send him into a tailspin.

He closed his eyes and forced slow exhalations. Recalled how he pulled his bag from the taxi in the marina's gravel lot that night, there beside the truck Eden should have driven to pick him up. How he'd opened the dock gate and laughed at his early-to-bed wife. *Overslept her alarm,* he told himself. *Or set it for a.m. instead of p.m.*

Dock planks had groaned under the weight of his strides. Pontoons shifted. Water slapped their boat's hull. The breeze flapped a banner at the ship's railing with *Welcome Home, Daddy!* in his six-year-old's scrawl. He whiffed creosote from pilings and diesel exhaust from the throaty generator that warmed his family this chill spring night. He boarded the *Safe Seas* and stepped over three starfish on the deck. Opened the locked cabin door.

Inside, the quiet, stuffy cabin. The girls' bunks, empty. Portholes closed tight against the clammy air.

Then, in his and Eden's bed, his girls—curled against his wife. Lucy, her thumb-sucking stilled as if in sleep, but, like her sister and mother, as dead as the carbon monoxide detector he'd failed to check.

He no longer howled with grief. Nor did he travel the memory every day. But when he did, their deaths smacked him, riddled him, dropped him. Changed him.

Only recently had he recognized that some of that change was good.

10
LUKE

JANGLES

TEN MILES. THEN FIFTEEN. Luke's pain retreated with the distance he put between himself and Port Angeles. Clouds overhead dissipated, too, as the rainy forests that covered most of the Olympic Peninsula gave way to fields of lavender and hay and grazing cattle and his own twenty acres—complete with barn and farmhouse, tractor and irrigation piping.

He'd chosen the place specifically because of the land's location in this rain shadow, away from heavy skies that cried as often as he did—and because he couldn't see any neighbors, or the sea, from anywhere on the hill-rimmed property. The sandy soil and sparse trees, the craggy mountain views . . . even the docile longhorn that came with the place were his life now, the home base for his fledgling carpentry business. If not for Miranda's post-divorce flight to Lake Sutherland and this new venture of hers at the Elwha Resort, he'd have avoided points west of Sequim altogether.

Even in April, his truck raised a trail of dust on his rutted driveway. In the rough pasture bordering the road, a brindle cow wagged a heavy head with every swipe of her tongue. When the broker had shown him the farm, the placid animal had stood ten feet from the fence while the owner's twelve-year-old daughter tied ribbons at the base of curved horns Luke swore were six feet, tip to tip.

The girl had looked at Luke straight-faced, stoic. "We can't take her with us." She rattled a large bell hanging loose at the cow's neck. "Her name's Jangles."

The girl's gap teeth. Those tangled red curls. *Quinny, six years older.* He'd keep the cow forever. Promised the girl, there on the spot.

Thirty-four days from his accepted offer, escrow had recorded his deed to the farm. With the deal done, he loaded his truck with a sleeping bag and the essentials Miranda had retrieved from his boat when he couldn't. Funny the things a guy remembered. That *thwack* of his brother-in-law's nine iron hitting golf balls from their yard onto the fairway behind their house. Miranda at his truck bumper with a box of glassware bound for Sequim. Her saying, "I can help, Lukie."

His reply: "You already have, Mirs. Still alive, aren't I?"

That day, without looking back, he'd driven the hour and a quarter to his new farm and ducked through barbed wire into the pasture. With his back to a cedar fence post, he'd sat in the dry October field and watched the longhorn graze and chew her cud and suck from the trough at the gate. At dark, he pulled the agent's tag from the brass key and, two years and six months after the funeral for his wife and girls, entered the empty three-bedroom farmhouse alone.

At least the rooms didn't echo now. He tossed his keys and phone on the counter, opened the fridge, and slapped a sandwich together for dinner. While he ate—standing—he opened his phone to a scripture app and clicked, listening. *So you have sorrow now, but*

I will see you again; then you will rejoice, and no one can rob you of that joy.

He'd fought that hope like a bluefin, but the braided line held. Miranda had hooked him with it, all right, then strapped on her harness and nursed the rod until he was played out. She'd proven the line's strength again when her own pain struck.

From a pocket he pulled the measurements of his sister's studio. "You want shelves, Mirs? I'll build you a hundred."

―――

The next day, he swigged water and crossed his bumpy lawn to the barn's back door. A northern flicker landed near the stovepipe he'd punched through the roof and patched in with shakes from a cedar bolt he'd found in a stall.

Luke eyed the bird, its cheeks streaked with the male's trademark mustache. "You again. Keep it down this time, will ya?" Inside, he strode past the tractor, yard tools, and a hay-filled stall before he heard the first peck on the metal chimney. He propped the door open to the workshop at the barn's far end as the bird tested tentative patterns of sound.

Frenetic taps for a mate erupted as Luke lifted a birch plank from a curing rack and studied the board's length for warps. He smiled at the speckled woodpecker's drumming, its echo loud in the pipe and megaphone stove, and his thoughts returned to shy Hildy.

"Dang, woman. Don't know how, but you're as loud as that bird."

11

HILDY

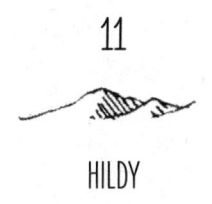

ENCOUNTER

JUNE FLIPPED ANOTHER EGG, then tapped the calendar by the phone, counting. "Six days until you start that new job, Hildy girl. You'd best see your momma before you lose yourself in that river."

At June's kitchen table, Hildy mopped yolk with the last of her toast and nodded. She'd been home a week already without stopping by Hillview.

"You don't need to stay long. She won't know the difference, but I expect the visit will quiet that conscience of yours."

Hildy glanced at the clock. Only seven a.m.—and a Tuesday. If she left now, she'd be back before eight fifteen and the rest of the week would stretch before her with only warm days and mountain trails as companions. Besides, June was right. Guilt niggled at her. Time to check this visit off her list.

"Yeah," she said. "Good idea."

In a rush, she brushed her teeth, donned sunglasses and her waist pack. Then she slid Butterness's floor tray from beneath him and lowered the cage over a bowl. Sunlight caught the canary's feathers as he dropped from the rim into tepid water, dunked his head, and shook droplets onto wings and cage and a towel floor. When Hildy turned to go, he cheeped.

"Take your time, little bird. I'll be back in an hour."

At Hillview, Hildy signed in. Pushed open the buzzing door when the bolt clicked free. A nurse pointed her to the straight-backed chair where Violet watched the courtyard fountain like a movie.

"Momma?"

Violet shifted in her chair. Brushed her cheek as if swiping a fly.

"Mom?"

Her mother twisted, swept a vacuous sightline past Hildy, then refocused on water spilling from tiers.

Pity eclipsed Hildy's discomfort. Her hand hovered above Violet's shoulder before she rested it there.

"Mom!" Louder this time, but her mother was elsewhere. Two minutes later, Hildy was, too. Outside, she absorbed the bright morning and felt only relief.

She was speeding through town when colored lights flashed in her rearview mirror. On Peabody Street the officer checked her license. Studied her eyes when she explained. "My mother . . ."

"Get out of here," he said. "And slow down." For four blocks, she did. Until the boulevard, when she raced around two cars. On the highway, she passed four more. At eight ten, as fatigued as if her own legs had been speeding, she pulled into the resort, caught her breath, and wished herself invisible. Miranda's Audi and Luke's black Dodge nosed Cabin 1 like horses at a hitching post.

Luke turned from his tailgate when Hildy pulled in. Her rearview showed him striding her way, his tool belt swinging at his hips.

She shrank in her seat. Waited. Palpated her braid and checked pockets for rocks. Had no clue what she'd say when she got out.

He was beside her door before she mustered the courage to open it. At least he didn't swing it wide. Instead, he stood back, arms at his sides, watching violet-green swallows rocket overhead. Rested his gaze on her when she climbed out.

"Perfect timing, Hildy. Miranda and I—we could sure use your input. I have one idea about these shelves, and she has another." He laughed, shook his head. "Ah. Big sisters. You have one? If you do, you'll know what I'm up against."

She toed the ground, angling for a piece of granite. "I do. Four years older. Tess."

"Hm. My good friend Bingo's wife is named Tess. I never met a Tess before her."

She looked at him then. "My sister's that Tess. You *know* her?" Agitated fingers traced her phone's outline in the waist pack. Oh, to call Tess then and there and ask about this man who was so . . . so . . . so *what*? She couldn't remember the last time she'd described a man, even to herself.

"Yeah, Bingo introduced us after they'd gone out a few times. She was still in high school. He asked me to stand up for him when they got married, but I was working in the Bering Sea and couldn't make it to Vegas on two days' notice."

"They were in a bit of a hurry."

"I'll say." His laugh felt like warm rain. "No shotgun needed, though. He sure loves that woman."

Bingo loves Tess? Bossy Tess? The thought had never entered her mind. Tess had been pregnant, and they'd married. End of story. Sure, Bingo was good to her sister, but Hildy had always assumed her jovial brother-in-law stayed for his boys and nursed beers for tolerance.

Her thumb played a cuticle like a fiddle. "H-how did you meet Bingo?"

"Met right out of high school when we crewed a purse seiner together for a guy named—wait for it—" He poked a cheek with his tongue. "Ulysses Diller."

Violet's surly old dad? Surely he was joking. "You lived on a boat with my *grandfather?*"

"Small world, right?"

"How frightening."

"You got that right. I almost swam home. Would have, too, if we hadn't been in southeast Alaska in heavy seas. I'll have to tell you that story sometime."

Sometime? She'd tried that once. Ever since, she didn't do *sometimes* with men. Her notebook was inside the cabin, a jar of pens on her desk, fifteen feet away. She sidled toward her door.

He narrowed the distance between them. "Before you go . . . Got a minute to give us your two cents over there?" He raised a bent elbow toward the studio.

Hildy puffed her cheeks. "Sure." *Good. A task.* Enough of this one-on-one. Shifting direction, she strode briskly to Cabin 1, consciously reassembling the persona she'd worked hard to create. When Luke opened the door for her, she'd regained her erect posture, her aloof mien. Untouchable, she hoped.

Miranda met them laughing. "I see my baby brother brought reinforcements." She slung a graceful arm around Luke's neck and held him in its crook, their affection obvious.

Luke ducked free and mussed her hair. She didn't try to smooth it. "See what I mean?" he said. "The woman's a tyrant."

Familiar longing pierced her. *Keep your distance, Hildy.* One problem: these two had drawn her inside their friendliness and now held her there. Did Luke sense her discomfort? She felt his eyes on her.

"So, Hildy. You're our arbiter. Miranda wants to jam every free inch of these walls with display shelving *and* fit her wheel, greenware drying racks, that little water closet, *and* the checkout counter in this twelve-by-sixteen box. Likes things *cozy*, she says."

For the first time in forever, Hildy fought back a grin.

"I told her that if I build out her plan, there won't be more than a foot-wide path through the store. Customers will be knocking things over. Get an animated student on that wheel, and mud'll be flying on the few souls brave enough to come inside."

Now Miranda suppressed a smile. "So Luke suggested an expansion."

"An expansion?" Hildy tried not to squeak, but this was getting away from her. *Give 'em an inch and they'll take a mile.* A favorite Violet line, when campers knocked at all hours.

Luke crooked an index finger, beckoning them to the neglected patio at the cabin's south wall. Hildy bent and pulled grass from cracks—listening. "I could frame a little addition here, facing the highway. Ten-by-twelve or so?" He wagged a hand at the concrete. "The size of this old slab. Lots of glass on three sides and freestanding shelves to display your finished goods and those souvenirs you talked about, Mirs."

Did they realize how little time they'd have here?

"Two rooms," he said, "The original cabin for the messy stuff and a gallery in the new addition, with an exterior door to each." He pointed. "With a half wall there, customers can watch potters work the mud without getting in the way. They'll be lined up for lessons."

Miranda's smile was wry. "My brother the marketer."

"Dam right." He poked Miranda's arm. "No *n*. Pun intended."

"Expensive to build all that," Hildy said, then berated herself for fretting again. She wished it weren't so, but all this—the investment, the hype, the man—scared her. "You do remember they're tearing down our resort in a couple of years. Every structure will go, including this addition you're proposing."

"We know. Don't worry about the money, Hildy. This is my gift. A thank-you to my sister and a tribute to . . . uh . . . someone who's been rebuilding us since life knocked us flat."

Miranda's eyes filled. "Okay, Lukie. You win—if Hildy agrees."

Knocked them flat? Both of them? Hildy didn't dare ask. "As long as you realize it's temporary."

Luke's face lit. "We've got a deal then. I can knock it out in three weeks. Have you up and running before Memorial Day, Mirs."

He squeezed his sister's arm, then shot his palm at Hildy, who shook it as any professional would.

That warmth again. How could she record a touch like his? What would she find on the riverbank to lock it in her brain?

"Don't you need a permit?"

"I'll get something in the pipeline at the county. See that edge around the patio? Used to be some sort of structure attached here. Permitting's easy if you build on an existing footprint. Besides, you think the county will care? This little project will be history in no time." His tape stretched across a new wall, then rattled as it retracted.

Hildy remembered the slat enclosure once attached to these footings—how it afforded guests privacy from the highway and from fishermen at the bridge until an RV bumped a corner post and it buckled from rot. She and Dad had dismantled the whole fence, thrown boards and spongy posts on the burn pile.

Miranda was tapping her chin, walking the proposed room's perimeter. "Few certainties in this life. I'm sure it sounds strange to you, Hildy, but knowing this cabin's short-lived helps us both.

This dream's for *now*, and we're going to make the most of it, right, Lukie?"

He plucked a pencil from behind his ear, a notebook from his chest pocket. Jotted. "Dreams take lumber."

12

HILDY

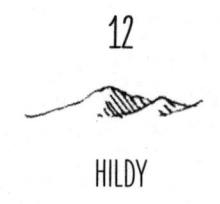

FRAME

IN HER DREAM. Dad ran a SKIL saw alongside a penciled line as Hildy held the plywood flush against the guide. She was young, learning, and the scent of sawdust was the scent of her father. Sprawled under her crumpled duvet in Cabin 2, she burrowed into her pillow and gripped the image until the irresistible scent and feel of wood faded.

But the pulse and whine of a saw persisted. She opened her eyes, read her bedside clock, and crept to the window. Two-by-fours, the longest red-flagged, projected from the bed of Luke's truck. "Only six thirty, Mr. B." Her bird fluttered when she uncovered his cage. "The man's out there already."

She dressed, brushed and braided her hair, replenished the canary's seed and water, and wished she could construct the addition herself. She'd honed her skills on Everett's place, and loved every cut, every nail, every stroke of a brush. *Be practical, Hildy. You start work in five days.*

Well, she could at least keep tabs on the project. June would be up by now. If Hildy ambled over for coffee, she could sit at the wall and peek.

"Good, good, good morning!" Arms raised, June called from her open door, loud as a trumpet. Hildy winced, glimpsed Luke looking their way, and quickly stepped inside. Across the table from Otis, she sat beside the window, where she could duck if she had to.

Otis talked through French toast. "Them two are like kids, buildin' a fort with refrigerator boxes," he said. "It'll take a year or two and bulldozers, instead of a month and rain, but that hideout's still comin' down."

"I don't think they care." Hildy said. "I get the feeling that studio's symbolic of something that happened to them, and how they survived it."

June handed Hildy a warm mug. "Miranda didn't tell you then? You want some egg toast?"

Hildy looked at Otis's plate. "Sure. Didn't tell me what?"

June dunked bread in batter, laid it on the griddle. "About their two hells. His first, then hers."

"What sort of hells?"

"Hell is hell, sweets. Just different addresses for the same enemy. Luke's came with the deaths of his wife and little girls, Miranda's when she caught her skunk husband with a fresh young thing at his pediatric clinic after hours. An RN, so green her pin was still shiny."

Hildy studied the carpenter, laying two-bys on sawhorses. *His family? Dead?* Her breathing stalled. "I guess I knew about Miranda's. But Luke's? How long ago?"

"Gotta be five or six years now. Miranda's, not so long. They're a powerhouse pair, those two. But they'll be the first to tell you it's not their own power. If you live through what they have and still want to see mornin'? You've been *carried*." She flipped the toast, watched it cook, and slid a plate to Hildy.

June nosed the air in Luke's direction. "I liked seeing you talk to him the other day. You two have a lot in common. He used to love salmon as much as you do. Caught 'em an' sold 'em, but still."

Otis carried his plate to the counter and poured more coffee for June.

She added cream. "He turned his back on the sea after everything happened. Sold his boats and market connections for a bundle, but Bingo says the price was fair. It's worked out fine. Luke stays busy now doin' just what you see out there, though finish work's his specialty. Man's an artist."

His wife and little girls. A firebomb of pain.

From June's kitchen, she studied Luke to the whine of his saw and the squeak of nails clawed from old lumber. Watching his hands, she saw her father's guiding her first seven-ounce hammer and whittling finials for the posts on her bed: raccoon, fish, doe, robin. She'd helped Dad sand that bed, then rub it with tung oil. Had slept in it ever since. Happy memories. Good ones—from the start of her lifelong pleasure of working with wood. Good *feelings* instead of burning ones.

Over two days, Luke tore siding from Cabin 1's south wall, pulled wood shingles, and trimmed the roofline to its stripped exterior. Nailed two-by-four framing until ready walls lay flat. While he worked, Hildy hung out in June's kitchen, where she wrote notes in her diary, played cribbage with Otis, folded laundry. And stole glances at the carpenter's progress.

On her third morning at the window, June tapped her with a wooden spoon. "He won't bite, missy. Why don't you offer him a hand?"

Hildy gaped. "I couldn't. I *can't*."

"Why not? Simple project out there. You got the skills. You're out-and-out droolin' over it."

"But—"

"You think he's gonna rassle you to the ground? Take away your hammer?"

"That's not fair, June. I—"

"Push yourself a little. You stand in front of classrooms all the time."

"That's different."

"No harder, though. Two more days and you'll be burnin' daylight on that river and miss your chance."

"June."

"Now I know I'm not your momma and you're no longer a child, but I want you to walk out of this store, pass that little cabin, and take a good look up close at what that man's doin'. I'm gonna watch for words comin' outta your mouth."

"No way, June. I—"

"I'm cashin' in my chips, Hildy. You owe me. Go." June's growl belied her care, and Hildy knew it.

"Only this once. For you."

"That's my girl."

At the gas pumps, Hildy paused, checked over a shoulder for June. Alone, she considered the cabins around the building to her right, then ducked left, where the path behind the woodshed and shop would loop her to her cabin unseen.

Instead, she smacked into June at the corner. "Nuh-uh, girl. You might even like him."

Hildy bit her lip and turned on a heel toward Cabin 1.

Where was Miranda? With no escape route, she trudged toward Luke, dead ahead, his back to her. A guillotine, that man, and she Marie Antoinette. She chafed at the absurdity and walked slower still.

His bare, sweaty back. He would finish that drink from his Thermos, then spot her, expect her to talk to him. How, when she could scarcely *look* at him?

Too much. Scuffing to a stop, she pivoted. June knocked on the window and shook her index finger.

"Hey, Hildy."

His voice stung her. Hand pressed to her belly, she turned and blinked at his sweaty cheeks and forehead. At least he'd pulled on his shirt.

She acknowledged him with a nod. "Luke."

That shirt lifted to mop his brow. Her gaze bounced to his muscled stomach, then to the trees.

He dropped the fabric and grinned. "Your timing's perfect. Could sure use some extra hands. I thought Mirs would be back by now, but she got held up in town. Walls will go up a lot faster with two of us."

Without speaking, she eyed the socket wrench, the waiting heap of bolts, and stepped through the two-by-four wall in the gravel, inspecting. Then she hefted one side of the frame, testing the wood's weight. "Okay," she said. *For June.*

"On three," he said. They hoisted the wall and settled the treated base over the shallow footing. While she held the frame upright, Luke tacked one end to the stripped cabin and positioned braces at its opposite vertical. He tapped the base, aligning it with the concrete rim. "Now to bolt this puppy." His eyes moved from her hands on the frame to her face. "You good holding that?"

"I'd rather run that drill."

He hiked an eyebrow. "You've done this before."

When she nodded, tense, he seemed to be fighting a grin.

"Your jaw's set. You're not kidding, are you?"

Hildy shook her head and glanced furtively toward June, still at the window.

"I marked the centers." He checked the bit, tapped the battery, and laid the drill on the concrete. Gripped the frame mid-wall. "All yours."

Hildy almost leapt to the drill. At a penciled V on the base plate, she positioned the bit and bored the first hole through the wood and into the weathered concrete. Luke and June both shrank in her mind as she secured the anchor bolt, moved to the next crowfoot, and drilled again.

Her socket wrench tightened the last bolt before Luke released the frame. "You're hired. Got a question for you, though."

She rose to her feet and brushed shavings from her pants. Shot him a cautious look.

"Don't worry, woman. It's an easy one." He chuckled low.

Warm, relaxed. His . . . way . . . made her believe him. She exhaled through her mouth.

"Just wondered where you learned to do that. I've known a few biologists in my day, and most of them aren't builders."

Well, that's not true. Plenty of her colleagues could build all kinds of things. "From my dad."

"Ah." Luke's head tipped a few degrees. "I remember your dad. Liked him."

She frowned, suspicious. "You knew him?"

"Bought flies from him when I got my first fly rod in grade school. Worked with him the summer I was sixteen. I painted those rowboats you guys rent out."

"How old *are* you?" she asked. *So blurty—and rude.* Heat crawled her cheeks.

"Turned forty-one last week, a few days before Miranda introduced us."

If he minded her asking, she sure couldn't tell.

"Though it's possible you and I met that summer I worked here. I remember a little blonde girl bringing me water one day out by your shop. She never said a word, except to chirp at that puppy of hers. Think that was you? Do you remember me?"

A fuzzy scene arrived in fragments. So much forgotten or confused in those years, but yes! She did remember him! A man—young, but still a man, swiping red enamel over green. And Cocoa, her chocolate lab puppy, with that dab of red paint on his waggy tail.

"Mom made me bring drinks to workers."

"Huh. Never saw your sister, though. Didn't know you had one."

"Mom always sent me. Tessie was too . . . uh . . . never mind." Too *everything* for Mom.

"Huh. So, if I may ask, how old are *you*?"

"Thirty-four." The question felt fine coming from him.

"Then you'd have been nine."

"I guess."

"And now here we are, practically age-mates."

His eyes startled her. Hazel-colored, like his sister's, but with a smile in them.

"Seems that way to me, at least. How about you, Hildy? You looking at an old man?"

Easier *not* to look. She plucked a nail from the slab and shoved it in her pocket for that spot on her window ledge. Last time she'd guessed a man's age, Cole had been crossing the UW's HUB lawn past her clustered group of brand-new freshmen. He'd moved like someone older. Since him, personal data about men, any men, had been irrelevant. No point in wondering.

But Luke was *way* off. "You're anything but old."

That turn of his mouth. His disarming grin upped the heat of self-consciousness—and attraction—already coursing her face and neck. She directed her attention to the two-by-four skeletons in the gravel, and her hands itched—either to raise the walls or to hurry home and write about all this. *Too much talking.* "Those ready?"

13

LUKE

WORKER

THE WOMAN COULD DO EVERYTHING. While Miranda came and went, Hildy bolted the opposite wall to concrete and helped him position the farthest, southernmost frame. She anchored that side, too, before they ran another two-by-four top plate that overlapped the three new walls and tied them together. By three o'clock they'd cut rafters to the cabin's six-twelve pitch. Ready for more, Hildy stood on the slab with hands on her head.

But Luke unplugged his saw and began coiling the extension cord. "Wish I could stay," he said. "But I've gotta check another job."

Lit by the amber afternoon, she nodded once, fingered the hammer in her tool belt, and edged toward her cabin. Wind off the river caught a stray blonde strand and sent it past her nose. He imagined tucking it behind her ear.

"Think you can help again tomorrow? You don't start work for two days yet, right? On May third, Miranda said? No worries if you have other plans, but—"

"I can help," she said, then slipped like a blown leaf behind the cabin. His breath hitched at her quick exit, but he restrained his impulse to follow, to seek a proper closure to their day together. He waited, listening until her door squeaked and thudded closed. He'd offer to oil the hinges for her. Maybe tomorrow.

He was parking the next morning when a braid-wrapped head showed above the riverbank. Only six fifteen, but Hildy, her face to the trail, was climbing the steep slope toward Miranda's new studio—with her tool belt strapped to her hips. She smiled shyly and shoved something in her pocket.

Luke narrowed his eyes at the sky, then walked toward her. "Gonna be hot today. That river might feel pretty good, come lunch." He raised his chin at something behind her. "You ever jump off that thing?"

Hildy turned to the rope swing that hung near her porch. "Used to."

He knew better than to pry. "Care if I do?"

"No."

"We'd better rumble, then. Finish those rafters, then see how much sheeting we can lay before that water yells so loud we can't resist."

He was even more impressed this second day with her. With every new task, Hildy anticipated steps, calculated quickly, cut boards to the millimeter. Drove 16d nails with three or four swings. She worked fast, too, and though as flighty and quiet as the feral cat under his farmhouse, she seemed eager to help.

She was pushing plywood toward him when he realized that, for once, he didn't shrug off the company of a helper, but welcomed it. For the first time in all those years alone, he felt contented with companionship. Specifically, with *hers*.

When she wasn't looking, he watched her; when she passed near him or held a brace steady or hammered an arm's length away, he breathed her in. For hour upon hour, everything, *everything* about her awakened him. No surprise he reacted physically to the woman. Working that close to her delicate, breathtaking beauty? He was a man, after all, not a stump.

But it was his emotional response that caught him off guard. If recent years had taught him anything, they'd instructed him to intuit hearts—especially the ones made vulnerable, made *beautiful* through pain. He'd seen hurt's effect on his own sister, when her husband's betrayal broke her, and when her reassembly began. Was this Hildy in process, too? He sensed as much. *A bruised reed*, he thought. *Fragile. Fascinating.*

Also surprising: Hildy didn't rouse memories of Eden, as he'd feared she would, but instead stirred him with curiosity about what went on in that mind of hers—a place he glimpsed as so winsome and mysterious he would drink her down in great gulps if he could.

Only a fool would try that. Either she was the shyest girl he'd ever met, or someone had scared her. A former boyfriend, maybe? Or family, if her grandfather gave any clue to their dynamics. Miranda said that uncle who'd died at the bridge was rough, too.

Across the slab, she raised a board to eye level, sighting its span for warps.

Who are you, Hildy Nybo?

High noon and, as forecast, pushing past eighty in the shade. Luke heaved another sheet of plywood onto the roof, and Hildy snugged it into place. Was the woman even human? Not a trace of sweat on her, and he was dripping. Stinking. "Enough of this. How deep's the water under that swing?"

Hildy looked toward the river, slow to answer. "Eight, maybe ten feet. Gets shallower midstream."

"Perfect. You in?" He dropped his cap and jumped to the ground. Unbuckled his tool belt and draped it on a sawhorse. Stuffed socks into one boot and emptied his jeans pockets into the other.

She drove another nail. "You go ahead," she said, but when he stripped off his shirt, she skittered down rungs, berthed him wide, and trotted toward her cabin without a look. When he rounded the studio, the half-open blinds at her windows wiggled and clamped shut.

Oh well. He hobbled barefoot on gravel and patchy grass to the bank, sent his thoughts from Hildy to the water, and grabbed the swing. Airborne, he whooped, then plunged deep into the clear, delicious river. The delicious, *glacial* river. Submerged, he saw trees and a cabin's log walls and Hildy all bending in the watery lens as he swam upward. He surfaced, gasping from the cold, and looked again as she carried a cage onto her porch, lowered it to a shady table, and sat beside it, her feet propped on the low rail.

"You could have warned me about the icebergs." He treaded below her, his kicks awkward in the soggy jeans.

She smiled as he swam to shore. "You bring a towel?"

"Figured I'd drip dry."

"Could take a week." She disappeared inside, returned with a bath towel, and tossed it over the rail.

Banter from the girl. A broad-beamed smile. A pretty one, too. A crack in that tough little nut, and he liked what he saw through it.

Careful, man. Don't get ahead of yourself. This had to be good for both of them, not all about him, like it was when he talked Eden into a life on the boat. *So they could be together,* he'd told her, then deluded himself into believing she loved the water as much as he had. Never mind that she'd been seasick for a year.

What a goon, thinking his wife would want to raise two babies without a shred of grass for them to play on unless they stopped in a port that had lawns. He'd offered his daughters no bicycles or swimming pools or consistent playdates or, once they got older, normal school or, for months on end, church with other families.

Their life had even excluded connection with his wife's close friends. He'd been dumb enough to believe her when she told him he was all she needed.

Yeah, she'd always made the best of their life together. Not like her to fake things, either. The woman had jumped in with both feet, deciding to *delight*—her word—in how he provided for them, even as she delighted in homeschooling their daughters and, it crushed him to say, in *him.*

Sure, his drive to protect and care for them had served his family well, but his ambition was another animal entirely. *Gah.* He'd been blind as a bat before they'd died. Then hindsight had stripped his self-centeredness to its skivvies. Grief had finished the baring.

He'd stay in the wheelhouse this time, on high alert for his own myopia, for submerged logs of egotism and appetite. No illusions on this go-around, if it even became one. Ignore those deadheads and they'd sink him and anyone he brought close.

No more. Never. So help me God.

Hildy busied herself with the cage while he dried his hair and skin and wound the terry cloth like a twist tie around each leg, squeezing water from his jeans. He climbed the bank toward her porch and caught sight of the bird.

"Thought you lived alone," he said.

"I've had him since college. Going on twelve years now."

"Didn't know canaries lived that long."

"Yeah, he's old, but another two or three years wouldn't be strange." Her lips puckered, and she kissed at the bird. "I wish he'd live forever."

To be that bird right now. "I'd bank on it, if I were you."

Her snapping eyes. "How's that?"

"If that little wonder isn't made new when the Creator reboots things, I've been hugging the wrong tree."

"As in *all things made new*."

A restatement, not a question. He hid a smile. "Yeah. A big *new*. Mighty enough to heal all the crap we've lived through. Where'd you learn that verse?"

"Dad took me to Awana for years."

"Where you cleaned up on those memory badges, I'm guessing."

"I have a few. I couldn't keep a lot of things straight back then, but I could memorize." She shifted the cage so sunlight reached it. The bird swiped chaff from his beak on a perch.

"Gotta be more to that story."

Another kiss to the canary. No sign she'd heard.

"You believe them?" His fingers combed damp hair to the side.

"Believe what?"

"Those promises you memorized. Those verses."

Hildy sighed. "I want to. Need to. Said I would."

"But?" He propped forearms on the rail.

"But . . . nothing."

"But *what*, Hildy?"

She sank deeper into the chair's faded cushions. Her hands ran the length of the wooden armrests until her elbows locked.

When she didn't answer, he again ran fingers through his drying hair, then turned toward his truck. Turned back when he heard her.

"I don't know. Stuck, I guess. Seems to me I should see more power in those promises. Maybe that's one of the reasons I came home to the Elwha. A gamble, but if that river can be restored . . . It would help me a lot to see *something* made new."

He ran a palm along the mossy rail. "Well, Miranda's studio's a good start."

Her quick smile was unguarded.

"But I'm gonna eat first," he said. He draped the towel on the railing. "See you in thirty."

───

Luke closed his lunch box as a rusty Ford towed a skiff past Cabin 1. Hildy joined him at his truck, hands pressed to her ears. "Ouch. That muffler."

He finished his apple and tossed the core in a bucket. "I'd lay odds he has a Harley in his garage." He flicked a wrist as if revving a throttle, then watched the elderly man drive past. "More like a '57 Chevy he bought new, if that's Kor Visbeek. I built a garage for it." He lowered his tailgate, donned work gloves, and sent the old man a two-fingered wave.

Hildy peered after the truck and boat. "I remember him. Another regular. June said we're full up with longtimers the next few weeks. Both sides." Her line of sight went to three more cabins across the river near a rustic, low-roofed structure. "Mostly fishing guests now, but square dancers show up Memorial Day weekend. Good for Miranda's opening."

"How many come for that?"

"A bunch. They reserve cabins a year ahead, but with Miranda's and mine out of play, there'll be more tents and RVs. Otis rents porta potties, and they shower in the laundry building or at the dance hall."

"Or jump in the river with soap, right?"

"I've seen that."

"Sounds like a hoot. When you were a kid—you ever go?"

"Yeah, but we worked, too. Mom handled the store and rentals here. Dad, Tess, and I ran the kitchen at the hall. Tended the campgrounds. Kept an eye on things."

"So you didn't dance?"

"I don't dance."

"At *all*?" *Unfathomable.* When she winced, he pulled the shingles from his truck bed, wishing he'd held his tongue. "You roofed before?"

Her hammer tapped her palm.

"Of course you have."

14

HILDY

CEDAR

WHEN HE ASKED AGAIN, Hildy snatched a shingle from Luke and pounded the roofing nail too hard, her mouth a thin wire. "I said, I don't dance."

He lowered his hammer. "Whoa, whoa." He caught her tool's claw on an upstroke. "Last I heard, *square* and *dancing* weren't fighting words. Neither was a man's surprise that you didn't partake. What gives?"

She shrugged, tried to wrest the hammer, but he held firm. "Nothing," she said.

"Nothing? I don't work that way, Hildy. With paid workers, volunteers, friends, enemies—with anybody. Life's too short."

Her head jerked as she sought escape. *Finch on the lookout,* Otis teased every time she did that. She wished she could fly now. The ladder behind Luke? A jump from the roof? Neither feasible. Silence—her third, most-practiced option—seemed appropriate.

A minute passed. By the second, she knew she was sweating, and not from the heat. Luke had come too close, sniffed out history she'd tried to bury. Unless she wanted a scene, she'd have to answer.

"Hot and tired is all. Going too slow."

He rolled back onto elbows, his legs straight. Midday heat activated and lifted the fragrance of cedar shingles between them. Along the river, sparrows sang to mates.

"What else?" His ice cream coax. *Soothing.*

"M-my dad had two left feet."

He stretched onto the felt underlayment. Lowered the cap brim shading his eyes and looked at her, waiting.

"Dad loved music, but couldn't sing or dance or play an instrument to save his life."

"Which caused a problem?"

She inhaled sharply and nodded. How did he—?

"And it affected you. Am I right? I don't want to assume."

"Yes. Mom danced all the time. I hated watching her. Hated how she taunted him." Fine hair on her arms stood on end. Had she just betrayed her mother? Aloud? Why was she telling him this?

Luke lay back on the incline, his face to the sky. Islands of river water still darkened his jeans. "I hear you, Hildy."

He does? With twitching fingers, she checked the plait under her straw hat, pulled cotton sleeves to her wrists against sunburn, and adjusted her sunglasses, glad for dark lenses that let her watch him. She braced for his next comment, fearing a word from him would undo the gift in those four words.

He swept hands at swallows chittering overhead, folded them at his belly and closed his eyes. "Who needs the radio?"

Unobserved, she studied his thick shoulders and felt a fleeting urge to touch those folded hands. No—to hide from them. No, not from them, but from this confusing man who helped her forget that she couldn't remember. She slid a sliver of broken shake under her hatband like a feather. The day's memento, for her pencil cup.

"Who needs what radio?"

He sat up, reseated his hat, and pointed at the swallows. "Don't need one. Good music right there. Better those birds singing than me. When it comes to carrying a tune, I guess I relate to your dad. Dancing's a different story, though. I've even danced while cleaning fish. And in my dreams. Alone, with a partner—"

She snatched another shake from the bundle.

He laughed. "More fun with a partner." He slid the wide slabs between them. "Aren't these beauties? I cut 'em from an old-growth cedar bolt some old-timer left in my barn. Got fifty years plus in them on a roof."

"Why use them here?" Her fists relaxed and opened. *Back to work.*

"Because we have them today. Because we can. I did enough hoarding for 'just in case' in my old life. Stuff, emotions . . . Don't get me wrong, I pay attention, plan, but stingy doesn't work for me anymore. I'd roof this shed with gold for Miranda, if I had it."

Longing punched her. Who would roof anything with gold for her? "Think I could take a shake home, then?"

"Sure, but why?"

"They smell so good." She'd hang the shake above her bed, between that 1907 bulk nailer and that steel square, if there was room. The wood's scent would help her remember.

※

Quitting time, she tucked a straight-grain slab under her arm and surveyed the new roof.

Luke threw scraps in a pile. "We'll finish the ridge in the morning. If we work late tomorrow, we can hang the plywood on all three walls and get the place wrapped before you ditch me."

"Ditch you? I—"

He raised his hands in surrender and smiled. "Good help's hard to find, you know? Who'd have guessed my competition would be a *river*?"

Too large for the crowded wall above her bed, the aromatic shake stood propped against her lamp, already marked with the number she also jotted beside the briefer-than-normal day's entry, her hands and mind gone quiet after a few short lines. *Cabin 1 at 6:30 a.m., roofing with Luke. Luke on rope swing at lunch. Dad, Mom. Dancing. Luke said he heard me.*

At quitting time the next evening, she stood by his truck, where Luke's elbow jutted from the window that framed him from the chest up. "Will you just look at that. Sheeted and wrapped in record time."

Hildy glanced at the studio, then unbuckled her tool belt. With their project nearly finished and her river work beginning, would she see him again? *Not like this.* When she shivered, Luke's eyebrows crouched.

"You okay?"

"Yeah." *Not really.*

He watched her, apparently unconvinced. "What time you get off work tomorrow?"

"I don't know yet."

"Stop by Cabin 1 when you do? I may need my fave coworker's advice."

Like calling an only child the favorite kid. "All right."

"Good. Best workdays I've had in years, Hildy, and you get all the credit. I'll miss—I'll miss your help."

That night she laid a numbered scrap of house wrap in her notebook as a bookmark and wrote.

Worked with Luke.

15

HILDY

DAVE

THE COMMOTION OF WAKING BIRDS roused Butterness first. At four thirty a.m., the bird's feet pinged the cage and woke Hildy, who knew he clung to vertical bars beneath his cage's cover, his head tilted to a chorus from the open window. *Canticles,* she thought, parsing the outdoor chirps and whistles of finches from those of chickadees and sparrows. The chirrups of grosbeaks from those of robins.

"Wishing, little guy?" She slipped from her bed, corralled her kinked, shiny hair into a loose rope, and checked the window screens for gaps. "Pretend you're outside with them," she said and unlatched the canary's gate.

Butterness hopped to the opening and perched there, cheeping, before he flitted. She silently reviewed her acquisition of each perch he chose: boot, willow branch, hand drill, plane, paint roller, wool sock, and the year-old hummingbird nest on that alder branch. The canary pecked at a twig's lichen before he flew on, a yellow blip in the jungle on her walls, then her crowded floor, then two of her carved bedposts: salmon, raccoon. A yellow laser pointer, testing her recall.

"Such a memory hopper. Thank you, little bird."

He sang from high on the wall while she changed his water, filled his seed, spread grit on a fresh floor. He flew to the cage top and cocked his head.

"No hurry, Mr. B. It's my first day on the new job, so I'll be gone for a while. Stretch those wings while you can."

An hour later, the bird entered the cage for the millet spray and a slice of apple she clipped inside. She snapped the door closed, blew the canary a kiss, and slung her day pack over a shoulder. When she stepped onto the shady grounds, June's head bobbed over her sink below sunrise-draped foothills. Campsites stirred with anglers. At the lane's far end, fishing lines bent into the lake from the dock and boats like insect feelers.

That dazzling, awful lake.

Was she jealous? Who wouldn't be? How many times had that reservoir won over her mother, its peacock water a siren call that trumped her, Tessie, and Dad?

A soup of feelings she didn't understand and couldn't describe washed over her. She swiped hands down her body as if she could shed them, then hurried back to Cabin 1, perusing the new, dew-wet roof until her breathing calmed. Luke would return with his tools soon. She pressed fingers to the stapled house wrap, tapped a sawhorse, then straddled it while she relived the last five days. *Miranda. The sawing. The rope swing. The hammering. The words.*

A beep at six thirty. She pulled her phone and read the text from Dave Cloud, likely up before she was. **Heading to the estuary now. Meet you there, if you can come early.**

Luke waved when they passed on the highway. His truck retreated in Hildy's rearview mirror above her bright red cheeks.

Her foot touched the brake and released it, and she sped toward the reservation.

Minutes down Place Road, she parked, hiked to the estuary, and waved to a man in chest waders. Tall, gangly Dave Cloud splashed toward her, his arms spread in a disproportionate wingspan. His spaniel looked up, then returned to nosing rocks.

"You know what Ben says about all this." He had the good sense not to hug her, and she was glad. No other greeting, either. Just Dave, immersed in the consuming passion of his life.

"Tell me."

"That before long, our salmon will swim the river's length again. That they'll slap their tails in the shallows and lie on their sides digging nests, laying eggs in those redds. I see them too, Hildy, every species, shooting through those emptied reservoirs. Chinooks, spawning in the headwaters."

A mental clip from fifteen years earlier played in her brain, and she saw Klallam Elder Ben Charles Sr.'s eyes crimp with hope for the Elwha. Despite the fact that the Tribe had convinced Congress to restore their river, by then three years had passed since the 1992 Elwha Act, and those dams still blocked fish passage. She had needed Ben's unwavering confidence to bolster her own.

"You been here in a while?" Dave asked. Behind him, the Elwha spilled into the Strait of Juan de Fuca.

"Not for years. Early college." She remembered the date.

"I figured. Best way to help you start this job is to reintroduce you—show you this beach, then the dams, firsthand. See them through the education and experience you've acquired since you left here." He pointed at a heron, stalking shallows bedded with grapefruit-sized stones. "You can see why fish have trouble down here. Those reservoirs are flat-out constipated with sediment that belongs in this stretch of river." He flipped a large rock with his heel. "We don't draw spawners with rocks this big."

The heron lifted on slow-motion wings and they watched the bird pass. "Not much woody debris, either," Dave said. "How can smolt hide from big boys like that?"

Her eyes swept the river's mouth, where channeled sand bars that should have sheltered the estuary were conspicuously absent. "Any clams left? Crabs?"

"A handful. But with the first dam only five miles upriver, what would you expect? This habitat's been starved for a century. There's enough sediment behind those dams to stack a football field three miles high, though. Just wait 'til a few million metric tons of that stockpile wash down here. When the water clears? Hoo-ee. Happy beach, happy seabed."

"Fish won't be able to breathe in that silt, Dave. Species mortality—"

"Another reason for the hatchery. And before the demolition crew dynamites anything, we'll sling-load coho upriver by helicopter and release them mid-reach—above Lake Aldwell—where they can access Little River and Indian Creek. Clean tributaries, gravel spawning beds."

Indian Creek. Hildy saw her mother, thirty years younger, wading the shallow stream, picking the watercress she mixed into salads.

"We'll implant transmitters in those fish, right?" A given, but she had to ask.

"Right. We'll track them." He shoved a stick between stones. "And yeah, death rates will be ugly for a while. They'll dismantle the dams in increments, but even pulsing the water's release, sediment will clog gills, stress filter feeders. No way to avoid losses until the river stabilizes."

Gulls stood one-legged on the coarse shore, their beaks aimed into wind stirring chop on the strait. Hildy waded the floodplain, assessing. "That baseline data you've accumulated so far: fish counts, habitat. You've got it for me?"

"Years' and years' worth. Flash drive's on my desk."

She raised field glasses to the far shore. "Where've you been setting up your sonar?"

Dave laughed. "Upriver, where the cameras can read the whole span. At least we've got two of them. Seventy thousand bucks apiece and we park them on *ladders*. Numbers seem to be accurate, though. I'll have you monitor those counts."

"Duly noted," she said. A nearshore fogbank wafted inland, gauzing river and sky. Hildy shivered in the marine air as she scanned the water for young fish. "It's like a graveyard out here."

"For now," he said. "Let the dream propel you, Hildy." He shaped index fingers and thumbs to frame the strait. "Picture it like the early 1900s. A million wild fish, sniffing their way home to the Elwha. Pinks so thick they bump each other onto shore."

"It happened once, Dave. That count was an exception."

He dropped his hands and turned to her, earnest. "Destroy that hundred-foot blockade, then the two-hundred-footer at Glines? I'm morphing a movie line here, but if we rewild it, they will come."

He seemed more certain than she that fish numbers would surge again. Every year now, only two to five percent of the historically typical four hundred thousand salmon returned from the ocean, and those numbers were mostly propped up by hatcheries. This whole effort was a high-odds gamble.

"I've met my share of naysayers, Dave. Some think no matter what we do, this river won't amount to more than a museum fishery."

"Yeah, yeah. Like runty bison at tourist stops." He tapped his watch. "Time to prove them wrong. Follow me to the office. I'll load you up with bedtime reading before we head upriver." Fingers to teeth, he whistled. The dripping dog splashed to them from the opposite bank, shook, and leapt into the ancient jeep's passenger seat.

Minutes later, Hildy walked through the foyer of the Klallam Tribe's Natural Resources Building to a long hallway and Dave's window-lined office. Elevation maps of the Elwha Valley and Olympic National Park, photos of field teams, and posters of each of the river's ten sea-going fish runs spanned his walls, unchanged since her internship as a UW junior.

"As if I were here last week," she said. "Even your dad's Marine Corps Willys. Camp Pendleton, 1953, if I remember right." A small smile bent her lips. "Isn't that jeep getting tired?"

"What *don't* you remember? Bet the serial number's stowed away in that big brain of yours, too." He plopped behind his heaped desk and passed her a thumb drive. "Got a paper file for you here, somewhere."

While Dave riffled through folders, Hildy browsed his walls and paused at a framed yellow document. "Aha. There it is." She tapped the glass, traced *The Elwha River Ecosystem and Fisheries Restoration Act* with a pinky.

He looked up from an open file drawer. "It's why you're here, my friend."

"Signed by H.W. on October 24, 1992—with no idea where the money would come from."

"Happiest day of my life."

"Almost eighteen years ago. Hasn't happened yet, Dave."

"It will. If you'd witnessed all those polarized groups deciding the dams had to go, you'd have a lot more confidence. I tell you, Hildy, the way they listened and heard each other was a real miracle. And to reach a *consensus* on how to save the fishery? Think of it—a consensus! Even from mill owners who profited from the dams' electricity. Of course, ongoing licensing problems leveraged them, and the Elwha Act promised compensation for pricier wattage from the City of Port Angeles, but they eventually came on board, too. Unbelievable."

He wagged his head, clearly still amazed. "To have *all* parties agree to demolish those dams? Two *functioning hydroelectric dams*?

Nothing short of amazing. When they took the vote, *every single player* agreed that healing the river was worth the cost of removal."

Healing—worth the cost. "Right under my nose when I was in high school, but I had no clue." *Dad was missing in the mountains.*

"Most didn't," Dave said.

"Who paid? How'd they afford it?"

"They couldn't afford it. Still can't, but they're determined to find the funds. Private and government monies have moved around, but not nearly enough yet. Demolition and rehab may cost upwards of three hundred fifty million bucks by the time everybody hangs up their shovels."

She sat, tapped her armrests. "That much, h·h?"

"At least."

"Hope we're in time."

"Aw, Hildy. Those native genetics in our hatchery? National park habitat? Our stockpile of native plants for those lake beds? The way nature heals? C'mon. You know those fish will be back."

"How long do you think it'll take? Projections are all over the place."

"Hard to say. A restoration of this scope is uncharted territory."

"For the Tribe's sake, I hope it's sooner than later. When their moratorium goes into effect next year, *nobody* will fish in that watershed until enough of those salmonids return."

Dave's voice rose. "You can learn a lot about patience from the Tribe. Sure, we're champing at the bit, but healing's in sight, Hildy. We've got to give the river every possible chance to recover."

He was making her nervous. "You don't have to convince me, Dave. As a kid, I watched salmon slam concrete every year trying to jump that dam, then swim loops and die at the base, while tankers drove through our campground and dumped trout into the reservoir. *Trout*, thousands at a time, for crying out loud."

While Mom rowed the lake with that scary shadow in her boat.

"Yeah. So many trout. Not the bears' first choice, but better than nothing. And rainbows fed a lot of kingfishers, osprey, eagles." He snorted. "*And* those herons."

He shuffled more papers, then waggled a thick manila file folder. "Got it." His eyes shone with the small triumph. "Everything you'll need to bring you up to speed. If the data's not on that thumb drive, you'll find it in here. Wade through it and I'll shoehorn you right in. Team members have read your work, so expect an open-arms reception."

Oh, she wished she could work alone. "No welcome party."

He suppressed a laugh. "You know me better than that. Just our regular meetings. Apart from those, you can slither wherever you like, eel girl. If you don't want one-on-ones, email works. Just get the job done and I'll be happy as Frodo here."

Stretched flat on the rug, the dog slapped his tail twice.

"Gotta say, Hildy Nybo, working my job and yours for the last couple of months has been tough, but I'd do it again if it meant getting you here." He handed her a key. "To your office—end of the hall. Unless you'd prefer Grand Central. The one right next to mine's open, too."

"You know *me* better than that, Dave."

"Figured as much. Ready to see the beasts? I'll drive."

16

HILDY

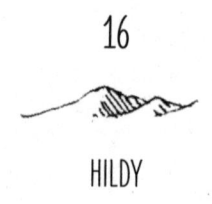

TOUR

FRODO LEAPT TO THE DRIVER'S SEAT. Dave tapped the dog to the jeep's rear, snagged a towel from a footwell, and wiped the cushions. While the spaniel panted behind them, he shifted into gear and watched the road. Hildy, however, took in the reservation's mobile homes and mossy ranch houses in damp alder groves, where children's toys mingled with crab pots, drift boats on trailers, and larger boats on blocks, their hulls green with algae and waiting. Fishing nets, their elliptical floats strung like berries, draped from large racks in side yards or from porches or the eaves of cavernous metal shops,

Lives on hold, she thought.

They turned upriver, and she shifted her gaze to the Elwha Dam. Once the heartbeat of the early Port Angeles settlement, its concrete jammed the steep gorge where generators still hummed like a wild hive. On the walkway at the dam's crest, she gripped the chain link barrier mid-span and peered over the downstream edge. "For all its heft, this thing looks kind of rickety," she said.

Dave bumped his heel as if testing the walkway for rot. "It does leak, you know. There were shortcuts in construction from the outset. Builders didn't reach bedrock the first time they built it. The thing failed almost as soon as the water rose. Next go-around the foundation seeped. A wonder it's held all these years."

She knew the history. "Bet that collapse was wild."

"I'll say. It blew out from the bottom. Cost overruns for replacement almost ate Thomas Aldwell's lunch."

"Too bad he didn't quit after that first breach."

He tapped his phone and handed it to her. "Yeah, what a bulldog. Gutsy, coming all the way here from Toronto thinking this territory was his to conquer. The guy crawled the valley for twenty years buying land cheap. Believed if dams could power Port Angeles and points beyond, he'd vault the peninsula out of the Stone Age. He fought hard to get his hands on those canyons."

Hildy scrolled photos of Aldwell's well-documented life: homesteader, merchant, entrepreneur. "Different mindset back then. Think of it, Dave. No fish ladders in either dam."

"They weren't part of his equation. In those days, if a few salmon died for the sake of progress or a bottom dollar, oh well. Plenty more where those came from."

Hildy sighed and turned to the walkway's upstream fence. Past the log boom barrier that distanced boats from the spillways, the reservoir ran aqua to a forested bend. She'd watched Violet row past that jog from uplake for years, convinced she'd never see her mother again. She shuddered and forced her thoughts to Luke's happy drop from the rope swing.

"We have one more year to wrap up our final readings, Hildy. The more documentation we have pre-removal, the better our post-removal analyses will be a year, ten years, fifty years from now. We're writing the manual for river reclamation everywhere. Hopefully, those making ecosystem decisions at the top will agree."

Hildy pinched her braid. "I took the USGS job to avoid politics, Dave. To gather data and present it without manipulation. To help fish by letting facts speak."

"Precisely what we'll be doing, and it's sure going to be fun. Now let me show you a few things here before we head up to Glines."

When they rounded the curve toward the Elwha bridge, Dave slowed at the turn to the upper dam. Hildy craned in her seat, intent on a glimpse of the studio and Luke's cap and curls.

"Need to stop at your place?" Dave asked.

"No. Thanks. Checking progress on a new building is all."

"At your resort? Why on earth—"

"It's a gift." She folded into her seat as he turned onto Olympic Hot Springs Road. "From a renter's little brother. A studio for her. For a year or two."

"Pretty nice gift. You better cover their eyes when the excavator shows up."

"They know the clock's ticking."

Dave accelerated past Madison Falls' trailhead and the pack mule barns. More familiar landmarks fell behind them as he drove deeper into national park foothills thick with old conifers. Tumbling from headwaters in the rugged Olympics, the Elwha sprinted headlong in and out of view.

And then, Glines Dam. Hildy whistled low when they reached the spillway overlook. "So tall. Gets me every time." Concave against the glacial water of Lake Mills, the structure sealed narrow, jagged Glines Canyon in an imposing arc.

"Over two hundred feet. Twice the Elwha's height. The razings will be the biggest dam removal project in US history." He cleared his throat. "Sorry. You know all that. I'm used to giving tours to dignitaries."

"It's going to be a mess, Dave."

"A controlled, necessary mess, but yes."

Blue-green water from Lake Mills sluiced the spillways and tumbled in a series of churning curtains to the boiling river below. Mist shrouded the canyon walls. Hildy snapped photos of the lake, the dam, the precipitous drop. "You have bathymetric maps for me? Shoreline samples? Watershed assessments? Mid-reach fish counts from here to Lake Aldwell?"

"All on that little drive in your pocket." She followed his gaze to two black-tailed deer hock deep in the reservoir. "Scientists from the NOAA and some of your former colleagues from the USGS arrive next week. Come July first, the river will be crawling with research teams from all over. You and I will coordinate interagency efforts, direct traffic, and join them with our team from the Lower Elwha Tribe. Another snorkel survey's planned for late August, so get your gear up to speed. I want your eyes and brain in that river, Hildy."

"I can do that." Her heart was already there.

Frodo snorted at the window's gap as they returned to the jeep. Hildy plucked and smoothed a brown and white flight feather from the side of the road and tucked it in her fleece, noting details for her diary.

"Osprey?" Dave asked.

"Yeah. Decor for my new office, unless you turn me in for keeping it."

He laughed. "I've got a few more you can have."

After work, Hildy trained her gaze on the clicking gas pump meter, determined to avoid an awkward, cross-lot hello to Luke. Only when she flipped off the lever and reseated the nozzle did she finally glance at Cabin 1. New openings for windows and doors yawned from the sheeted exterior, but Luke's and Miranda's parking spaces stood empty.

Her shoulders sagged. *Gone home.* She replaced her tank's cap and drove the short span to her cabin, where June was crossing the grass from Cabin 3, a bucket of cleaning supplies on her arm.

Hildy waited for her at the porch. "He left already?"

June pinched a smile. "If you're looking for Otis, he's sprucin' up the dance hall. Shindig's only a few weeks off now."

Hildy felt her skin go pink. "I didn't mean Otis."

June elbowed her and giggled. "Won't kill you to say his name, sweets. He went to get somethin' to eat. I told him I'd fix him a burger, but he declined. Said he'd be back by four thirty to wrap up."

Hildy checked her watch. She had time to freshen up. Maybe he still needed help.

"You go. Put your feet up until he gets here, girl."

Hildy didn't move. "After I say his name. What then, Junie? I'm out of practice."

June studied her for a moment. "Ask him a question or two. Near as I can tell, the man's an open book. Regardless, I'm sure he'll be happy to see you."

To see me? Not just have me work with him? Hildy frowned. "I'd better check my bird."

"You do that. Just don't lock yourself in there. I bet Luke'll want to show you everythin' he accomplished today. Sure looks nice."

Hildy's hand was on her latch when June called from the road, "How was *your* day, girl? Job good?"

"Job's good." she said, and slipped inside.

By four thirty, she'd brushed her teeth, run a warm washcloth over her face, and hurriedly rebraided. By four thirty-five, she'd tuned the radio to music for Butterness and was peeking through slats when Luke's truck rolled into the yard. When late sun struck him through the broken clouds, an electric wave rolled from her chest and raised the temperature in her face and neck.

She swigged water, donned sunglasses. Then she jumped from her porch and walked to Cabin 1. To see if she could help.

He stopped walking when he saw her and smiled, arms at his sides. "Hey, you're home! How'd your first day go?" Even through dark lenses, she felt him meet her eyes.

She stepped backwards, rubbed her elbows. "Okay. Nice, actually."

"I hoped it would be," he said.

His attention spotlit her, made her squirm.

"You stay in the office or get outside?"

Her tongue wouldn't move.

He hiked his eyebrows and looked away, then raised an arm toward the studio in slow motion, like she would to avoid startling Butterness. "Finished a few things out here today. Gotta say, I missed hearing your hammer. Want a quick tour?"

Her held breath escaped. "Sure."

He waved her through a second entrance, new since morning. Took her shoulders and guided her to mid-room to views through openings on three walls, then swiveled her to the pass-through he'd cut into the original cabin.

His hands on my shoulders. That spin. She'd write them down.

"Windows and doors arrive tomorrow, so we can zip the place up. More rain coming by Thursday."

"Seems bigger with those cutouts," she said.

"Doesn't it? Miranda's pretty happy with the ambient light." He toed a bundle of insulated wire on the floor. "I ran a line from that new breaker box for some display lighting and outlets. Might get to those by Friday."

"I like it." What else could she say? Fingers found her braid. She pushed a hairpin deeper, felt for wisps.

"I'm done for today, though. My stomach's been growling for an hour. You hungry?"

Come to think of it, she was. But why was *he*? Hadn't June said he'd gone for food? Hildy followed him outside. "I guess."

"Thought you might be. Got a couple of Subway footlongs in my truck, if you'd like one."

A whole foot? "Kind of you. Thanks."

"I can send it home with you or you can join me, if you want. I thought I'd hike to Madison Falls to eat. Nice walk. Change of scenery."

"I used to ride bikes there with my dad," she said. "Haven't gone since."

"About time then, don't you think?

She pulled a twig from her pocket and pretended to study it. "Uh. Sure."

A new smile split his cheeks. "Good deal. Let's go. I'm going to fall over if I don't get some food in me."

She touched her sunglasses, wished the lenses were darker. "We can eat here, if you'd rather not wait."

"Aw, I'm exaggerating. It's only two miles." He grabbed a Subway bag from his truck console, held it aloft, and tipped his head at the mountains. "C'mon. We'll be there in no time. Food'll taste better in that little glen."

A hike and a sandwich. Something to *do*. She waved shyly to June at her window and matched his strides. At the highway, she fell into step beside him and, when he didn't start blabbing, didn't ask questions, she relaxed. As when they'd framed or roofed or sheeted, he was so . . . *easy*. Comfortable, whether or not either of them spoke. Such a *relief*.

For the next mile and a half, she heard only birdsong, the river's clatter of water over stones, and the slap and scuff of feet on the two-lane Olympic Hot Springs Road she'd traveled with Dave earlier that day.

At the trailhead, Luke turned from the pavement to the river fifty yards off, the water's earlier gray now azure with the clearing sky. "That riverbed will sure change when those dams are gone, won't it?"

Would it ever.

"Everything will ch-change."

She cringed. All the times she'd taught ecosystem restoration, and now she was *stuttering*? Her tongue felt downright spastic. If he pressed her to explain . . .

Ask him a question or two. Above the buzz in her ears, she heard June, whispering from her kitchen.

Okay. Okay. Her exhale blew from puffed cheeks.

"June said you're a commercial fisherman?"

"Used to be."

"So you know the life cycle of salmon, right?"

"More or less. I know they return to home rivers anywhere from eighteen months to eight years after they go to sea, and that I like—liked—to have lines in the water when they headed there." He looked at her quizzically. "Why you asking?"

She wrung her hands, suddenly overcome with the importance of what she wanted him to understand. "Because opening this river will let them do that. Let those fish return here, after so, so long away! After they breach those dams and the grit washes out of those reservoirs and resettles in the riverbed and the estuary and strait, and after sediment quits clogging the water, our beautiful salmon will find their way home for the first time in a hundred years. A hundred *years*, Luke."

At her sudden, passionate gush of words, Luke feigned being blown backwards, his shoulders and elbows upraised, his mouth an O. "Oh *yeah*. Now we're talking."

Was she ever. She felt herself blush. Overwrought, she thought she might cry when she looked at him, thought she might grip those muscly arms of his and leave bruises of emphasis. "And they'll bring the ocean back to the mountains. Do you know what that *means*?"

At that moment she didn't care that this was the first man she'd wanted to spend time with since Cole. Didn't care that her attraction to him made her stutter. Didn't care if this speech of hers drove him away. She only wanted him to *understand*, and, if this man who said "I hear you" on that studio roof heard or cared at all about anything, she wanted him to care about this river and the wonder of its fish.

"Maybe I don't, Hildy. Tell me."

A fast inhale before she squared to face him. And though she braced herself for resistance, she'd never seen eyes kinder.

"Those fish will fight rapids and leap cataracts to get upstream, some all the way to the river's beginning, to lay those eggs of theirs. Carnivores will feast on those spawners and grow stronger, and the animal scat will carry sea minerals into the forest to help the trees. Fish will die in those reaches and their bodies will make birds healthier and other fish bigger, and their offspring will grow in the river." Her lungs heaved as if she'd been running. "The ecosystem will function as it did before those dams cut it to pieces."

Abruptly self-aware, she swallowed. Slowed. "That's the short version, but everything, *everything* about the Elwha will be better."

"I believe you." His expression concurred. "I don't understand it like you do, but I want to. I'd like to see that healing."

She hoped he would. A sigh pressed from her belly, and she went quiet again. But the floodlight of his attention waited for more from her. She groped for another question.

"You don't fish at all now? Why not?"

Luke scrubbed his beard. "For all our tiptoeing so far, you sure cut to the chase, don't you?"

Her brows knit. *How? What did—? Ohhh.* His career change came after his family . . . Now she'd done it. "Luke I-I . . . I'm so sorry. I was just trying to—"

He sloughed a weary laugh. She hung on it, hoped he wasn't angry, then felt certain he was. Her fish lecture, then this? She turned to go.

He caught her arm. "I don't mind, Hildy. You surprised me, is all." He scanned the sky as if reading it, searching for words.

"You don't have to—"

"Yeah, I do." He hoisted the paper bag toward the woods. "What do you say we walk a quarter mile that direction first, though. Let a little food and the beauty up there fortify us both before you hear it. I'll spare you too many details, but there's nothing pretty in the short version, either."

He opened the bag and looked inside, then raised his head to catch her gaze. "I take that back. The rescue was breathtaking."

17

HILDY

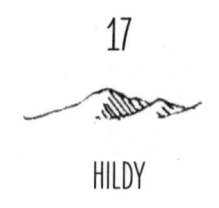

HISTORY

HILDY PLUNGED PAST THE AIRY FOLIAGE at the Madison Falls trailhead. *Please, Luke. Don't tell me.* If he wanted a confessor to ease his mind, she wasn't his girl.

She hurried ahead of him into thick-bodied firs, maples, hemlocks, and cedars, their limbs an arbor above the trail. Shade-loving trillium, their white-and-pink blooms a constellation on the forest floor, infilled crowds of understory sword ferns and vine maples, snowberry and red osier dogwood. The fairyland around her and the waterfall's white noise did little to soothe her. When they rounded the bend, worry blinded her to the fifty-foot cascade.

Luke strolled into the mossy alcove after her and sat on a damp bench. When he offered a sandwich, she took it and paced.

She blamed June. Hadn't the woman pressed Hildy to talk to the man? What a tin of worms—and Hildy had tossed the lid by asking stupid questions.

Luke tapped the rough wood beside him. "Here. No need to wear yourself out. We still have to walk back, you know."

Arms crossed, she stood feet away, scowling as he bit his sandwich, chewed, then rewrapped the unfinished food and returned it to the sack. He again patted the bench. When Hildy perched stiffly, he set the open bag between them. "Got some chips in there, in case you change your mind."

Her fingers twitched to write all this or to pluck something, anything, from the clear pool at the foot of the tumbling water, but Luke's nearness immobilized her. Working together was one thing, but sitting beside him with zilch to distract her, to occupy her hands? With nothing to *do*? "Luke, please don't—"

"Five years ago. Remember when your brother-in-law went out on his own, bought those boats?" He stretched arms on the bench's backrest, laid an ankle on his knee.

"Yeah." She snatched a bag of chips, tore it open with her teeth.

"Thatta girl. Don't want you wilting on me." He pinched a fallen chip from her knee. She tracked it to his mouth, composing her day's entry.

On bench at Madison Falls. Dropped a potato chip. Luke took it from my knee.

"Bingo bought those boats from me." A scoff escaped his nose. "Not exactly a fleet. Only three of them—one's a charter, the other two trollers—but with the sport business and commercial contracts, it's a good gig. He's done well with it."

That day at her table, June had said Bingo approved Luke's sale, had called it fair, but did she mention the buyer? "I didn't know you sold to him."

"I'd have given everything to him, the state I was in. Bingo's a good man. Did right by me. Paid market value with a buyback option in case I changed my mind. He hoped I'd return to the sea, fish with him again. Didn't finalize his ownership for three years."

She crunched a chip. *Too loud!* Cringing, she shot Luke a look as her saliva pooled around the salty flakes. With her tongue she rubbed the pieces small and swallowed as Luke shifted, crossed forearms onto knees, and frowned into his story.

"We'd fished for the better part of twenty years together by then. He knew how much I loved the water, the fish, the work. All of it."

"No need to explain . . . June told me your family died."

He looked at her. "Did she tell you how?"

Hildy shook her head.

"We lived on the *Safe Seas*—one of our trollers. My wife, Eden, our two girls, and I. Quinny was six—and Lucy." He rubbed his nose. "She turned four two days before I left."

"Babies," Hildy whispered. She tucked a calf under her thigh, her hand to her mouth, wishing his pain into the mossy cliffs. "Where'd you go?"

His Adam's apple bobbed. "Ah. Only Hawaii, so why would they possibly want to go with me, right? I should've brought them along. Could've, you know. Thought I'd be too busy with all my meetings, big-shotting. All those fancy restaurants, buying my fish."

That snort again. He stared at the tumbling water.

"I killed them, Hildy."

What?

"Didn't mean to, of course, but my fault just the same. The ship's upkeep was my responsibility, not Eden's, but with that trip coming up?" He shrugged. "I was too blasted preoccupied to check systems. Didn't pay attention. Didn't tend simple details that would have saved them."

His hands hung limp between his knees, and he looked at the ground. "Too busy prepping for *Hawaii* to check the batteries in the monoxide detector. It got cold while I was gone, so Eden closed the portholes. Coroner figured they died an hour or two before I found them."

Hildy pressed knuckles to tears, warm at the corners of her lids. Neither spoke for minutes.

"I lived like an animal after that. Shunned everybody who tried to help—Miranda, Bingo, longtime friends from our home church in Forks. Blew them all off. I'd maybe had five or six beers in my life before then, but after the funerals? Suffice it to say, the Bible didn't numb me, and I wanted to numb everything. So when I ran into an old fishing buddy who let me bunk at his place in Clallam Bay, we hit the bars, hard. I drank around the clock."

Numb. That, she understood.

"I'm so sorry, Luke," she whispered. She fought the impulse to brush him with her sleeve—as if fabric could wick the mess.

"Fast forward. Noonish on the one-year anniversary of the funerals, Miranda and Bingo tracked me down at the Hang-Up—a dive in Forks—and hauled my wasted self to her place in Bremerton to dry out. I spent the year after that remembering who I was, who God was. Until I could dodge the Accuser's hammer enough to start over." He shifted, rolled his shoulders. "Still hurts though. Always will, most likely. God can wash a person clean, restore hope, but consequences can scar a heart up pretty bad."

Accuser?

"I've got a long way to go, but I'm all in, Hildy. Not with some God I tap for favors, but with a living Tsunami who raises the dead. Who washed my sorry carcass onto a better road."

He paused then, and Hildy sat in the spillway of his story. A response was impossible.

He stared at the waterfall before he locked eyes with her. Gave a small smile. "So much for my icebreaker."

Hildy shivered in the damp shade, rubbed her upper arms. So many years alone, so many years since she'd talked with anyone besides June or Otis about more than the scientific, visible world. Quickened, she hunted for a reply, ashamed that her vocabulary about anything personal or spiritual had so atrophied since her dad died.

Her voice squeaked. "Faith was an elephant between my parents—the kind neither mentioned, at least in front of us. Mom went to church with us sometimes, but that's about it. If not for Otis and June when Dad disappeared . . . They have what you're talking about."

She rose, wandered past tree roots to the pool, where she bent for a pebble and shoved it in her pocket. "But trust's—"

Ki-ki-ki-ki-ki . . . Sudden and loud, a dozen staccato cries punctured the air. Out of nowhere an enormous bird flew toward her—fast.

Startled, Hildy ducked the outstretched black talons. Luke appeared at her side as the raptor sailed into the trees. "Almost got you," he said. "Goshawk. Big female, from the size of that wingspan. Four feet at least."

"Yeah. Her nest must be close." Hildy scanned the trees, breathless from the attack. "There." Forty feet up and as many feet distant, a twiggy nest bulged from a narrow crotch in the trunk. A few trees away, a flick of wings and a single, longer *kee-ah* drew their attention to the perching mother's gray-streaked breast, her banded tail feathers.

Luke eyed the trail. "We're on her turf. We'd better—"

Too late. More screams signaled the bird's second launch straight for Hildy. Yellow-orange eyes, the hooked beak, those yellow feet spread wide—Hildy gasped as black razor claws caught her braid and sliced her forehead. The impact knocked her backwards.

Like a phantom, the raptor melted into the woods. Warm ooze dripped past an eyebrow as Hildy got to her feet. Luke held her chin and lifted hair from the blood. "She got you, all right." He studied the injury, tested its borders with thumbs. "Not deep enough for stitches, but you've sure got a bleeder. Hold on." He hurried for napkins from the Subway sack and dabbed. "Here. Put some pressure on it. I'll take a better look when we're not in her bullseye. You okay to walk?"

Bears had chased her off rivers. "Yeah, good to go."

Hovering, he steered her to the trail, then to a weathered cedar stump near the trailhead. When he cradled her cheek, inspecting, she closed her eyes, smelled the salt of him, heard him swallow. His breath and the late sun brushed her as his fingers again tried the cut. "I have some butterfly bandages in my truck. I can snug up those edges."

She nodded, reluctant to budge. She had to finish telling him. "Trust's hard for me."

She'd holed up with a canary, for crying out loud.

He pressed a fresh napkin to the wound and held it there. "Maybe I can help you with that."

What? She was only telling him, not asking for help. Alarmed, she pushed his fingers off the cut. "I've got it," she said and, without another word, streaked down the trail. At the road, she stuffed the paper in her pocket and jogged until blood dripped from her chin.

Luke caught up to her when she stopped to tamp it. "Maybe I can't."

"Can't what?"

"Help you. But at least let me close that cut?"

She'd overreacted. "Okay." Without a butterfly from his truck, she'd have to drive to town for Steri-Strips. Sure, he could patch her up.

But fixing her trust was a different issue entirely.

18

HILDY

EVASION

SHE DIDN'T SEE LUKE ON TUESDAY. On Wednesday, she left the resort before he arrived. That afternoon, she returned from work to drive straight past his truck, lock herself in her cabin, and peek through slats until he departed. Then she crept to the studio to try its new latch. *Locked!* She glanced at June's empty window, then hurried home and splashed water on her blazing cheeks.

When he left Thursday evening, she circled to the cabin's far side. Out of sight, she peered through a window at new electrical outlets and light fixtures and imagined him installing the rustic, knotty plywood that covered three walls of the insulation-pillowed studs.

After he drove off on Friday, she lingered on his plumb lines and the tongue-and-groove pine on the ceiling, and on the trim boards that lay across sawhorses, their cuts precise.

Awake until two a.m. one night, three the next, she lay in her bed and heard him, saw him. Her skin remembered his careful fingers as he cleaned and closed the gos's mark.

With every recollection of his kindness, his story, his beliefs, and his interest in her, events from her own history tightened her throat. But, unlike all the other times they nearly choked her with anxiety, this time Luke was a porch light in their midst, and she a moth, unable to divert herself.

Maybe I can help you with that, he'd said.

Could he? Only one way to find out, but could *she*?

Saturday morning, a truck's rumble woke her. Hildy tripped to the window, hugged her chest, and watched Luke stroll to the cabin next door. When he went inside, she dressed quickly, tended Butterness, and braided her hair so tight it hurt. Then she stared at herself in the mirror, nodded once, and strapped on her tool belt. Ignoring the rubber in her legs, she walked to the studio.

Across the room, Luke measured a board, extracted a pencil from behind his ear, and scribbled on a wood scrap. She stood at the door until he looked up.

"Hey." He chewed a lip and pondered her until she grew uneasy. Had a slow smile not risen into his cheeks, she'd have split. "How's the cut?" he said. He laid pencil and tape on a sawhorse, but stayed where he was.

She touched the scab. "Good."

He squinted at it, and moved closer. "May I?"

"Uh. Okay."

Thumb to her forehead, he leaned in. She felt his breath on her cheek.

"No infection," she said.

"I see that." He stepped back and seemed to absorb her. She'd looked at fish like he was looking at her. And at birds. And flowers.

She shifted. "Thought you could use some help."

"Could I ever. Got another job in Sequim next week, but I'm determined to have this place ready in time. If we can wrap things up by May twentieth, Miranda will have time to do a little decorating before those dancers get here."

"Okay."

"Think you can come after your workday? I can stay longer."

"Yeah."

"And the next couple of Saturdays?"

"Yeah. Sure." She wouldn't think past the work they'd do here or she'd faint. Had no clue how this would play out. Convinced herself to stop guessing.

Through the window, she saw an Audi's hatch open to clay pots, flats of flowers, and potting mix. Miranda knocked on the glass. "Lukie, can you help me . . . Oh! Hildy!"

Luke opened the window and pointed at the sawhorse. "In a sec."

Hildy hurried toward the door. "I can, Miranda."

They were unloading bags of soil and knee-high clay flowerpots when Tess's SUV turned in from the highway. Hildy shaded her eyes for a clearer view when her burly brother-in-law slammed the driver's door.

"Hey, little sister."

Hildy dodged his hug. "No Tess?"

Bingo ticked his head at his rig. "She sent a pie instead. Girl's been cooking up a storm, can you tell?" He pinched a belly roll through his shirt. "Last-minute cancellation for my boat today, so she gave me a honey-buy list long as my arm. I figured if I was making a Port Angeles run, I'd stop in for a read on Miranda's little project. Luke's been texting me updates."

"Bingo Brink." Miranda appeared around a corner and stepped into his beefy arms. He squeezed. She wriggled free, patted his head. "Bone-crusher. Come see Luke."

Hildy would be a spare tire in there. She made a show of checking her watch. "You visit and I'll grab some breakfast. Back in a half hour. Tell Luke?"

Thumb on her latch, she heard Luke shout. "Bingo! Son of a gun." Her door clicked closed behind her.

19

LUKE

NOTES

LUKE CLAPPED HIS OLD FRIEND'S SHOULDER as they crossed the studio. His closest friend, who, along with Miranda, had saved him from himself.

"Checking up on you, man." Bingo bent to an outlet, roved the walls like a house inspector, touched window casings. "Looks good."

"If I'd poured concrete for this place, I'd have scratched your name in the slurry. If not for you, I wouldn't be building anything."

"Returning the favor, bro. Don't forget, if not for *you,* old man Diller would've quit looking for me when that net pulled me overboard. Seas like that? I'd have been deep-sixed with the bottom-feeders and you know it."

"Mean old bugger." Luke wagged his head. "Ketchikan never looked so good. Never thought I'd jump anyone's ship, but that boat? That skipper? Should have listened when Dad tried to talk us out of going."

Outside the open door, Miranda tamped a geranium. "Ulysses paid you guys, right? Dad told me he tried to stiff you."

A nod from Bingo. "Took a while, but yeah."

Miranda jabbed her trowel into the soft earth and talked past the jamb. "Mom said he terrified Violet. I think Gram even reported him, but apparently feeding your child and getting her to school qualified you as a legit parent back then."

She brushed potting soil from her hands. "After he screamed at Violet right in front of Mom for leaving her toys outside in the rain, Gram insisted the girls play at her house—under her supervision. Ulysses took offense, of course, and kiboshed any further contact."

Luke moved a ladder. "I bet Mom missed her. It could be lonely out there."

"Yes." Miranda stared toward the highway. "Remember hide and seek? How we used that property line post in the woods as base? Mom said she'd spy on Violet from there, hoping she'd come close enough to talk. One day Mom saw Ulysses and Violet's older brother—the one that died last winter—throw toys, books, clothes, even Violet's bike on the burn pile. When the old man torched them, Violet ran toward our place, but her brother caught her and hauled her back to Ulysses, who made his little girl watch."

Bingo scowled. "Where was her mother?"

Miranda shrugged. "Who knows? Meek as a mouse, Grammie said. That man probably browbeat her so badly she couldn't defend anybody, herself included. She got sick, died early."

"I bet he did more than browbeat." Luke sighted down a trim board. "When that man got mad . . . A little girl, growing up with that? Had to affect Violet. You think Mom ever had second thoughts about leaving us with her?"

"I don't know. A lot of years had passed. Violet didn't have kids yet, but she must have seemed okay. You remember what her husband, Lars, was like, right? As kind as they come. They both were."

Bingo peeked out the door at Hildy's buttoned-up cabin, then straddled the threshold and spoke low. "Something's not right in that family. Wouldn't want *her* to hear this, but that girl's packing some sort of hurt even her sister doesn't understand. Tess tolerates her mother at best, but you know my Tessie's a strong one. She never let Violet get under her skin. Hildy's different. Around her mother, she's raw. Got even worse after their dad disappeared."

"What got worse?" Luke asked.

"Don't tell me you haven't noticed. When you texted that she'd been helping you, I thought you were kidding. She went out with some guy her freshman year in college, but apart from Otis, Tess says she hasn't said more than two words to a man outside of work in who knows how long. Avoids most women, too. Doesn't trust anybody. Even worse, she's convinced she's losing her mind. Well, her memory, at least. Which makes no sense, superstar biologist and all. My Tessie talks to her by phone, but otherwise, Hildy even keeps her offshore. Go figure. Bet she won't invite either one of you inside of that little house of hers."

"Why's that?" Luke asked.

Miranda seated another flower in the pot and glanced toward Hildy's cabin.

Bingo jingled change in his pocket. "Fort Knox, wherever she lives. She doesn't let anybody in."

"I like her, Bingo." Miranda brushed her hands and stepped inside.

Luke closed the door behind her. "I do, too."

"That's what worries me." Bingo gripped his friend's shoulder. "You watch that heart of yours, Luke Rimmer. There are other kinds of pain than the ones you've been through."

Luke considered the warning—but only briefly. Over the next two weeks, he caught himself counting hours until Hildy arrived to work beside him. During May evenings and two long Saturdays—while they finished the studio's floating floor, interior trim, board and batten siding, painting and shelves and counter laminate—he glimpsed her mind and heart and, here and there, pieces of her faith. He liked what he heard and saw and felt when he was with her. And apart from her skittishness, he found nothing he didn't.

But that skittishness? On May 17 he topped off Jangles's trough before the sun rose. "Moving day for Miranda, young lady. Won't see you 'til late. Got three trips to make from Lake Sutherland to the river, and it'll take a while." He scratched the longhorn between the eyes. "Fragile dishes for Miranda. Fragile everything with Hildy."

Hadn't she warned him at the falls? The woman could flit away as quickly as she'd landed in his world. He understood Bingo's caution now. He didn't want to blow this—*them*—up. He really did like her. But if whatever bothered her was too much . . . If she couldn't trust him, couldn't open up more than she had so far, they were going nowhere. And if *he* couldn't trust *her*, he'd have no choice but to bow out.

Late afternoon, Miranda sliced packing tape on another box of plates at the studio. Her hand-painted *Toes of Clay Ceramics* sign hung between copper spinners on the eave fronting the highway. Luke was tightening the last rack of shelves when Hildy showed at a window. With an arm stretched toward the blooming pots and pinwheels on sticks, she wandered the studio perimeter. Then she came inside, past the kiln and potter's wheel and empty greenware racks in the original cabin to new shelves in the addition, each filled with displays of place settings and decorative bowls, serving platters and mugs. So many mugs.

Sidelong, Luke watched her mouth their inscriptions: *Elwha*

River, Lake Aldwell, Lake Mills, Olympic Peninsula. Heard her breathy laugh.

"What's funny?" he asked.

"This one." She raised a hefty mug.

Etched in clay, oars hung from a skiff. He squinted at the caption. "What's it say?"

"R-O-E . . . *Roe your boat?*" Hildy coughed another laugh.

"Ahhh, a closet punster." Miranda aimed a finger. "I've got your number now, Hildy Nybo—and more wordplay where that came from."

Puns. Who'd have guessed? Luke pulled a smaller mug from the shelf. Below a school of fingerlings, he read, *"We're practicing small talk."*

Hildy's eyes lit, and she lifted another, glazed green and etched with a hook-nosed salmon. A giggle, then *"You're such a chum."*

Game on. "Well, here you go then." He plucked a blue one with two fish on it and set it at Hildy's eye level. *"Hey gill, what's up?"*

Her lips pursed against a smile. Small, beautiful lips.

Luke's face pinched at another. "So bad, Mirs. Where'd you get all these?"

His sister shrugged.

Hildy was full-on grinning now. *Good sign.*

"Ring this one up for me, will you, Miranda?" He raised a smooth, fish-covered mug the aqua of Hildy's shirt.

"Which one?" Miranda said.

"Two fish on it. Caption: *There's salmon for everyone.*"

He held the mug toward his sister, then handed it to Hildy. "For you," he said.

Her face went pink. Those river-water eyes of hers darted left.

Uh-oh. He took the mug from her and set it on the counter. "Miranda and I thought we'd head to town for dinner. You want to come?"

Was this the first time she'd looked straight at him without dodging? The silken skin at her throat rolled when she swallowed. "Yes," she said. "I'd like that."

20

HILDY

DANCE

MEMORIAL DAY WEEKEND began with shouts between cabins, as friends from Seattle and Bremerton, Olympia and Mukilteo reunited, and as more of the square dancers who'd booked campsites a full year ahead rolled into the Elwha Fishing Resort in vans and motor homes. While pickups towed travel trailers to both sides of the river, June welcomed more registrants at the store counter. Otis waved RVs into the field between the dance hall and the highway and directed tenters and boondockers into the woods.

All of them, every one, arrived not for the trout or the boats or clear-water swims—though few could resist, eventually—but for the hall across the river, where twelve squares of eight dancers each, plus a caller and the usual tagalongs, would jam inside through the long weekend. A hundred or more would scuff that hardwood maple floor in the hall her dad had built before she could walk.

Hildy scanned the slew of vehicles at the studio. *Luke should be here by now.* Down the lane, a handlebar-mustachioed man in cowboy boots and a Johnny Cash T-shirt raised a hand as she passed, then plugged an extension cord into a hookup site. Behind the man's RV, she spotted Luke's truck and darted to the busy studio to find him.

Inside, Miranda boxed a mug for a noisy redhead. "I love, love, *love* your new shop!" the woman said. Her perfume wafted when she patted Miranda's cheek. She bumped past Hildy, turned at the door. "Tomorrow I'll bring *friends.*"

But Hildy didn't see Luke. The only man in the room handed Miranda his credit card and a sturdy mug—red, with the Glines Canyon Dam in dark relief. In small script, a sentence above the picture. "Good one," he growled. Dark, tangled eyebrows jumped twice. "The wife'll love it."

Hildy tracked his exit and crossed to Miranda. "I missed that one. Know the caption?"

Miranda rang up a plate. "Education through humor. *What does a salmon say when it hits a wall?*"

Not funny. Hildy sidestepped a customer and drifted into the hallway. No Luke near the kiln or wheel either, or—she eyed the lightless gap under the restroom door—in there.

The dancing would start at seven. "We can watch, right? Come with me?" he'd asked.

Why had she agreed? By morning, she'd wavered. **Changed my mind,** she almost texted at noon. *Should have.*

Though clumsy, Dad had taught her and Tess the patterns, the calls. He'd grinned ear to ear when they executed them flawlessly with others at the dance hall, the last time in her fourteenth summer. The next year he was gone, and she hadn't stepped foot in that hall since. How could she *watch?*

Through the back door, she spotted Luke throwing rocks in the river like a ten-year-old. She leaned against the building, then bent for a clover she'd press in her diary—to hold in her mind this sloped light, the sparkling river, and *him*, there on the bank, *playing*. When had she last done anything of the sort?

"Luke." Her *I can't* and *I won't* poised to leap.

"Hey. There's salmon I like." He crossed the twenty feet between them with hands lifted in greeting, a smile stretched to his ears. He aimed a thumb at the dance hall. "You know, I've always wondered about that place. How about a tour before the show starts?"

"Luke, I—"

"Jumping the gun again, aren't I? How about a bite at the store first?"

Warmth rode her shoulders when she looked at him. How could she say no?

After burgers, they walked the highway to the river. Mid-bridge, Luke propped elbows on the rail. Two boys cast lines between the abutments below. Thin filaments from their reels caught sun and floated the air like spiderwebs before they landed.

Luke bobbed his head as if to music. "I fell in love with fish doing that."

In love with fish? Could he startle her more? Had she heard anyone say that other than herself? Even at work, where fish were the bedrock of careers, her colleagues never talked about *loving* them. They teased her for saying as much.

She gazed at the water, whispered. "I think I was five when I fell in love with salmonids. Caught kokanee fingerlings one spring with a tadpole net. They were so beautiful, I named them. Hauled them around in a jar."

"Bet that didn't end well."

"Dad saw them by my bed when he tucked me in. In the morning, we walked to the creek to let them go. Pretty sure I cried."

"Your dad. You two were close."

"Being home again reminds me. I hear him all over the place. See him."

"Search teams, hikers, rangers—they never found him?"

"Nineteen years since he disappeared, and nothing. Dad didn't say what trail he'd take. None of us knew where to look. He . . ." Her throat squeezed, pinched her words.

"What?"

"He loved the mountains. Hiked a lot. If he didn't tell one of us where he was heading, he always left a note. But that time—when he vanished—I was away on a school science trip to California. Tess was living in Sekiu with Bingo and baby Joel. Mom said he left in the morning. When he didn't show after dark, she checked his gear. His overnight pack was gone, so she didn't worry. Not until the next night. Not like him to stay gone when campers were coming in."

Luke propped on an elbow and faced her, frowning. "He didn't tell her?"

"They . . . he . . ."

"What?"

"Mom was pretty hard on him. He took off sometimes to clear the air. Didn't like to fight with her."

Luke nodded and sent his gaze to the river. "I'm sorry."

The memory dropped lead in her gut, and the awful story grew monstrous, needed telling. *Like Luke's did that day at the falls.*

"He'd been gone two days when Mom reported him missing. I got home that afternoon to search and rescue teams, neighbors, and volunteers coming, going, marking trails and quadrants on a wall map they hung at the store. They couldn't tell which direction he'd gone after he crossed the highway, though, so it was anybody's guess."

She was talking too much. Saying too much. "Those mountains, Luke. This valley. They swallow things. People."

A throaty rumble. Harleys, growling, interrupted as they passed on the bridge. Three, four, five. Her shaking hands. Luke's scowl. Her toes scuffed the concrete barrier rail as she peered over the edge and let her sightline run with the current. After they'd halted the search for her dad, she had jumped from this bridge every day for weeks. Twenty-five feet of air to the fishing hole, to water that closed over her head and dulled her senses with snowmelt.

"I can't keep talking about this." She resumed walking, and Luke fell into step beside her. When his hand clasped hers, she didn't shrink. He'd been underwater before. He knew how it felt.

Across the river, shouts and laughter rode the low smoke from campfires. Hoots erupted when a tossed horseshoe rang metal. Luke and Hildy turned from the highway into the meadow to scents and sounds of dinner picnics and cornhole toss, dogs and robins, and the splashes and chatter of waders in shallows. Hands clapped time to a harmonica.

"Getting primed for tonight, sounds like," Luke said. Ahead, the hall squatted at the field's far end and a VW van with Oregon plates rolled toward the woods behind it. "That dance floor's gonna rock."

He doesn't know the half of it.

At the south wall, Luke tried the door. Peered in a window. "Guess we'll have to wait."

Otis rounded the corner. Startled, his voice hitched. "Progress, you comin' here, Hildy girl." He waved at Luke before he hurried on. "Side door's open."

Luke followed Hildy down the back hallway, past doors to the storeroom and bathrooms, to where the familiar washed her:

windows lining three ballroom walls; the dropped ceiling and its fluorescent bulbs, for when those windows weren't enough. Hildy watched a woman carry pitchers from the kitchen to a table under an eighties stereo speaker hung in a corner. On the stage, a rangy, sunspotted old man in a blue neckerchief and plaid shirt stood at a table and sorted vinyl 45s beside a portable record player.

"No way. Is that what I think it is?"

The man heard Luke. Saluted.

"It is," Hildy said. "And that's Clarence. I bet that's the same turntable he had when I was little."

"Old school. How great is that?" He eyed her cautiously. "Didn't you *want* to learn to dance?"

"Oh, I learned, Luke. Dad couldn't keep time, but he taught us the steps." She knew every call anyone could throw at her. "Tess and I filled in wherever groups had odd counts."

"But you said—"

"I said I *don't* dance. Anymore." She sighed. "Without Dad, it stopped being fun. Tonight's the first time I've been in here since he went missing." Because she cried at the mere thought of dancing. Might cry again when the music started.

"Wish I knew these dances. Maybe we could find that fun for you again."

"About as likely as my getting you in a boat again—to land a big Chinook."

"Touché, Hildy."

"No going back, Luke. Losses like ours kill joy. Shrink us."

"They don't have to. Not permanently, anyway. You ever learn that verse about restoring the years the locusts eat?"

She shook her head.

"It's coming true for me. I'll send it to you."

The old man left the stage, unlocked the double front doors and snapped the wrist holding a four-inch cowbell. Outside, heads swiveled. Dancers whooped. RV doors and tent flaps opened and unzipped.

Luke was grinning. "Oh, yeahhh. Here they come." He grabbed Hildy's hand and pulled her to a row of folding chairs along a wall.

In twos and fours, then a steady stream, they barged in. Men, their hair banded or parted or smoothed or oiled off foreheads, wore kerchiefs rolled and knotted at the neck or sterling-clasped bolo ties at collars of western shirts embroidered or painted or woven. Shirts in every color of paisleys and plaids and solids, the snaps on plackets and cuffs pearlized or metal. Tidy, ironed shirts, deferentially tucked into belted jeans or slacks or pleated trousers. And at the hems of those pants, boots or oxfords or loafers—all with slick leather soles to keep dancers' footwork nimble.

Luke elbowed her, spread a finger and thumb from the philtrum below his nose past the bearded corners of his mouth. Oh yes, and the men wore *mustaches*: chevron and Dalí, lampshade and pencil. Walrus, toothbrush, and curled, waxed handlebars.

And, on their men's arms, or trailing, or clucking and flitting ahead of their partners, the women. *In full plumage.* She had forgotten how, as a child, she'd held her breath at the female dancers' first flamboyant surge into the hall, how she'd studied the flowers and swirls and buffalo checks on those full-fabric skirts tenting over layers of petticoats. How the dancers' sleeves ballooned and fluttered.

At age six, she'd begged to copy them until, *finally*, she fluffed new petticoats under a daisy skirt that puffed her into a bell. *Like a hollyhock,* Dad said when she tried it on. She and Tess had twirled on the lawn by the river until they collapsed giggling in their fancy new dresses, dizzied from their spinning flight.

The elderly caller made a show of donning a blazer. And when he seated a cowboy hat, the crowd whooped and stomped. He stepped to the microphone as ninety-six dancers clapped, standing ready, two to a side, four couples in each of twelve squares spanning the polished floor. Volume up, black speakers crackled loud in the seconds before he lifted the tonearm, set the stylus on the spinning disc, and began to sing.

As if moved by a giant hand, the kaleidoscope of humans pivoted and swerved, wove and twirled. *Like fish,* Hildy thought. Schooling, synchronized, shifting directions, flashing colored scales. Her eyes grew wet.

"A right and left around the ring. While the roosters crow and the birdies sing."

Luke threw himself back in his chair, mouth ajar. Clearly delighted, he elbowed Hildy, clapped and toe-tapped to the easy, rolling rhythm of the caller and dancers and fluid squares.

"All join hands and circle wide. Spread right out like an old cowhide."

The music, the happy crowd—she stole glances at the man beside her, laughing, clapping. How would she write this when she got home? She tasted the descriptions that crossed her tongue. Landed on *merry*. She caught herself tapping her foot. Arrested it. Looked around and leaned to Luke's ear. "He's big on patter."

"Huh?"

"Patter. His color talk. Like a sports guy. The roosters and cows."

The play in it all. Gray-haired women with wrinkles no iron could smooth wore the flounces of girlhood in calico and red pettipants that peeked when they whirled. Fret-weary mothers on getaways and career women with spreadsheet faces joined clerks and hairstylists and pharmacists, their other worlds molted away on their drives here and in those RVs and tents, from which they emerged as the birds of American folk dancing, flitting, flying.

Box the gnat. Allemande left. Slip the clutch. Step to a wave. More calls, more steps until Hildy forgot she couldn't be there without hurting and allowed the man beside her clapping and tapping, the silly, happy women in their silly, beautiful dresses, and the courteous, caring men to sweep her into forgetfulness that she didn't mind at all.

"Corn in the crib and wheat in the sack. Meet yer partner and turn right back."

On the turn, a jiggly, flush-faced woman wrenched, yelped, tipped, and sagged into her rawboned partner. In a flash, couples in the square cinched around her like a purse string and helped her to a chair. While her man removed her shoe, a woman hurried to the kitchen, reappeared with ice.

"Her ankle," Luke said. The dancing went on. On a difficult combo of calls, two groups lost step and folded, their underarms and brows ringed damp.

"All go home now," Clarence called. Dancers returned to their start points to await instruction, but the caller raised the tonearm from the vinyl. "Now help yerself to some of those delicacies Mary's set out for y'all over there. She's got cookies, juice, water." The crowd hummed like bees, then swarmed to refreshments and restrooms.

A brush-whiskered man strode to them. "Well, little Nybo, all grown up. Good to see you again. Thought we'd lost you *and* your dad." Hildy scrambled to place him as the injured woman propped her foot on a chair. "She's out of commission," he said. "Don't think it's broke, but we'll need another couple. You two game?"

Hildy bit her lip. Luke's gaze questioned her before he replied. "I'm game, but I couldn't follow all that if you paid me."

The man howled. "Well, if that ain't torture. What were you thinkin', Hildy? Bringing him here without teachin' him."

Hildy felt herself blush.

Luke intercepted. "My doing. I dragged her here."

"This girl knows the ropes. Have her give you a lesson and come back tomorrow. Old Clarence'll call basics every night running. Good for beginners, too."

"Thanks." Luke patted Hildy's knee. "I'll see if I can talk her into it."

Hildy looked behind the man, then toward the restroom, as fear arrived from nowhere. "Excuse me a minute."

There would be no dancing for her.

21

LUKE

SASHAY

THE MEN WATCHED HILDY hurry toward the restroom before the mustache turned to Luke. "Or you could come back in the morning for a lesson. We'll get you up and running so you don't step on that pretty girl's feet."

"Lessons?" Luke's eyes lit.

"At eight to ten the next two mornings, right here. Come to both and we'll have you twirling that girl with the group by Sunday night."

"I'll be there," Luke said. He'd do his part. Getting Hildy to join him was another question. He snagged two cookies from the table, ate one, and intercepted her at the hallway. He wagged the second oatmeal wonder under her nose. "This'll make you want to dance."

A glower had replaced her ease. "I'm leaving." Her words pricked him, but he held steady, wouldn't react. He'd guessed coming here would challenge her, but had hoped he could pull her through.

"I'm with you. Let's get out of here," Luke said.

Released, she darted from him, wove past dancers regrouping into squares, and shot through the double doors.

He caught up with her on the lane. He thought about pretending nothing had shifted in her, as he had other times clouds like these scudded in those mysterious eyes of hers. A chess game, this relationship. He could call it a relationship now, couldn't he? And however tentative, hadn't they reached new squares on the board? Could he bump her, ask, and get an answer? It depended. Was the piece she held back a pawn or her queen? He needed to know.

"Hildy." He touched her arm, but she walked on, as if he weren't there. "Hildy," he said again, then stopped. Hands at his sides, he stood in the gravel lane and watched her walk through failing daylight to the highway.

While new calls and the shuffle of lively feet thrummed through the hall's open doors, she crossed the Elwha bridge. He followed, but she'd evaporated into the campground when he reached it. *Fair enough.* He'd leave quietly. Let her be. Maybe he'd been playing God, cocksure of his ability to reach into that broken heart of hers and glue it back together. Maybe Bingo had been right.

But when he clicked the key fob to unlock his truck, the blink of his parking lights lit a crouched figure: Hildy, between his bumper and the trunk of a high-limb fir, sniffling. Wet runnels on her cheeks shone in the flashes.

"I'm no good at this, Luke. I don't know how." Her sob hitched.

Pained, he sank hands into his pockets so he wouldn't reach for her. Sensed her impending bolt if he came any closer, though he suspected touch was exactly what she needed most. "Takes time for people to get to know each other, Hildy."

"No, Luke. You don't get it. There's something *wrong* with me. Sometimes anxiety flat-out blindsides me. Tonight, you and I are sitting there, and I'm actually enjoying myself. Then that guy comes over and within seconds, I can't breathe. Logically, I think one thing, but my body reacts."

Luke frowned.

"If I'm within a half mile of this resort, I can't trust myself to stay calm for a stupid *hour*! And I start seeing things nobody else does."

Was she delusional? He moved toward her cautiously. "Hildy. I want to hear more. But first I'd like to wrap my arms around you and hold you. Hear you tell me more while I keep you safe. Is that all right with you?"

She stared at him wide-eyed and got to her feet. At her tiny nod, he eased within reach of her and, as if catching a fluttering, wounded finch, encircled her in the perimeter of his arms until his hands hovered behind her. Gently, so gently, he placed his palms on her shoulder blades before he pulled her toward him. She dropped her head, rested her brow in the curve where his neck met his shoulder.

Was it two minutes he held her like that? Twenty? He didn't know, didn't care as he rocked her, felt her sink into him and settle. His mind raced while he pressed his cheek to her hair and felt her chest expand and contract with each stuttered breath. His shirt absorbed tears.

"Hildy." He lifted her chin with a thumb.

In the dim, their eyes met before she closed hers and pivoted. He gripped her shoulder and held her against him, their sides a long seam.

"About these things you see."

She wiped at his damp shoulder, then her cheeks and nose. Her words came slowly. "They're more like sensations, with shifting shapes and textures. I don't really see them, but they feel dark, like shadows. When I was little, one followed my mother around sometimes—in the boat, at church. They come out of death wrecks on our corner, too. I really noticed them after I turned nine."

She pressed her temples. "Then I didn't see any for a long time. I thought they were gone, hoped they were gone, but when a van crashed the summer before I left home, there they were again. Last winter, two more came off my dead uncle's truck."

The back of his neck pricked. *Keep talking, sweetheart.*

"Tonight there was one trailing that guy who talked to us."

Luke stared into the gathering dark. "What changed when you were nine?"

Her laugh was humorless. "Otis says holy Light moved into me then."

"Moved into you *when*?"

"At church. The preacher said the Comforter would shrink my worries and be my bodyguard if I trusted and asked. First time I'd really listened when he made that offer. All those verses began to make sense. I was too shy to go up front, but I took him up on it anyway."

She shuddered under his arm. "Sounds wacky, right?"

"You ever talk to that preacher about those shadows?"

She shook her head. "Only to Otis, but I know he told Junie."

"Why didn't *you* tell her?"

"I just didn't. Only reason I told Otis was because we went to help after that van hit the bridge and three of those things flew straight toward me. Almost scared *me* to death. He tells me they're lie-makers from the pit of hell, but I don't know."

She exhaled through puffed cheeks. "I've spent the better part of my life hiding the fact that I'm crazy, Luke. *Crazy.* If people knew what goes on in my head, I'd lose what little credibility I have. And my job, most likely. I may be scaring you off, too, but it's for the best, I guess. Why waste any more of your time?"

"Why do you think—?"

"But my job? I live for that job. Doing what I do—helping those beautiful fish—makes me think even Nutso Hildy has some value somewhere."

She hiccoughed. "If I lost my work . . . I'd lose hope. Those rivers . . . the salmon . . ." She was whispering now, her eyes grown enormous. "I get to take part in the wonder of them. Right alongside . . . God."

She clapped a hand over her mouth, as if she'd revealed another secret. "At least I never see those things outside of this valley."

"Who said you were crazy, Hildy?" No exaggeration on Bingo's part. She seemed convinced.

"Otis said I see dark *spirits*, Luke."

Luke shrugged. "I've known Otis a long time. I bet he doesn't equate seeing spirits with being crazy."

"Doesn't matter. Who sees spirits unless they're wacked?"

"People can sense the unseen without being mentally ill, Hildy." In his own dark season, he'd felt them himself. Kurt, his neighbor and pastor, said those liars were everywhere.

She straightened, raised her voice. "Well, there's more. How about this, doubter man. All through my growing up years, I lost things. Forgot where I put them. Not only that—I'd recall an event I absolutely believed was true only to be told otherwise, and when I'd hear what actually occurred, I couldn't for the life of me find that sequence of events anywhere, *anywhere* in my memory."

Where is this going? He slowed his breathing, hoped she'd subconsciously match the pace.

"It didn't just happen once, Luke. It was the story of my childhood, over and over and over. I realized I wasn't trustworthy, even to myself."

"But who—?" Those shadows could be legit, but this forgetfulness? What in the world was that?

"Then Dad got lost, too, and nobody could find him. My daddy. I was so desperate I decided to take his truck, drive to Seattle and . . .

well, maybe live with the family of a girl I met on that math-science trip right before he died. Anything to escape, to go where everything didn't remind me of him."

"Can't say I blame you for that."

"I asked Mom for the keys. Told her I was going to the library in Port Angeles. I'd lost so many things she didn't trust me one bit, so when I grabbed my purse, she asked if I had my license. Of course I had my license. I'd had it for a month, safe in my wallet. That license meant freedom. You remember that feeling?"

She snatched a breath, lost in her story.

"I do. Like having wings."

Small nods. She exhaled through her mouth. "Mom held the keys, waiting for me to show her. But I couldn't show her, Luke, because my license *wasn't* in my wallet. I even lost my brand-new *driver's license*, and my mind was an absolute blank as to where."

"Did you ever—?"

"No! I never found it! After that, concentration on my schoolwork was my only escape. No crazies, just details, formulae, and facts—which, unlike everything in the rest of my world, I could recall perfectly. I held on to God by a string, but I couldn't feel him."

He knew about that. Knew God did the holding.

Her trembling grew more pronounced, and he gripped her tighter.

"I learned to dive so deeply into my studies, to compartmentalize and concentrate so hard, I could have long stretches of clearmindedness—full weeks, even a month once—without any confusion or anxiety at all. Then my freshman year of college ended badly, and both returned with a vengeance. After that, when I wasn't working, I stayed home, mostly, where I developed tricks to help store my days. To help me remember my *life*. Not seeing the shadows helped, too. They didn't follow me to Seattle."

She sniffled. Swiped at her nose.

"But now I'm here on the river again, the shadows are back, and my agitation's worse. Half the time I'm home, my palms are sweaty, or I breathe like I'm at high altitude. My heart pounds harder than it has in years." She turned to face him straight on. "Otis thinks some lie-maker's got his finger in the pie of my life, but I sure don't know what that lie could be."

Her breath seized, and she looked at him. "I dare you to tell me I'm not losing it, Luke Rimmer."

He ran two fingers along the braid pinned to her head. One down her nose. Was Otis onto something?

"A lie, huh?"

He thought of a game he and Miranda played when they were kids. She'd hide a button in the woods and direct him to it with temperature readings. He could still hear her: *You're warmer, Lukie. No, colder, cold, warmer, warmer* . . . Hildy's symptoms were worse here, and the shadows—at least ones she could see—were *only* here in the valley. If the lie were a button . . . Was she closer to uncovering it in the Elwha?

"Who diagnosed you, Hildy? Who said you were crazy besides you?"

"That actual word?" She scrunched an eye. "Nobody needed to."

He hugged her again. "That *Nobody* is wrong."

Come morning, Luke rounded the curve and glanced at the bustling store and studio before he crossed the bridge and parked by the dance hall. A half hour early, he brushed bakery muffin crumbs from jeans and tee, swigged the last of his coffee, and bent to double knot leather-soled chukka boots.

At the hall's side door, he wrote a long text to Hildy, then erased most of it. Instead, he tapped a brief one: **That locust verse I** promised to send you, different version: **"I will give you back what you lost."**

And on its heels, a second: **Haying from noon until dark tonight. Thinking of you.**

Inside, he sat a few chairs away from a lean, compact man flanked by preteen twin girls baiting him with spelling words. "In-SOU-ciance, Dad," the girl closest to Luke pronounced slowly. Her sister giggled.

The man hunched, cocked arms and jutted his chin. Vulture-squawked, "In-sue-chants."

"Daddy!" The asker rolled her full-moon eyes.

Her sister zeroed in on Luke. "I bet *he* knows."

Luke raised hands, palms out, and thought of his little Quinn when he quizzed her spelling after homeschool and the day's catch. How she'd already loved books, loved words like he did. In his mind he kissed the memory, then he spelled the twin's word as fast as he could spit letters.

"Told ya." One girl elbowed the other. The pair was standing now. He couldn't say which one had asked.

Two more couples crept inside as the previous night's caller carried the record player to the stage and plugged it in.

"A good Saturday mornin' to you intrepid souls," Clarence crowed. "Come on over. Eight of you's exactly right, 'specially considerin' my fill-in wife's still in our trailer sippin' coffee. A fill-in for lesson squares, not the other." He chuckled, rolled a wrist to his watch face. "On time, too. Eight, straight up. Ya ready? If we're goin' to jam a course worth's of learnin' into two two-hour sessions, let's go home."

⛰

Turned out that *go home* meant the same as in the Monopoly game: start over. Next came *circle left*—the twins rolled eyes at the obvious, then made short work of *allemande left* and *do-si-do*. The second hour all faced each other and alternated hands through *right and left grand*, *promenade* and *swing*, and disintegrated into hysterics when Clarence set their new moves to music and they tripped, collided. Men and kids high-fived four rounds later when, at last, they nailed a set.

"You're quick studies, all a ya." Clarence propped doors and admitted the waiting, experienced crowd dressed in day two's get-ups. He turned back to the learners. "After tomorrow? You'll be dancin' with the big kids."

"Spell *promenade*, Dad," twin Lacey said.

⛰

Afterward, Luke spotted his sister when he drove the bridge to Cabin 1's crowded lot. Miranda pulled a box from her car, hitched it to her hip, and waited while he double-parked behind her. "Here, Mirs. I've got it." He pecked her cheek, emptied her arms.

"Where've you been?" She eyed his truck cab. "And all by your lonesome?"

"You won't believe it."

She hoisted another box from her tailgate and followed him into the studio. "Try me."

He lowered the box behind her counter and scanned shelves. "You got any bolo ties tucked away anywhere?"

"You're not."

"Took a lesson from a master today. More tomorrow morning. Hoping Hildy'll join me for the Sunday night finale."

"You're a dreamer, Luke. You told me—"

"Yeah, well, last night . . . She might. Either way, it's a hoot. You know dancing and me, Mirs."

She laughed, dodged a customer to pinch his cheeks. "I'm so *glad*. I thought you'd lost that, too."

"You're not the only one." He eyed her car's open hatch through the window and looked at the sky. "I'll close your rig, then I've gotta run. I'm making hay today. Neighbor's baling around dinnertime, so we'll be bucking bales 'til dark."

She walked him outside. "Look at you, farmer boy. Supposed to rain like crazy here tonight. Bet you won't get a drizzle out there in dryland."

"That was the idea, buying that place, remember? Didn't need a sky full of tears, too. If you see Hildy, let me tell her about . . ." He swung an invisible partner and grinned.

A fragrant first cutting. Sunday morning Luke stopped at the field on his way out, pulled dewy hay from a broken bale, and tossed it past barbed wire to Jangles. The cow's horns seesawed as the animal swiped a tongue and lifted a drape of drying grass from the well-drained ground. *No clay, no mud.* Luke reached, rubbed the animal's smooth, wet nose. The mighty head tracked him as he walked to his truck.

Driving west through the valley's farms, he eyed the clear, bright sky. *This place.* It had taken some getting used to, all right. Sunshine, three hundred days a year. And sixteen inches of rain. Not seventy miles away, Sekiu topped a hundred. Even at half that distance, Mirsy at Lake Sutherland and Hildy at the Elwha both expected sixty. Some years west-enders didn't see the sun for months.

Moody light, angry clouds, and near daily, sullen rain: just the way things were, growing up out there, and afterward. For him, for Eden. For their girls. Until . . . well, he'd hadn't needed abusive weather reinforcing his own storms. Though he didn't feel shadows as Hildy described them, he'd known a few out there, along with suffering's dark cloak and bone-chilling cold. Had he stayed at the west end, the weather might have finished his undoing.

Boats, sea, maritime gloom—he'd said goodbye to all of them in favor of this land-bound fresh start. *All things new?* He was working on it. At least now he had tools—and help.

He drove ten miles, fifteen, and as the Olympics' rain shadow retreated behind him, clouds thickened, curdled, and started to spit. At the outskirts of Port Angeles, he flicked windshield wipers on low and felt wind buffet his truck. By the time he rounded the Elwha hill's curve, trees bowed to the heavy blow. The wipers' rubber blades whapped like a terrier's tail.

A dog. Maybe I should get a dog.

He peered through the glass. A bedraggled couple hurried into the store, where two more huddled under the gas pump awning. In the storm's false twilight, lights dotted RVs' windows as water sheeted from the roofs of cabins and trailers. Gusts billowed and collapsed tents, sent ripples down the puddles and river, and frothed the lake into a white-capped frenzy. Cross-river, campers rolled soggy gear and shoved it into car trunks. A departing pickup slowed at Luke's approach, and the smiling wet-headed driver dropped his window. Two more rigs tailed him.

"No quitting for you, right?" The middle-aged man brushed a drip from his nose. Beside him, a petite woman wiped condensation from her side window. "Us either." He glanced past his shoulder at the vehicles behind him. "If you see Clarence or Otis, tell 'em us tenters are hunting motels in Port Angeles. Tell 'em we'll be here with bells on tonight, though."

Rolling forward, Luke saluted the man, then parked in the rain-flattened meadow. His phone dinged, and he opened Hildy's reply to his text the prior morning. A thumbs-up emoji. Only that, and after twenty-four hours. Good thing he liked to dance. Who knew if she'd ever join him?

Inside, steam rose from his damp cohort, assembled and raring to go. Clarence set the needle. "Roll away to a half sashay," he called. And they were off. They passed through, separated, went home. Ladies curtsied, converged, yelled "Whoo!" *Weave the ring, box the gnat, wrong way grand.*

Shortly before ten, Clarence swiped his hands in loud, brushing claps. "That's yer toy box, kids. Let's put 'em together and see you play. You ready?"

The twins stomped. Their father stretched his neck and crowed, flapping elbows like a rooster. A broad-shouldered woman scrunched her voluminous perm, put fingers to her mouth, and whistled.

Clarence set the needle and sang. Five short rounds and twenty minutes later, he stopped the music and pointed at the floor below center stage. "Square up right here tonight," he said. "Where I can keep an eye on ya. Come seven this evenin', y'all are leavin' the kiddie pool."

More whoops, as Clarence opened doors to raincoats and umbrellas and more dancers blowing in on the freight-train wind.

Luke snagged him before he returned to the stage. Mouth at the man's ear, his hand swept the room's east windows. Their heads turned to a speaker on a corner shelf.

"Worth a try, if she don't come," Clarence said. "Depends on the weather, though."

22

HILDY

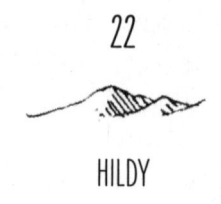

BREACHED

SUNDAY MORNING. Hildy backed the Yukon to her stoop, cinched her hood, and stepped into the storm as Miranda emerged from her car at Cabin 1, thrust a wave at her into the wind, and hurried into the studio.

Good, no talking. And no one else outside to further jam her brain. The campground and dance hall, the busy market on this morning's grocery run—their noise and hubbub crawled her like spiders, and her tearful revelations to Luke had left her ragged. Three bags of groceries to get inside, and then she'd hole up through tomorrow—until the holiday passed and all these pressing, invasive people returned to wherever they came from.

A drenching gust slammed her as she opened her liftgate. With her back to the howling wind, she sidestepped to her door, balanced the paper bag on one hip, and fumbled for her key.

The lock clicked open. Hildy shouldered inside just as Luke appeared at her elbow with groceries in both arms. He backed the door into the interior wall and held it for her. "This rain," he said. "Glad I saw you out there."

What? No! You can't— Thunderstruck, she couldn't speak, couldn't move. Behind him, her empty car, shut tight. He'd even closed the hatch without her hearing him. Now, in plain view, in front of him, were Butterness, her desk and chairs and messy table, her neatly made bed.

And all of her *things*.

Gasping, she shriveled over the groceries she hugged to her belly. *No warning at all. How could he—?* He'd stripped her, gut punched her, violated her most carefully guarded boundary. He'd tricked her, appearing like this. Proved once again that she couldn't trust any man who showed interest in her. Even worse, he wouldn't care if she did or not after . . . after seeing this.

Still hunched, she minced to the counter, lowered her bag, and propped herself against the laminate edge. Luke kicked the door closed, set his bags beside hers. She shrank when he reached for her. "What is it, Hildy? Can you stand? Look at me."

Rain slammed and sheeted the windows. Butterness cheeped between agitated hops. Hildy stared at a row of stones along the backsplash and ticked her head his way an inch.

With his fingers on her shoulder, he waited. His touch reached her lungs somehow, slowed her drowning. When his thumb hooked her chin and turned her face to his, she saw only kindness in his earth-streaked eyes. Still, she looked away.

"What's the matter?"

Didn't he see? Elbows bent, she raised flat palms to the ceiling and swiveled at the waist, presenting her cluttered space like an offering. Or evidence.

"You should have called first." Then she could have left and met him elsewhere. Or hidden behind her locked door. Anything to keep him from . . . this.

At least her distress over his presence was dawning on him. He removed his hat, held it like a penitent. "Oh. Uhhh. Yeah. Sorry. I hadn't planned to . . . This storm. Saw you out there and . . ." He shrugged. "Your groceries were getting wet." She didn't know what to say, so she stood with arms crossed as he scanned the room. But instead of the horror or disgust she expected, his raised brows and open mouth showed only . . . surprise?

"So . . . are these the tricks you said you developed? To help store your days? To remember your life, I think you said."

What could she say? Her lips stretched flat and wide as a baby robin's rostrum. She cringed as he strolled the room's perimeter.

"Ingenious," he whispered.

"Tess thinks I live in a mess. Says I'm nuts to keep this stuff."

"She's the one? Defines you as crazy?"

"No, Tess doesn't understand me, but she doesn't question my sanity. She just wouldn't want to dust it all, streamlined as she is. Like Mom that way, though similarities end there. I don't mind the dusting. Feather dusting keeps me in touch with everything."

"I see."

His reaction—well, his *lack* of one—astonished and calmed her.

The back of Luke's hand skimmed a row of her notebooks; his fingernails clicked on their bindings. "So many," he said. "Journals?"

"Diaries. Lists, mostly." Her arms scooped air as if gathering her walls' contents. "I won't forget a single day, a single event ever again, Luke. Haven't for years now."

He inspected a duck decoy that hung from a cabinet. Read its underside. "Number 462?"

"Corresponds with a diary entry."

"And this?" A narrow piece of shale on the window ledge. "Hashtag 1423?"

She felt herself blushing again. "Likewise."

"Your good days, bad days, they're all here?"

"Or in there." She pointed at the closed bedroom door. "Except for the rocks I left at my last place, every day's here and accounted for since I left home . . . uh . . . sixteen years ago. Written records and visual prompts of all my waking hours."

"Huh." From the center of the room he considered her wooden chairs, the bed, then walked to her love seat and moved a pillow. "May I? I just danced for two hours."

What? He planned to stay? And sit on her *couch*? Still reeling, she lowered herself into her usual chair at the table. "I guess."

Luke removed his boots, aligned them near his feet. Punched the pillow and rolled his ankles. "Much better. I'm all ears, Hildy."

"For what?"

"The backstory on this stuff. I'm interested. Very interested."

Something beneath his words. She believed him.

She tracked his sightline across the collection on her ceiling, along her walls, and over every available ledge. Surreal, seeing him here, knowing his eyes roved her history, told in hundreds and hundreds of items from roads and rivers, mountains and trails. Gatherings from yard sales and hatcheries, lakes and beaches and little streams. *His soft eyes.*

"One for every day," she mumbled.

"And they each have a story."

She nodded, smoothed a crease from her jeans.

"If you've got time, I've got time. How about you start by the door, work your way around, top to bottom? See how far we get? I don't have to go anywhere until seven o'clock."

Seven? He wanted to stay for the next *nine hours?*

"Chronological order could work, too." He sat up, tapped his chin. "Or what about grouping them by themes?"

"Themes?" Her hand shook as she plucked a box from behind Butterness's cage and refilled his seed.

"Yeah. Like hobbies." He slung his gaze over the dozens of antique hand tools she'd hung. "Woodworking? Or childhood. Family. Boyfriends?"

"I'd rather not."

"Which?"

"Boyfriends. Boy*friend*. Just one, and I don't want to talk about him."

"Okay then." He adjusted the pillow as a backrest. "I see quite a few toys here. How about . . ." His eyes scampered the baseboards. "That?"

He pointed at a doll's metal high chair, white enameled, with a Nordic design painted in red on the seat back and tray lip.

"It's like the one I lost."

He studied her. "Like the things you mentioned the other night. Lost things. Now there's a theme. You have more replacements in here? Of other stuff you lost?"

She nodded. "Not everything, though. I haven't found copies of everything yet."

"How old were you when you lost the chair?"

"Four, I think." *Groceries can't sit out.* Hildy opened the fridge, stowed orange juice, eggs, pizza dough.

He watched her, thoughtful. "My Lucy was four. Hard to imagine her losing something that size."

Is he doubting me?

"I'm not questioning whether or not the chair was gone, Hildy."

Reading my mind!

"Just that the logistics seem improbable. A four-year-old wouldn't be likely to stray very far carrying something the height of her chest. You sure nobody stole that chair? Lots of kids pass through campgrounds."

A can of beans slipped from her hands and rolled toward him. Hildy stooped, then dizzied when she stood. "It was winter. I remember a patch of snow, bare trees. We lived in the store apartment then."

How did he do that? Get her talking?

"Tess was at school, Dad gone somewhere. Sticks in my mind because Mom bundled me up, sent me outside while she cleaned upstairs. I stomped puddle ice, got bored, I think, and sneaked back in. Hauled my doll and that little high chair out to the yard, then ran back inside, got a sheet, and spread it over a rake handle I propped across the fence and a yard chair. A tent house, all set up. I played out there quite a while until Mom called me inside."

Her voice trailed off. She sat at the table.

"I can picture it. Then what happened?"

"She was worried. Said I was too cold. Made me come upstairs and take a warm bath. I remember because of how my frozen fingers hurt in the water's heat. And because Mom was so nice. She turned on the tape player with kids' songs she knew I liked. I had a squirt gun in there, and bubbles. She usually said no to long baths. Usually made me hurry."

Birdseed chaff littered the table. Hildy swiped it into a palm, then crossed to the trash.

"While I was in the tub, Mom was changing beds, cleaning down the hall. I made a mess, so she helped me dry off, then mopped my splashes. Told me I could pick fresh clothes by myself. I remember because she rarely let me."

"Why not?"

Hildy raised an eyebrow, chuckled. "You had little girls. Wildest outfits ever, when I got to choose. It surprised me that Mom let me pick, but I was glad. I wanted my doll, so I pulled on some warm clothes and ran back outside." The scene was vivid before her. Her confusion, more so.

"And?"

"I couldn't find her. No tent. No doll. No rake or sheet or chair by the fence, either. Gone, all of it. As if I'd never been out there."

A sofa spring creaked when Luke leaned forward, elbows to knees, intent on her. "Your mom. She do something with them?"

"She was upstairs, cleaning. Like I said."

"Huh. Did she help you look for them? What'd she say?"

"She heard me crying on the porch and ran downstairs. I remember how worried she looked when I told her. Chewing on her lips. Then she sat on the stair and petted my head like I'd break or something. Told me I'd been riding my bike outside, not playing house, that she'd been keeping an eye on me from an upstairs window. That she'd called me in when she saw my red ears and nose."

"Hildy—"

"Still, I insisted we hunt, so she indulged me. We scoured the yard before we found the doll in the toy closet where it belonged. The sheet was in the laundry basket, as if I'd never taken it. That rake, the lawn chair—back in their spots, too. We never found the high chair. Searched high and low for the longest time. I spotted this one at an estate sale. Identical, except the detailing on mine was blue."

"Strange."

"I know. I am. Happened a bunch of times."

She batted a pair of steel roller skates strung from a hook on the cabin's center beam and watched them swing. A metal adjustment key dangled by yarn from one wheel. "Tess and I each had a pair of these. Dad took us to sidewalks in town sometimes. So we could skate on concrete. One day we'd been at Erickson Playfield, pretending that big slab was frozen and we were stars in the Ice Capades."

She caught Luke's smile and nod. As if he knew about skating.

"When we got home, I distinctly recall setting my skates in the kitchen—to the side, so no one would trip on them. Dad called us into the store, scooped us some chocolate cones. We twirled on those stools at the counter while we ate them. After, my skates had up and vanished. Nobody stole them, Luke. They were on our linoleum, away from the door."

Luke's gaze traveled to the replacement skates overhead. "Huh."

"Mom heard me wailing and came in from outside. Looked sad when I told her. Resigned, I guess. Said, 'Oh, Hildy. Not again.' All four of us scoured the house, the yard. Even Dad's truck, in case I'd left them there."

Luke was frowning. At the stories or at her? She didn't ask and didn't stop the telling, afraid she'd lose her courage. One after another, she recounted two hours' worth of detail-laden narratives about disappearing toys and books, clothes and tools. Even her *puppy*, for heaven's sake. All where she'd left them until they simply *weren't*. She told him about lost belongings and her fabricated memories of *how* she lost them, so different from reality she learned secondhand.

She was pacing, chewing her fingers. After all this, Luke would know the biggest loss was her brain, her mental marbles. All her rambling . . . She'd taken too much of his time.

Pausing for breath, she steeled herself against his judgment, dismissal. Expected him to tie on those leather boots of his and stroll right out her door. Prepared, she faced him, looked him square in the eyes.

And caught her breath at his tenderness. Was he sorry for her losses? For *her*, more likely. *So be it.* At least he'd know what she was contending with if they spent more time together.

More time? Unlikely, after this.

"The stories don't add up." He tapped the skates, sent them swinging again.

"No *kidding*, they don't add up. That's what I've been trying to tell you. I don't remember my life correctly."

"I don't mean that, Hildy. You ever look for a common thread?"

Her mind was quicksand. "I lost stuff. I don't recall how. All my misplaced things, my skewed recollections—they're ropes, not threads."

"Not those threads."

"What, then?"

"Still thinking on it. I'll process better over a little lunch, though." He sauntered to the counter, eyed the folded Safeway bags, apples, a loaf of bread. "May I?"

She hurried toward him and reached for the bread, but he swung the bag. "I'll make you one, too. Got any peanut butter?" He tapped a drawer. "Knives?"

Hildy yanked the next drawer open, dug a jar from the refrigerator, and watched Luke smear bread, wash two apples, and carry the food to the table. She hovered by the fridge until he looked over his shoulder and smiled. Patted the chair perpendicular to his.

Eat? How? She slid into the seat, pressed a fist to her belly. What did he mean, a *thread?*

Luke chewed slowly. "I doubt your memory's the issue here."

"What are you trying to say?"

"Otis believes a lie's in play, right? And he calls those ugly things you sense *lie-makers*? Says they might link to your anxiety? You said both shadows and anxiety are worse for you in this valley. *Warmer, warmer* . . . You could be closer to the truth than you think."

"I don't know, Luke."

"Your family's been in the Elwha for what, three generations? Four? Some lies get handed down, become strongholds kids are raised with."

Her eyes went wide. "Like what?"

"I don't know, but I worked for that old man. Bingo almost died under his watch."

"Grandpa Diller is dead. I don't—Let's change the subject."

She picked at her food until they locked eyes.

Luke broke the gaze first. "Okay. New subject. I have a surprise for you."

Wary, she lifted her chin.

"Guess where I've been the past two mornings."

She licked peanut butter from a finger. "You said you'd been dancing."

"Right over there. Took lessons."

"You *what*?"

"After seeing those dancers the other night, I couldn't resist. And don't deny it, woman, you wanted to get out there right along with the rest of them."

"I told you, Luke, I don't—"

"*Didn't* dance, for a season or ten—well, twenty years. What's stopping you now? Last I saw, your legs worked fine."

"You know what's stopping me."

"Hildy. You want to feel better? That dance tonight is a good place to start. Come with me. Let's add a happy memory to the good stories you have about your dad in that hall."

Her chair scraped as she thrust herself from the table. "I can't. I—"

Luke leaned on forearms, smiling, relaxed. "Sure you can."

"I don't have one of those dresses."

"Who cares? These'll do." He pulled two crumpled bandannas from a pocket, both blue. He shook them out, tossed her one.

For the longest time, Hildy stared at the kerchief in her lap. Rolled it, unrolled it. Fingered the hem and, finally, giggled.

23
LUKE

DOCK

HOME FROM HILDY'S BY TWO. Luke rubbed Jangles's ears, and while the longhorn burped and chewed her cud, he sat in the shade of a poplar until the cow's galvanized trough overflowed. Hildy's stories were only now catching up to him as fully as he'd known they would. The unknown behind them pressed him.

He guessed their talk would be soaking her now, too—and wondered if its impact would change her mind about the evening ahead. If she'd go with him at all.

The hydrant squeaked as he lowered the handle, cutting the water's stream. He walked to his barn, cool inside and, but for a row of small square windows, dim. Through each, yellow beams slanted to the floor, his workbench, and the empty wheelbarrow awaiting woodworking scraps. He leaned against a rough-cut post supporting the hayloft, watched dust float in the light, and prayed for answers to be as clearly lit as those specks.

He'd sleep awhile before tonight. Turn off his phone until he knocked on her door. No text from her would keep him away.

⛰

Subdued but apparently willing, she met him on her stoop as the sun ducked below the day's heavy clot of clouds, now empty of rain. They set out for the bridge, where Luke took her shoulders and turned her in a full circle. "Wow. Look at this," he said, as a firehose of the late light sprayed tree-stacked hillsides and the river and a billion drops on needles and leaves. She smiled and rotated a second three-sixty on her own before they walked on.

But as they neared the hall, her steps slowed. Fifty feet out, she stopped altogether. Dancers walking behind streamed around them. "You're asking a lot of me here, Luke. I can't go in there again. Not yet."

Her *can't* was softer than before. The door she'd been slamming stood ajar. Hopeful, he took her arm and swung them both back toward the highway. "I'll take *yet*. I have a better idea, anyway."

The background cream of Miranda's *Toes of Clay* sign had gone bronze in the thick light when he guided her around the studio, down the lane, and past the other cabins. In the residual warmth of the long May day, trees steamed, ethereal with gold light and evaporating rain. Apart from swallows hunting low over the shimmery lake, when he and Hildy reached the dock, they were alone. Soon fiddle music and Clarence's rhythmic calls traveled through the hall's open doors and windows and over the lake's narrow neck, its rising mist a megaphone.

"This idea of yours." Bewilderment hiked her cheeks.

Luke laughed and gestured to the dock. "Wide as a square with room for swings. Edges will keep us in line."

He grabbed her hand and pulled her onto the planks. Rowboats tied to the pontoon dock bobbed like cows in stanchions.

"Here?" Two steps onto the weathered wood, she halted. "With just two of us?"

"We'll pretend the other six." He turned, grabbed her other hand, too, and backed her onto the makeshift dance floor.

"The dock's too narrow, Luke."

"Not for them." He swung their clasped hands toward the invisible pairs forming the rest of the square. "They can dance on air, you know?"

"Go on home, y'all," Clarence droned from across the water. "Now let's make room for one more square. Newbies, get out here. Raise those paws of yours so we all know who you are. Let's hear it for 'em, folks."

Through the hall's windows, whistles, stomps. Hands clapped in unison. Hildy blew from ballooned cheeks.

"Easy one, comin' right up. Pat your pillows goodbye, cause we're about to leave the homestead. Bow to your partner . . ."

Hildy faced him and notched at the waist in a small, stiff bow. *A rusty hinge,* Luke thought. *Seized up.* How long since she'd moved to any music at all?

"Join hands now, circle to the left . . ."

As Clarence sang, Hildy shuffled a do-si-do, her circle tight, then scowled through the next three calls. Luke questioned the wisdom of bringing her here, pushing her to dance, certain she'd flit away. But when she cocked an ear, listening hard, he understood her frown as intensity, not dislike.

She wasn't quitting. She knew every single one of these moves.

"Birdie in the cage," Clarence called. "Let's see those wings."

Luke danced around her, clapping, whistling, as Hildy lifted elbows in a meager flap.

"Birdie out, crow hop in." In a smooth rotation, they traded places—now he bird-stepped in the center of the imaginary square. As she circled him, mist and swallows and a thousand ancient firs bore witness with Luke to her rising brow and a thaw in the ice of her movements. To her small extra twirl as she orbited him. Arms folded, she arched her back and threw shoulders into another do-si-do, while he turned with her, his elbows flapping. When her shoulders swung as if oiled, he tossed his chin and crowed through a wide-beak grin.

"Hop out now, and promenade. Go around town."

Her hands relaxed in his as he retook them, and her wrists and elbows and knees broke from the rust. She floated like that steam over the lake—her fluidity a descant to the foot-stomping fiddle music. *Like her river,* he thought, surprised, delighted. *Escaping the dam.*

The beginners' dance ended. Luke caught her at the waist and spun her. Didn't want to let go.

As if watching, Clarence's lighthearted command flew across the water: "Y'all go home now, ya hear?" Rhythmic clapping rolled from the speakers and Luke imagined the dancers setting up, eager for the next stylus placement on the next disc in the caller's sizeable stack.

Through five sets, Hildy led Luke, demonstrated unfamiliar steps, doubled over in mirth at his impromptu inventions for steps he didn't know. Easy, the beginner sets now. He added flair, and her laugh was a bell.

Another break, then another hour of music. They sat out none of the tunes as Clarence's singing rolled downlake and echoed off hills. And while the sun dropped into the forest behind the hall, Hildy's giggle, the waning light, and the slap of the water on the dock's underbelly joined the double-stop fiddle in the gladdest music Luke had heard in years—maybe ever.

Venus shone above the hills by the time Clarence lifted the needle from the final song. "Give yourselves a hand, y'all." From across the water, applause, background rustle, murmurs. "Watch yer step heading out now. Stairs might still be slick from all that rain. Stir pickles into yer potato salad. Picnic's tomorrow at three, right out front a here."

Luke scooped Hildy under the arms and swung her again, then draped an arm over her shoulder. Under his biceps she felt supple; her spine bowed her into his side. *No ice, no rust.* He dropped his elbow down her back and held her neck in horseshoe-arced fingers as they left the dock. Near a fat maple, he looked at her sidelong. "Excuse me, ma'am. There's this pie in my truck begging for plates and forks. Think I could find some in Cabin 2?"

She looked at him straight-faced. "Depends. What kind of pie?"

"Not telling. It's a good one though. Nothing but the best for those delicious lips of yours."

Her face went rosy, and she scuffed to a stop. From behind her fingers, a challenge: "How do *you* know they're delicious?"

Luke shrugged, his grin uncontainable. "Just guessing." He stepped in her path, reached under the shield of her palms to cradle her flaming cheeks. "May I confirm?"

He heard her sharp intake of breath as her eyelids closed. Saw her small nod before he brushed her mouth with his, caught his own breath, and tenderly pressed his lips onto hers. He felt her reply as he lingered. Then he eased away, licked his mouth and eyed the shining planet overhead, assessing.

Hildy blinked blonde lashes, and he traced her cheekbone with a slow finger. "Looks like we're going hungry."

Her pout clobbered him, and he laughed.

"If there's a pie fine enough for those lips, I've yet to taste it."

She toed the ground, her smile a wisp. "I'm starving, Luke. I vote for the one in your truck."

24

HILDY

VITAMINS

"YOU SHOULD HAVE SEEN US, BUTTERNESS." The bird hopped from the cage floor to a low perch. Crown feathers lofted, he cocked his head at Hildy in her chair at the table, then swiped his beak on the perch. "The dock was our dance floor." She squinted at the bird's hyperextended toe knuckles, his nail arcs too tight for a clean grab at the perch. Outside, a man shouted a greeting, and another replied. A car door slammed.

Memorial Day.

"Time for a trim, little guy." The canary flitted from her slow-moving hand until she caught him at the cage bars and brought him close. Gauging the distance from each nail's thin red vein, she threaded Butterness's translucent claws into the jaws of her clipper, snipped, then gently returned the bird to the enclosure.

The canary pecked seed while she spread a hand towel on her table, filled a shallow bowl with cool water, and set it on the cloth.

She rolled her lower lip over the upper, reviewing Luke's kiss there on the dock and again after pie. The berry taste of him.

After everything I told him. And after all he'd seen here in her cabin. Her eyes swept the room, its clutter exposing her mind, illustrating it. Then she removed the bird's paper-lined floor and set the cage over the bowl. "Why does he like me, Mr. B?"

Luke already knew more about her than she'd ever told Cole, but he kept showing up. *Why?* More confusing: how on earth had he bypassed her evasiveness? And why had she let him? *Never again,* she'd sworn after Cole. Until now, she'd kept that vow.

The bird hopped to the edge of the bowl, then into water as deep as his underside. He dipped his head and splashed, his flutters and flaps spraying drops to the towel and cage bars and to the nests, fir cones, and papers littering the table, until his black crown feathers parted and his yellow breast clumped wet. When he flitted to his high perch to shake and preen, Hildy twisted the wand of her blinds to the early sun, aiming rays to warm him.

A scouring pad, she thought. That sun would scrub the forest, the store roof, the flowers in Miranda's pots, the skin on Hildy's bare arms. *Here it comes.* She hurried to her riverside window and yanked the blinds' pull cord until the wooden slats stacked at the top of the glass, opening her view past her porch and the trees and the rope swing to where sun struck water, bounced, and polished her ceiling.

Her mind went to the prior day: the groceries, the rainstorm. Luke, bumping his way into her cabin, learning her walls and her stories. Their walk to and from the hall and their dance on the dock in the bright mist in time to the fiddle and the sunset and his arms around her and the smell of him and the electric current coursing from him, warming her until her fingers didn't itch.

She clumped her loose, kinked hair to the top of her head and let it fall before she spotted her current diary, unopened the day before. Gasped when she realized she hadn't written. Hadn't felt the need to.

―――

At nine a.m., she pulled on shoes. Busiest weekend of their year, and she'd promised Otis she'd help. With free time for dancers until today's midafternoon picnic, every inch of the resort would hop.

She leaned into the store and mouthed *Otis?* to June at the till.

"Check the dock, sweets."

Before the door jangled closed, Hildy was on the lane with campers fresh from the showers with totes and wet hair. In campsites, others soaked up early sun and sipped coffee in lawn chairs near RVs. More strolled toward the lake with fishing poles, trailed by scents of bacon and cottonwoods. A boy on a bike whizzed past.

Hildy caught up with Otis on his way to the dock. "Where do you want me today?" she asked.

He shifted an armful of oars and studied her, his grin wry. "I detect a little less aversion to the Elwha anthill this morning." He spat into the grass. "Wouldn't have anything to do with that heel-toe action on the dock last night, would it?"

Heat rushed her face, and she shrugged, almost glad he'd seen them. "I remembered how, Otis."

"Good thing, dancin'. You and him. All of it." He glanced at the waiting boaters then back at her. "You willin' to spell June at the counter for a bit?" He stepped sideways toward the dock, the oars like giant whiskers from his elbows.

"I'm on it," she said. "You go." Her phone buzzed when she pivoted back toward the store. "Hey, Tessie."

"What time's that picnic today?"

"The usual. Three."

"Good. I'll pick you up then. Mom's talking."

"What do you mean, 'Mom's talking'?"

"As in words, Hildy, and she's recognizing people. Can dress herself again. The Hillview nurse who called me couldn't believe it either. When I agreed to the treatment, I sure didn't expect this."

"What treatment?"

"Mom's naturopath contacted me with sixty years of studies on vitamins improving brain function in dementia patients. Said her own patients have benefited. Doesn't work as well in advanced cases, but she thought it was worth a try. The stuff's cheap, so I told her to have at it."

"Which vitamins?"

"A multi and some other stuff, but mainly B-3. Niacin, I think."

"No kidding."

"I'm skeptical, but I gotta see. You're coming with me, little sister. Maybe she'll know us."

Hildy sighed. "Three then."

Seconds later, a text. **You working, dancer girl?**

Her reply to Luke was quick. **For now. Tess coming at 3:00. Visiting Mom at Hillview.** Suddenly, she wanted him there with her. Did she dare ask? Yes. Yes! **Come with?**

⁂

From Hillview's portico, Luke hurried to Tess's car when she pulled in, and he opened Hildy's door when they parked. "This visit's spur of the moment, right? Last night you thought you'd be on duty with campers all day." He swiped a hand toward Tess. "And both of you here? What happened? Is your mom okay?"

"Hey, Lukie." Tess slung a bag onto her shoulder and slammed her door. "Violet's making a comeback."

"What does that mean?" His eyes locked on Hildy's, questioning, and he gripped her hand. She held tight, siphoned his sturdiness.

Tess hitched and dropped a shoulder. "Improvements, I guess. She's buttoning, zipping. Putting shoes on the right feet. More aware."

"They're giving her megadoses of vitamins." Hildy dropped her voice as they walked the hallway. "B-3's the ticket. I found research spanning decades. Healings, reversals, mitigated symptoms."

He looked doubtful. "If it's that good, why don't they—?"

"You tell me. No money in it, I guess. Medicine's big business."

Ahead of them, Tess turned at a door, and Luke released Hildy's hand. She snatched it back and pulled him into her mother's room.

Near a window, Violet sat in a swivel recliner, staring blankly at a half dozen goldfinches fluttering at the courtyard feeder outside.

"Bet they're eating thistle seeds, Mom." Tess's voice boomed in the too-warm room. The birds scattered as she turned their mother's chair to face her visitors.

Violet's frame had gone knobby, but her eyes sparked with recognition. "Tessie!" When she snagged Tess's blouse, her sister braced like a bull.

Too close in here. Hildy's ribs stretched with a high-volume breath, hunting oxygen.

Tess peeled their mother's fingers from the cloth just as Violet spotted Hildy and Luke. "Lars?" The woman threw a hand to her mouth, and wailed. "Hildy, you found your *father*?"

Tess matched her volume. "No, Mom! No! That's—"

Hildy squeaked, slipped to the corridor, and pressed her spine to the wall. She slid to sit, folded knees to her chest, and chewed a thumb, six again. In seconds, Luke was beside her, his hand on her knee like ballast.

Muffled voices seeped between the floor and Violet's closed door. Hildy again drank air, hugged her chest. "What's wrong with me, Luke? Mom took care of me, *raised* me, for heaven's sake. She can be a little annoying at times, but she was always kind. From the way I responded in there, you'd have thought she was one of the mean ones. I couldn't escape fast enough."

Luke studied the ceiling. "Do I look like him?"

"Like who?"

"Your dad."

Frowning, she ingested his face, torso, and the long-boned legs folded beside hers. Did he?

He rolled his arms, inspecting elbows. "Anything?"

"Maybe your hands?"

He spread his fingers. "Yeah? That's it?"

"I'll show you some pics." The sudden need to hide Luke from her mother stole more breath.

Luke laughed. "Good. You start thinking I'm your dad, I'm outta here."

That laugh. Her chest filled with it.

"Deal?"

"Deal."

"Good," he said again. He pulled her to her feet, stuck his head in Violet's door. "We're going, Tess. Call you later."

"Lars? Lars! You can't take her!"

"Mother. Look at me." Tess in charge, gruff.

"Leaving *again*, Lars?" Violet's cries screeched after them.

25

HILDY

GATHERING

WHEN LUKE FIRST INVITED HER to meet "his people," she'd shied. The second Sunday he asked, she drove to the property she'd visited twice with Miranda and turned uphill on his gravel driveway, where she knew he'd be waiting over the rise.

At the crest of his first pasture, she slowed, stopped mid-lane, and stepped from the car to calm herself. Like she usually did. Even after their six weeks of near-daily contact, if she didn't settle herself before she saw him, she still clammed up, and it took precious chunks of their time together before she found her tongue.

"It's as if you came to the Maker's party that year you turned nine," Luke had told her over coffee, "but you stayed in the foyer. Time for you to meet more of the family, dancer girl. See the rest of the house."

She agreed reluctantly. With her new Elwha colleagues, she'd repeated the professional distance she perfected in her jobs at the UW and the USGS, the moat around her private life a mighty one.

But that moat was draining. Kindnesses from Luke, Miranda, Junie, and Otis had begun to penetrate her mental hideout, and she now shared bits of herself in return. Four people. Six, if she counted Bingo and Tess. More than enough.

Meet *more* of the family? *Don't wreck this, Luke.*

From the hilltop, her eyes swept the Dungeness River's alluvial spit and the sky-bouncing strait, then roved the watershed's farmland and, in the little town of Sequim, houses full of families. She and Cole had imagined their own family once, before she locked that wish away, too.

She turned to the Olympic Mountains behind her, sentinel crags above Luke's two-story farmhouse and the weathered plank barn—both buildings solid, simple, old. Luke stood on his porch, shading his eyes as he watched her. At his wave she raised a hand, returned to her car, and drove toward him on the poplar-lined lane. Her mirror's rearview of water and valley dropped beneath the crest.

Near the driveway fence, Luke's mild longhorn lay on folded legs and rolled cud in her jaw. A cowbird walked the animal's back, its head low. Hildy lowered her window and listened for the bird's gurgle. "Sing to me, brownie," she whispered. The bird pecked an insect from Jangles's withers before Hildy proceeded toward Luke and the calico winding a tail around his leg.

He opened Hildy's door and eyed the Bible in the passenger seat. "Hey, you brought it," he said.

She handed him the leather-bound gift from her dad. He fanned pages, thumbed to her underlining, and looked up at her. "Awana verses?"

Her cheeks heated. "Some," she said. "Some new."

He nodded, read her tidy script in the margins, and touched a passage. "He's talking to you," he said. "Can you tell? Words like these?"

A smile cinched into fans at his eyes. "We'll shortcut through the field," he said. "We're back and forth so much Kurt and I put a pass-through in the fence."

At a stand of firs, they slipped through a narrow gate in the barbed wire. Behind the trees, two couples sat in lawn chairs on a ranch house's patio. "Warm days like this, we meet outside."

Hildy bit a thumb.

"Kurt and Jill worked in South American medical missions before they retired, then Kurt finished seminary. They bought this place a few years before I got here. I met him on the road when he was walking his dogs." He shrugged. "The rest is history."

She'd heard that history. How the man had worn a pasture trail to grieving Luke, packing comfort like salve.

Two more couples rounded the house with children. When Hildy hesitated, Luke caught her hand and pulled her into the group. Introductions blurred, but she sorted and assigned the children to their parents and heard of others grown and elsewhere.

She attached names to the banker, lavender farmer, homemaker, and golf pro. Then to the pickleball champ, gardener, birdwatcher, and kayaker, before she escaped with Luke to the shady lawn, where some had already toted chairs, and others spread blankets. Luke sprawled on the grass, and when Kurt perched on a stool and talked, Hildy sat cross-legged and absorbed his stories, underlined verses, and scribbled notes.

Her childhood meetings had felt something like this, when she and Tess flanked Dad on folding chairs at the Crescent Grange Hall, then plucked donuts from the back table afterwards. Here, kids beelined for cobbler as fast as she and Tess had gone for maple bars—two each, on days Mom stayed home to help campers.

Hildy elbowed Luke as a couple herded four young children to their car.

"They're patient," she said.

Luke laughed. "Yeah, they're learning. Those kids give 'em a run for their money, but coming here helps."

And so the weeks passed and, rather than recording her days, Hildy lived them. Around her fisheries and resort duties, the Elwha summer unfurled into time with Luke. After work and on weekends they hiked to the riverside cabin at Humes Ranch and to alpine wildflowers and panoramic views from Hurricane Hill. Ate dinners out or prepared them at their homes. Walked beaches and Luke's land, where he'd tie Kurt's lessons to stories from her walls and from his life since boyhood, and to fishing, and nature, and building things with wood. Talking she now craved, to her surprise.

Before long, her need to review each day compressed to bedtime, after she closed her eyes. Then her skin would remember Luke's physical gestures, too—thousands of affectionate touches that thrilled her, steadied her, and—when he never wavered—sprouted trust.

Touch she now warmly returned—and initiated.

Except around Miranda.

She didn't know why she froze up around his sister. She almost idolized the woman.

Luke certainly showed no such restraint. Whether Miranda joined them for lunch in Sequim cafes, seafood dinners on the waterfront, or meals at his home, he'd invariably sling an arm around Hildy, kiss her openly on her cheek or hair. On hikes when his sister tagged along, he'd hold Hildy's hand. Touch or hug her like he always did.

But as much as she wanted to, around Miranda, Hildy couldn't respond.

One evening the three of them shared salad, garlic bread, and chowder from clams they'd dug together. Hildy had served her berry sorbet, and they'd laughed, played rummy. But when Luke playfully caught Hildy at the waist, she went fence-post stiff.

"What gives?" he asked, as his sister's departing car dropped behind his hill.

"I don't know. I can't help it."

"She doesn't bite, Hildy. She likes you. Likes us together."

"It's not that."

"You want me to leave you alone when she's around?"

"No." *Absolutely, no.*

"What then?"

"I really don't know." And she didn't. Eventually she had to chalk up her response to yet another feeling she didn't understand and couldn't explain—just as she couldn't clear the murk from her own stories—or explain why some affected her so deeply.

And one story was too packed with emotion to tell. She'd torn its page from the diary and ripped it to shreds.

26

LUKE

WINDOW

HE'D GIVEN HILDY TIME, hadn't he? Been straight up and affectionate with her, respectful and interested? Tried his best to be fun—and interesting? He took care of himself, looked good enough, he hoped, for a woman as beautiful as she was, and he knew they had chemistry. They both loved the outdoors, and their brains and beliefs connected on any number of levels. He even liked the mystery in that shyness of hers, tantalizing him with curiosity about what she'd say or do next.

But with each passing day, he grew more convinced that, shy or not, she was evading him. Not in all ways, of course. They could talk for hours on a wide range of topics. At the other's touch, they had to tap willpower and avoid situations that could take them too far. Intellectually, physically, and spiritually, they were on a good road.

But emotionally? Though he hated comparing the two, if Eden had been this dodgy, his younger self would have been long gone. Whether aware of it or not, Hildy was hiding something. *Why?* And *why*, with that near perfect memory of hers, did she question the veracity of every childhood story she told him?

He was falling for her—fast. Any more time without a resolution to this, and he'd be in a real mess. *Time to fish or cut bait, Hildy.*

For both of them.

With the tide low on this July Saturday, they'd started early, hiked the ten-mile round trip to the Dungeness Lighthouse before lunch in Sequim. On Luke's patio now, Hildy pulled off her hiking boots, shook her sandy socks.

He carried ice water from his kitchen. "Trade?" He handed her a glass, lifted her bare foot into his lap, and rolled thumbs over her arches.

Hildy sighed, closed her eyes. Her chin bobbed to the slow tempo of his massage.

"You good for another outing? A short one? Got a surprise for you."

She looked at him, waiting.

"Wild blackberries. Native ones, not those Himalayans."

That same look from her.

"Top of my hill. Vines crawling the ground, loaded with little half-inch beauties."

She lowered her foot and grabbed a sock. "They ripe?"

"Ripe and sweet as they're ever going to get. I'm thinking shortcake tonight. You in?"

Berries thunked the bottoms of buckets when Luke pinched a plump one between his fingers and raised it toward Hildy, who was hinged at the hips and calf deep in thorny vines.

"For your thoughts," he said. He was going to chase his hunch. He'd considered it for days.

She eyed the berry and swung her bucket toward a dense mound behind him. "I was thinking we shouldn't try to pick over there."

"Why?" Over *there*, more blackberry vines sprawled the hillside in a tangle of toothy leaves.

"Male brambles. Only female blooms bear."

"No kidding." He ambled toward the heap, inspecting. Not a berry in sight.

As good a lead-in as any. "Some guys are like that." He smiled at the segue and watched her closely. If his words registered, he couldn't tell. "Ever know any?"

Her nose crinkled. "Huh? Any what?"

"Guys who didn't sweeten your life." He pointed to a thorn's scratch down her shin. "Guys who made you bleed."

Her lips parted, fingers sped over vines.

"Maybe just one guy? That boyfriend you mentioned but never talk about?"

"Still don't want to."

"One conversation, Hildy. That's all I'm asking. A point on our map. We can pass right through it, but we need to go there, if I'm to understand you, know you better."

"What for?"

"Because I wonder if whatever happened is still affecting you."

"What if it is?"

He wove through the brambles to her. When he took her bucket and lowered it to the ground, she remained stooped, hands on her knees. He touched her arm until she stood. "Even the short version is fine," he said.

She left the berry patch and faced the mountains, her back to him. "I swore I wouldn't."

"Swore you wouldn't tell me?"

"I swore to more than that."

"I don't bite, Hildy. Haven't I proved that time and again?"

"Yeah, but I—I like you, Luke. I don't expect this—us—to last forever, but once you know, you'll—"

"I'll *what?*"

She resumed picking. "Quit wasting your time."

"Try me."

Bingo's warning resonated, but Luke had to know.

A Canada jay perched on Hildy's bucket, then glided to a mate in a nearby fir. Luke added his berries to hers and watched her. Five minutes passed before she spoke.

"Cole."

"Who?"

"His name was Cole. He was a senior in engineering at the U when I met him. First week of my freshman year."

Luke upended his empty bucket and sat, eight feet from her.

"We were together ten months. He was amazing. Never gave me a reason to believe otherwise. Thought I'd be with him for the rest of my life."

She went silent, studied purpled fingernails.

"But here you are."

"Yes."

"Because . . ."

"We'd gone out six months when he asked me to marry him. I told him I would. No date set, but he gave me a beautiful ring."

"And then?" *Like extracting slivers.*

"We made plans. I was really happy. We both were, I thought."

Her tears erupted, and he went to her. "Hildy."

She raised a hand. "If you stop me, Luke, you'll never hear it."

He pressed his lips together, returned to the bucket.

"End of the year, he graduated and I left for a summer internship in Maine. We talked every day, but I didn't see him for six weeks."

She wiped an eye. Stood like a soldier and frowned.

"Then what, Hildy?"

Her lips trembled. "I decided to surprise him, so I came back a day early. I parked by his truck in the alley so he wouldn't see me drive in, then sneaked into the kitchen. He never locked that door during the day. I couldn't wait to see his face when he saw me. I thought he'd be so happy."

"What did he say?"

"Nothing. He didn't. See me, I mean."

"But—"

"I heard him and a girl laughing. My freshman roommate before I moved off campus, actually. She dated one of Cole's roommates, so she was around there a lot. Dumb me, I didn't suspect a thing. I tiptoed into the living room and—"

She swallowed. Looked at the ground.

"They were on the couch. They were—"

"Oh, man."

"Yeah. Neither saw me. I yanked off my ring, threw it in a bowl on the kitchen counter. Slammed the door on my way out."

"No doubt."

Resignation rode her exhale. "You've got to know that I've been over him for a long, long time, but back then I was so upset that when I couldn't reach Tess, I called my mother."

Her mother.

"We talked for an hour, and she reminded me that relationships with guys were tough enough for normal women. Said that given my lifelong issues and the character of most men, catching

Cole red-handed was the best gift I'd ever receive. She said if I didn't stay away from the whole lot of you, I'd be sorrier than I could imagine. I'd never heard her be so blunt.

"'But Dad was a good man,' I told her.

"'And where is he now?' she asked. As if she knew.

"I couldn't answer her. I'd known Dad had gone hiking that morning, but something in Mom's tone, the innuendo in it . . . What if he hadn't gotten lost after all? What if she knew he'd gone somewhere else? Now I had the rotten hope that if my dad wasn't who I thought he was, maybe he was alive somewhere. Maybe I'd see him again after all. But would I want to?"

Luke groaned.

"Once she brought Dad into it, I didn't know what to think. Mom knew me better than anyone did—and she knew my dad. If I couldn't even trust him . . .

"Cole called me, wrote me. Apologized so many times. Cornered me outside my apartment and at my part-time job and begged for another chance. But what was the point in talking? Mom was right. How could I possibly trust him again? How could I trust any man—or myself? I vowed I'd never get involved with anyone again."

She finally looked at him—with dry eyes this time. "And now here you are, and I'm playing with fire."

A double whammy. This Cole guy and, worse, her mother's ridiculous advice—her *insidious* advice.

"Just because one guy goes sideways on you doesn't mean they all will, Hildy." What would it take for her to believe that?

Was he the one playing with fire?

27

HILDY

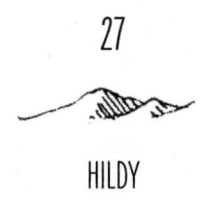

LEAP

THE AUGUST DAY after Dave briefed them at Olympic National Park headquarters in Port Angeles, the twenty-one members of four Elwha survey teams headed for their assigned staging areas on the river. In this final survey before the dams' decommissioning the following June, researchers from myriad agencies would record water temperatures, depths, and quality; the physical condition of the river's creatures; sediment makeup and accumulation; and other ecosystem data.

But their most critical assignment? Counting. From the mountain headwaters near Chicago Camp all the way to the strait, snorkelers would swim the river, lay eyes on fish, and count them—one at a time.

Awake by four a.m. on August 20, Hildy arrived at the Whiskey Bend Trailhead an hour before the others converged.

"You're like a thoroughbred in the gate," Luke had teased the night before.

She parked her rig smiling. *That grin of his.* Since she'd told him about Cole and Dad and her mother's take on things, something had shifted in her. *For the better,* she thought, though she couldn't say why.

"A racehorse?" She'd suppressed her own smile. "Hardly."

But here she was, about to bolt upriver. As she waited in the awakening forest, she knew Team One was setting up below the lower dam. Within the hour, Team Two would bivouac here at Whiskey Bend, and she would set out with Teams Three and Four for predetermined positions on the river's upper reaches. While all teams would begin shoreline data collection as soon as they got situated, the swimmers would wait for Hildy's call. To avoid double counts of the same fish, once her Team Four reached the headwaters, she would set the simultaneous start time for all four teams. Only then would snorkelers enter the river and begin their counts.

Near a heap of rope-wrapped parcels, a string of three mules and a saddled quarter horse mare with a bell at her neck twitched sleek shoulders against flies. Slouched in waiting, the animals straightened cocked legs as the mule skinner lashed bundles of food, camping gear, dry suits, and survey equipment to their backs, balancing loads, checking for rub points. Like wind, the Elwha swished and murmured beyond them.

A few feet from the pack string, Dave Cloud's roan gelding kicked at biting insects on its belly. Dave rubbed an insecticide wipe over the horse, then looped reins on the saddle horn and tightened the cinch.

Hildy walked the line of animals briskly, touching lash ropes that secured khaki-covered equipment to the pack saddles. Early sun flossed trees as she referenced the clipboard list at her hip. Team members assembled around her.

Her impatience was rising. For weeks she had evaluated reports from the Cessna's flyover, monitored logjams, and gauged weather and water conditions, antsy to enter the steep, wild river and swim with those fish. Delayed twice by storms, their time window was closing. If they couldn't complete the survey before the fall storms arrived, they'd lose their low-water opportunity to access the canyons—and the essential data they hoped to collect before the demolitions—forever. Now, finally, the river's clarity and depth were again at seasonal norms, and a strong high-pressure ridge promised a week of fair, dry weather.

Time to go, she thought. *Now.* Around them, tails of moss floated from trees like seaweed in the air's soft current. She sniffed for rain, skeptical of the blue patchwork through the woods' canopy. In this country, a nose could often predict coming weather as well as meteorologists or sky, and even in August, storms could rise fast.

Another downpour could force more delays, compromise their research accuracy, and jeopardize teams' safety. Snorkelers could only swim narrow, bouldered Carlson Canyon in low-flow conditions; heavy rain would render that sheer-walled stretch nearly as dangerous as the river's Grand or Rica Canyons. And anywhere along the Elwha, logs and unstable woody debris could trap, batter, or drown them.

"What's that barometer say, Dennis?"

A tall man checked a gauge. "Lower than an hour ago." They looked at each other, then at the sky.

"Watch conditions," she told the gathered teams. "Surveyors have flagged whitewater. Team Three . . . obviously, bypass the major canyons. There's no way to climb out of those chutes if you get in trouble. Team Four, we'll stay out of Carlson Canyon until we're sure it's tame enough."

A lean-muscled biologist whispered to a bearded colleague shouldering his pack, then ran his gaze down Hildy's body. She glared at him. "I heard that, Bryce. Kayak all you like off-duty, but we'll read Carlson when we get there. I don't care if you're wearing

Kevlar or medieval armor under your dry suit. Stay out of crazy whitewater. All of you—get to high ground if the weather turns. Everything else is a go. Track each other. Stay within range. Where the river's wide, add a third diver so you don't miss swaths."

She ran a finger down her clipboard. "You all ready?" Mules ambled onto the trail behind the skinner's mare. The group hoisted packs. "Good. We're off then."

Amused, Dave spoke low as she approached. "Kudos, Trail Boss. Big cake of a reprimand, coming from you." His saddle creaked as he mounted.

"They need to be careful," she said.

"We handpicked those teams, Hildy. They know."

She bit a thumb. "But Bryce . . . Do you think he'd try to float Carlson if the water's high?"

"Don't be gullible. He's getting a charge out of your reactions, is all. The man's your age, with enough river wrecks kayaking in that freestyle playboat of his to teach him a few things. You let him, he'll bait you all week."

He nudged his horse onto the brown seam of trail.

Gullible?

She donned her pack. With mules carrying the bulk of their loads, her gear didn't weigh much. They'd make good time.

She brought up the rear, distanced from the others' banter. Alone with her thoughts, her gaze swept the understory, the damp, mossy boulders, and the dark sea of tree trunks, and she assembled observations she'd share with Luke. He'd be curious about *everything*.

So how'd you feel about that, Hildy? She could hear him.

She was learning to answer. This time, she'd tell him about the trail's voice, calling her. The parental hover of stiff-limbed spruces and firs. The river's moods—its pensive turquoise, its white, narrow rage—and the ache in her over both. She'd also mention the elk calves browsing near their mothers and bulls dangling bloody velvet from new antlers, once she could name the feelings about family they evoked in her.

And she'd tell him how she watched for something, anything, of her dad's. For clues on his cold, mysterious trail.

Lunch, rest breaks, and eleven miles were behind them when the trail veered to a low-bank stretch of river. Dave directed Team Three's attention to the gravel shore. "Our first put-in tomorrow, right there. This section's a clean run—and the first long reach, so we'll split our counts, start a new one at the surveyor's flag. C'mon. Let's unload."

At nearby Elkhorn Cabin, the packer loosened diamond hitches, and others carried gear from the mules. Dave and the skinner pulled saddles, then watered and staked the animals to graze the meadow. Teams made camp in the cabin and around it, cooking, laughing. Hildy walked the field's perimeter, reading the trees and air before she slipped into her tent early.

After breakfast, Hildy's radio beeped. She replied to a downstream team, then frowned at scooting clouds and hoped the weather would hold. "We'll see you in four days, Dave," she said. The pack string set out, and Dave waved her and the upriver team on.

Along miles of gradual ascent between Elkhorn and Hayes Cabin, Douglas firs gave way to the elegant silver firs Hildy loved, and Team Four followed the river past floodplain. *A liquid dream,* she thought, as she tried to ignore the shifting air. By late morning, however, the rising wind sent a steady *whoosh* high overhead, and she eyed the swaying canopy every few minutes.

They had passed the Hayes River confluence when Bryce slung his pack beside a landslide's uprooted fir and crashed through brush to peer over a canyon's lip. "There's Carlson," he shouted. Seconds later, Hildy heard Dennis whistle and watched him and wiry, dark-haired Liz lower backpacks and skirt more downed logs to reach indigo huckleberries dotting shrubs like jewelry.

Time for a break anyway. Hildy shrugged free of her load, pulled trail mix from a zip pocket, and scaled a boulder for a clearer view of the river, the terrain, and the changing weather. The skinner untied his mare from the string, quickly staked the mules, and remounted. He called to her from the trail. "Wind's picking up. I'll get on top and take a quick look from that crown. See if more sky can tell us what we're in for."

The packer's concern heightened Hildy's. Her backcountry team could handle a storm without issues. But could she? A rogue squall could force delays, and rain would mean shared tents or decrepit shelters and more time in the close proximity she did her best to avoid.

At the riverbank, Bryce eyed treetops. "I'm not digging this," he shouted. "Looks like that blow off Cape Flattery veered east."

Hildy craned toward the sky. "Let's hope those clouds are bluffing. If they emptied their buckets even an hour ago, we'll be okay."

Twenty yards off-trail, Liz and Dennis ate berries as fast as they could pick. Bryce peered into the water fifteen feet below. Hildy was reading GPS coordinates when a wild bray arrested them all.

Below her boulder, the mules screeched. Lines taut, they huddled, loads pressed to one another. Their brown-streaked teeth bared as a pair of black cubs scampered from the berry patch straight toward Bryce.

No, not toward Bryce. The cubs hurtled toward their *mother,* as she charged the man between her and her half-grown babies. Hildy clapped hands to her mouth. Dennis yelled, waved, and trampled brush as if to intercept. The mules swiveled long ears and kicked air.

Slack-mouthed, Bryce stood frozen between the advancing bear and her cubs for a full two seconds. Then he crouched, leapt toward the icy river, and disappeared.

28

HILDY

KNIFE

THE SOW LURCHED TO A STOP at the bank's edge, then spun to six-feet-four-inch Dennis, who spread his windbreaker overhead like a sail and bellowed. Liz pulled bear spray from her belt and sprinted toward him. Hildy clambered from the rock just as the mother bear wagged her nose, grunted, and cuffed the first cub to reach her. When Dennis roared again, the sow stood on hind legs, raised her muzzle, and sniffed. Then she dropped to all fours, circled wide, and, with cubs in her wake, loped up the talus hillside and over the ridge.

Hildy, Dennis, and Liz scrambled to the cliff at Bryce's jump-off point. Intent on the churning water, Hildy shielded her eyes, wishing for her field glasses stowed on one of those mules. She scrutinized the boulder-strewn river below. "Water's low enough. He can swim it."

"If he's conscious, he'll *have* to swim it," Liz said. "No way in or out of that gorge for more than a kilometer."

"He'll have to ride the cataract." Dennis squinted into the distance.

"A two-meter drop. He can handle that," Hildy said. Or could he? The cold would be paralyzing. He'd have to swim that frigid water without his dry suit.

If he was conscious and could swim at all.

Dennis stretched taller, teetering. "There he is!" Forty yards downstream, a drenched head rounded a boulder. Legs behind it flailed, but whether from the current or Bryce's effort, Hildy couldn't tell. Dennis cupped hands to his mouth. "Ride it, Bryce! We'll get you out!"

No sign the man had heard.

Reckless, stumbling, they reached the mules. Dennis blew his whistle for the skinner. The sound bounced every which way in the trees and canyon, but no horse rounded the bend. Where was he?

They couldn't wait. If the river hadn't already killed Bryce, the icy water could. They had to get him out. Dry him. Warm him. Liz and Dennis bolted downhill.

Breathy with fear, Hildy pawed at the mules' wrapped loads. *No time!* She snagged Bryce's pack, tore his rain gear and a fleece from inside, and set off after them at a run.

She'd followed for at least a mile before the pair ahead of her left the trail. All three clawed through brush to where the frothy river left the tight gulch, then pooled, spread, and slowed, its surface now as gray as the thickened clouds above them.

And where, humped like the sow he'd evaded, Bryce staggered toward their side of the river. Hildy dropped the clothes she carried. All three splashed the knee-deep water toward him.

Then Bryce stumbled, pitched into Hildy, and plunged them both into the glacial drink.

"I'm okay. You tend him." Though Hildy had never been colder in her life, at least they'd crouched behind a boulder, out of the wind. Beside her, Bryce shuddered, his lips blue. Contusions purpled both his cheeks. Already clotted, a two-inch gash on his calf gaped.

Liz squeezed Hildy's arm. "Put this on." She opened her rain jacket, untied the fleece at her waist and zipped Hildy into it, then cinched the hood over Hildy's dripping braid.

"Wear this, too. Hold in a little more heat." Liz removed her cap, seated it over the hood, and turned her attention to Bryce.

"If you'd taken a snorkel and slate, we could record that reach." Liz cocked a dark eyebrow at him.

Bryce grinned crookedly as Dennis lifted his colleague's wet shirt, exposing a bruised shoulder blade and ribs scraped raw. "Yeah, what was I thinking?" Bryce said. "Would've been fun suited up." He winked at Liz, pursed his lips.

"Don't get fresh, buddy. Stand up, now. We'd better make sure nothing's broken before we hit the road."

He dropped eyelids to half-mast and raised his chin. "Take your time, baby."

Hildy's teeth chattered as she watched Liz check Bryce's pupils, palpate his back and belly, and test his limbs' range of motion.

"Bumps and scratches is all." Lips flat, Liz watched him work arms into the sleeves of his recovered fleece and rain jacket. "Bryce, you're an animal, you know that? You just bodysurfed Carlson in nothing but cargoes and a tee." She tugged Hildy and turned toward the trail. "C'mon. Let's find those mules. Get you dried off."

They'd scarcely set out when the clouds opened, and wind spanked them with a horizontal deluge. In river-soaked boots, Hildy already couldn't feel her toes. By the time they reached their abandoned packs, rain saturated the fleece Liz had loaned her, and cold reached her bones. She donned her rain gear, but needed more than waterproof nylon over her soggy clothes. Layers of shirts, pants, warm socks, and her towel waited in that second beast's canvas pack.

But the stakes, tie-line, and mules were gone. Farther upstream with their handler, Hildy figured. But how far? Shivering in her raincoat, worry niggled at her as she spotted Dave, ascending fast behind them, his horse blowing hard. His dripping poncho flapped.

"Glad I caught you guys," he said. "I passed your mule string two miles ago, heading downhill. He heard a whistle, thought you were ahead of him. From the looks of you, that would've been a good idea."

"Yeah." Hildy's teeth chattered. "This squall's no help. It's a cold one."

"It's no squall, Hildy. We've got ourselves a gully washer. An atmospheric river for the next two days, at least."

"Oh, no."

"Every team's called off. High water's expected the entire length of our study area. Fast runoff will be turbid." Dave shifted in the saddle. Water dripped from his poncho brim and ran in rivulets past the horse's flaring nostrils. "If you can get to Hayes Cabin, the packer and I will unload your gear there."

"We're so close. All those miles . . ."

He propped an elbow on the saddle horn and looked at her. "You're not thinking straight. You don't even have tents."

Dave's roan stood behind her, eyes closed, head low against dollops of water penetrating the canopy. Hildy blinked away drips, her brain cloudy. "No. We don't."

"The four of you wait this out at Hayes. The skinner and I will look after the animals at Elkhorn and stay in the cabin there with Team Three." He scanned the forest, the thick trunks of evergreens like bars in a basement cell. Moss and needles from their branches dripped and bobbed in the wind. "You better get going. Already feels like twilight in this gloom. I cached more food inside Hayes Cabin with your name on it. There's dry wood on the porch."

"Gotcha," Liz said.

Hildy nodded and stuttered her thanks. Bryce and Dennis angled downhill.

Dave took up his reins, his smile kind. "We'll debrief later. Just get to Hayes while you can still see the trail."

Dave and his horse were long gone when the hikers splashed through gathering dusk and crossed the clearing to the Hayes River Patrol Cabin. On the covered porch, Hildy stumbled on the heap of packs left by the skinner and smacked into the primitive log wall. Liz eyed her with concern.

Dennis pulled a headlamp from his pack, took two buckets from hooks, and headed toward the sound of rushing water. Fumbling with the latch, Hildy's hands shook as she shouldered the door open. Liz hurried past her into the single room, shone a flashlight at the cookstove, and passed a large pot to Bryce. "Fill this, too," she said. Liz's face blurred in the dark; her voice seemed far away. "We'll get you a fire, Hildy. No running water or toilet in here, but at least you'll be warm."

Her tongue thick, teeth rattling, Hildy nodded. Clumsily, she grasped tinder and kindling from a crate and stuffed it into the cookstove's firebox. While Liz gathered fir rounds from the porch, Hildy broke the first match, her pressure against the abrasive strip unmeasured, her fingers useless. Clenched against tremors, she scuffed a fresh stick. The flame popped to life, but as Hildy thrust it to the fuel, she fell against the stove.

Liz dropped her armful of wood, caught her, and pulled her upright. "I gotcha. Let's get some heat in you."

Hildy mustered a dull nod and stood at the open firebox. Liz gripped her tighter as the kindling quickly caught, crackled, and popped.

The orange glow lit Liz's angular face. Her eyebrows pinched into the crease between them as she studied Hildy. Boots thumped the planks outside, and Dennis elbowed the door open, his buckets dripping. Bryce followed with the soup pot.

"Back of the stove," Liz ordered. "Then hang on to her, Bryce. She's struggling."

"Oughta be me, not you," Bryce said. "Sorry I knocked you down." He blurred in Hildy's vision as he lowered the pot, threaded arms under hers, and propped her against him. Liz added wood to the fire.

Her mind like cotton, Hildy watched Liz scoop water from the soup pot into the kettle and set it above the flame. Voices reached her—muffled, dreamlike. She thought her clattering teeth would break.

Liz reclaimed her from Bryce. "Give us five minutes," she said. Bryce brought Hildy's canvas tote and sleeping bag inside, then joined Dennis on the porch.

Liz sprang into action. "Dry clothes, hot tea. You'll be as good as new." She shook Hildy's sleeping bag onto the bunk closest to the stove, then rummaged the pack for dry undies and socks, a fleecy sweatshirt, leggings, and beanie. "Think you can put these on?"

Hildy's nod was spastic. When she reached for—and missed—the string to loosen her hood, Liz took over, untying, unbuttoning, unzipping. She sat Hildy on the bunk, stripped her saturated boots and socks, raincoat, fleece, shirt, and bra, then wrapped her sleeping bag around her while she stood her again and pulled off her lower layers. Liz directed her as if she were a child, and Hildy responded like one, reaching, stepping, turning as Liz dressed her, tucked her into the bag, checked the water's temperature, and brought a mug of warm tea.

"Drink," Liz said, when she helped Hildy sit up. She held the mug while Hildy swallowed, then poured her another, hotter one that Hildy wrapped with cold fingers. Outside the window, a headlamp beam illuminated a shadowy wall of firewood stacked between two trees. More wood thumped to the porch.

Liz sat on the bed at Hildy's hip, leaned close, and shone a flashlight at her face and the empty mug. "Good. Not shaking so much. I almost stripped down and got in there with you. Can you talk yet?"

Hildy swallowed hard, licked her lips. "I think so. Thanks, Liz. Sorry. The wind. I was too wet." *My brain, AWOL again. Now they'll know.*

Liz waved her off. "Blame it on the bear." A knock sounded and Liz leapt to the door, swung it ajar. The bedraggled men hurled more bundles inside and latched the puncheon door against the storm. Water pooled under dripping coats they hung on pegs.

The monochrome twilight dissolved. Bryce shone a flashlight over the corner bunks, a rough table, chairs, and shelves laden with kitchen paraphernalia, canned goods, and lidded plastic tubs snugged against the wall beneath the shelves. "Matches, Lizzie?"

Liz tossed him the box. He lit the Coleman lantern on the table. The room flooded with white light as Liz draped wet clothes on a drooping line strung near the stove. Bryce added wood to the fire.

Dennis cupped hands to the window and peered into the night's ink. "Sorry I didn't notice you were in trouble, Hildy," he said. "Thought you warmed up when we started walking. Too focused on Bryce . . . How's that leg, Superman? Anything left of that brain of yours?"

Bryce waggled eyebrows above his bruised cheeks. "Regenerating as we speak. Part crab, y'know." He emptied a bag of dehydrated soup into the steaming pot of water, dug through Dave's tote for bread, and opened the communal cache. "Never know what you'll find in these things." He extracted a package and laughed. "Well, I'll be. Cornmeal mush. A true 1950s breakfast, compatriots. I dig this stuff. Last time I ate some was . . . uh . . . from a cache at Upper Lena Lake, boiled and sugared." He held the carton to the light and squinted. "And get this: only expired six months ago."

Hildy pulled her bag to her chin, watched Dennis add a can of chicken to the soup, and closed her eyes. He was doling out bowlfuls when Liz roused her, filled her mug. Silent, she dunked grainy bread and ate. A half hour later, the others played poker while Hildy rolled to the wall and burrowed into her bag.

⛰

They all slept in. At eight o'clock Bryce rekindled the fire, set coffee to boil. From her bunk, Hildy watched through slitted eyes as Liz sliced into the cornmeal packaging and stirred it into a saucepan. Bryce zipped and rolled his bag and secured it with a bungee. Dennis tidied and stowed, making room for them to wait out the storm.

"How about these knives, compadres?" Bryce leaned over a log round in the cabin's far corner. Several midsize fixed blades and a couple of multi-tools projected from the sawn surface, their tips embedded in the wood. "I've seen clothes and food for the taking in these cabins, but never neck blades. Some nice ones here. Anybody need to trade up?"

Liz inspected the assortment, unsnapped a sheath at her belt and pulled a shiny blade. "From my fiancé," she said. "The man reads my mind. Feel the balance of this thing." She handed the knife to Dennis, who tested its heft, nodded appreciatively, and handed it back to her.

Hildy crept from her bag and retrieved her dried boots from beside the stove.

Bryce crossed to her, nudged her with an elbow. "Morning, sunshine. You sure were out. I checked you a couple times. Made sure you were still breathing."

Checked me how? She scooted from him and thought of Butterness, vacationing with June and Otis at the store. Oh, for the privacy of her cabin, or on the trail or river with nobody talking to her—unless it was Luke. "Good. Thanks." She zipped her parka, fingered her pocketed multi-tool and yesterday's pebble, and slipped outside to pee.

Dennis handed her a bowl of mush when she returned, and she wandered to the shelves, perusing. She ate standing, swallowed dregs, then strolled to the assortment of knives. She had pulled, inspected, and reseated two when a third caught her eye, and she tugged the five-inch blade from the wood. "My dad had one like this," she said.

Dennis poured more coffee, stepped closer. "Yeah. That Buck knife. Can't imagine anybody swapping out a knife like that."

Hildy carried it to the window, ran a finger on the engraved blade, and read the inscription. Felt the blood drain from her face.

"It *is* my dad's."

The other three bunched around her. Hildy handed the knife to Liz and sank into a chair.

Bryce leaned close and read aloud. "*HBD, my Lars. Your V. 1980.* So Lars is your dad? What's *V* for?"

"Violet. My mother."

Liz swiveled the knife, inspecting. The blade glinted light from the rain-spattered window. "Pretty conclusive, that's for sure.

Amazing nobody's taken it. Your dad's been gone since you were a kid, right? Wonder how long it's been here."

How did Liz—? What else did these people know about her? "Lost it hiking, I guess." Her lungs heaved as she rummaged a pocket and stabbed the tip of her multi-tool into the log. On a shelf she found a water-stained sheath, snapped her father's knife inside, and clipped it to her whistle lanyard.

Her mind raced. When had Dad hiked this far upriver? Or had he lost the knife only to have some other hiker find it and bring it here? And when? She hugged the sheathed blade to her chest, felt her underarms drip. *If he left it here himself, why? Did he think he wouldn't need it again?*

The log walls, these people, the shingles thundering with rain—oh, they pressed, pressed her, and Bryce . . . he crowded her, looked at her too much. Eyeing the door, she considered flinging it wide and running under the angry clouds, into the pummeling rain. Anywhere but here. Her lungs shrank.

She crawled onto her bunk and faced the wall, her fingers itching as she forced herself to breathe.

29

HILDY

SNORKEL

FOR ANOTHER FULL DAY, the deluge trapped them. Like caged cats, Team Four paced, fed the fire, cooked, ate, napped, washed themselves from buckets, played cards, radioed Dave and the teams farther downriver, and stayed in the cabin a second night, waiting.

At first light on their third morning together since they left Whiskey Bend, Hildy at last woke to silence. While the others slept, she slipped to the clearing outside in her bare feet and lifted her face to a cloudless, pink-tinged, windless sky. She minced her way to the river and read the currents before she returned to the cabin and beeped Dave at six o'clock.

"No hurry," he said. "Did you look at that water?"

"I did. Turbid and too fast, but it'll be better upstream. Send the mules?"

By nine forty a.m., they were following the packer and his animals over land steaming in the return of August's heat. At Chicago Camp, they unpacked, pitched tents, prepped equipment, hung food out of bears' reach, and hiked to the coordinates for the survey's uppermost start point—to check the river.

"Hear that stream chatter?" Dennis paced the bank where the narrow headwaters bumped over loose stones. "A real talker. We could start now and—"

"Tomorrow," Hildy said curtly and turned toward camp. Dennis took a step backwards as she passed. Liz and Bryce lagged to give her wide berth.

At Hayes, she'd sat on the porch for hours to escape them all. At the rickety table, when Bryce dealt cards and patted the chair beside him, she'd snarled her *no*. "Hoo-ee. Got ourselves a little wolverine," he'd said. Dennis and Liz had studied poker hands and pretended not to hear.

Wolverine. If only. But flippers and fins would be better. *Tomorrow, fish.* She rechecked maps, confirmed markers in her memory. At twilight, moss hung limp over their tents as Hildy crawled into hers, relieved to be alone.

Camp robbers squawked early. Bryce brought her coffee. While the jays pecked torn pancakes from Dennis's hands, she read the shallow, cobbled span at their start point, radioed Dave, and gave the others a thumbs-up. An hour later, she tugged neoprene gloves over her dry suit's cuffs and turned to Liz, whose waterproof waders reached her armpits. "Remember to georeference my position as you go.

Confirm all landmarks, riverbed features. We want to match the segments from the earlier studies as closely as possible. Let me know when we hit two hundred meters on those longer sections, okay?"

Clipboard at her hip, Liz nodded and jotted notes on a laminated tally sheet.

Dennis hitched wader straps over his shoulders. "Pace yourself, Hildy. If you need a break, we probably will, too, so if you're feeling it at the end of a stretch . . ." He patted a day pack at his feet. "Concession stand, right there."

She scanned the pair, then called to Bryce, taking measurements and soil samples cross-stream. "Join me when the river widens?"

"Hey, Boss Lady. We've been over this how many times? Flash bulletin: I'm not one of your green-gilled UW students." He tapped his temple. "I have forty miles of Elwha bathymetry stored right here. Humor me a little, will ya?"

Hildy scuffed a stone underwater and almost bent to retrieve it. "Sorry, Bryce. I just—"

"Knock it off, Bryce." Liz's tone was sharp. "Don't apologize, Hildy. The Klallams are running this team's show, Dave assigned you the lead, and every agency represented here agreed to that. You're doing fine. Better to review protocol than get sloppy."

Mouth tight, Hildy nodded at her data recorders. *Teammates.* "Let's go, then," she said. She seated her goggles, secured her underwater camera, and swiveled the dive slate attached to her arm. Then she spread lips over the snorkel's mouthpiece and lowered herself face down into the frigid Elwha.

And entered the world she loved.

While the others recorded shoreline data and trailed her downstream, Hildy left them behind to crawl, float, and pull herself through the glorious water—and to imagine herself a smolt on its silvery dart to the sea.

Hours passed. At length, Bryce joined her in the river, wider now with the inflow of new tributaries. Swimming parallel, he and Hildy navigated around rocks in churning, oxygenating riffles and runs, then floated quiet pools and glides. Though woody debris rerouted them and logjams sometimes spit them to shore, survey stretches accumulated as they swam or crawled their way downstream.

Segment after river segment, Hildy floated and tallied on her forearm slate and snapped underwater pictures of everything. As she did, her dad, that knife, annoying Bryce, and every other troubling thought fizzed and dissolved into aqua clarity. Suspended weightless in translucent pools and drifting face down in floodplain flows, she sensed the river's incipient freedom as if it were liquid itself. As more hours passed, her watery world finned with hope, and she felt only joy.

Soon, river. Her index finger wagged toward each fish she counted—a stroke for every big-headed bull trout, olive-backed and speckled yellow-and-red. A caress for each black-spotted rainbow trout—red or blue or green or yellowish, banded with rose from gills to tail. *Soon,* she thought again. How many of those rainbows would loop to the sea and back again after the dams fell, their steelhead genetics unleashed?

When the dams fall.

She measured the time in months now, not years. Ten months until the transformation would begin. *Ten months.* Around a pebbly bend, an elk cow and calf waded a tributary, sighted her, and fled into the wall of trees. On her feet for a rest, Hildy eyed the gravel where they'd stood and pictured spawners slapping tails in the pristine shallows as they scooped redds for their peachy eggs. In her mind's eye, newly hatched alevin dangled yolk sacks. Flashy fry and finger-striped parr ventured farther, exploring the little stream.

Her thoughts followed bigger smolt downriver and into the ocean, growing as they did until, hook-nosed, rock-scarred, and striped by teeth of seals or orcas, those Chinooks, cohos, pinks, and chums, those sockeyes and her imaginings all schooled at the mouth and in the estuary until their kidneys could welcome the river's fresh water.

Water that would carry them home.

Soon, beauties.

In a sparkling pool, she pulsed her mouth around her snorkel as if drinking great gulps, then kicked her flippers like a tail and pretended herself one of those home-going fish, pushing through rapids, leaping waterfalls. When she passed more gravel beds, she imagined herself a mother, with ova as orange as the eggs that would hatch there.

Glorious, those dreams. They swam with her for the rest of that day and two and a half more, though the only fish she saw were trout.

With no further hitches, the last team completed their survey nine days after Hildy's team left Whiskey Bend. The packer returned to that starting point to unload the surveyors' equipment, then took the mules and mare home to their stable on the Olympic Hot Springs Road.

Hildy went straight to her office, where she updated counts as numbers arrived. From the headwaters to the mouth, teams had laid eyes on 7,300 rainbow trout, 220 bull trout. From below the lower dam, they added 545 adult Chinook and 26 pinks. Weary, she double-checked the data. No surprise, but the numbers cried with urgency. The magnificent Elwha was gasping.

30
LUKE

WARNING

AS HIS TRUCK ROUNDED THE CORNER from the east, Luke saw Miranda collapse the A-frame *Open* sign and carry it from the highway shoulder toward the entry to Toes of Clay Ceramics. She looked up when he pulled into the empty lot. Seconds later, the Brinks' SUV rolled in behind him.

Miranda leaned the sign under a studio window. Arms spread, she hurried toward the vehicles as their doors opened. "All of you? What a surprise!" Then she saw them, and halted, her face slack with confusion and concern. "What—?"

Arms folded, stances wide, Luke and Bingo stood at the Suburban's bumper and scowled. Tess's expression resembled the men's as she crawled from the passenger seat, slammed her door, and extracted a box from the rear seat. But when Bingo pulled a pitch pipe from his pocket and blew a steady C, their feigned gloom crumpled into grins, and Tess's alto, Bingo's bass, and Luke's baritone launched into an off-key rendition of "Happy Birthday."

Miranda giggled and batted a hand. "You got me. I thought somebody died or something."

Luke squeezed his sister to his side. "Not a chance, Mirsy. We're having us a little *party* for my number-two woman."

Tess's head snapped toward him. "Does that mean what I think it does?" Her frown was genuine this time.

"Relax, Tessie." Bingo pulled another bag from the back seat and headed for the door. "I never thought Hildy would sit in her place, but I've been waiting for somebody to dethrone his sister for years." He aimed a finger at Miranda. "So has *she*."

Miranda adjusted shoulders to a regal posture. "On one condition."

Luke followed her inside. "And that would be?"

"That she's right for him. If she hurts you, Luke . . ."

"Save it for the wish, Mirs."

At the narrow counter, Tess pulled a cone-shaped party hat from the bag, stretched its elastic, and settled it on Miranda's head. Bingo lit the single candle, then carried the cake to her on flat palms. "Blow," Tess said.

"Now?"

Bingo raised the cake to nose height. "You think you'd get us to sing *twice*?"

Miranda shrugged, tapped her chin, and contemplated the ceiling. Then she puffed out the candle and swiped a fingerful of frosting.

"Hold on, cavewoman." Tess pulled plates and napkins from the bag. Handed out forks and party horns, then waggled a knife above the cake—now perched precariously on a barstool.

"Whoa, Tess." Luke caught her knife-wielding hand. "Care if we wait a few minutes? They're down from the mountain. Hildy will be here. She texted me an hour ago from her office."

Tess heaved a sigh, lowered the blade, lumbered to a window. She glanced up the highway hill, then thumped Luke's chest with a forefinger. Spittle rode her whisper. "You be careful with my sister, Luke. She's as tenderhearted as they come. Like a baby sometimes. If you do her wrong . . . if *you* hurt *her*—push her, scare her . . . *dump* her when all her weirdness outweighs her gorgeousness, I'll have your hide."

"I wouldn't think of it. I—"

A rig on the highway arrested him. His eyes darted from Tess as Hildy turned at the store, and he flew outside to wave her SUV alongside his truck. When she stepped to the ground, he pulled her into his arms and swayed her.

Her "Hey, Luke" was music.

"I missed you." He ran a knuckle down her cheek and kissed her nose. "You were gone a year."

Her smile was tentative, but she raised her chin and let him in. Her white-blonde brows, those pale lashes. That navy rim around her ice-flecked irises. His gaze rested lightly lest he spook her, but she held it. *Oh, this woman.* Without a word or a touch in reply, she leveled him, owned him.

He glanced at the studio and pulled her out of sight. Their lips touched lightly at first, then full on the mouth, eager, joyful. A passing highway driver laid on the horn and she pulled away, flushed.

"Tess brought cake," he said.

Hildy leaned to view the studio. "Was she surprised?"

"Seemed to be. Fun, regardless. We waited for you." He opened the Yukon's hatch, slung her pack over a shoulder, and watched her sidelong as they walked to her cabin. But when she fingered a leather case at her neck, her shoulders slumped, and he felt her retreat.

"You okay?"

Somber, she pulled the lanyard over her head, handed him the attached sheath, and unlocked her door. He carried her pack inside. She crossed to the sink as he extracted the Buck knife, its blade gleaming.

"My dad's," she said, squirting soap into her palm. "Found it cached at Hayes Cabin—where we rode out that storm."

He tested the blade with a thumb. "Still sharp."

"I know." She lathered her hands, rinsed. Splashed her face.

"Any idea how it—?"

"You'd better get back to that party."

He nodded, touched the blade's engraving. "You coming?"

She dried her hands, ticked a *no* with a head shake. "I have to think. Can't tell Tess yet."

He slid the knife into the sheath, placed it on the table, and stared at it.

"Save me some cake?"

He kissed her on the forehead. "I'll call you tomorrow."

⌂

"I can't believe it. Ten steps away, but she didn't even stick her head in the door." Tess licked her fork, folded the paper plate around it, and shoved both in the trash.

"Tessie, Tessie. Think about it." Bingo brushed a crumb from his wife's lip. "When's the last time you remember her at anybody's party?"

"That storm delay. It was a long week. Took a lot out of her," Luke said.

"*Pshhhh.* No wonder she likes you. You cover for her like Dad did." Tess bustled to more empty plates. "C'mon, my man. Let's get home before birthday girl here gets out her Hula-Hoop."

When they turned to go, Luke's clasp at Bingo's neck was quick, warm—another in their countless see-you-laters. For five years—well, four—he'd paid attention, memorized every farewell, aware that each could be more than that.

He looked from Bingo to his friend's abrupt, usually lovable wife, and to his sister, celebrating another year, before he thought of his Hildy next door. When she'd told him about Cole, he'd doubted they'd make blackberry shortcake together that night, much less see each other the next day. But since then? Somehow telling her story had softened that vow of hers, and she hadn't ditched him after all.

Nor he, her.

Quite the contrary. In subsequent weeks she had fallen toward him, not away. And he toward her. Weeks ago he'd asked himself if he dared to love her. Now the answer was obvious.

His eyes welled, and he blinked fast, absorbing the night, his friends, his sister. Miranda looked at him and nodded, her own eyes full.

31

HILDY

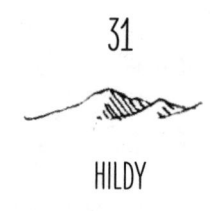

SPLIT

LEAVING FOR WORK. Hildy startled at Miranda on her stoop, poised to knock. Quickly, she stepped outside and pulled the door closed behind her. She glanced at her watch and frowned. *Only six thirty.* "I wanted to come to your party, Miranda. I'm sorry."

Miranda stood tall, a plastic-wrapped piece of chocolate cake in her hands. "We missed you. Luke missed you." She held the paper plate toward Hildy. "I told him I'd bring this."

"You came from your lake house this early to bring me cake? Nice of you, but—"

"We need to talk, Hildy. I wanted to catch you before you left. Before you saw Luke again." Without the plate in her hand, Miranda rubbed a thumb, fidgety. Shifted side-to-side.

Nervous? "Talk about what?"

"About him. And you. I'm only here because I care. You've got to realize that."

"Okay." A shiver ran Hildy's backbone. She eyed the scudding clouds, gripped the plate tighter.

As if steeling herself, Miranda filled her lungs, then straightened even taller. "Luke and you . . . He's the finest man I've ever known, Hildy. A man who doesn't want to scare you off. For some reason, he and Tess think you're some sort of baby needing protection, not a thirty-four-year-old woman. He thinks you only need time to warm up to him."

Miranda sputtered, balled her fists. "But patience has its limits. Do you have any idea how he feels about you? I've been watching you for months now, and I honestly don't see you warming up to him at all. He could serve you his heart on a platter and you wouldn't reciprocate. Last night, after he'd waited for days to see you? You blew him off. Blew him off! When he came back from your cabin, he had disappointment written all over him, and it was the last straw." Miranda's neck and ears blazed. "Absolutely the last straw."

What? Miranda had been *evaluating* her? Yes, and had found her lacking. *Not good enough for Luke.* Hildy sank to a stair, paid no mind to the cake that tipped and sagged onto her lap.

"Appears to me, Hildy Nybo, that you're toying with him. Killing time at his expense, and I won't have it. I watched his heart break once. You'll break it again over my dead body." Miranda crossed her arms and thumped them to her sternum. Fierce. Protective.

And rejecting me.

The wind swirled an alloy chill between them. Hildy couldn't look at her, and for a moment, couldn't move. Then she brushed the upended cake to the ground.

"Talk to me, Hildy." War glinted in Miranda's eyes. "I need to know you'll leave him alone."

Hildy had no answers. No words at all. Wasn't even sure she had a tongue. She stood on trembling legs and walked to her SUV, her mother's caution loud in her head. *Right all along.*

At the Natural Resources Building, Hildy slipped through a side entry and hunkered in her office with the lights off, the door locked. For an hour she rearranged papers on her desk, their print too blurry to read. Accusations spun through her brain.

Miranda rose large in her mind. Miranda, the woman she'd come to consider a friend, and with so many qualities Hildy admired. Discernment, for one. For her to say all that, Luke's sister clearly saw Hildy as Mom did.

As I am.

Strong, determined Miranda had revived Luke after his tragedy and loved him to his core. The woman always spoke her mind and acted on her convictions, traits that left Hildy in awe. Luke's sister could never, ever allow him to attach himself to someone like her.

Her breath hitched. She had seen his sister's discomfort that morning. Telling Hildy her concerns had to be so, so difficult for her. But how courageous of her to intervene on his behalf. How wise of Miranda to guard him.

And how foolish of Hildy to imagine she wouldn't.

Miranda had begun her explanation by saying she cared. No question about that. She wanted what was best for her brother, and like it or not, Hildy had to agree: Luke's best life would not include the *real* her.

But her friend . . . her *former* friend . . . did have one thing wrong: Hildy wasn't toying with Luke. Quite the opposite, in fact. Her care for Luke had grown vast and deep, and she wouldn't hurt him for anything. If she had to give him up to keep from doing so? Well, better to end the charade now before she caused him any more pain.

But oh, the hurt in *her*.

When he called that evening, she let her phone buzz. His text arrived as she covered Butterness's cage for the night: **Did you get some cake?**

Haunted, she'd crawled into bed when another came through: **Where are you, dancer girl?**

How long until he'd leave her alone? When tears wouldn't stop, she buried her face in her pillow and lay awake for hours.

32

LUKE

EMPTY

FIVE DAYS. SEVEN. He'd gone ten days without Hildy answering his calls or texts or knocks to her door, though Miranda assured Luke she'd seen her come and go. After dinner, he tried Hildy's line yet again, and heard four rings to the same voicemail message: *Nybo here. Leave your info.*

His text then: **Hildy.** Only that, knowing she wouldn't answer this one either. Praying otherwise.

Awake at three a.m., he crept over their interactions the night of Miranda's party for the hundredth time, examining the ingredients of their last moments together and her reaction to each: Her understandable dis-ease over the discovery of her father's knife. Her request for cake. Didn't the latter say she'd see him again? He'd left her with a promise to call, and she'd leaned into his lips at her forehead.

And then, without a whisper of warning, she'd dropped from the sky of their life together. *Fallen off the planet, more like it.*

Without a breath of explanation.

At four a.m. he made coffee, filled his Thermos, and drove the now joyless forty-five minutes to the Elwha Fishing Resort and her empty Yukon. She had to go to work, didn't she? He'd catch her on the way, between her cabin and her rig. Ask her for two minutes . . .

He slid his driver's seat backwards and stretched his legs, poured coffee into the Thermos cap, and sipped. In the gray pre-dawn he watched her door and the window beside it, his hand to his aching chest.

At five thirty, the slats of the window blind opened partway, and a silhouette crossed behind them. *Not long now,* he thought. By design, her seven-to-four work schedule had mostly matched his, granting them hours of summer's late daylight together.

But seven o'clock passed, then eight, with no Hildy. He waited another hour—until Miranda arrived, and he followed her into Toes of Clay. "I don't get it, Mirs. She dropped me like a hot potato, and I do not know why."

Miranda looked up from her till, a bundle of bills in her hand. "I guess it's good she did this now rather than later, Lukie. You can't make someone care about you."

"That's what's so confusing. I know she does." He turned to the window in time to see Hildy's vehicle, leaving fast. His lungs constricted. "There she goes. Have you connected with her at all?"

Miranda's sadness was palpable. "Not since the morning after the party. I took her that cake."

"What did she say then?"

Miranda sighed. "Not much, and she's avoided me ever since."

"Gotta have something to do with . . . Never mind." If Hildy hadn't mentioned the knife to Miranda, he wouldn't either.

"With what?"

"Nothing. Just speculating."

"Careful, Luke. Face facts. She doesn't want to see you, and lacks the relational wherewithal to tell you why. Maybe it's better to let her go."

"I thought you liked her."

"I do, Luke. I really do. But something's not right there. To treat you like that? To refuse to talk, when . . ." She shuddered, joined him at the window. "Surely you saw this coming, though. She's never been warm. Not like Eden." She adjusted a row of mugs. "Be patient, little brother. Wait for a girl who can love you back. At least now you know."

Eden? He refused to compare the two. "At least I know *what*?"

"That you still have it in you to care about a woman, to find someone else."

Her words slapped him. Incredulous, he stared at her. "I thought you got us. Understood her, me. Don't you realize I don't want anyone else? Can't you see that? I want Hildy. Only her. I might even love her, Miranda."

"You've known her since April, Luke. The end of April. Love? Really?" She pressed fingers to her temples. Rubbed slow circles.

"I believe she feels the same way about me."

"Has she told you that?"

"She doesn't know how yet—how to get past this . . . this thing in her way. But she will."

"Luke, please. Don't. Haven't you been hurt enough?"

"Hasn't she? I thought you—"

"Groveling won't help."

"Groveling? When have I ever groveled? This isn't about me anymore, Miranda."

"Don't pretend you aren't hurting."

"Of course I'm hurting, but so is she. I'm sure of it. And I will not fail her when she's in a rough patch. She needs me right now. Just doesn't know it yet."

"And how do you propose to come alongside her when she

won't even talk to you? Listen to yourself, Luke. Face the music: she's written you off, like she has me."

"Good grief, woman. What makes you think—?" He shoved hands into jean pockets and paced. "I know you think you're helping, but I'm the one to decide if I'll walk away. And as far as I'm concerned, if she's breathing, there's hope. I'll figure out how to reach her."

"Oh, Luke, no. If for no other reason, imagine what your house would look like."

He stared at her, dumbfounded. "You went in her place?"

"I looked inside. Enough for me. Should have been for you, too. I didn't react, but that room? She's a hoarder, Luke."

"Dang, Mirs. You have no idea . . ."

"I think you—"

"I heard you the first time." He reached the door. "I may be back, depending."

"Where are you going?"

"Damage control."

⛰

At her workplace, Luke slipped past the front windows to the back hallway, toward the office Hildy had shyly shown him before her trip upriver. He hesitated at her closed door, then tapped twice.

"Come in, Dave. I've got that—"

Luke locked the door behind him and was at her desk when she turned. He expected her surprise, but not her horror. She shrank as if expecting a blow.

He took a step backwards, tilted his head, his hands raised palms up at his waist. "Hildy."

"Wha-what are you doing here?" A gully formed between her eyebrows, the blue beneath them gone dark.

"I think you know."

She stayed at her desk, hugged herself as if she were cold. Wouldn't look at him. "I didn't know what to say. How to tell you."

He sank into the chair across from her. "You can tell me anything, Hildy. Haven't I shown you that?"

Her eyes met his with sadness so profound he thought she might break. "Miranda was right, Luke."

"Miranda?" He propped forearms on his thighs. "What am I missing?"

"She doesn't . . ." Her chest jumped in little hitches.

"Doesn't what?"

"Want us together. Thinks I'm . . . Thinks I'm bad for you. Thinks I'll hurt you."

"She told you that?"

Hildy snuffled with her nod, wiped tears. "When she brought cake."

Luke flinched as if from gunfire. "Really."

She nodded again. "Said you're handing me your heart and I don't give anything back. That she wouldn't stand for me hurting . . . you after . . . after all you'd endured."

"Did she now? Hard to believe she'd—"

Hildy's low, wobbly cry interrupted him. "It's all right, Luke. I understand. Why would you believe me? Who knows if any of my stories are true? You should thank your wonderful sister. I mean that. She's wonderful. And whether my brain twisted her words or not, she's right. Absolutely right. If you keep coming around, I'll mess with your head. Heck, I mess with my own head. How could I not wreck yours? *And* your heart."

She wrung a tissue, her hands tight. At her sobs, a knock and a man's voice: "Need any help in there?"

"No," she said.

The locked handle jiggled. "You're sure?"

"I'm good, Dave. Thanks. Talk to you in a bit." She walked to a window, and Luke caught her by the waist, set his chin on her shoulder from behind. She peeled his hands away and faced him. "You're not taking me seriously."

"How could I not? You've avoided me for almost two weeks."

"Go away. Get on with your life. Leave me alone, Luke Rimmer."

The strength in her resolve frightened him. *Now or never.* As effectively as she'd avoided him so far, would he get another chance?

"I won't force you to do anything, Hildy. You want me to leave, I'll leave. But hear me out, will you?" When she stared at the ground, he took her chin and held it until she looked at him. "Will you listen? I'll be quick."

Her "okay" rode an exhale. Reluctant.

He stepped away, rubbed his whiskers. Hung his hands from the back of his neck and studied trees outside the window. When he looked at her, she slid down the wall and hugged her knees.

"First off, I know Miranda means well, but . . ." He gritted his teeth. "I'm not happy with her at the moment. Saying I'll be better off without you? Rocks in her brain. Second, the way I see it, Hildy, *you* haven't wrecked a thing in your life. Third, I believe every word of your stories, just as you recall them. Few people I've known remember as much, or as accurately, as you do. Yes, you're dealing with some lies, but I don't believe they're yours."

"Whose are they then?"

"I don't know yet." Then again, he might.

She parted her lips to say more, but he raised a hand.

"Fourth, I love you, Hildy Nybo, and once I love someone, good luck getting me to quit."

She stared at him. "How can you say that?"

He shrugged a shoulder. "Easily. With all of me. I hope you take *that* seriously."

She groaned. "I waited too long."

"That bad, huh?" He roused a smile and nudged her to stand. "C'mon, sweetheart. Unless my radar's been off, you feel something like that toward me."

"I'm not good for you."

"But you are, Hildy. Not only good for me, but *good*." He took her hands and kissed the palm of each. "Let's imagine you believed that."

"You're wasting—"

"If you believed you were good for me, could you look in my eyes and tell me to go away? Would you say you never wanted to see me again?"

Her gaze darted to him, then the door. "I don't know."

"Not my style to chase you, Hildy. But unless you can say with certainty that you want me gone from your life, I'm not going anywhere." He ducked for a broader view of sky through her south windows and pointed at the crescent moon, translucent in the morning light. "I've lived in the dark of the moon, dancer girl. There were months I thought it forgot to orbit. Times when I could only see that shiny thumbnail out there. Or, when I was really hopeless, nothing at all."

Her forehead pressed the glass.

"But phases pass, Hildy. Picture a big round moon, still tugging at the tides even when you can't see it. Always solid, regardless. Can you do that?"

She closed her eyes.

"Better yet, think of it full and bright without a shadow hiding it. Then think of us without the dark blocking us from each other."

It was her turn to shrug.

Withdrawing from me.

"Keep learning, Hildy."

"I'm always learning."

"Keep tending that heart of yours. For your own sake, don't quit, you know?"

"I'll do what I need to."

"I'm choosing to trust that. I'll text you now and then, see how it's going, but like I said, I won't chase you either. Reply or not, your choice."

The door blurred as he grabbed the knob. "But do one thing for me, will you? If you decide we're through for good, tell me to my face." He extracted his phone and waggled it. "Not on this thing."

At her desk again, she rolled a pen.

"Take care, dancer girl." Quickly he pulled the door closed behind him, before a reply took him out at the knees.

33

LUKE

SIBLINGS

"MIRANDA!" Luke slammed his truck door. Fists tight, jaw clenched, he approached the studio.

His sister plunged a trowel into a pot of blooming echinacea and bolted upright.

"What were you thinking, derailing us like that?" He spat the words.

"I don't see it that way. *Helping* you is more accurate." Hands on her hips like a dictator.

"Don't pull that, Miranda. We're way past denial. Why didn't you tell me you'd talked to her?"

"I did tell you. When I took her some cake, remember?"

"Look. I know hurting me's not your end game, but Lord knows you did. I thought you quit trying to manipulate my life a long, long time ago."

"How dare you." She bent again at the pot, yanked a weed with fury.

"Quit the huffiness, woman. Your defensiveness won't work either. Are you going to spill the beans and hope I forgive you or pretend ignorance and wreck the best friendship of your life? I'm all you've got for family now, in case you've forgotten."

She dropped the trowel, propped hands on the pot's rim. "When she didn't come to my party, Luke . . . I saw your hurt and frankly, I saw red."

"Mad at *her*? What for?"

"Dismissing you yet again. Thinking only of herself. When I saw how much she hurt you that night, how you'd waited for her and she still didn't join you, I . . ." She growled, stood with arms stiff at her sides. "Hildy treats things that matter to you like they're . . . disconnected from her. You do something thoughtful for her and she barely reacts. Doesn't care. She treats you like you're the paper boy or something."

Luke folded his arms and leaned against his truck's grille, studying his sister. "Honestly. Couldn't you have asked me? All the talks we've had about the dangers of making assumptions. About taking matters into our own hands. She tell you what happened to her while she was gone upriver?"

Miranda scowled.

"Yeah. I thought not. Did you think to ask her why she didn't come to the party?"

Her head shook an inch left, then right.

"You don't have the slightest idea what she's thinking or how she feels about me. Or what she's going through. Instead of finding out, you sic that tongue of yours on her, send her back to her shadows."

"Luke, she's wrong for you. She's a stray cat. A rescue. What kind of wife would she be? You'd pour your heart and soul into her, trying to rewrite both your failures, to make up for . . . ways you think you didn't love well before. What's she got to give you back?"

His jaw hung, his mouth stretched sideways. "Is this a repeat of your save-Luke-from-taverns crusade? Geez, Mirs. How'd that work out? I'd eat those meals you brought and down another six-pack. I can't rescue Hildy any more than you could have dried me out before I owned what I was doing to myself, acknowledged that I was powerless to change it. Until I let God do the heavy lifting."

Miranda tracked a crow toward the foothills. Bit her lip.

Luke's voice dropped. "She's scared as a rabbit, and you've driven her into a thicket. Thorny in there."

"Luke." She sighed wearily.

"I love that woman, Miranda. I see who she'll be when she's free. Like you saw who I would be, even if your plan to get me there was screwed at first."

"I'll talk to her."

"No. You won't. Not a word, you hear me?"

"But I—"

"No. Leave it alone. Leave *her* alone. If you want us—you and me—to be okay, you will stay out of Hildy's and my business from here on, understand? Talk to God all you like about this—and I'd be glad if you would—but stick to the weather with her, if she'll engage you at all. Am I clear?"

"But—"

"I mean it, Miranda. Am I clear?"

The trowel whapped her thigh. "I didn't . . ."

He turned on his heel and left her. His anger wouldn't help anyone right now.

⛰

Home by noon, Luke postponed a door installation in Discovery Bay, ate leftover stew and threw hay to Jangles. In his barn, he climbed the loft ladder and dropped beside a broken bale—first to his knees, then prostrate, forehead to hands.

He hadn't moved for two hours when his neighbor found him there. "Only place left to look," Kurt said. "You doing battle?"

"In full armor." Luke rolled upright, sat on a tight bale, brushed hay from his shirt.

"For Hildy or yourself?"

"Her, me, us. Miranda tossed a grenade."

Kurt stirred loose fodder with a toe. "Sorry to hear that."

"Yeah. Now Hildy suggested I stay away. Insisted. In so many words."

"So you've been asking."

"For insight, yeah."

"Jill and I will as well. I'll bring the others on board, too, if you're good with that. We don't want you going backwards. If you don't pay attention, next beer you run across could look pretty good."

"Huh. Right."

"I set those tools on your workbench. Thanks for the loan."

"Anytime."

Kurt's foot found a ladder rung. "If you need me, call. I mean it."

Luke got to his feet. "Remember those shadows Hildy saw? Pray against those, too, will you? I think Otis is right about a lie somewhere."

"Will do. Stay the course, man."

Luke bit a cheek. "I used to play trumpet."

"Hah. Yeah. Like that. March around the walls. Blow hard."

34

HILDY

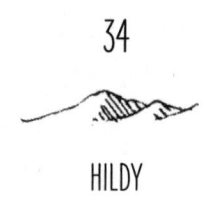

SOLO

"FRIEND OR FOE?" In Luke's wake, Dave stood at Hildy's elbow. She turned from her office window and sighed. "Who?"

"That guy who just left. You two weren't playing cards in here."

"A friend, but I don't think I'll see him again. Goodbyes are hard, you know?"

"I've said a couple of those." He assessed her, his eyes gentle. "Fine with me if you need to get out of here. Clear your head."

Hildy crossed to her desk, took her bag from a drawer. "I'll take you up on that. I won't get anything done today, anyway." Her fingers trembled as she dug for her keys.

Dave watched her from the mudroom, then waved an envelope. "Before you go . . . may I run something by you?"

She looked at her boss, then down at her chest, expecting blood from her ruptured heart. *Back to business, as usual.* If she didn't leave soon, she'd collapse right in front of him.

"Of course," she said.

"Good, good. Picking your brain here. Hannah stopped by with this." He handed Hildy a letter from a biologist she'd met only once before the woman took maternity leave. "Her resignation. Three kids now, so she's going to stay home. Can't blame her, but I sure don't want that position empty. I'm thinking about offering it to Bryce Dixon. He sent his resume last week. Wants to be on our river for the long haul."

"What about his research?" Her survey teammate's work was getting noticed. His latest paper had crossed her screen only yesterday.

"Good stuff, right? You see his abstract on osmoregulation? His salmon gills will be right at home in our lab."

"So he'd take Hannah's workspace?" No question Bryce was qualified, but to share an office wall with him? The vacancy next door had suited her.

"You'll be collaborating, so why not?"

She looked at her feet.

"Don't fret, Hildy. Your door closes and locks for a reason. If you need space, you'll have it, but you'll be glad he's here. There'll be lots of hats to wear around here the next few years, and you won't want them all. Bryce has the energy and then some. His competency's on par with yours . . . almost. I'll be relieved to have you both in place before I retire."

"Sounds like you've already decided."

"Subject to your approval." He clasped hands behind him and waited.

What could she say? Her beef with Bryce wasn't a professional one. She simply had no interest in dating him. In Seattle he'd pestered her with the same tenacity Dave appreciated. She'd only allowed him to join her snorkel team after he pledged to behave himself.

"No other contenders?"

"One guy, but he's a distant second, so . . . no."

"Then Bryce it is."

"Good—no, *great*! You go now, Hildy. Treat yourself to something nice. I'll get the ball rolling with our new hire."

Our new hire? How long before that decision haunted her?

By October, her preoccupation with Luke hadn't blurred, as she'd hoped. Instead, he inhabited the front of her mind when she commuted or bought groceries. He swept her skin when she hiked rivers and worked at her desk. Memories of him sharpened her longings until they frightened her.

And strengthened her resolve to stay away.

As wrong as she was for him, how could she do otherwise? If they were together, it would only be a matter of time before she hurt him when her brain went sideways. To wish for him now? To go to him—at his expense? Doing so would be selfish, plain and simple. If she truly cared about the man, she'd avoid him at all costs.

Most days, she opened her phone to tell him that, to cut their connection for good. *Get it over with,* she thought. But then his *tell me to my face* rang in her ears, and she didn't dare.

And a forever goodbye in person would kill her.

No question he'd helped her. Daily she heard him: *Keep learning, Hildy. Mark every verse that reaches you.* The first time he said it, they'd hiked to Humes Ranch and were eating trail mix under that old apple tree by the cabin. *Works for me,* he'd said. *There's Love in that book. It's a road map out of the dark.*

Out of her anxiety, too? Mornings she'd uncover Butterness, change his water and seed, then dress, brush, and braid. She'd eat oatmeal and open that Bible from her dad as a tug-of-war wrenched her thoughts, and her dad's knife lay like a threat on her table. Every now and then, though, a fresh shift in her understanding arrived. A week ago she'd looked at the crescent moon and had seen the whole orb.

⛰

Mid-month, a beep. Static. Outside her cabin, Hildy dropped a bamboo rake in a pile of leaves and pulled the walkie-talkie from her belt. "Hey, Junie." As she always did now, she turned her back as Miranda set her *Toes of Clay* sign at the road.

More crackling. "You got a minute, Hildy girl? Man here wants to rent Cabin 6 long term. Says you're his reference. Over."

"Me?"

"You. Over."

"Did you tell him the resort's closing after the Fourth of July?"

"He knows. Doesn't care. Says he's gonna be working with you. Over."

Uh-oh. "On my way."

Unseen, she slipped through the store's back door to the kitchen and peeked. At the lunch counter, Bryce Dixon leaned toward June on muscular forearms, and they whispered like spies. Below the counter, his knee bounced double time.

At an apparent punch line, June laughed, then spotted her. "Is he telling the truth, Hildy girl? This the guy you hired? Didn't picture him like this from your description."

Bryce's twinkling eyes locked on hers, their mischief familiar. "I'd like to hear that description, Trail Boss."

Oh, to quit blushing at every little thing. "I couldn't tell you what I said, Bryce. Something generic, I imagine."

Generic? Hardly. How had she not noticed him before? He looked like a tawny, green-eyed puma—without the twitching tail.

Sinewy, strong. *Feral.* His appeal surprised her. Clearly, what Luke had reawakened in her refused to sleep.

"But first, let's talk rent," Bryce said. "I'm guessing it's sweet, with this camp on its last legs and all."

"Not sure it's available. A logger's been—"

"According to this lady right here, the logger is in Cabin 5. Cabin 6 is the one I want. Wide open and ready for me when I arrive on New Year's. Care if I bring some things over before Christmas? Prorate my rent, if you need to. I start work Monday the third and don't want to be hassling with setup once the job starts."

"Honestly, Bryce. That cabin's nothing special. Why there?"

He spun a full circle on his stool. "No reason to live in Port Angeles for a slug more rent. Besides, I like the scenery around here better. Figured you could use some help now and then, too." He grinned and raised a dark, luxurious eyebrow. "No charge."

Maybe he wasn't as self-centered as she'd thought. All the dismantling coming up? Extra muscle could be useful. At least he'd be four cabins away. More space than the wall they'd share at work. "Whatever. Work it out with June. I've got leaves to rake."

35

HILDY

BRYCE

HE ARRIVED IN A SNOWSTORM. But when Dr. Bryce Dixon pulled into the store on December 23, 2010, he looked more like a surfer from that Pismo Beach she had visited after a seminar at Cal Poly—golden somehow, his hair streaked, those green eyes the color of his down jacket. Hildy dropped her gaze to his sockless ankles as he snagged a six-pack of Pabst Blue Ribbon from the cooler and carried it her way.

She punched the price into the old register. "You look like you've been to Tahiti."

"Nope. Costa Rica. Back yesterday. Last chance on those waves before the job starts." He studied her face and frowned. "I should have invited you. You look like you could use a little sun."

"I get plenty of sun." An icy blast gusted the door wide, and she rounded the counter to latch it. Snow drifted around the pumps.

Bryce sidled next to her, caught her pale hand and held it next to his tan one, comparing. "Just sayin', Ghostie."

She snapped it away and peered through the door at his jammed Toyota 4x4. A kayak and surfboard leaned in the roof rack like a rooster's comb. "Won't take you long to move in."

"Still a futon and a couple of tables in there, right? Stove, fridge?"

She handed him the key to Cabin 6. "Not much else."

"Cool. I'm good to go. What time you done in here?"

She glanced at the wall clock over the door. *Only four thirty.* Flakes swirled in the gloaming above the foot-deep accumulation. "Won't matter today. Nobody's stopped in hours."

A snowplow passed on the highway. Bryce raised the six-pack and flipped the store's *Open* sign to *Closed* before he pulled a pizza from the freezer. "Join me then. Watch how a pro moves in."

She bunched her fingers to quiet them. June and Otis would be with their daughter in Idaho for another three weeks. With Luke gone and Miranda estranged and no fish work until after New Year's, a new sensation had been plaguing her, despite cheery Butterness and plenty of the solitude she considered medicinal. The odd malaise had hounded her for a week before she ID'd it as *loneliness*.

"Okay."

Bryce feigned a startle. "No way. A yes from the ice woman? More things new than a job around here." He grinned and pinched a puffer coat from a stand by the door. "This yours?"

When she nodded, he snatched the parka, held it open for her. She slid arms into sleeves as a truck slowed, passed the store, and turned to the studio. As Bryce settled the jacket onto her shoulders, she glimpsed Miranda next door in her bright gallery, boxing items, closing shop for the season. Seconds later, she saw Luke stomp snow from his boots at the studio's door.

Oh, to run to him.

At the storefront, Bryce balanced sweating cans on the frozen pizza. His fingers poised at the light switch. "Got everything?"

She pulled out her keys, wouldn't look up. "Yep."

Lights flicked, and the store went dark. While Hildy seated the store's deadbolt, Bryce opened the passenger door, and when she sat, he set the meal on her lap. He revved the engine, and the rig rounded the store, pushed through snow.

Hildy glanced in the passenger side mirror. Luke was standing at Miranda's window, watching them drive by.

Past her cabin, Bryce sped up, busted drifts, and pulled in aslant at Cabin 6. "Wait here," he said.

Hildy bent over a heater vent on the dash as he opened the cabin and carried the food and three large boxes inside. Five minutes after that, he shut down the engine and offered a hand she refused as she left the rig. Snow filled his docksiders.

"Looks good in there. Tha-a-a-nk you, June."

What am I doing? Twitchy, she crossed the floor to the compact woodstove, the blaze he'd started while she sat in the car not yet dispelling her breath's visible fog. She held hands to the fire while Bryce kicked off his shoes and dug in a box for socks.

She waved a hand toward the kitchen range. "Want me to—?"

He leapt toward the second box, extracted a cookie sheet, clicked an oven dial, and smiled at her. "Yeah. Good."

Not Luke, but not bad. He'd help pass the time, anyway. Besides, a girl like her couldn't be choosy.

She slid the pizza into the oven. Bryce popped two tabs and handed her a can.

"No, I—"

"C'mon, Hildy. You're not twelve."

No, she wasn't. She stared at the beer as Bryce flopped on the futon and propped his feet on a drum-shaped ottoman. By a drop leaf table, Hildy perched on a wooden chair, the beverage untouched as she thought of Luke, five cabins away.

Bryce aimed his chin at her beer, then swigged his own. "We're off the clock, Ghostie. Loosen up a little. Try it."

"No, thanks."

He shrugged. "Big storm, long day. Roads were bad. Took me twice as long to get over here from Seattle." He stretched an arm atop the sofa's backrest as firelight capered the length of him. His half-lidded gaze. Those dimples. Agitated, she stood and walked to the bank of windows.

He loaded more wood on the fire and, at the timer's ding, pulled the pizza from the oven, cut it with a pocketknife, and served her on tripled paper towels. While they ate, he drank the rest of his beer and gestured at hers.

"I don't like it," she said.

"You ever tried it?"

"Don't need to."

He raised his brows, chugged hers, and got another from the fridge before he joined her at the window, watching the snow.

"Getting worse out there," she said.

"Or better. Near whiteout." He bent to her ear. "Wish you weren't within walking distance. A night snowed in with you could be kind of fun."

"I'd better get home. Check my bird."

"Just kidding, Ghostie. Criminy. You don't have to go yet."

She was already at the door, zipping her parka to her chin. "Yes, I do."

"I'll walk you back."

She stuffed feet into snow boots. "No need."

"You ski?"

"No."

"Snowboard?"

"No."

"Never? You from the moon?"

Maybe. She shook her head.

"Outdoor girl like you, I'd a thought for sure you . . . You got any sleds?"

"Sleds?"

"Yeah, for tomorrow. What else we got to do?"

"In the shop, maybe."

"You look in the morning."

"I don't know, Bry—"

"I'll text you when I get up."

"Aren't you going home for Christmas?"

"No home to go to besides this one. You're my Christmas."

Hoo boy.

A sheet of powder blew into the room when she opened his door. Without a glance or goodbye, she stepped through it and slogged a calf-deep trail to her cabin. The snow stung her cheeks as if she'd been slapped. She deserved it. What on earth was she doing with Bryce?

Luke had shown her the moon.

Blowing snow heaped her porch, draped her door, and hid the white plastic bag leaning there. Her toe caught it when she stepped inside, and the bag slid into her entry. Still rattled, she ignored it, closed the door and hurried to Butterness, feather-puffed in the dark, chilly room. His head popped from under a wing and he crouched on his perch, startled.

"Just me, Mr. B. Sorry I'm late." Light pooled when she flicked a lamp's chain, and she checked the thermometer, adjusted the wall heater's dial. "We'll turn it up a notch, hm?"

She hung her parka, set her boots on a tray below it, and toweled the quick-puddling snow. Pulled the fitted winter quilt over her bird's cage.

Only then did she remove the dripping bag and carry the box to her bed. A Christmas box, untagged—its paper red plaid, the ribbon a distinctive holly pattern. From Toes of Clay—the wrapping, at least. Customers had carried like-packaged gifts from the studio for weeks.

The wrapping was Miranda's, but the container? Hildy hung the ribbon on a hand drill hooked to the wall, tore a plaid scrap for a bookmark, and frowned at the label before she studied the large photo of a gooseneck barn sconce glued to the cardboard. *A light fixture?* She turned the package, inspecting, and smiled. Royal blue duct tape anchored cardboard flaps. *Luke's tape.* He'd joked about the color.

If only she hadn't gone with Bryce.

Luke would have come inside. We'd have talked. She pictured him stretched out on her couch, laughing, listening, his strong legs crossed at the ankles.

No! She pressed the heels of her hands to her temples and closed her eyes. Time with Luke would falsely encourage him and that wouldn't be . . . loving.

Loving? She felt herself blanch. Was that how she felt toward him, even after all this time? *Patient. Kind. Not just a feeling, love.* Luke had said it at the gate in his upper field. They'd been walking home—to his home—after her second or third Sunday meeting at Kurt's. *Not self-seeking.*

She washed her hands and splashed her face, dried both and tried not to care. Then she pulled a tissue-wrapped bundle and a sealed envelope from the box and opened an unlined paper to Luke's scrawl—bold, scratchy. She ran fingertips under the message and mouthed it in a whisper.

To keep you warm until I can, dancer girl.
Luke
(Alpaca. Jill made it.)

Hildy pictured Kurt's quiet wife, Jill—her shuttle flying, the thumps and clacks from her giant loom a soothing rhythm. *She made this?* With a tug, she freed a jute strand from layers of tissue paper. They opened like petals to a soft wool cloud.

"Oh, my." She touched her mouth and unfolded the lap throw, drapey and scrumptious and the most beautiful gift anyone had given her, ever, ever, ever. The loveliest thing she'd ever owned. She scrunched it to her face and breathed for a scent of its giver.

Like cashmere, she thought—and in that color she'd picked for her beanie and fleece. She'd shown Luke the hue on a sunset hike. *Over there,* she'd said. *That warm aqua riding the gold.*

Weeping, she unpinned her braid, undid her hair. Folded her duvet at an angle to open her sheets, then tossed her clothes on a chair. Goose-bumped, she wrapped herself in the kitten-soft alpaca blanket and scooched under her thick down comforter.

A dreamless night, for once, but she awoke before daylight, scowling at the necessity formed in her mind. She dressed quickly, spread the still-warm throw on top of her unmade bed, and swiped it smooth with her hands. As if tending an altar cloth, she folded the magnificent blanket lengthwise and stroked it until the fight went out of her.

The blanket was a piece of her history now, best displayed where she wouldn't reach for it.

She hunted her walls for a vacancy. Finding none she liked, she took a ladder from the spare room and screwed a new hook into her overhead beam. When she'd draped the throw on a hanger, she hung it there, above her head. At daybreak, she opened her phone and punched in Luke's number.

36

LUKE

SLICK

"WHO'S SHE WITH, MIRANDA?" Luke tipped his head toward the resort's gas pumps as the lights above them went dark. A man held the door of an SUV for Hildy, then set something in her lap. Lit by the white ground and the rig's dome light, he seemed to be talking nonstop.

Luke's sister brushed snow from his shoulders and followed his sightline through the gallery window. "He's new to me. I saw him buy something at the counter a few minutes ago, but he obviously knows her. I probably shouldn't comment on how good-looking he is. Have you talked to her lately?"

"Texted, but she hasn't answered. I told you, Mirs, I can't chase a rabbit. She'll come to me when she's ready."

"And you believe she will."

"I do."

"It's been four months, brother. Patience is a virtue, but stubbornness isn't."

"Depends, Miranda. Take you, for instance. Worst snowstorm in fifty years and we have to close shop and haul goods to the lake house *now*. Not tomorrow or the day after, but *today*, late. I'm sure you've got your reasons, but if not for that plow, I'd be in a ditch between here and Sequim."

"You never go in ditches. Besides, tomorrow's Christmas Eve, Lukie, and you were coming out here anyway. And, in case you've forgotten, I leave the day after Christmas for New York."

He shook snowmelt from his hat. "I rest my case. Who's to say my rationale for hope is any less valid?"

"So you have a rationale?"

"I do, but I'm not telling you. You're minding your own business, remember?" He pulled a box from the bag he carried. "You could do a little penance, though. Wrap this for me? I'll deliver it, and we'll head for Sutherland before this weather gets any worse. I hope you've got food out there. I'm staying over."

Ten minutes later, he trudged to Hildy's dark cabin and left the bag on her porch. With his back to the swirling storm, he returned to the lane, obscured but for the SUV's filling tracks—parallel swerves from spins and skids in the slickness.

He followed them down the row of cabins hunkered in the cornice of snow at the riverbank, each unlit like Hildy's. But at Cabin 6, where the white-blanketed Toyota sat askew, a flickering glow bronzed the windows, and he knew it was warm inside. For less than a breath, he considered a closer look, then pivoted into the wind.

37

HILDY

SETTLE

HILDY GLANCED AT THE SHAWL she'd hung overhead and tapped her text to Luke, hoping her **Thank you** wouldn't wake him on this dark, sleepy morning. The short days and late dawn drugged everyone but her, it seemed.

How long until Bryce woke after all those beers? Those parties she'd avoided in college, all that hangover talk in their wake—her frame of reference was secondhand at best.

She looked at the clock and grew edgy. *Already seven fifty.* Bryce would surely be up—and headed her way any minute. When they'd camped on the upper reach, he'd brought her coffee before she'd wiped sleep from her eyes.

Her gaze swept the crammed space around her, and her pulse quickened. Best to head him off, deflect him from her secrets here. Though Luke's hours in her home had led to repeat visits from both June and Otis, Bryce came nowhere near that trusted circle. She'd burn her cabin before she'd let him inside. No doubt he'd try though, if she didn't act. Keeping the man off her porch called for drastic initiative.

She'd knock on *his* door.

But first, the sled. Long ago their saucers and snowshoes had sold with her dad's tools, but she knew the steam-bent toboggan still hung by its curled nose on the shop's back wall. She'd seen it not two days earlier.

She bundled up, hefted the small sleigh to the shop's doorway, and plopped it in the snow, sending a quiet puff of powder into the blue-white insulation that had fallen through the night. Then she took up the loop on the tie-around rope and trudged to Cabin 6.

Bryce didn't answer at her first knock. At her second, he held the door wide enough for her to see half of him. Five bare toes. Tartan flannel bunched at a foot, its green plaid topped by a gray crewneck sweatshirt. Sleeping clothes.

"Found the sled," she said, surprised that she spoke first.

Bryce scratched his chest. "I see that. Want some coffee?" The door creaked wider to all of him, and he swung an open palm toward the interior. Chin-length, streaky hair tangled on one side, lay flat on the other. He looked . . . accessible. Quite nice, actually.

The room, however, was freezing. "June warned me," he said. "Shoulda picked up a space heater."

Hildy panned the room. Two sport boards—one for surf and the other for snow—leaned near the door. Clothes and boxes mounded in the center of the room. Except for that kayak, he'd emptied his rig. *In that storm*. She eyed the tub of kindling—Otis's welcome in cabins with woodstoves. "May I?" she said.

Stiff fingers roughed his hair into symmetry. "Have at it." She stirred coals and lit split cedar sticks and watched from the corner of her eye as he filled a stainless percolator at the tap, scooped ground coffee into a strainer basket and seated lids. Turned a burner to high as she sat at his table.

"You're lookin' good this morning, Ghostie." He stretched, sauntered to her. At her ear he rubbed her beanie's wool between two fingers. Behind him, a sleeping bag hunched like a worm casting on the futon. "You? Waking me up my first morning here? I'd never have guessed."

"Don't bug me at work," she said.

He chuckled, raised palms to her. "You made that clear before we swam the river, Ghostie. No worries. I know the code: professional to the max when we're working. Off-hours are another story. Wouldn't be my first secret life, if that's what you're offering."

"I'm not offering anything. You said you wanted to sled."

He pulled a breakfast bar from a box and tore it open. "You're here, aren't you? Admit it, Hildster, you can't resist me."

When her face burned, he laughed. "Gotcha."

"There's a hill past Cabin 7 my sister and I liked. Short, but steep enough."

He chewed the bar, pulled snow pants and a wool Henley from a duffel, and looked outside. "Playground out there. Virgin powder. You sure you don't snowboard?"

"I don't."

The pot perked and he stripped his sweatshirt, grabbed the Henley.

Hildy looked away, the coffee forgotten. "The toboggan will pack the hill. I'll get started."

He stopped dressing and studied her, arms half into sleeves. The shirt bunched at his tan belly. "You do that. Give me five minutes. Gotta brush my teeth in case you make me kiss you after a run."

"I'll do nothing of the sort."

Bryce pitched with his laugh. "I'd lay odds you will."

She flicked a hand on her way out, dismissive—and stronger than she imagined. The man was good practice, at least. And a measure of her growth. If he'd said that last winter, she'd have sprinted for home.

Crystalline puffs rolled from her knees as she waded to the hill. Around her, the sunlit snow held fast to trees and roofs in the frigid air, and she shifted her thoughts to the chill.

Unusual for here, this cold. Storms in her childhood had dropped wet, leaden flakes that slushed within hours. But this? Floaty high-country snow her dad had loved. She thought again of their bentwood snowshoes and how she'd hunted duplicates at yard sales and on eBay. Still hoped to find their matches.

She'd made two solo runs of the sloped sixty feet before Bryce trudged to her with an insulated mug.

"Ten degrees," he said. "Your gullet will thank me."

She opened the lid and sipped. Frowned. "What's in this?"

"A little Baileys. Like it?"

"In the *morning*?"

"Made for weather like this. Hildy. How else we gonna stay warm?" He slurped, laughed. "Well, I proposed another way, but you vetoed it."

"I—you—" she sputtered and set the mug in the snow.

"Aw, drink up, girlie." He flipped the narrow toboggan, stood it on end, and rubbed its underside with wax before he dropped it to the snow. "We're going *sledding*." He drained his coffee, took the rope, and preceded her to the top of the run. "Curl up. You brought a kiddie toy here. Not much room for two of us."

Knees to her chest, she gripped the side rope as Bryce dropped behind her and placed feet on the curled bow, his legs sturdy rails on either side of her. Then he tipped the sled over the brink into a straight, quick drop. "Oh, yeah. Short and sweet," he said at the bottom. He jumped to his feet and dragged the little sleigh to the top.

Hildy followed, breathless, not from exertion, but from . . . fun.

Eight runs and Bryce eyed the back side of the hill. "No offense, Ghostie, but that looks like a better course. Steeper, longer. Ever been on a luge?" He glanced at her and smirked. "Don't answer that."

More stomping, more packing, until their new, banked run ended in the trees. He downed her mug of coffee and rewaxed the sled. Hildy climbed on. "Hang tight, chicky, and get low." At the sled's stern, he powered them forward and leapt behind her when the sled caught the chute and dropped. His feet found hers and he pulled her into him, backwards, flatter for speed, the rope taut at their sides.

Hildy laughed out loud.

But on the next run, when he rolled them into the snow at the bottom and aimed his mouth at hers, she turned her cheek, wiggled free, and got to her feet. "I'm going home now," she said, and pressed a mitten to lips that had last felt Luke's.

"See you soon," he said. "Higher fruit's tastier, anyway."

Oh, the man annoyed her. The sledding was fun, though.

On a Saturday in late February, Otis stopped the UTV as Hildy stacked firewood on her porch.

"Hey, Otis."

"Got a few minutes, Hildy girl?"

"Of course. What's up?"

He patted the seat beside him. "Come along then, missy. Got a broader view to show ya."

In the open vehicle, wind shrank her into her parka as he accelerated. She pulled her knit cap to her eyebrows against the chill, and they crossed the bridge toward the dance hall. Otis drove the

UTV to the river's edge and a panorama of the seven cabins on the opposite shore. He raised an arm and opened his hand toward Bryce's Cabin 6. "Been together for a coupla months now, you and that one."

"I wouldn't call us *together*, Otis. I work with him. Hang out now and then."

"Don't take me wrong, Hildy girl, but that ain't what I see."

Hildy bristled. "And precisely *what* do you see?"

"He don't mean well. Tryin' to wear you down, he is. What would make you give up that carpenter for him? You like this'n more?"

"We're not serious, Otis. He's just . . . around. First you and June worry that I don't see anyone and when I do . . ."

"You're smarter 'n that, missy. You know good and well we didn't mean for you to unplug from that beautiful heart and faith a yours. I only hope you ain't helpin' him empty our cooler. He's keepin' us in business."

She'd wondered. Though she was used to it now, Bryce did pack a can or bottle most everywhere. At least they'd struck a balance since he started going to town a few evenings a week, drinking elsewhere. And since he'd toned down those pushy come-ons, she didn't mind him so much. Nights he was home, they played cards and board games, talked about fish. Kissing him felt nice, and he made her laugh. Without commitment, he was no threat to her vow. What more could she ask for, given her . . . limitations?

"We're not . . . involved, Otis, though it's really no business of yours. You're the one who said I should have more fun now and then."

Truth was, Bryce filled hours she no longer wanted to spend alone, when thoughts of Luke arrived unbidden. Now that he fixed her coffee most mornings, Bryce consumed her learning time, too. She hadn't underlined verses for weeks.

Otis looked thoughtful. "So you trust him, then?" His voice fell off.

He had her on that one. No, she didn't trust Bryce. Not enough to believe he'd ever care about her—or anyone—more than himself. Especially since she found that hair tie in his car a month ago and that angora sweater behind the seat a week after that. Even so, when he kissed her, she believed a little more that though she couldn't be right for Luke, she *might* be compatible with a man like Bryce, who laughed off feelings and loyalty, and trusted science as his god. If she had to split herself in two to avoid the isolation she no longer yearned for, so be it.

She shrugged.

Otis looked at the river. "Ya don't get stronger or wiser or freer by compromising, Hildy. By giving yourself to the wrong man. Fake food for your deep hunger. A poor swap for love."

What choice did she have? To be alone forever? The irony struck her. That's what she'd pledged to herself—until she met Luke. Whom she wouldn't allow herself to think about, and pushed from her thoughts when she did.

"What about happier?" she asked.

"Nothin' happy about it. You got a voice, Hildy girl. The right man'll hear what you stand for and love it as part of ya. Worth waitin' for."

She clenched mittened hands. *What voice?*

Otis waited, his eyes on the far shore. When she didn't say more, he turned the UTV to the highway toward the home she no longer worried Bryce would breach. As long as she went to his place, he didn't bother to come to hers.

38

HILDY

LUNCH

WHILE THE LECTURE HALL EMPTIED, a mixed group of Peninsula College biology students remained behind and peppered Bryce with questions. Hildy closed her laptop and slid it into her bag, then touched his arm as she left the podium. "Keys?" she whispered. He gave her a fob from his pocket, and she slipped past them into Port Angeles's April drizzle.

She texted Bryce from his Toyota thirty minutes later. When another quarter hour passed and he still didn't show, she retraced her route to the hall and spotted him with a foot on a bench under a sheltered walkway, nodding at an animated coed with long copper hair. Smiling his sparkling, irresistible best, he tapped something into his phone, but Hildy's didn't buzz. And he didn't see her. Instead, he watched the girl walk away, her hips swinging. Hildy observed them both, then slipped behind a stand of trees and beat Bryce to the car.

He was whistling. "Hey, Ghostie. Got us some new recruits for the revegetation team. Good feedback on our presentation, too. You shoulda stuck around."

"You had it covered." *Ghostie.* That name was wearing on her. She dropped the visor and checked her braid in the mirror. Tucked erupting hairpins and assessed her pale skin.

He squeezed her knee. "Next up: waterfront. A late lunch at the Crabhouse."

Did he care if she liked the place? He didn't ask, and four minutes later, they walked inside.

Water, sky, her affect—gray, gray, gray. Heavier now, rain pelted the window beside their table as the steely drab of strait and clouds absorbed her. Matched her, more likely. She swung her gaze to Bryce, his exhilaration the only bright thing for miles. He rocked his chair back onto two legs, and his eyes darted the room.

"This gig today? Last thing on my slate before I take off, Hildster."

"You're leaving? Where?" In the four months since that Christmas snowstorm, when had he mentioned going anyplace?

"Don't you listen, woman? Tomorrow morning. You've known since I arrived I'd be outta here all May. Part of my contract negotiation with Dave. I committed to a consulting job on the Klamath before he hired me."

What? Oh, her unreliable brain. "I didn't—"

"Ever think of slotting my plans into your tidy little schedule, Trail Boss?"

She shrank—meek and off-balance. "You're right, Bryce. Thoughtless of me." Her shoulders bowed like saplings. "Fill me in?"

Her softness seemed to temper him, and his charisma revived. "Perfect timing, isn't it? River data's submitted, plans are set. We're ready on every front. No way I'll twiddle my thumbs until they shut off those turbines. Don't worry, Ghostie. I'll be back in time for them to throw those breakers at the dam on June one."

Don't call me that. "Good to hear." Every word of this was new to her. Risky, but she had to ask. "So where besides Oregon?" Klamath wouldn't take a full month at their phase of restoration. Blinking, she gave him the smile he liked, the one she'd stumbled on by accident. She ventured a guess. "Seattle?"

"Yeah. Like I told you. Stopping there first to see my parents for a few days. They're on holiday."

His parents? *No home to go to,* he'd told her.

Her stomach pinched. "How long since you've seen them?"

"Aren't you nosy today? Not since Dad transferred overseas."

"Transferred."

"Where's your brain, girl?" His mouth stretched and rounded—slow, exaggerated, each S a hiss. "US Department of State? Denmark?"

"But last Christmas . . ."

"Better to surf in Costa Rica than hang out in some Danish flatlands. Besides, my sister's a pain."

He had a sibling? Had he told her that, too?

"Ah. Your sister. What bothers you most about her?"

"What doesn't? You remember she's a tenured prof at that seminary, right?"

No, Hildy didn't remember. When had he—?

"Teaches theology. In Dallas. Been hassling me to read her work. Said she reads mine, so I owe her."

"You don't? Ever? Read her stuff, I mean."

"You kidding?" He gulped water, set his glass in its sweaty puddle. "Pauline Epistles are her specialty. I read some of it a few years back, but that Paul dude's dry, I tell ya. Out of touch." He arched a brow and a grin. "All Greek to me, anyway."

Hildy stared out the window. A chill ran her spine, and she heard Otis. *You have a voice, Hildy girl.*

"A joke, Hildy. Greek, get it? Geez. Have a little fun, will ya?"

She forced a swallow. "I like him, Bryce."

"Who?"

"Paul."

"That prehistoric dude? The two-thousand-years-ago *preacher*?"

"I've learned a lot from him."

His chair's front legs hit the floor. He leaned toward her on forearms. "You believe that stuff?"

"Yes, I do."

"Ahhhh. I get it now."

"Get what?"

"Your mixed messages, Ghostie. Why you won't—Going religious on me wasn't part of the deal."

"What deal?" How could she tell him all the ways those holy words exposed and undid her, the ways they described real love? *When I bother to read them.*

"I've been wasting my time, haven't I?"

She wished she were strong enough to confirm that.

"Your coming over all the time? I've been patient, haven't I? Almost embarrasses me, how patient I've been." He ran fingers into his hair and held them there when he leaned toward her, working his jaw. "But you've been playing me, Hildy Nybo. You have no intention of putting out, do you?"

His voice carried. Heads turned. "It's for marriage, Bryce," she whispered, but her words felt hollow. She knew as well as Otis did where Bryce wanted to take her. The destination had nothing to do with commitment.

"Marriage, Hildy? *Marriage?* Why? We've got a good thing going, right?" He took her hands, rubbed them with thumbs. "I thought you liked me."

"I do, Bryce."

"Yeah?"

When she nodded, her chin stayed low.

"That's my girl." Eyes twinkling, he relaxed into his chair, past this ugly discussion, she hoped.

But when the server arrived with their food, Bryce stabbed an oyster and held it poised between them. "How about you show me, then? Before I leave for an entire month, give me something to come back for. Criminy, woman. Let me give *you* something to tide you over while I'm gone. Tonight. No, today. Soon as we get back. I'll keep you going 'til we leave for work in the morning."

She scanned the room furtively. They were attracting attention. She twisted her napkin, her food untouched as her tears erupted. "Bryce, stop." She dabbed wet cheeks before the middle-aged hostess led two men their way. One wore jeans and that shirt she loved on him. No way to hide.

When Luke saw her, he slowed and brightened—until he searched her face, and his countenance dulled. He ran eyes over Bryce, intent on his food, then found hers. "Hello, Hildy," he said. He touched his cap and continued to his table somewhere behind her.

39

LUKE

STRAIT

THE HOSTESS VEERED toward a view window, but Luke pointed to a table mid-room. "Mind if we sit there?" He'd have a direct sightline to Hildy—the back of her head and shoulders anyway—and a clear view of her companion, as engrossed in his meal as if sitting alone. Luke studied him, confirming. Yes, the guy he'd seen through Miranda's windows in that snowstorm. Who took Hildy to his cabin.

And now she was crying.

The hostess flapped a hand at the dreary waterfront. "No problem. Kinda dull out there today, anyway."

Luke eyed the monotone sea and sky and the blinking Coast Guard beacon at the tip of the three-mile spit, surprised at the ease in his glance at the bay. *Long time coming.* Eating at this harbor-view restaurant would have been unthinkable two years earlier, difficult even a year ago. Eating here, a short mile from the marina where he'd docked the *Safe Seas*, where he'd last seen his family alive.

His breath snagged at a flash of them curled on the bunk.

In another lifetime. He stood at his chair, squeezed the top slat. Now his future possibly sat there, a few tables away, with a man paying no mind to her distress, no attention at all.

"Hey. Luke." The man with him gestured at Luke's seat, took his own, and checked his watch. "Catch the view later. We've got work to do. I want to be at my office in an hour."

Luke cleared his throat, swung eyes to the blueprint spread between them, and sat. "Sorry, Matt. Hijacked for a minute there." They read menus before Luke ran a finger over an architect's elevations and traced exterior windows. "On your high bluff site? Amazing."

The server jotted Matt's order and turned to Luke. "What're ya hungry for?"

If only you knew. "Number three's fine. No mayo."

Past them, the man with Hildy flipped his streaked, sandy hair off a high brow. Sharp cheeks, thin nose, his eyes a sultry squint. Miranda would notice this guy. Well, she already had, months earlier. In that snowstorm.

The man stood when Hildy did, draped her blazer over her shoulders, and laid a guiding hand to the small of her back. He was *with* her. Obviously.

Until Hildy looked sidelong as they walked toward the door, and her eyes locked on Luke's. Mouth pursed, her shoulders rose and fell, and her attention clung to him. At her sideways shift, the man tracked her gaze, bypassing Luke as he hunted the room.

God help her, Luke thought.

He finished a sandwich and the plans review with his client and returned to his truck, resting his forehead on the steering wheel for a moment before he texted her. Another message she likely wouldn't answer, but for months, every one he'd sent her showed *Read.*

You were crying. Need a shoulder, I'm here.

Skies cleared as he neared home, but he couldn't shake Hildy's lingering gaze—or the foreboding he felt. For the next hour he walked his land, pleading, and felt himself at war. He resisted the impulse to drive to the river and find her and instead located Jangles, lying sphinxlike in the south pasture, her jaw grinding rich spring cud. Massive horns tilted when he sat. And when he leaned on her withers and wept, she didn't get up.

40

HILDY

CAPTURE

OUTSIDE THE RESTAURANT. Bryce threw an arm around Hildy and brushed his lips to her neck. Her gooseflesh rose with heat different from what she'd known with Luke, but heat nonetheless. In reply, she laced her arm around his waist and wished she'd never met either of them. Wished she'd never reawakened to the complicated power of touch.

He opened her door, wiped rain from her brow, and kissed her, on her lips this time. Nuzzled her braid. "Mmm. You smell good. Let's get home, hang out. We can fill Dave in on our presentation tomorrow." He pulled the belt over her lap and buckled her in. "I'll fix you an early dinner, beauty."

Not Ghostie. *A new angle, hm, Bryce?* She smiled at him, pressed her nose to his cheek. The man didn't quit, but she'd hold her own with him, like always.

Minutes later, he emerged from Safeway to hoist a wine tote and grocery bag to her window and settle them behind her seat. "Bet you'll like this Riesling."

She laughed. "You don't give up, do you?" Unlikely she'd drink this one, either. But his buoyant good nature, his whistling, their comfortable silence the rest of the way to the Elwha—the familiarity soothed her, stifled her dis-ease.

He sheltered her from the rain with his coat and hurried her into his cabin, then retrieved the bag and two bottles, draped her blazer on a hook, and closed blinds against the drumming downpour. "No point in looking out at that, is there?" When she hugged her upper arms in the room's chill, he hurried to light a fire. She warmed herself at the woodstove screen while he opened the two bottles, poured from each, and handed her a glass of golden liquid. He raised his glass of red. "Don't know why I never thought of it."

"Thought of what?" Hildy peered at her wine. Swirled it.

"A white. Like soda. You'll like this one."

"Is that right?" So many of the times she'd hung out with him, he'd suggested she relax and share his ever-present drinks. But though heaven knew she needed *relaxing*, they tasted awful. She'd shuddered and quit at every first sip.

"To us," he said, and clinked her glass.

Us? She touched the drink to her lips and licked them. Sampled it again and bent an eyebrow. Eyes wide, she swallowed a mouthful, and on its heels, another.

"Whoa, whoa, whoa." Bryce grinned, took the glass from her, and held it out of reach. "Small sips, gorgeous. Take your time, or you'll be sorry. So will I, when you're snoring on my bed—or . . ." He waved his hand toward the bathroom. "Holed up in there."

"Okay." She swirled the wine. *Nectar.* And he was right. Just two swallows calmed her.

He set her glass on the counter, filled a small plate with crackers and hummus. "Better get some food in you before you drink any more. You ignored that lunch." Bent to the open fridge, he extracted greens, a tomato. Sprouts.

Looking out for me. More progress. "Want some help?"

"Nope. The gift begins now. Put your feet up and watch the chef work. Tonight's dedicated to the most stunning woman on the planet." He set the plate on the end table beside her, spread a fleecy throw over the scratchy upholstery, then brought her glass. "Eat first, then sip."

More whistling while he made salad and vinaigrette and sliced a thick-crusted loaf. She giggled at his flourish of the bread knife, a salmon pun like Miranda's, and his deference. Studied him while he connected a speaker, filled the room with Vivaldi and Ravel, and refilled her glass. He set the steaks to broil, laid out place mats and napkins, utensils, and a pair of elegant dinner plates. She examined the underside of one. "Limoges?" She'd eaten from plates with this pattern at a Seattle colleague's private dinner welcoming her to the UW. "Where'd you—?"

"Mother's. A couple of extras from her set. I crack them out for . . . nights like this."

"Wonderful," she said. All of it was. The music, the fire, the tender preparations. The wine and, to her surprise, this man. When he shoved a candle in an empty bottle and lit it, she blinked slowly, watching him. Her mind, body . . . and even her heart were warming.

He held her chair, spread her napkin across her lap, and bowed, a towel on one arm. When he again filled her glass, she tugged him toward her, but he wagged a finger, then abandoned his fleeting primness, kissed her crown, and sat across from her. Doting. Irresistible.

They ate at a leisurely pace, and while the light of candle and fireplace flickered a connection she felt in her belly, he filled the quiet with his questions and kindnesses and observations. Did he hear her replies? The reciprocity with Luke had been electric and melting. Respectful and trusted and beautiful. Was this similar? Momentarily, her vow forgotten, she wanted it to be.

Plates empty, he cleared them, then took her hands and pressed lips to her fingertips. Then he emptied the bottle of red wine into his glass, plopped beside her, and they thumb wrestled, laughed. When he dropped to the floor and pulled off her shoes, she swallowed the rest of her Riesling, sank into the cushion, and closed her eyes, as sleepy as she'd ever been.

When she opened them, night had fallen, and only the fire lit the room. She lay on her back on the fleecy blanket, her head on a sofa pillow. Bryce sat in a chair watching her. He'd turned off the music.

"Well, thass a first." He swigged his beer and wiped his chin with the heel of his hand.

"What?"

"Never had a chick fall asleep on me like that before. Waste of perfeckly good steaks."

Hildy stretched. "The meal was great, Bryce. The entire night was."

He snorted and swilled again. "The *night* never got rolling." He got to his feet and steadied himself before he plucked her refilled wineglass from the counter and crossed to the futon. Swaying over her, he set it on the end table and dragged a finger down her cheek. "Now, where were we?"

Hildy rose on one elbow, eyed the bathroom door. "I'll be right ba—"

Mid-sentence, Bryce pushed her hard against the futon's backrest, and dread bit her like a trapped animal.

41

LUKE

ALERT

FOUR HOURS AND NO REPLY from Hildy, though Luke had watched his text send and its status change to *Read*. Her parting glance at the restaurant haunted him. What was she trying to say? The foreboding that settled on him when he watched her leave had grown oppressive as the afternoon stretched on.

Through failing twilight, Luke tracked Kurt's hurried course across the field and checked his phone. *Huh*. The tractor had drowned Kurt's call.

His friend leapt to Luke's porch, breathing hard. "Just heard from the group. Three of them were weighed down as they prayed for Hildy. Her name's been on the list since you two split, but tonight they were *burdened* for her, man."

Luke slapped a post and blew from puffed cheeks. "I knew it! Four months with only one glimpse of her, but today we end up twenty feet apart at the Crabhouse. Think that's a coincidence? She was with that guy I saw last winter."

"At the resort."

"Yeah, him. She was crying, Kurt. What time did they get those warnings?"

"They met at seven. Liam called a few minutes ago."

Luke glanced at his watch. Was he too late?

Kurt frowned. "What are you sensing?"

"That I should go to her. But when haven't I wanted to do that? I told her—"

"I know what you told her. Anything different this time?"

Luke dug in a pocket for keys. "That she's afraid."

"Go, friend. Now."

42

HILDY

CUT

BEFORE HILDY COULD GATHER HER WITS. Bryce stooped, gripped the futon's frame below her hip, and pulled. Something clicked, the backrest fell flat, and she found herself lying on a full-size mattress—the convertible bed Bryce slept on in the one-room cabin. Jolted, she sat upright and eyed the door, but just as quickly he shoved her to the bed and straddled her, hands on her shoulders, holding her down, his mouth alive on her lips and cheeks and traveling her neck as one hand clamped her wrist flat beside her. His forearm pinned her opposite shoulder as he worked the placket of her shirt.

"Bryce! No!" She wrenched her mouth from his demanding one and clawed his back where she could.

"Not thish time, chicky. All your games—I've waited long enough." Muttering, panting, his torso immobilized her as his free hand abandoned her resistant buttons and his weight compressed her lungs. He grabbed her neckline in an iron fist.

In the next second, he reared up and jerked her shirt in a quick, downward snap. Sensations and sounds: the sharp pressure at her neck, the rending cloth, the crush of his weight again. His whiskers at her bare shoulder as he tore her shirt away.

Somehow, she freed an arm, flailed, and swept the lamp and wineglass to the floor.

A split second of chaos and breakage. Bryce bucked and cursed, and Hildy writhed to the bed's edge, twisted, and flopped backwards, her head and one shoulder onto the floor, her other shoulder, the bare one, onto the jagged bowl of the broken glass.

She shrieked with pain. Bryce pushed himself upright and swore again. Dizzied, she rolled to her knees, clamped a hand to her injured deltoid, then winced and snapped it away. "Glass in me," she gasped, and scrambled to her feet. Scowling, Bryce swiped at her arm, but she slipped from his reach, lurched wide over wreckage and again touched the cut.

Fingers dark with blood, she hurried to the bathroom and locked herself inside, where she pulled her ruined shirt over the wound. But when fabric caught on an embedded shard, she whimpered, retracted the cloth, and inspected the gaping slice in the mirror. Found splinters and plucked.

Bryce's voice at the door. "Let me see, Hildy."

She shrank, stared at the lock button.

He rattled the handle. "I'm sorry."

Her heart thundered as she twisted toward the mirror. Below her frayed braid and pale face, a three-inch arc bloomed raw. Blood dripped to the counter and sink.

The hollow door thumped. Hildy jerked as if shot. She froze when Bryce shouted her name, then tiptoed to the small window, hoisted herself to the frame, and squeezed through.

Barefoot, she tiptoed beneath the dripping eaves of his cabin as a light flicked on inside and its glow seeped past edges of the closed blinds. Muffled now, Bryce called her again, and she heard pounding. She crouched, clenched the ragged cloth across her chest, and minced on tender feet over gravel.

At Cabin 5, then 4, wet grass gave her softer footing. She crept faster, bent into driving rain that soaked her and plastered loose strands of hair to her brow and cheeks and the back of her neck.

A truck rounded the store when she reached her stoop. Blinded by headlights, she cowered. *Hurry,* she told herself, and fumbled under the stair for her hidden key. Quivering fingers aimed for the lock, missed.

"Hildy!" A man's voice. An image of Bryce loomed in her mind and she cried out, shrank to her knees.

She flinched when hands pressed her upper arms, pulled her to her feet, and helped her inside. Eyes squeezed tight, she bumped a jacket slick with rain before she felt the warmth of him, smelled the scents of cedar and sweat and kindness she loved.

Luke. Still bunching her shirt, she fell into him.

43

LUKE

VOICE

"MY BIRD," SHE SAID. as Luke helped her to a chair at her table. Butterness flitted, clung sideways to his cage. Hildy spoke through chattering teeth. "His quilt."

Luke covered the cage and assessed Hildy's unsteadiness, her shocky tremors. The bird wasn't the only one needing a blanket. Scanning the room, he pulled the alpaca throw from its hanger. "Give me your shirt," he said. She didn't move. "C'mon, Hildy. I won't look. It's wet. You'll warm up faster without it."

He raised the throw like a curtain until green linen hit the floor, then wrapped all of her upper body but the wound. Below it, the weave caught fresh blood in a swag of red. He dialed the wall heater to high, moved a floor lamp to her shoulder, and slid the strap of her sports bra farther from the cut. He drew a chair close behind her, sat, and inspected. Her shivering wasn't merely from the cold.

"Wine glass," she said. "Hurts."

"No doubt. It's a deep one, Hildy. I can get the bigger splinters out, but they'll flush it at the ER. You're going to need stitches." He rummaged kitchen drawers for clean towels. Scrubbed his hands and dried them, then wrung a fresh cloth and dabbed blood from the perimeter of her torn flesh. "Tweezers?"

"Medicine cabinet. Zipper bag."

He found the implement fast. "A wine glass didn't shred that shirt."

"No," she said.

"He hurt you anywhere else?"

"I got away. I didn't think he . . . He never acted like that before."

"Who's *he*?"

"B-Bryce Dixon. I work with him."

A light tap at the door. A man's voice. "I don't bite, Ghostie. You didn't need to run off." *Slurry.* "I'm coming in. From the looks of my bathroom, you're bleeding like a stuck pig."

Luke switched on the porch light, and when the latch clicked open, he filled the doorway and frowned at the man he'd seen at the restaurant. "No thanks to you."

The man stepped backwards. "Who—? Where's Hildy?"

"None of your business, unless she decides otherwise."

Bryce wiggled a finger at dark drops at his feet, then tried to peer inside. "She's bleeding. Lemme in. I can help."

Luke stepped in his path. "I don't think so. I suggest you turn around right there."

"Like you said, that's for her to decide, isn't it?" Bryce staggered, whapped a zippered case the size of a shaving kit against the jamb. "Hildy? I brought my med bag."

"Go away, Bryce. Leave me alone."

Luke cringed at the phrases that had burned in him for months.

Words so wrong when aimed at him, but at this lowlife? *Thatta girl.* She sounded stronger than she looked.

"You heard the lady." Luke closed the door inches from Bryce's face, threw the deadbolt, and pressed a hand to the frame, breathing to calm his anger. Praying. If Bryce took this further, Luke would do whatever the situation required, but Hildy needed help, not more conflict.

Outside, planks thumped as the man muttered profanities and paced. Silence followed his thunks down the stairs, but Luke didn't bother to look. *I'll deal with him if he shows his face again,* he thought, and turned his attention to Hildy.

Two triangular shards. A thin, inch-long splinter. Luke tweezed more glass to a paper towel, patted the congealing blood, and ran a tissue over the wound, testing for snags from additional fragments. Though her shaking had subsided, she hadn't said a word as he worked and only squeaked at the third extraction. Instead, she watched the wall, listless.

"How'd you know to come find me?" she asked.

"Got a nudge. Like we talked about." He touched her porcelain cheek with a knuckle, absorbing her.

She turned to him wide-eyed, nodded, and drew an enormous breath. Focusing. *Finally.*

When he laid a fresh cloth over her shoulder, she didn't flinch.

"Good," he said, and eyed her bare skin and the afghan that wrapped her like a shawl. "Time for a little embroidery, sweetheart. Got something to wear to the emergency room?"

Arm tight to her side, she rose and claimed a hoodie from her closet. Moments later, she emerged from the bathroom zipped to her chin and holding the bloodied afghan. Her voice was birdlike. "Rinse this first?"

He took it from her. Knew he'd wash the sky for her if she asked.

Luke shifted to Park, glanced at Hildy, and peered through the windshield at three stories of gleaming hospital windows. "They'll ask for details in there. You want to file a report?" If it were up to him, he'd have the guy arrested and booked, her torn shirt tagged as evidence.

"No-o-o!" Almost a wail.

"You think he'd have quit if you hadn't escaped?"

"I don't know."

Luke scrubbed his cheeks. Pressed his hands' heels to his eyes. "Dudes like him . . ."

"He's not usually like that. He drank more than usual. And I went over there a lot."

"You're making excuses for him, Hildy. And taking blame."

She fixated on the window.

"A man who cared about you would have guarded you, not used your vulnerability for personal gratification."

Hands clenched in her lap, Hildy wagged her toes in the truck's footwell. Watching her squirm, Luke blinked at a sudden insight: a picture of her as a child, yearning to please. Trained to accept mistreatment, then to pack another's wrongs as if they were her own. No wonder she settled for Bryce.

At least her dad had loved her. In every story she told, Lars treasured her. Luke had watched Hildy's body language and eyes for mixed messages about him, but had seen only clarity and bright sparks of being cherished. If not for Lars, Luke doubted he could have connected with her at all.

Who then? Who had sideswiped all that? He had an inkling.

"He assaulted you, sweetheart."

"I don't want to report him, Luke. I got away. I learned. Besides, he won't bother me again. I expect he'll replace me pretty fast."

"And try again with some other woman who isn't as strong as you are."

"I'm not strong."

"All those years you kept to yourself? You could've caved a long time ago. Even this time, you showed up on your porch with only . . ." He swiveled in his seat to face her. "Now don't take this wrong. I'm not minimizing the seriousness—but when I found you, you were fully clothed, with only a torn shirt and cut shoulder. He could've hurt you a lot worse. Grace on God's part, Hildy. Courage on yours. You escaped him."

"I was drinking wine."

"His idea or yours?"

"First time he found something I liked. He'd been trying for a while."

"What's that tell you? If not for the Spirit staying my hand, I'd kill him. C'mon, Wonder Woman, let's get you sewn up."

44

HILDY

HAIR

ELEVEN STITCHES LATER. Hildy dozed in Luke's truck until they passed the curve to the Elwha bridge. When Luke's headlamps flooded the resort's lane, the exterior light flicked on at Cabin 6. Bryce stood in his doorway until they parked, then pivoted and disappeared inside.

"He's waiting for you." Luke threw the deadbolt behind them. "Think he's got the stones to see how you're doing?"

"He's drunk, Luke."

He shook his head. "Another excuse. Why?"

"I don't know. I don't think he cares all that much about me."

Luke swiped as if at wasps. "Then why do you—" From a window he again scanned the dark. "Never mind. Drunk or not, he's more likely to leave you alone if I'm here."

"I won't let him in."

"How many times did he light up your phone the last few hours? That lock won't stop him."

Her eyes filled. "You'd better get home. I'm guessing you've got a full day tomorrow. He's leaving in the morning, anyway. For a month."

"He can't leave soon enough. With your permission, I'll be here to watch him go." He plumped a small pillow at the armrest of her love seat, then retrieved the aqua throw draped on a chair, its edge still damp from his rinsing. His stockinged feet hung in air when he lay on the too-short sofa and spread her favorite blanket over himself. He grinned at her and winked. "When he takes off, I'll wave at him from right here. Now if you're going to wake up for breakfast with me, you'd better get some shut-eye. You good with that?"

Sleep? With Luke on the couch all night? The warm room, her relief at his presence, the ache in her shoulder as the lidocaine wore off—all quelled the protest that reared in her. She had no fight left. "Yeah. I am. Thanks."

"Mind if I read awhile?" He chose from a stack of books on the floor. "Will the light bother you?"

"I don't think so." Still dressed, braided, and too tired to care, she crawled into bed, rousing only when Luke, later, tucked her duvet around her, touched her cheek, and clicked off the light.

At dawn, rattling hardware startled her awake. Her eyes swept the quiet room and the empty love seat, and she heard her shower shut off. Beneath his cover, Butterness cheeped. As quickly as it began, the noise at the door stopped, flooring thunked, and a vehicle revved. She crept from her bed in time to see Bryce's Toyota turn onto the highway.

She paced until Luke emerged from the bathroom, fully clothed and rubbing his head with a towel. She hurried to him, clutched his shirt. "He was here," she said, as he held her. "Tried the latch."

She pointed toward the highway, and realized how worried she'd been the night before. "Drove off."

"Huh." He swung the door open. The blazer she'd worn to Peninsula College threaded the door handle, and tan leather flats sat at the threshold. Luke checked around the porch and inside the shoes for more. "You'd think he'd at least leave you a note. I don't need specifics, but did he text you anything decent since he sobered up?"

Messages from Bryce the night before—insistent, demanding—littered her phone.

"No, nothing today at all."

"Not my business, Hildy, but I suggest you tell your boss."

Tell Dave? Her employer thought of her as a daughter. He'd be livid, and Bryce would be toast. "I couldn't."

"Working with the guy's going to be untenable. At least say you'll think about it? If not for your sake, for the next woman's."

She looked at her hands and nodded. "I will. Consider it, I mean."

Luke handed her a steaming mug and sat across from her. "Enough about him. How's that patch job this morning?"

Hildy rolled her injured shoulder and winced. "A little sore."

"I'd be surprised if it weren't. You going to let me change that bandage?"

"Already?"

"Later today."

"Don't you have to work?"

"It's Saturday, Hildy. And a holiday."

She frowned and dug for the calendar in a pile of papers. "Uh, I don't think so. I'm a resort kid, remember? I know holidays."

"Call it an anniversary then."

She tipped her head and squinted at him. "Whose?"

His smile sent a surge through her. "Ours. We met a year ago, plus a few days, but who's counting? Worth celebrating, don't you think?"

And just like that, here he was again. "Why, Luke? After all I've..."

He reached across the table, laid hands on hers. "Because we can, Hildy. Let's just see what happens, one day at a time. Think you can do that?"

Her cheeks burned. "I don't know. What if I can't?"

"I'm a big boy. I'll risk it."

Twenty-four hours earlier, she'd sat here alone, reviewing notes for the presentation she and Bryce would give at the college. Fingers quiet, her brain ran the prior day's—and night's— details. No need to write.

Butterness pecked at millet, scattering seeds onto papers and the cleared surface between her and this astounding man. She opened the door to the bird's cage, and when he flitted through the opening and clung to a dangling skate, the accumulated tension, her fear, and a swell of relief commingled, and she burst into tears.

The bird flew to the child's high chair and perched on its metal backrest. Luke rose and rounded the table. Kneeling, he stroked her wet cheeks. "Copy him, Hildy."

"Who?"

"That bird, leaving his cage."

She shrugged and fingered her sleep-frayed hair. "I don't know what you mean. I'm too much of a mess to go anywhere."

Luke tapped a loose hairpin. "May I?"

"What?"

He ran fingers along her braid. Pulled a pin. "Brush it?"

My hair? She shook her head.

Luke dropped the pin to the wood. "Okay. I won't."

But the sensation of his touch remained. His fingers on her

braid, his release of one of those bent little wires she jabbed into her hair every single day of her life.

For what? To protect her hair—*herself*—somehow? How was *that* working? If last night was a test . . .

"No one besides me has handled my hair in years."

"Maybe it's time?"

Maybe it was. "My brush is in the bathroom."

An urge to run. She gripped the chair seat, held herself in place. Rigid, she clamped her eyes closed until he brought the brush and slowly pulled each pin. As a small pile of golden wires accumulated, he unwound the yellow coil and removed the clear band that held its tail.

"My girls liked braids," he said, and she was sure he was with his daughters, not her. But then his fingertips loosed the plait, and she knew otherwise. He shook the strands and spread the waves at her nape. A shiver ran her neck.

"Wow, Hildy." He smoothed her hair's length and batted it side to side. "Magnificent. Your hair. You."

She felt naked—and bathed by his words. The two perceptions arrived *together* and, to her astonishment, *linked*. The exposure of her freed hair. The safety with him who had freed it. Shameless and euphoric, she could have swooned.

"Here. Turn," he said, and she shifted, the chair's back slats to her side as Luke bunched, lifted, and began slow, gentle, rhythmic brushing she leaned into like her long-ago pup had leaned when she rubbed his ears.

So different from her mother's rough, hurried tending. A scene she'd not thought of in decades charged in: Violet's sharp jerks of the brush through Hildy's snarls, her muttered threats to chop off the whole mess and throw it in the lake. Seven-year-old Hildy's cries at the pain. Her learning fingers fumbling to braid and pin the plait to her skull. She'd never worn her hair down again.

"Did you brush theirs like this? Your Lucy and Quinn?"

"Often. Did your dad brush yours?"

"No." *Why didn't he?* So many blanks in her remembering. "Mom did. But not like this."

"When did you last see your mother?"

"Not since I was with you. Too long ago, I know."

He studied her. "You don't say much about your mom."

"Nothing to say." She pulled her head away. Fingers taut, she divided her hair into three strands and yanked three passes of a tight new braid.

"Whoa there. I won't push you." He rested hands on hers. "May I?"

She paused in his calm. Breathed.

"Thatta way." He caught the strands in one hand and massaged her good shoulder with the other before he twined a long, loose braid down her back, reattached the band, and scooped the pins away when she reached for them. Then he flipped the braid so it swung at her waist. "You up for a little breakfast in Sequim?"

She pulled the braid over her shoulder. Butterness cheeped from a rusty wagon beside her bed. Clear to Sequim with her hair down? She may as well be in pajamas. "Like this?"

"Absolutely. Catch that bird and we'll go."

She'd try it. Once.

45

HILDY

OFFLINE

"STORE'S BEEN A GHOST TOWN TODAY." June set a warmed cinnamon roll and fork in front of Hildy, then rounded the counter with a stack of mail. "Couple a fisherman earlier, but that's it. Nobody here on a warm, beautiful May morning? Odd." She riffled through envelopes and flyers, sorting.

Hildy lifted the plate to her nose and inhaled. "Mmmm. Who cares? A slow day lets you make *these*. You sure won't be baking come Memorial Day. Last dance hall convention before those turbines shut down? This place will be insane."

"Got that right. And soon as the lake drops, I 'spect lookyloos'll come out of the woodwork for a piece of history. End of an era." June poised an invisible walkie-talkie at her lips and crackled static in the back of her throat. "Hundred years of Elwha electricity, over and out." She tossed junk mail in the trash, then wagged an envelope. "Good thing he's not bringin' me his rent in person. I'd throttle him. How's your shoulder doin'?"

There was only one renter Hildy knew of who would mail a check. Only one male renter, period. "Better. Got my stitches out."

"Glad to hear it." With a knife from a countertop caddy, June sliced the seam of Bryce's envelope and tapped his handwritten note. "Can't say I'm sorry."

"For what?"

June flapped his check and letter like wings. "He's paid in full—for the very last time. Dr. Bryce Dixon has given notice." She dropped the letter beside Hildy's plate and touched a scrawled line. "Says he'll be outta here month's end, soon's he gets back from Oregon. I told ya, girl. You shoulda given him the boot. Now he got the last word."

Luke had wanted her to evict Bryce, too—and offered to haul Cabin 6's contents to the highway with a *Free* sign.

"I don't care about that."

June's eyebrows arched. "You oughtta. More ways to set boundaries than hidin' out, Hildy girl. Stand up to that man."

"I did."

June's look was dubious. "You tell that boss of yours about him yet? How you expect to work with that creep?"

"He's not—"

Her mouth grim, June raised a stop-sign hand. "I don't care how handsome, smart, funny, or whatever it is you saw in him, the man's a creep. The farther he gets from this place and from you, the better. I'm tempted to call Dave myself, but with you bein' thirty-five now . . . Won't stop this from happenin' again if I care more than you do. C'mon, girl. Step up. He was usin' you."

"Well, likewise."

"That's usually how it works, Hildy. You wouldn't be the first at the potluck swapping yourself for junk food. The girl comes out sadder and hungrier, every time. Nothin' but fake love in that trade."

"We didn't . . . I didn't."

"Only a matter of time, the way he was anglin'. You want to continue workin' with the man?"

"Not really, but he's the best—I don't want to mix my private and professional lives."

June snorted. "Too late for that. Dave needs to know. If not for that glass insultin' your shoulder, sure as I have a nose on my face, that man would've—"

"I guess."

"I mean it, girl. Tell Dave. Tomorrow."

Hildy expelled a long sigh. "I'm not promising."

But she'd try. *Yes.* To placate Luke. To protect others. And maybe for herself. Maybe telling Dave could perch her at the door of her cage, prep her for liftoff.

Monday, when she finished the telling, Hildy dared to look across the desk at Dave. Lips clamped, he leaned back in his chair, his face slack with sadness, his eyes sparking with the emotions she'd recognized in both Luke and June when they heard. Anger. Indignation. *Care.* Clear as the river, she recognized each one, because, freed in her voicing, each welled in her, too.

At last.

"Wait till he gets here." Dave gritted his teeth. "I'm sorrier than you can possibly know, Hildy. Thankful it wasn't worse and sorry. You report him?"

She turned her gaze to her knees. "What would I report, Dave? Think about it. A public accusation? No thanks. The guy's not a criminal."

"Depends who you're talking to." He stroked his chin and typed on his keyboard. "There it is. His email this morning." He turned the computer to her. "Beat me to the punch. Must have sniffed us about to talk and skedaddled."

Hildy leaned toward the screen, squinting as she scanned the lines. "He got his old job back?"

"Apparently. Read on. Says NOAA made him an offer he couldn't refuse. He'll show up here on their river teams, but effective June first, Bryce is off our payroll."

He quit? She'd spilled her guts to Dave, and now Bryce was leaving of his own accord? The whole sorry event could have stayed secret. A wave of regret rolled over her. "I wish I hadn't said anything."

"Rats smell traps, Hildy. Your bringing this info to me? Bet he sensed it soon as you decided. Things work that way sometimes." He shrugged. "If you'd kept this under wraps, you'd be working here alongside him, with me none the wiser. Heartburn material. Or worse."

As she listened, her doubts—and that awful regret—shrank. A new strength couched itself in Dave's observations. Clarity too—about Bryce's role, and hers. She could see the demarcation between them better now, and she refused culpability for Bryce's actions outright. She pictured Butterness flying.

And she couldn't wait to tell Luke.

"Well. I guess that's that." She stood and turned toward the door.

"Not so fast, Hildy. You won't press charges, but I'm going to document what you've told me and include it in his exit interview when he clears out his office. I'll respect your wishes and not go public at this point, but I'm flagging his file. I expect my written statement and a little face-to-face discussion will incentivize him to toe the line, ambitious as he is."

He peered over half-rim glasses. "Sure you won't let me throw the book at him?"

"I'll deny it if you do, Dave. And I won't sign that report of yours." Telling Dave was one thing. Going public, quite another. Formal charges would keep Bryce and her snarled for who knew how long, and then everyone would know. Her privacy was at stake.

He clicked his tongue as if urging his horse. "Have it your way."

Memorial Day weekend dawned overcast. By Friday afternoon, the gloom deepened as dancers' rigs rolled into the campground. Across the river, boondockers crowded the woods behind the dance hall as more RVs stacked into the overflow lot past Hildy's cabin. She waved a backing trailer into a narrow slot, then raised her buzzing handset. "June."

"Don't want ya broadsided, Hildy girl. You oughtta know there's a red Toyota in that lineup, headed for Cabin 6. Over."

"Got it, June." Hildy stepped between a camper bus and a tent trailer as Bryce's rig passed within ten feet of her. Beside him in the passenger seat, that redhead from the college. Rapt in the auditorium's front row, the girl had trailed Bryce outside the day of their presentation. A *recruit*, he'd called her.

For more than fish, Hildy thought. She peeked past the trailer as the Toyota stopped at Bryce's cabin and the pair went inside. Twenty minutes later, she nearly collided with the girl exiting the store with a six-pack in each hand.

"Sorry, I . . . Oh! Hey! It's you! Bryce and I—" She hoisted the beer between them. "Want to join us?"

Too bright. Hildy cringed at her tinny voice. "Other plans, thanks." Without looking back, she found June behind the crowded counter, checking in guests. "Heard from Tess yet?"

June glanced at the clock. "Said she'd be here by six, so any minute. You leavin' for Miranda's?"

Hildy pushed her walkie-talkie across the counter. "Soon. She's closing the studio at six and wants to eat by seven, so I'm chopping salad. Luke'll meet us there."

"Glad to see you patchin' things up with her." June handed a receipt to a skinny middle-aged woman and circled a site on the resort map between them. "Luke's ankle any better?"

"He's limping, wearing a brace, but he's getting around." He'd called Hildy from a job on Hurricane Ridge Road when he wrenched it, and she'd driven him to the Port Angeles clinic for X-rays. "He'll be fine."

"No dancin', though."

"No dancing." Not for Luke, anyway, and she wouldn't go without him.

"Tessie and us can handle things here, girl. You go with that man a yours. Have fun."

That man a yours. Was he?

One day at a time, Luke had suggested, and though she dared not look beyond the next twenty-four hours with him, as their weeks together accumulated, her emotional footing stabilized. This morning she'd dusted the shelves vacated by her packed-away diaries, her torrent of need to record and gather mementos slowed to a trickle. Even better, now she rarely gave shadows the time of day, counting each hour too precious to waste.

Usually.

At nine o'clock the next morning, music and the caller's drone wafted cross-river when Hildy left an early shift at the store for a late breakfast at home. Mid-lane, she spotted Bryce, who slammed the hatch of his loaded vehicle before the redhead closed the door of Cabin 6 and locked it. Bryce grabbed the girl from behind, pressed her to the wall, and kissed her hungrily. He took the key dangling from her fingers as she pulled him closer.

Embarrassed, Hildy looked away. She neared her door when Bryce broke his embrace and spotted her. Trotting her direction, he tossed the key near her stoop. "All yours, Ghostie. We're outta here."

She turned her back, ignored the key, and slipped inside her cabin. Bryce could have been a stray dog, for all she cared. And she'd have felt like one, had she stayed her course with him. Stirring oatmeal at the stove, she glanced through the kitchen window when a horn blared outside. Bryce's hand stretched high, waving from the red SUV before it turned onto the highway toward Port Angeles.

After breakfast, she toed Cabin 6's key in the gravel, pinched it from the ground as if it were a dead squirrel's tail, and carried it to the store.

The morning of June first, Luke and Hildy stood on the Elwha Dam as a small group in hard hats filed into the powerhouse. "Park employees, dignitaries," she said. Some held cameras. "And those reporters. This'll make national news by tonight."

Luke leaned on the rail over the spillways. "Don't you want to go inside? See him flip those switches?"

"No, thanks." Fingers wide, she stretched arms toward the foothills. "I'd rather hear those turbines go quiet. Get an earful of the valley the second the voltage leaves those wires."

Luke limped to mid-span. "Yeah. Only been ninety-seven years."

They both went silent. Their ears pricked—and were rewarded when the powerhouse whine dimmed. "One down," Hildy said. "Two to go." She pinched Luke's shirtsleeve and again panned the forested hillsides and the lake. "I've prepped mentally for this day for years, and I still find this hard to believe."

"Oh, it's happening." His head tipped. "There goes another one."

Twice, Hildy hopped in place, then walked to Luke and stared at her watch. At 9:19 a.m., the pitch of the remaining live turbine dropped, then the hum quit altogether. She dropped her forehead onto Luke's shoulder and listened. The collective shout she expected from the station never reached her ears, though her inward cheer lasted for hours.

46

LUKE

SHORELINE

"A LONGHORN. HUH? Ever think of breeding her? A calf could be fun for you. Not as entertaining as landing fish off Neah Bay, but you've got the land, Luke, if you've got the time." The Sequim dairyman had run a hand over his barn's new siding, inspecting Luke's handiwork. "I can match a sire for you, store the semen in my nitrogen tank. You see her in heat, ring me. Breeding her in June or July's best, if you want a spring calf."

"A calf?" Hildy had patted Jangles's withers when Luke told her. And when her eyes lit, he'd sent a check for that semen. Now, mid-June, Jangles was bellowing along fence lines when Luke haltered the animal, snubbed her to a post in a corner of the field, and held her tail. While the farmer threaded a long pipette through her cervix, the cow wagged her monstrous horns and swayed foot to foot. Twenty minutes later, Luke was on the road to Hildy's.

She met him at her door in jeans and a tank top, boots in hand. "You'll call me when she's in labor? Day or night, I'll be there."

Nine months until that cow would deliver, and Hildy was planning that far out? With him? He hadn't dared hope past tomorrow. Happiness rushed him, and he kissed her nose.

"Absolutely."

Hildy's attention darted. "Only two weeks since those turbines quit, Luke, and the reservoir's already dropped eighteen feet. Our dock's high and dry. You good hiking that new shoreline today instead of the hill? I've been trying to get out there all week."

Anywhere they went together agreed with him. "It's dropped that much, huh? Those shallows must be dry then."

"Yeah. Now the river cuts sediment way past Mom's old cabin. The actual lakeshore's quite a ways out." She thrust her thumb downriver and tied a hoodie at her waist. The tip of that braid hung at her slender waist, with no pins in sight. "Scavengers are showing up. One guy found a hundred-year-old wagon wheel. Sold it online to a ranger."

"Uh-oh. He get fined?"

"Yeah, hundreds of dollars. Won't stop people, though. Illegal or not, treasure hunters will raid that lake bed. Can you imagine how many tribal artifacts they'll find out there?"

"And how many more they won't find after teams replant that forest?"

She chewed her thumb, then curled fingers around it. Grinned wryly. "I'm bringing excavation tools. We'll call it soil testing."

"You get busted, I won't admit to knowing you."

She grabbed his hand, pulled him to the waiting UTV, and added a shovel to buckets and a metal probe. "Oh, yes you will."

"We'll see about that."

She laughed and boarded the rig. "Nah, you're safe. I'm authorized. Next stop, the vanishing Lake Aldwell, with my partner in crime."

Partner. Oh, he could be, if she'd let him. And she might. His optimism grew every day her receptivity to him lasted. But would it stick? He knew the change in her was too remarkable, too fast for all the emotional ground she had to cover yet. But he was beginning to believe it would.

Hildy hummed as she donned work gloves and pulled on a cap. In the distance, a grouse drummed for its mate before she drove them past the cabins, the stranded dock, then read the sediment and rounded the mudholes on firmer, gravelly ground. At the retreating lake she rolled them to a stop and leapt from the rig. Hands on hips, her sights roved the glistening water and the rim of conifers before they landed on the evacuated shore.

Luke tracked her gaze to the exposed lake bed. *Artifacts? Right. More like a bathtub ring.* All he saw were waterlogged stumps and the thick trunks of windfalls, each layered with a gritty brown-gray film he felt an absurd inclination to scrub.

But when Hildy reached for a five-gallon bucket, he grabbed shovel and probe and followed her onto the drowned wasteland she and those teams would spend years resuscitating. At least he could walk with her, jab the probe here and there.

"Easy with that thing, Luke. We want to find stuff, not wreck it."

Pointless, he thought. Until Hildy hurried across the forty-degree slope and grasped an oxidized metal pipe projecting a foot above the water. A pipe with a handle.

"I thought it was a branch at first." She planted her heels in the heavy earth, crouched, and pulled. The item budged, barely.

"Here, let me." Luke waded the river to his boot tops, probed underwater, and dug.

Hildy bent toward him, hands on her knees as he excavated. "What is it?"

When the object came free, he sluiced it with lake water, rubbed, and sluiced again. Beneath mud and algae, a child's wagon emerged, patched with rust and flaking red paint. Wheels, their hubs sclera white, seemed to stare from bolt pupils as if surprised.

"Not exactly an antique," Luke said.

"But way out here?" Hildy seemed delighted. "No buildings within a mile. No roads smooth enough to pull it on. You think it floated?"

Luke carried the toy to shore. "I doubt this thing was buoyant."

"There's a mystery here, Luke. I'm taking it home."

"You're going to get canned." He laughed. "I'd better hire you. Keep you out of the breadline."

"Nobody'll care if I take it. Those wheels? You're right. It's not that old."

Luke rinsed and drained the wagon a third time, then hiked the handle over a shoulder. "I'm not packing it all the way to the dam. You see enough for today?"

A wheel spun when she tested it. "Yeah. We can head back." Her eyes narrowed and skimmed the lake. "Can you imagine what's hiding out there?"

A corner of Luke's mouth hitched as he reversed direction. "Might compete with your yard sales."

It already is, he thought. He'd tagged along on a couple of stops at garages and yards filled with loaded tables. She had the same jittery focus out here.

Upbeat, Hildy dogged his heels on their quicker return, and she didn't say much. But the occasional weight of her hand on the wagon gave him pause. Why her interest in this rusty old thing? He sensed more than a mystery. But did she?

The wagon dried while he carried it, then dropped silt and rusty debris when he set it beside the painted wagon in Hildy's cabin. From a chair by the woodstove he watched her kneel, frown, and run hands along the corroded bed.

"Same size," she said. "And the same make, from the looks of it."

He leaned onto knees. "You keeping them both?"

A grin cleared her storm. "Of course." She scrutinized her walls and located a narrow strip the width of the wagon's handle. "There's room. We can hang it right there."

Luke nodded. Plucked a hook from her table and screwed it into the space. She hung the wagon, her face tight with concentration.

"You're working a puzzle," he said. "Am I right?"

"A puzzle," she mumbled. "I don't know."

"Stay on it, Hildy. See how the pieces fit."

"You think they will?"

He took her hand from a wheel, pivoted her to him, and kissed her. "Yep. And when they do . . . ?"

They'd need an archeologist's tools, for one. And somebody wise about this stuff. His arms wrapped her and lifted her to tiptoes, his nose at her neck. She fell into him, nuzzled his cheek until he turned, and replied with lips on his.

That missing piece. Should he broach the possibility with her? If only he had proof.

47

LUKE

CEREMONY

ELWHA DAM. SEPTEMBER 17. 2011

At the bluff above the Elwha Dam, Hildy pulled Luke aside for a shuttle cart that wound through the gathering crowd. A park ranger unfolded a wheelchair, and a wizened Klallam woman disembarked from the cart and sat. The woman's grandmotherly companion leaned on a cane and called to friends seated in folding chairs. The shirtsleeve September day was warmed even more by the crowd's high spirits and, Luke noted, a glaze of collective disbelief.

"Elders." Hildy gestured toward the women, then the two front rows. "They've waited a lifetime for this."

She skirted the crowd and ducked to seats in the rear, her lips tight, her sunglasses hiding the discomfort Luke knew she felt among so many people, though she'd talked of this ceremony for weeks. Of how the festivities would commission the excavator and dynamite and launch the beginning of freedom for the river she loved.

Freedom for the Tribe, too. "The Strong People," Hildy called them. Luke hadn't thought about them much before he met her.

His thumb ran tendons on Hildy's hand as he scanned the dignitaries and politicians behind the podium and the security personnel flanking them. An eclectic crowd of locals, park employees, Natives, and what he guessed were reporters, scientists, and environmentalists chose rows and found seats in front of them.

He zeroed in on the Native men, their hair shiny black, peppered gray, or ponytailed and white with years. Hildy said many were fishermen like he had been and, also like him, many knew personal sorrows. Unlike him, however, they—and the women and children seated around them—packed a *century* of collective, unbearable griefs.

But they had borne them—and survived. Hildy said they buoyed each other with better stories of what was and what could be again, traveling their sadness to arrive at this day, flush with hope for the river and the fish and their lives.

For the first time since he sold his fleet, he missed his boat.

Klallam dancers advanced uphill. Family groups, he realized, in red-and-black garb and woven cedar hats and long button robes adorned with art and feathers and mother-of-pearl. All bearing stories Luke suddenly wanted to hear with new ears and with the dancers' reverence. They treaded uneven ground toward the crowd, their feet bare on the late-summer earth, their song rhythmic and low to the drumming sticks on deerskin stretched over bentwood hoops.

Luke settled as he listened and translated their songs by feel. Songs of canoes and river, fish and earth and trees, he guessed. All pulsing beats of the valley and its original dwellers. The chanted melodies entered him like roots pushing through soil—tendrils of beauty and longsuffering, welcome and return, faith and release, until he could hardly bear their collisions.

On his knee, Hildy's fingers entwined his. He bent over their hands and closed his eyes.

Another song. A new pattern of drumbeats. She squeezed his fingers, and he sat up, drank a breath. When a stooped, smiling elder in a beaded neckpiece made his way to the microphone, Luke looked at Hildy sidelong. From under her sunglasses, tears streaked to her jaw.

"Ben Charles Senior," she whispered. "He'll level you. You'll see."

Within minutes, Luke understood what she meant. He tuned in to the man's hands working the air, then to his reflections about grandparents, aunts, and uncles. About relatives—heartbroken and praying when "progress" stole their river. About tears and shortened lives and the great cloud of witnesses from generations past.

In every row, listeners nodded, wiped cheeks and eyes.

Prayers with no apparent answers, Luke heard. *Hopes flying away.* Immersed, he felt as much as heard Ben's voice, its linguistic rhythm the soft Coast Salish staccato.

"But Creator was watching. Creator saw and said, 'I'm taking care of it . . .' A hundred years—that's a long time to us. But to Creator . . . a blink of an eye."

The elder swallowed, considered the crowd, and spoke through tears. "Prayers are answered, even though so many times we weep, we pray, we weep some more, we pray some more. We think, what's the use? What's the use? But Creator says, 'Aw, come on. You're just about there. You're just about there.'"

Come on. You're just about there. Were he and Hildy, too? A flicker's call pierced the air like punctuation.

And then Ben prayed for those who had blocked their river, destroyed their fishery.

Luke sat transfixed.

"I ask, Lord, that you be with them, keep them in your hand. Help them to know we pray for them, we love them, and we thank you that they keep us aware of things that could happen."

Luke reeled. *Love? Gratitude?* After a century of misery, Ben was *thanking* the perpetrators for what his people had learned through their suffering? *Mind-boggling.* One thing was obvious, though: despite all the events that could have caged and crushed this elder and his Tribe, the man speaking in front of them was *free*.

He stroked Hildy's knuckle. *I want that for you, sweetheart. For both of us.*

When chairs emptied, he trailed her to the chain-link barricade. Seconds later, a cry erupted from the crowd. Below the bluff, an excavator bucket took its first bite of the dam.

48

LUKE

DISCOVERIES

AT DAWN. November rain pummeled the Elwha Valley. Luke cinched his hood tighter in the gray, widening lake bed. Alone among the waterlogged stumps, he and Hildy plodded, intent on the gravel underfoot. At the base of an exposed silt terrace, she plucked something and held it aloft.

The wind whisked her shout downlake as he hurried toward her. Finally, another discovery. Every one of the seven Saturdays since demolition began, they'd hunted this wasteland and come up empty. He'd begun to question his theory.

Hildy beamed, elated. "An old one, Luke."

He bent close to the stone she held and touched the wider of its two tapered ends. "Whoa." Indentations riddled its flat face. "Looks like a primitive grinder. A pestle."

"Nope." She turned the object in her hands and tapped a riddle of indentations on the flat face of the tool's wider end. "Strike marks. It's a hammer. Archeologists found one like this at the Klallam village they've been excavating by the mill. Called it a spool maul."

Her head snapped toward the shoreline. *Hunting landmarks,* he guessed.

"Here." She handed him the stone and pulled the lanyard from her neckline. On the attached GPS, she saved the artifact's location coordinates and stowed the tool in her pack. "Gotta report this one. There may be more under all this sand. Every storm now, high water will turn another page of sediment. This lake bed's like a huge old book."

Luke prodded the discovery site with his shovel blade, but Hildy grabbed the handle. "The tribe will send somebody." She walked backwards and tugged, then turned and skirted a cedar stump the size of a toolshed. Outlined by fabric, the maul shifted at the small of her back. "C'mon. So much new ground opened up this week. And the river took a blade to it. There's more in those cuts. I can feel it."

She was calf-deep in shallows when her eyes locked on a spindly pair of metal rods that jutted from an avulsed bank. "What's *this?*" she cried. Luke splashed to her and plunged the blade into sediment beside the nearest piece of metal. As if waterskiing, Hildy gripped the rods and leaned back. When Luke leveraged the shovel, a mound of gray-brown grit and a small chair fell into the river.

Hildy laughed.

Luke didn't. He watched her closely as the water muddied around a metal high chair no taller than his thigh. *A doll's chair,* he thought, not forty yards from where they'd found the wagon. He laid the toy on its back in the storm-driven flow and when he splashed and rinsed and exposed the flaking white paint and its blue, hand-painted design, Hildy gasped.

"It's yours, isn't it?"

She pressed silty fingers to her mouth and nodded. "That tole painting. Blue."

Confusion shadowed her face. And something else, dark behind her frown. He returned his attention to the chair.

Identical. Apart from its trim color, it matched the one in Hildy's cabin, clear down to its heart-shaped footrest. A confirmation of his suspicions? Probably, but the accusation would be serious. He forced himself to bite his tongue. Without proof, it could drive a wedge between them.

"I wish I could remember, Luke."

"You told me about that chair, Hildy. That camp you built outside. I'd bet my right arm you remember it just fine."

"Then how . . . ? Mom said—"

"You can't expect to remember something you didn't see. Something that happened when you were, uh, in a bubble bath with a squirt gun?"

They locked eyes. "I don't know what you mean."

He shrugged. "I didn't see what happened either, Hildy. You want to keep looking or go home?"

Still scowling, she stood the chair upright in the sand, inspecting it from every angle before she flicked a paint flake from the rusted metal behind it. Then she hooked the chair over an arm and turned on her heel toward a silty bend in the river. "Let's look for another half hour, okay? Then, Mr. Fisherman, we'll have French toast. I bought sourdough."

The first time she had called him that, he'd cringed. When had he stopped minding? Today, he'd let her call him anything for that toast of hers, its nutmeg and vanilla and true maple syrup. Her hair would smell of its deliciousness for hours. He checked the time. "Deal."

Twenty minutes later, she'd turned for home when he stooped toward foot-deep water where a stripe of pink poked from the sand. The band resembled faded surveyor's tape, only wider and stiffer. He easily pulled it free.

Fifty yards upriver and intent on the lake bed, Hildy hadn't seen him stop. He almost called to her, but rubbed algae from the pink vinyl instead.

And his skin crawled.

He darted a glance at Hildy, relieved at her steady progress upriver. Too far away to see the object he held.

A collar. A good-sized dog's, he guessed, as he considered its buckled circumference. He scraped slime from a brass plate, then spat and rubbed it on his jeans until he could read the etched letters.

Cocoa. And a phone number. No owner name.

In the distance, Hildy turned and raised a hand to her eyes, blocking rain. His lungs labored as he waved her to him.

Here was the proof he'd been hunting, though he'd never have suspected anything like *this*. Messing with Hildy's head was bad enough, but *this*? An urge to guard her seized him, and he raised the collar at the impulse to hurl it into the drink.

"Whatcha got?" she shouted, as if spotting a gift.

Maybe it would be a gift, in a twisted sort of way. He lowered his hand. "That brown lab you had when you were little. What was his name?"

As if through a tunnel, he saw her head tilt and her face, bright with curiosity, wet with rain. The slow-motion drop of her eyes to his hands. His heart thumped double-time as she lowered the high chair.

"Cocoa. Why?"

He shifted, swallowed air, his mouth dry. Answered by handing her the collar.

Her face was unreadable as she studied the neck-sized loop, the disturbed sediment swirling at his feet. She returned her gaze to the collar and read the plate's inscription, though he could tell she already knew.

"My puppy." He could hardly hear her over the wind. Her hands trembled.

"Who would—?" Beneath the straps of her pack, her shoulders jumped with a quick series of open-mouth breaths. "Who would—?" Water swirled past her thighs as she sank to her knees in the river, the collar clutched to her chest. "Luke, who would . . . ?"

He pulled her upright, and the collar slipped onto her forearm. "You tell me, Hildy. Not a lot of options, far as I can see."

"Couldn't be. No." Through their heavy clothes, he felt her grow rigid, her movements jerky. "She gave him away and didn't tell us?" She petted the collar, stared at it. "Tell me she gave him away. Found him a good home."

Luke turned her to him. Held her as her forehead thumped his chest.

Her eyes pleaded. "She wouldn't. Not this."

"Who, Hildy? Say her name."

"My *mother*."

He felt the confession split her. A breach, he thought, of her own unseen dam, then doubted, second-guessing, though he prayed it was so.

She pivoted, flailed, and the collar flew. "The lie! This is the lie, isn't it?"

He snagged the strap, rammed it in a jacket pocket, and caught her with one arm. Hooked the high chair with the other and plucked the shovel. She was crying, and wind snatched her words before they reached him.

"C'mon, sweetheart. Let's get you home. You're wet."

And she was cold. He aimed her toward the shower and listened for running water, then made a simpler French toast. Bread, with beaten eggs, browned in butter on the skillet. Nothing like hers, but he cooked and stowed the food in the oven until she joined him, her cheeks pink with heat and the silence now lodged between them.

He lowered plates and sat across from her, where he could see her eyes. Butterness sipped fresh water, then cocked his head, the cheer in his chirps from another galaxy.

Hildy's attention swung to the collar he'd set near the canary's cage. She fingered the buckle. "Cocoa slept on my bed with me, Luke. Got protective when he reached adolescence. He'd bark at night, jump on the window ledge, wake me up when Mom got home from checking the camp or from rowing all those odd hours. I kept my door closed, so he wouldn't run downstairs, but his bark got loud and deep. He'd wake Tess sometimes, too. And Dad. I heard my parents argue about him more than once."

Her fork clicked the plate as she toyed with her food.

"One morning he was just . . . gone. Mom said he was whining at my door early, so she let him out to pee. Said he ran off."

"Right. And your mother's rowing hid the evidence."

At least Hildy saw that now, though the truth immobilized her. Where was her fire over all this?

Had Violet sunk that, too?

49

LUKE

CONFRONTATION

ANGRY ENOUGH FOR THEM BOTH. Luke scowled toward the collar, benign in the table's clutter.

Hildy hugged her upper arms. *Chilled again,* he thought, though from more than the cool room. He felt it too. He stoked the woodstove as Hildy's glare sparked and her mouth clamped to an iron line. Her chair toppled as she lunged for her phone on the counter, punched a number, and shouted.

"Tess. Get over here. Fast as you can drive."

A protest from the phone. Luke couldn't make out the words.

"I don't care what you're doing. Come. Now. It's about Mom."

She ended the call, flung the device to her bed.

Mad as a cut snake. And man, was Luke glad to see it. In his experience, human anger did more harm than good, but for Hildy, right now? Well-placed dynamite. Before sunset, this new fury of hers could open the river to her soul.

Bring it on, girl.

He reseated the chair and carted Hildy's uneaten French toast and his empty plate to the sink. Arms crossed, he leaned against the counter while she paced and fumed, her tears a flood as she pieced the puzzle he'd begun assembling with every story that hung from her walls. Pieces he'd held close as cards. If he'd told her outright when he first suspected, she'd never have believed him.

How could she, something this bizarre?

⛰

"Don't get your hopes up. Last week, she called me Mrs. Beecher," Tess said two hours later. As Luke set the parking brake at Hillview, she unbuckled in the back seat and angled toward Hildy riding shotgun.

"Who's Mrs. Beecher?" Hildy asked.

"My third-grade teacher. She retired before you got there."

Luke turned in his seat. "At least your mom's talking. You girls want me to be there?"

Tess punched his shoulder. "Dang right, Luke Rimmer. We need a voice of reason in that room. If you don't come, I may eat that woman alive." She tugged Hildy's ponytail. "And who knows what this one will do? I don't care, either. You let her have it, Hildy. All of it. Three and a half decades' worth."

A voice of reason? Hah. His own rage steamed under an ill-fitting lid. If he went inside with hurricanes Tess and Hildy, unleashed, he couldn't promise anything.

He forced himself to lower his voice. "How about you test the water with the wagon, the high chair? If you slam her with that collar, she may shut down altogether, and where will that get you?"

As if they'd get anywhere at all with Violet. Even if the woman were aware enough for them to confront her, if they thought they could dump their anger on her and walk out of there feeling better? Well, a rude awakening awaited them both. No quick fixes for betrayal like this.

And no quick understanding of the deep-seated pathology behind it. What mother in her right mind would do this? What *human being* in her right mind would?

From behind his seat, Luke retrieved a paper bag and walked toward the tailgate, where Tess lowered the high chair and reached for the wagon Hildy pulled from the bed. Tess glowered as she seized the wagon's handle. "The collar. You got it, Luke?"

He swatted the bag. Hildy straddled the truck's bed above a wheel well, leapt, and threaded her arm between slats in the high chair.

Their heads close, mouths furious with plans, the sisters marched toward Hillview's entry as Luke, tight jawed, shoved gum into his mouth. They'd stick it to Violet, all right. Who wouldn't? But if either's anger curdled? He'd smelled that stink before. Hildy could get as trapped in this new rage as she'd been in her isolation and fear.

He lagged, praying they'd find Violet unresponsive—or at least incoherent. They'd be frustrated, sure, but at least vengeance wouldn't be feasible. They wouldn't be able to off-load ownership of their healing onto whatever Violet might say or do, either. Those were rabbit trails he knew all too well.

Without those options, Hildy could get on with business. Deal with reality head-on. Mend.

But would she? While he couldn't speak for Tess, he knew how unresolved anger could enmesh Hildy even more deeply in Violet's relational patterns and lies.

And what about them—him and Hildy? If she stayed stuck, he'd have to face reality: the two of them didn't stand a chance. Even with the door of her cage wide open, Hildy would fly back to it every time she felt afraid.

Tess and Hildy charged down the hallway ahead of him, their rusty toys in tow. He lost sight of them when they stormed into Violet's room, but their voices carried, and he listened from the hallway as the accusations amped. Part of him tasted blood, and cheered them on. *We're like wolves,* he thought.

Too much like wolves. This attack could devour them all.

He entered the room to Violet cowering in her chair, her eyes clamped tight. Hildy stood to the side, her arms a straitjacket around her, her mouth thin and hard. Tess towered over their mother, bumping the wagon handle against Violet's knees. "Open your eyes, Mother. Look at it."

Violet shrank from the contact and pulled her knees to her chest. A reedy cry escaped her throat. "No Daddy, no Daddy, no Daddy, no . . ."

As if struck, Tess reeled. Wide-eyed, she swiveled to Hildy, mouthed *Daddy?*

Luke had suspected as much. Years earlier, he'd have stood beside these women, demanding an account from their mother. Seconds ago, he almost did. But now? Compassion washed him. Generational sin took captives, and Violet was no exception. No matter what she had done, piling condemnation on her wouldn't help anyone.

"Enough, girls. We're aiding and abetting."

Violet flinched when he laid hands on her shoulders, then visibly relaxed as he massaged them. Tess and Hildy moved to the wall, scowling.

"Pfft. Traitor." Tess, still loud.

"Who? Aiding and abetting *who*?" Hildy's frown had turned to confusion.

"Those lie-makers, sweetheart."

Hildy stared at him, then looked at her hands.

"Fine." Tess stomped from the room, dragging the wagon.

Luke tucked an afghan around Hildy's mother, and her blank eyes tracked him. He bent and whispered, inches from her ear, "We're leaving, Violet. You're safe now." He pressed a hand to Hildy's back and guided her outside. "Hold on," he said, and retrieved the unopened bag on the bed.

50

HILDY

FIND

BY JANUARY, Lake Aldwell had shrunk beyond the bend, closer to the crumbling Elwha Dam. The lake holed up in deeper troughs, its waters opaque from sediment released as the Glines Canyon Dam fell, too. Miranda hiked the shore, her mittened hands swinging on her first outing with Hildy and Luke since she'd scared Hildy off. She dropped a stone in a murky pool. "How can anything live in that dirty water?"

"Some won't," Hildy said. "The silt from Lake Mills is too fine. Stays suspended longer. Hard for fish to breathe."

"So what's the point, if it kills them all?"

"Mirsy, she said some will die, not all of them. Besides, the demolition crews are pulsing the teardowns. They stop every so often to let the water clear and the fish move. You should see the excavator at Mills. It's perched on a floating barge at the dam's lip, eating concrete between it and the drop-off. Way I see it, the whole contraption could go over the brink any minute. An OSHA nightmare, I tell ya."

Hildy snickered. "The barge is anchored, Luke."

"Would you sit on that thing, work levers on that machine, not knowing if the next bite would put you over those falls?" He planted a foot in a logger's old springboard notch and hauled himself onto a silt-coated stump, his red beanie bright in the otherworldly grayscape.

Rushed again by her attraction to him, Hildy felt her face grow warm. A near-daily occurrence now, along with his welcome lips. And since they'd found the chair and the collar? She couldn't explain it, but now that she knew the truth about Violet, she'd begun to welcome memories she'd previously questioned or denied, and her "crazy" badge was fading.

"Tha-that storm last week." Her stutter caught her off guard, though the intensity of her feelings for him didn't. "The riverbed shifted a good fifty feet."

"Have a look from here." He crouched, extended a hand. She found toeholds, and he pulled her to the cedar platform eight feet above the lake bed. His arms reached from behind her, and he settled his jaw on her shoulder. "Your river's finding its course again," he said. Sure enough, a new meander carved a serpentine through the silt, bent on a fresh route toward the strait.

"I think I am too, Luke."

"Yeah, I'd agree." He rocked her. "Won't happen overnight, but my offer stands."

"What offer?"

"To help you with that. See what's in store for us when the water clears."

"In store for us?"

"Yeah, together. You game?"

She squeezed his arms at her waist.

Farther downriver, Miranda toed a terrace of sediment before she stooped, tugged at a flap, and shouted, "Cozy up later, you two. I've got something here."

They hadn't found a thing since the dog collar. Halfway down the stump, Luke jumped to the gritty earth. Hildy was seconds behind him. When they reached her, Miranda had loosened a triangular corner, blackened by mildew and time. Where she scraped deeper, the fabric continued into the bank.

"Nice try, Mirs." Luke flapped the grommeted corner. "Somebody's litter, is all."

"You don't know that." Not for months—since she'd first witnessed their sibling banter—had Hildy seen Miranda this imperious. "If it were a scrap, I could at least budge it, don't you think? It's got something in it."

"Yeah, like eons of mud," Luke said.

Hildy ran a stick along the embedded tarp until it caught. "Some kind of ridge. I think she's right, Luke. There's a line wrapping the tarp. Where's the shovel?"

Luke trotted for the tool, planted the blade and dug. Ten minutes in, the three of them pulled a waterlogged bundle free from the sediment. The diameter of a smallish culvert and the length of a love seat, their discovery resembled a grubby caterpillar—pooched and segmented by a thin cable wrapping it, and with several strips of that same cable strung like legs between grommets on the tarp and heavy bulbous feet.

Fishing weight feet, Hildy thought. Finned downrigger balls the size of her big river rocks, but heavy as lead. *Coated lead. Twelve pounds each,* Bingo had told her. He used them fishing saltwater on his charter boat.

"Good God," Luke said. On his knees, he lifted an attached weight by its cable, then let it fall. Where his hold rubbed away grime, stripes showed, multicolored.

Hildy crouched, rubbed a longer section of the wire, then curled her hands and shrank, as if the patterned cable were alive. The hair on her neck and arms stood. "That's our clothesline. There's a roll in the shop and a stretch of it in my cabin."

All three of them stared at the bundle before Hildy flopped onto the tarp in an awkward embrace. Just as quickly, she jumped to her feet and backed away.

From his knees, Luke lunged for her, caught an ankle. "Hildy. Wait. Don't run." He scrambled upright and held her, the vise of his arms the only thing that kept her from dissolving into the river, the sky, the horror itself.

Miranda stared at them both, then at the wrapped body, or what was left of it. "I'll call," she said. "Go, bring help. I'll wait."

51

HILDY

PROCESS

"'BOUT TIME," JUNE SAID. "A whole three weeks just to decide if those were his teeth?" With newsprint-blackened hands, she settled another cereal bowl in the U-Haul moving box and waved off the laptop Hildy had turned her way. "Summarize that report, Hildy girl. If I don't get this kitchen emptied before the truck gets here, I'll lose my bet. I told Otis if I wasn't packed up on time, I'd make him a pie every week for six months straight once we get settled in Hungry Horse."

"You already cook pies every week." *Words like a normal person's,* Hildy thought. But then, the truth and catharsis of recent weeks made for an odd grout. Patched with it, Hildy felt stronger today than she had since they found the body. Today she actually felt like talking to someone besides the therapist Kurt had found for her—and Luke, of course.

Poor Luke. That day at the falls, when he first offered to help her, he sure didn't know what he was in for. After every counseling session, she talked his ears off, and was pretty sure she was just getting started.

June pressed her tongue against a smile. "It's the principle of the thing. For forty-five years I've buffaloed that man. Can't let him think I actually *like* baking now, can I?"

"You'd be ruined. You don't dare refuse our help now. Tess'll be here at two." Hildy wasn't sure she'd have the energy to help June pack up, but she'd try.

June exaggerated a sigh. "Twist my arm, darlin'. Now tell me about the report from that *fo-ren-sic* dentist. Never knew there was such a thing before all this."

"There aren't any with that specialty around here. Dr. Tuppin took a while to find Dad's old records, but once he did, that Seattle dentist he sent them to confirmed the identity. Both Dad and that corpse had wisdom teeth."

"Lotsa people have them. How—?"

"Hold on, Junie. There's more." Hildy opened her laptop and leaned toward the screen. "*And* they both had MOD amalgams on tooth number 29, PFM crowns on numbers two and three, and MO composites on fourteen and twelve. It was Dad, all right."

"As if you doubted." June's touch smudged Hildy's hand.

"I'm going to miss you two, Junie."

The woman kissed the whorl at Hildy's crown before she stroked her loose yellow hair. "Ah. Glacier Park? Those aqua rivers? You can hike for years up there. Bring that man of yours. We'll have plenty of room. Nice lodge we're lookin' after."

"I—" Hildy couldn't speak for Luke, but couldn't imagine visiting without him. Couldn't imagine anything without him these days. "We will, Junie. Promise."

"Is that report you just read me public yet?" June closed flaps on the box and ticked her nose at the table. "Toss me that tape, will ya?"

"Any minute, most likely. Once it hits the paper . . ." Hildy wagged her head. "Wish they'd leave us alone."

Have at it, Hildy had told authorities, given no choice after they recovered the body. For weeks since, detectives and law enforcement personnel had scoured the resort for evidence of Violet's guilt. But with the trail twenty years cold, they returned to the toys and dog collar and corpse, the distinctive clothesline and those fishing weights. The case file wouldn't close for who knew how long, but that didn't stop circumstantial evidence from telling the story. Investigators assembled Tess's statement about their parents' arguments, their mother's physical strength and after-dark rowing, the patterned line's match to the coil in the shop and their laundry lines outside . . . even the route Violet drove to the dock nightly.

All of it implicated Hildy's mother in the murder of Lars Nybo and explained the feasibility of his transport in that green UTV to Mom's rowboat. Once word got out, few would give Violet the benefit of presumed innocence until proven guilty in a court of law.

"At least they aren't haulin' Vi off to some cell," June said. "Not sayin' I'd want to lose my mind like that, but bein' unfit for prosecution has a way of keepin' a person outta the clink."

"She's already in prison, June. Probably's been there her whole life."

But Violet's motive for killing her dad was anybody's guess.

⛰

"So you think your mother pitched your things because they troubled or threatened her," Miranda said over dinner. Hildy and

Luke had joined her for steaks at her lake house after goodbyes to June and Otis.

"That's what my counselor believes," Hildy said. "But I'm just beginning to assimilate all that. Most days I'm too busy being horrified or so angry I could spit. Wasn't until yesterday that I felt some sadness and pity for Mom—for about ten minutes. Honestly, I'm on a roller coaster right now."

Miranda thumped her glass to the table. "How could you not be? All those years Violet lied to you? She had to be copying her dad, don't you think? The way he burned things she loved? Who knows what mind games went on in their house."

"Yeah," Hildy said. "Luke told me about him. Mom wasn't cruel like that, though. At least not to me."

"That's debatable." Miranda reached for the butter. "She did to you what he did to her. Different costume, same party. I hope you told that counselor about your abominable grandfather."

"Mirs."

"Just saying, Luke. She doesn't have to agree."

"It's okay. Really." Hildy pressed a napkin to her lips. "Yeah, Sarah knows about Ulysses. She said we'll look at my extended family's relational patterns, too. Said strongholds can be broken. I don't understand all that yet, but I will."

Miranda nodded. "She have any thoughts on *why* your mother lied to you?"

"As of this morning, yes. Says it's possible Mom connected her little girl self with me—as if she and I were the *same person* at times. Anything of mine that was out of place—or that she couldn't control—sent her back into her childhood fear and powerlessness, and she *became* a child again, hiding from Ulysses. Became *me*. By purging my belongings and creating new stories she could inhabit through me, that little girl believed she could keep herself safe—something she couldn't do in her real childhood."

Miranda was wide-eyed.

"Oh, that's not the half of it." Hildy said. "Since Mom thought we were one and the same, I had to believe her fabrications, too, which is why convincing me became so crucial to her. Sarah thinks I was a redo of her early life."

"No kidding." Luke said.

"Almost too far-fetched," Miranda said. "But that old man sure scared me. If I were Violet, la-la land might have looked pretty good."

Hildy eyed her with surprise. "Tess used that term—*la-la land*. Said Mom lived there. But *I don't!* After all those years of feeling wacked, I'm pinching myself. I'm really not losing my mind."

"I could've told you that," Luke said. "Wait a minute. I did."

Hildy swatted his knee. "Apparently, it'll take a while for me to believe it viscerally, though, and to *trust* my memory—at least as much as any of us can. Sarah said my brain physically has to rewire, to grow new neural connections from truth, instead of all those lies. She *also* said . . ." She paused, flashed Luke a smile. "My anxiety should shrink as my brain changes."

Wax spilled from a candle, pooled at its base. "She can't explain why Mom killed Dad, though. I don't get it. He was no Ulysses."

"Reality wouldn't have mattered if fear twisted her brain," Luke said. "Her demons were working overtime."

Hildy heard Otis in his words. *Them shadows, missy. Lie-makers.*

Miranda salted her potato. "My goodness, Lukie. Where'd you get *that*? You'd better hide those books of his, Hildy."

"I'm not hiding anything, ever again." Her eyes waited for Luke's above the taper's flame.

52

HILDY

CONFESSION

A TECHNICIAN CARRIED A BUCKET of feed to the first in a row of the narrow exterior raceways at the new Klallam hatchery. Six lanes away, Hildy laid a net and clipboard aside and strode toward him to watch their spring hatch of coho, new to this outdoor pen. Elwha genetics, this batch. They'd moved them outside only this morning.

At the humans' shadows, the fish writhed subsurface, and when the tech strewed feed pellets, they boiled above it, silver bodies flipping, darting. Hildy nodded approval as she caught sight of a tall man crossing from the Natural Resources building toward them. His silver hair poked from under a stocking cap. She returned her attention to the fish until the man hooked fingers in the chain link fence surrounding the pens.

"Hildy Nybo?"

When she looked up, he dropped hands into pockets and hunched against the chill.

"May I help you?" She knew him from somewhere.

"If we could talk alone for a few minutes. I won't take long."

"You here with the team?"

"No. It's a private matter."

She waved toward the building from which he'd come and glanced at her watch. "I've got a team coming in twenty minutes. My office is—"

"Your receptionist told me. Thanks."

She backtracked for her clipboard and hung the net in the hatchery building. He was waiting at the side door, clearing his throat. His eyes snagged hers, then darted to the forest behind the building. His hand worked the inside of a coat pocket.

"I know you, don't I?" She angled her head, felt her eyebrows stitch into a line above her eyes.

"You were young. I doubt you'd—"

But in a flash of recollection, she saw him as a younger man, in a hard hat and the ubiquitous jeans and boots and plaid of manual laborers thereabouts. Behind him, a giant, electricity-generating turbine.

"You crewed at the powerhouse, right? Late shift. My mom brought Tess and me one summer evening and you gave us a tour. Mr. Lampere, right?"

"You remember that. Huh. You couldn't have been more than nine."

"You told us there were a million volt amperes in a megawatt. Your job matched your name. I guess I remember 'cause I thought it was funny. And 'cause Mom said you were nice. She didn't say that a lot."

She opened her office door, aimed a hand at a chair and sat in her own. He perched uneasily, ran a hand behind his neck.

"She told you that, huh? Yeah, worked there thirty years. I liked that shift. Read a lot. Watched the stars, when the clouds cleared."

"You aren't here to discuss stars."

"No." He coughed. "I'm sorry about your dad. Sorry about a lot of things." He fished in his coat pocket and extracted a white rectangle he pressed to his palm. A card of some sort. "Should have brought this a long time ago."

She was really curious now. "Brought me what, Mr. Lam—"

"Randy, please. Though you may not care what my name is once you hear."

"Hear what?"

"I—I—" His nostrils flared with a deep inhale, and for the first time since he'd arrived, he looked directly at her. "I got clean years ago. AA meetings every morning. Working the steps every day."

"Congratulations. Difficult to do, I hear."

"Some ways, but better in others. Not running away anymore, at least."

A sense of foreboding pricked her skin.

"Step number eight. I made a list of people I hurt. A long list, but you and your sister were right close to the top. Your mom, too, of course. Damage, all around. Not all the choices were mine, but mine aplenty. For years now I've been stuck on number nine, the one about making amends. I hold no grudge if you refuse. But when I read about your dad in the paper, and that Violet . . . Well. Before I knew all that, I thought it'd be better for you if I let things be. You didn't need more hurt after all you'd been through. Hoped you and your mom would have—that you'd have some peace, make some good memories with her. Didn't want to wreck anything more with what went before."

Hildy shifted in her chair, leaned on her desk.

"But reading all that in the news?" he said. "All those lies had to mess with you girls' heads. I can't undo what I done, but going forward? Well. Knowing truth can free a person from a lot of rot. I mean you—I hope you can get free."

What was he talking about? The guy had shown her around the dam, for crying out loud. His name brought her 4-H circuit breaker to mind, not psychological damage.

"My wife Dottie and me. Can't hardly believe she kept me around. Married forty-one years now, but we couldn't have no kids. No blame, just the way it was, but when babies didn't come, she left me for sadness and I left her for your mom. Didn't plan to, but one night in August I was sitting by the lake about midnight eating my lunch, like I did during summers, looking up at Cassiopeia in that deep starry sky. The Seated Queen."

Left his wife for my mother?

"Then your mom rows up like that queen come to life. Strange, a woman out there alone so late. I called to her, got her to come in. I knew who she was from buying gas at your store sometimes, and I remembered her from school, couple years younger than me, but out there she was like an apparition, like an angel come from heaven, all that blonde hair, those little shorts and her shirt all sweaty and sticking to her. Course I knew otherwise, knew better, but it was like neither of us had other lives. Talked an hour or so that night, and the next one, and the next. Wasn't long before we was doing a whole lot more."

They *what?* In her mind Hildy fought him, but she couldn't stop listening.

"I'm not proud of what we done, but we done it," he said. "For years and years. Weather got bad, we hooked up in the powerhouse or my truck. No more long nights for me alone, out in the middle of nowhere. I honestly didn't think anybody would find out. If they did and tried to stop us? I think I'd have killed to keep her."

Killed? Did he—? Her cell phone buzzed, a hornet on her desk. "Hold on a sec." She clicked it off, eyed her clock, beeped Dave on her intercom. "I've got a new team of volunteers in the lobby. Planters. You mind showing them the nursery? My meeting's going long and I—There's no way I can handle them right now." No way she could think clearly, either. Her hands shook.

"Happy to. Everything all right?"

"No. I mean yes. Maybe. Tell you later."

Would she? Though her office was cool, she unzipped her fleece to a sweat-damp tee.

"Sorry, Randy. Go on."

"Crazy, I know. I was crazy. We was crazy. Not with love, neither. I know now that I didn't love your mother, though if you'd asked me then, I'd've said I did. She was a drug, I tell you. Hours with her killed every pain I'd ever had, until after, when what we was doing to my wife, you girls, and your dad hurt so bad I was even hungrier for her, hungrier to kill everything about that pain by being with her again."

"Kill everything? Like my dad?"

"Good Lord, no, Hildy. I'd have done myself in before I'd do anything like that. I pitied him. Hated myself for what we was doing. Didn't enter my mind that your mom would have it in her to . . ." He held his head as if it would pop. "I went to see her last week."

"My mother?"

"After I saw that write-up. She didn't know who I was."

She gawped at him, but he studied his fingernails, his head tilted with the remembering.

"When you was in California for that school trip, Violet called me crying. Said Lars found us out, went to the hills, and hadn't come home. It was broad daylight, but she insisted I come there, to your house. Distraught as she was, I went.

"I was nervous, told her he could come through the door any second. Tells you how nuts I was, how nuts we was. It was two days since he left by then, and Vi said he'd took off in a rush. Hadn't taken stuff he'd need in the backcountry. Bothered me, him knowing about us. Not knowing what he'd do. Kindest man in the world to me when we talked at the store. I felt like crap. Worse than crap."

He rubbed his head and hair stood on end. "Now I know. He was already—she'd already—She told me he was going to throw her out. Not throw you out, Hildy. Only your mom. She said she couldn't do life without you."

A grimace Hildy couldn't control. *Too much, too much.* She eyed her phone, needed Luke.

"I checked the park register, and he hadn't signed. No record of where he was going in those mountains, so I went back to your house, dialed the sheriff's phone number for Vi. Stayed until I heard her report him missing, then hightailed it outta there. Didn't see her for a month after that. Never in all that time or all those years since thought for one second that she would have—Well. Makes sense now why she didn't worry about me coming there to your house."

She fought to breathe. "How'd Dad find out about you?"

"Who knows?" He rubbed the card he held absently. "I never put two and two together, but things wasn't the same after he went missing. You'd have thought I'd have been glad we could finally be together, but it didn't work like that. His upsetness about us . . . It drove him into those dangerous mountains unprepared. *We* drove him there, or so I thought. I couldn't help but picture him in a cougar's belly or broken up in a ravine someplace, or froze to death, all 'cause I couldn't keep my pants zipped."

She wanted to look at the ceiling, the floor, a spidered corner. Anywhere but at his face. But she needed to hear this story and knew it.

"Vi and I, we tried to keep it together. Talked like we would. But the fire I had for your mom went out, just like that. I was done with the whole mess. Last time I saw her in the old way was some months after you turned sixteen. She gave me a nice Buck knife of your dad's, engraved and everything. Asked me to take it upriver next time I went. Kinda like that knife was ashes she wanted me to spread at a place he loved, only there weren't no ashes."

Or a murder weapon Mom wanted in Randy's hands, not hers. After the last few weeks, nothing would surprise her. The police had that knife now. They could decide. "Did you go?"

"Not until last year. Those first years after your mom and I split, I drank myself silly. Didn't climb those hills for a long time after I got sober, either. My wife doesn't hike. Once I came clean with her, she let me back into her heart, but her trust in me was in the tank. I didn't go many places without her. We're better now. Last year, I spent a week in those mountains, hiking the backcountry with her brother. Took that beautiful knife and stuck it in a cedar block at Hayes Cabin for somebody without the history."

Only then did he acknowledge the card he held, bent while he talked. "And then there's this." He pinched and straightened the corners before he gave it to her.

Between her fingers, the photo of herself at sixteen took a moment to register. *My driver's license.* Hildy dropped her head to her desk. Nose to the wood, she mumbled, "Tell me."

"Your dad was gone. Vi said you was crying all the time and couldn't concentrate. And you, a brand-new driver? She didn't want you behind the wheel, so she took it outta your wallet. Said you was looking all over for it, so when she gave me that knife, she asked me to hang onto it until she could trust you to be safe."

Hildy reared upright. "Until *she* could trust *me?* Trust *ME?* And she never tried to get it back from you?"

"Like I said, I never saw her again. We never talked after that, neither. Guilty as I felt, I buried the knife and your license in a bunch of junk at my powerhouse desk, locked my drawer, and forgot about them. Compartmentalized, ya know? I've read us men are good at that. Found them when I cleaned things out a couple of weeks before I retired—the day the turbines went offline."

Water under the bridge. Dredging a whole lot of sediment. She refused to cry in front of this man, though water ran his cheeks as if from the river itself.

"If I told you a hundred times a day for the rest of my life, I couldn't begin to say how sorry I am for my part in all of this. If you ever find it in your heart to forgive me, I couldn't ask for a better gift, though I sure don't expect you to, and don't blame you one bit if you hate me instead. Knowing Vi, though, and how she messed with my head, I thought maybe she messed with yours, too, and thought that hearing a different story, a true one, might help you a little bit."

She stared out the window as Randy got to his feet and pulled another paper from a jeans pocket—a scrap he dropped onto her desk. "My cell number. You think of any questions later, you call. My Dottie knows I'm here, so anytime's okay. No more secrets. No more lies."

For an hour after he left, Hildy didn't move. When she did, she texted Dave. **Going home. Thx.**

She drove dry-eyed and shocked. Halfway home, she dialed Luke. More for them to process together. But they would.

53

HILDY

VIGIL

THOUGH THE SPRING EQUINOX dawned clammy and cold, Hildy had found the sweet spot on her heater's dial that kept the cabin at a steady seventy degrees. But even with the warmth and romaine and a slice of apple clipped to bars, even with fresh cage flooring and grit, new seed and the radio for company, Butterness sat on a low perch, his tiny body buried in a puff of feathers.

She brushed her hair as she assessed him, her mouth bent with concern. "You sleep if you need to, little guy. A good day for that." There wouldn't be eight hours of daylight that day, and from the forecast, every hour would be dim. She banded her ponytail low, opened a window blind for whatever light would make it through the clouds, and covered half the cage against drafts. As she zipped her parka, she kissed at the bird, then touched his door. "Back soon, Mr. B. Please hang in there."

Oh, this meeting. Ten scientists coming from out of town for the think tank planned months ago. She didn't dare beg off.

Luke answered the first ring. "Hey."

"Can you come? I don't want him alone. He's dying, Luke." Unsteady, each syllable. She cleared her throat.

"On my way."

When she returned home two hours later, she heard Luke reading aloud, his voice a hum of comfort beside the cage where Butterness now squatted on the floor, his eyes closed, his feathery head bobbing. Luke scooted aside. As if grasping fog, Hildy reached into the cage and cupped her hand around the little canary. With care she lifted him, held him first to her throat against her heartbeat, then her chest.

Nestled in her open hand, he was quiet as she petted his black crown and wings, his goldenrod body. Her fingers were gentle as air.

Her heart heaved as she memorized her canary here, now, and she scarcely dared blink. No need, anyway. With her eyes awash, she willed herself to a stillness that matched her little bird's.

Down, up, down. Luke's fingers traced her spine, and she felt herself a new midwife, learning, and him a doula, teaching her. When he rose and brought her water, she knew what she would tell him when this was over. When Butterness flew.

Luke read again: three psalms this time. A half hour later, when Butterness went limp in her hand, Hildy wiped bleary eyes, stroked her little bird, and pictured him fluttering, landing, peeping goodbyes. *Made new.* While she held his quiet body, she imagined his loft through the ceiling into sky, with freedom falling from his wings like sparks.

Flight paths. Luke was showing her one, too—and would, he'd said, for however long it took. He'd also told her that hard as her story was, its truth would strengthen the wings she was growing.

She walked her gaze to him. Oh, she'd waited too long to tell him another thing she knew was true. She touched his jaw, angled closer, and when her "I love you so, Luke Rimmer" came out in a whisper, she felt herself soar.

54

HILDY

AVULSION

WARM AND HEAVY WITH MOISTURE, the late March front rolled off the ocean onto the Olympic Peninsula from the southwest, across the ancestral beaches of the Chinookan peoples for which this wind, and the largest of salmonids in the Elwha, was named. The Chinook gale clobbered the west side of the Olympics with inches of rain in mere hours, but held plenty in reserve as it roared across peaks, melted snow, and soaked the Elwha Valley. In response, the river—tasting new freedom from the compromised dams—surged in its banks and writhed over lake bed floodplains.

Before work, Hildy pinched her raincoat hood against the pelting blow and pushed to the bridge. Nervous, she gauged the current's attack on the pillars. Hindered by the exposed delta at the lake bed's southernmost end, the water heaped against sediment and churned.

Fingers trembling, Hildy texted Dave. **Not coming in. Wild up here.** With June and Otis long gone to Montana and Miranda's studio closed and emptied, she was the only one to see it. Also closed for good, the resort store stood silent amidst dirt piles and a gaping hole, its underground gas tanks gone for a week now. Cabins huddled empty at the water's brink, unoccupied, but for hers.

She hung up and dialed Luke.

He answered first ring. "Where are you?"

"Bridge." Her back was to the wind, her hand a shed above her phone.

"Can't hear you. I'm at the top of your hill. Be there in five. "

"I've never seen the river like this, Luke. It's *ferocious*." She jumped as a tree slammed the pilings, broke free and surged past, its root ball bobbing in the froth.

Luke's shout cut through the wind. "Can't hear you. Stay off that bridge, Hildy."

"I'm good," she shouted back, though wind pushed her toward the river now gray with rage. A branch cracked and the rope swing fell into the water. Twenty feet past her riverside deck, a flank of earth collapsed.

Oddly, she calmed as the storm grew crazier, and as the turbulent river twisted and gulped and jumped in response. Her hood caught and blew to her shoulders when power—in the air, the water, her mind—unzipped her. She flung arms wide and wanted more: of the rending, the ridding. The purge of grit and mud and shadows from her decades and the river's century of entrapment. All around her, wind and water were brooms and scalpels and bulldozers. Making things new.

Her hair and clothes dripped and her coat hung from her elbows when Luke pulled her from the unstable bank, his mouth at her ear. "C'mon, baby." He pointed uphill. "We need higher ground."

Upriver, a swath of trees fell. Hildy resisted him to watch. She felt the crashing, then saw the currents readjust, carving deeper toward the cabins.

She cast an arm toward Cabin 2. "But my—"

"No time, sweetheart. We've gotta get out of here." He grabbed her outstretched arm, towed her to his truck, and closed her inside before he flung himself into the cab, threw the gearshift into reverse, and peeled onto the 101 Highway, uphill.

In the cab's quiet, the storm's spell broke. Hildy swung her eyes from the hypnotic river to Luke. "Please stop. Pull over. I need to know for sure, to see it happen."

Luke checked the rearview, frowning, gauging their elevation, she guessed. Calculating safety before he eased the truck to the shoulder and set the brake. Hildy jumped from the rig and ran to a gap in the trees seconds before the rope swing tree collapsed into the river. Next door to hers, Cabin 3 tilted, undermined.

Hildy's mind skidded, scrambled. Everything she owned was in Cabin 2. Her Yukon was parked at its stoop. The river had both in its sights.

If the water didn't reroute, and fast, the Elwha she loved would take her aqua throw, her diaries and collections, the furniture Dad made, and her only photos of him. Why hadn't she digitized them? Everything that grounded her and helped her remember was about to disappear into that river. Her computer, her lunch, her bag and wallet still sat by her front door. None had made it to her car.

Distance and the wind's oceanic rush muted the next collapse, but when the river ate the thirty-foot section of the bank she'd climbed since childhood and toppled another cottonwood near her deck, the sight nearly dropped her. Riveted, she held her breath until the water's next rending. Within seconds, Cabin 2 wrenched and leaned.

Luke enveloped her, his chin familiar at her neck. "You don't have to watch."

"Yes, I do."

A year ago, she'd have run down there, clung to a log wall, and screamed over the groan of her listing cabin, quaking with terror and grief.

Now only a heady anticipation swelled in her, and as her cabin jerked and slouched, she couldn't look away. When the structure sloughed into the water, where it broke apart and bobbed in pieces downriver, a peace she couldn't explain came over her. As a chaotic stream of her belongings boiled in the broken cabin's wake, she mildly wondered what she would find in the storm's aftermath.

If she chose to look.

Luke gripped her. Like hers, his head was bare, his hair a mass of streaming coils. His jaw left her cheek, and she knew he was watching her. "Hildy."

"I'm okay. Really." She turned to him, twined her arms around his chest, and thought of her glossy old-school calendar dissolving offshore. "Better than okay." Riddled with joy, actually. She imagined Butterness aloft and felt herself fly with him.

She pulled Luke tighter, looked at the sky, then into those eyes of his before she caught rain on her tongue and kissed him, full and deep. Then she opened a foot of air between them and swiped drippy hair from his forehead. The wind made her shout. "Seems my schedule's wide open, Luke Rimmer."

She raised an eyebrow, laid a finger to her cheek. "Come to think of it, I don't even have a calendar anymore. So. Remember that question you asked me—that day on the stump?"

He was laughing now, his mouth at her ear. "Oh yeah. About seeing what was in store for us when the water cleared. I asked if you were game."

She kissed him again. "That's the one. I'm game, Luke. Pick any day you like, the sooner the better. I want us to be home when that calf's born."

EPILOGUE

HILDY

DIPPERS

ELWHA RIVER, SEPTEMBER 2018

As if speed-squatting to a snappy tune, the gray bird bobbed on a cobblestone half buried in sand near the Elwha's mouth. When the movement drew Hildy's eye, she sat on a cedar log and raised compact binoculars above the corduroy pack on her chest. "A dipper, Luke. There. Same color as the rocks."

Luke propped a foot beside her on the weathering driftwood and trained field glasses on the bird as it plunged into a riffle, disappeared, and resurfaced ten feet closer. A glint of silver squirmed in its beak.

"It got a fish, Daddy!" A dark-haired boy hopped on one foot as he tugged on Luke's coat. Late September shone in his ruddy cheeks. "I wanna look."

Luke palmed the child's curls, lifted the boy to the log, and held one rubber-flanged optic to the child's eye. "Hold it with both hands, Larsie. Shut your other eye. Pretend it's your telescope."

"My turn my turn my turn!" Still plump from babyhood, a sandy-haired two-year-old snagged the dangling strap.

Six-year-old Lars braced, the binoculars tight in his hands. "The bird flew away, Maxy."

The toddler wailed. "Daddy, I wanna *see*!"

Luke scooped Max under an arm and pointed at the sparkling river. "Let's find fish instead, boys. Look for the big ones I told you about."

Lars's voice rose. "Those fishes are swimming way high to the mountains, Maxy. I'll find you a huge one. Bigger than the one I catched with Daddy in the boat."

Luke snagged the binoculars as Lars took off at a run. Max squirmed to free himself, but Luke tickled the younger boy under his parka. "You want to ride?"

The child slowed his squirming. "Run wif Larsie!" But when his feet touched sand, Max pouted toward his brother and the widening gap between them. He reached for Luke. "Uppy, Daddy. I drive."

Luke laughed, swung the child to his shoulders, and turned to Hildy. "You coming?"

Sun at her back, she stayed seated. "You go ahead. She's waking up."

The boy gripped his dad's hair and kicked. Luke grinned at Hildy and grabbed the child's ankles. "I'm not trotting, buddy."

Hildy stroked the fuzz protruding from her pack and watched the pair cross the beach toward her elder son. Max kicked his dad again. Luke whinnied.

A bird's long, lilting warble rolled across the water behind her husband, her boys. Hildy scanned the shoreline willows for a second dipper and lowered the carrier to her lap, shifting her position to shade the squinting baby. Eyebrows high, her smile open-mouthed, she curled over the wiggly towhead. "Bird music, my Annie. River music. Sweet songs for my sweet baby."

The infant cranked her downy head toward the cheek Hildy stroked, and she felt her breasts firm and twinge. She unzipped her parka, raised her fleece, and winced as the baby latched. "We'll get used to this, little one. Won't be long." She held her breath against the pain until her milk let down, and the baby gulped to keep up.

Hildy cradled the nursing child and hummed, remembering her Larsie's first weeks, her worry that her breasts wouldn't feed him. How Luke had laughed and reassured her she'd have plenty. *More than plenty,* he'd said. When his prediction came true, she'd wondered if—then had come to believe—love flavored her abundant milk, first for Larsie, then Max, and now for this little bug. Full as she was, how could she not spill over?

So full that though she tracked the river's progress eagerly, she hadn't visited this estuary or hiked above the dam sites since she'd quit her job seven years earlier. She ticked through the chronology of pre-resignation events: the April day one month after she lost her cabin when Kurt married Luke and her on the shore of Lake Sutherland and Tess, Bingo, June, Otis, Dave, and Miranda lit sparklers, toasted the newlyweds, and tossed birdseed as a send-off to their monthlong honeymoon to five national parks. Oh, those seeds! She and Luke shook millet from their heaped wedding clothes the next morning and found more in the truck for weeks.

She hadn't yet resigned her job that sunny day in August, either, when she stopped on the way home from work for fresh cod at the grocery, but retched in the meat aisle and went home empty-handed.

No, not until four months after she and Luke came home from Yosemite to their farm in Sequim did her career plans shift to motherhood. It was a September day, when two weeks of nonstop vomiting and an inability to eat resulted in a diagnosis of hyperemesis gravidarum—and the first of many IV drips from a visiting nurse. She emailed her resignation to Dave that afternoon.

In the distance, the boys jumped, screamed, pointed. Luke bent, his gestures animated. He lifted Max, then Lars to see. When he released them, his shoulders shook. *Laughing again.* How she loved that laugh of his.

Lars's arms slashed the air. "Big big big ones, Mommy!" reached her ears. He wasn't seeing summer steelheads. They'd passed through already—in *droves*, she'd heard. She thrust her hand high and returned his wave. The kings were coming home now. *Chinook.* Would they reach the headwaters like the others?

Lazy swells rolled the strait, fringing the new delta with lacy white waves. *Millions of tons of sediment,* she thought. All of it freed from those lake beds to build sandbars, shelter pools, and lagoons with bends resembling, in the aerial shots she saw online, a sandy womb all its own, welcoming from the strait the fertility of salmonids and their genetics in roe and milt.

She lifted Annie and kissed her nose, patted her back for bubbles, and changed breasts, her left side gone slack. On a slick track of riverbank mud, she watched a pair of otters skid into the river, here for the clams in the gritty new beach. In the years since she'd left her work with the Tribe, even Ediz Hook, the Port Angeles spit that sheltered the city's harbor seven miles east, was regrowing its shore strait-side with more of the sand from the Elwha that had built the riprapped spit in the first place.

Healing, everywhere—in the river, in Tess, and, for years and years, in her. In their mother, too, she hoped, though only God knew. Now bedridden and unresponsive, Violet lay waiting for the rescue that Luke, Hildy, and their boys prayed every evening she would receive. The mercy for which Hildy had also asked aloud the preceding day, as her hand, cool on her mother's warm forehead, petted her cheek and hair for an hour.

Hildy dug for her phone and clicked a photo—of her man and their sons on this magnificent river, this magnificent day. When Annie finished her meal, Hildy burped her again, zipped the baby into her chest pack, and crossed the beach to see the fish.

DON'T MISS THESE OTHER CAPTIVATING NOVELS BY CHERYL GREY BOSTROM

AVAILABLE IN STORES AND ONLINE NOW

JOIN THE CONVERSATION AT crazy4fiction.com

A Note from the Author

IN 1887, MY POETRY-LOVING great-great-grandfather Charles Amzon Wood pulled shallow Midwestern roots, transported his wife and children to the Olympic Peninsula, and replanted them in the Puget Sound Co-operative Colony, a "utopian" settlement crouched on Ennis Creek at the edge of the frontier town of Port Angeles. His and Emily's children—including my great-grandmother Mary Emma—spent their childhoods a mere shout from potlatches at the Klallam's Ennis village.

From land near that creek's mouth, my forebears looked through new, cedar-framed windows toward Port Angeles harbor and another Klallam village—Tse-whit-zen—at the base of Ediz Hook, the alluvial spit guarding the harbor. Mary Emma and her siblings played on the shoreline where Klallams beached canoes, camped, and smoked salmon over driftwood fires.

Even so, the broader coexistence of cultures was an uneasy one. Intense pressure from the USA's expansion had already forced S'Klallam Tribes to sign the 1855 Treaty of Point No Point, which ceded historic tribal lands to the US government. Ensuing years had seen tribal villages around nearby Port Townsend destroyed, driving the S'Klallams who lived there to new locations. A number of them joined the Lower Elwha Klallams at their ancestral home seven miles west of Port Angeles.

Consolidated into fewer, larger settlements, tribal members strove for normalcy, pursuing traditional occupations guaranteed them when they relinquished their lands. They'd been promised the right to harvest fish and shellfish where they had always found them, as well as the freedom to hunt and gather on lands that remained unclaimed and open.

Therefore, despite the government's umbrella of ownership, the Lower Elwha Klallams continued to fish in the Strait of Juan de Fuca, gather shellfish on its shorelines, and hunt the area's ample game. In the Elwha Valley, they harvested wood and bark from enormous cedars to craft many of life's necessities, and most crucial of all, they fished the river. Though encroachments on their treaty rights persisted, it appeared likely that as long as nothing harmed the cornerstone of their survival, the Klallams would preserve their autonomy and culture. That cornerstone? The Elwha River's salmon.

Enter Thomas Aldwell, who had been secretly buying Elwha bottomlands for years. In 1910—the year my great-grandmother Mary Emma gave birth to my grandfather Sydney Tozier, Aldwell tapped backing from Chicago investors, logged a reservoir site, and began construction of the Elwha Dam.

When the government failed to stop construction, the treaty's pledge to protect the salmon on which the Tribe depended flew out the proverbial window. Built without fish ladders and only five miles from the river's mouth, the dam blocked all salmonid spawning upstream of the Elwha's hundred-foot barrier.

Outside of the Tribe, however, few paid any mind to the dam's ecological consequences. The hydroelectric benefits to the Olympic Peninsula were simply too profound to allow fish—or The People who needed them—a voice. After all, upon its completion in 1913, the Elwha Dam carried the primitive peninsula into modernity and launched an unparalleled lumber industry. Prosperity arrived for most who had toeholds in that commercial growth, and Lakes Aldwell and Mills (once the Glines Dam was finished) became hubs of wilderness recreation.

The Klallams, however, saw few of those benefits. Instead, as the reservoir waters rose, they suffered cataclysmic losses—of sacred sites, culture, livelihoods, and lives, all of which had been shaped by and depended upon the wild river and its abundant fish.

Denied passage upstream to lay their eggs, returning salmon slammed the concrete barricade, circled helplessly at its base, and if they didn't die first, competed for limited spawning beds in the short lower reach. Since most didn't spawn at all, the seven runs of Elwha salmonids, historically ranging from a combined 400,000 to a million per year, began a precipitous decline.

By 1927, the Glines Canyon Dam upstream compounded the loss of fish by trapping even more of the sediment necessary for healthy redds—salmon nests. Starved of sand and gravel that typically washed downstream, lower reach spawning beds eroded to cobble. Without fish returning to the upper reaches to spawn and replenish the habitat with their mineral-rich carcasses, the Olympic Mountains' wildlife and vegetation suffered, too.

Meanwhile, members of the Lower Elwha Klallam Tribe were banished from ancestral fishing campsites outside of the Elwha Valley as if they were squatters. Natives collided with homesteaders in traditional hunting grounds. Industrial builders buried Tse-whit-zen and other villages under tons of fill and replaced them with pulp and paper mills powered by the Elwha River's generators.

Though crushed, the Klallams persevered. Rightfully called The Strong People, they pursued their treaty rights for decades, finally presenting the beleaguered fishery to 1991-92's 102nd Congress. Their breakthrough arrived with the passage of HR 4844, and when

President George H. W. Bush signed that bill—The Elwha River Ecosystem and Fisheries Restoration Act—the Elwha's renewal was at hand.

Or so the Tribe thought.

It would be another twenty years before the dams' demolition began.

Tribal Elder Ben Charles, Sr. died a year before I began my research for *What the River Keeps*. While all other characters in the novel are fictional, Ben lived not only to see the dams come down, but to inspire others with hope, patience, and forgiveness while they waited for the river's rewilding. The Klallam's prayers, trust, and persistence have been holy notes in the river's miraculous healing—and its song.

Whether you hear the Elwha's melody in person, through the abundant online accounts of the river's recovery, or in the pages of this book, I pray you'll emerge from your listening certain that if this river's dark strongholds could fall, yours can too.

You're just about there.

Acknowledgments

I THOUGHT ABOUT FLYING A BANNER inscribed with my gratitude to each of you who helped me with this book. A huge banner, flapping behind an airborne biplane that wouldn't land for years. Your gifts of time and expertise and encouragement have meant that much to me. If any of you hadn't been part of this effort, the book would be missing limbs. A million thanks and more to every one of you.

Bill Tiderman, not only did you introduce my teenage self to Lake Aldwell and your family's fishing resort, but decades later you brought that setting to life for me with your maps and stories and answers to my dozens of questions. Though I changed the date and reason for the Elwha Resort's demise, your enthusiasm for that beautiful river is timeless, and your rich rendering of the joyful life you spent there made all the difference in this story. I'm grateful.

Tracey Cloud Hosselkus, your connections to the Lower Elwha Tribe and the Elwha powerhouse introduced me to both. I'm thankful for your guidance, our childhood friendship, and your kind dad—who worked in that powerhouse, taught us 4-H electronics, and was *nothing* like the story's Randy. Dona Cloud, thank you, too. Your love has fed me down the years and your spot-on skills as a research librarian fed this book. I immersed myself in your Elwha offerings, and I learned.

Mike McHenry, your thirty-plus years' experience on the Elwha River and with the Tribe, your devotion to and knowledge about the river's ecosystem, your feedback on the manuscript... all informed and tuned the story and its characters. Your help was bedrock. Jeff Duda—with Mike, you've swum the river and painted its beauty with years of your accumulated research and hope. Your information, manuscript comments, and ideas were a bounty. Hildy's experiences needed yours. Many thanks to you both.

Patrick Crain, facts from your phone call and the materials you sent enhanced the story. Matt Bierne and Robert Blankenship, our early chats sent me in the right direction. Des Hatchard, I wore a snorkel and counted Chinooks through your descriptions. Felt the brain freeze, too. Thanks for all your thumbprints on these pages.

Dean Reed, your firsthand experience with the mills and your synthesis of their deep histories were worth gold. Your knowledge was the missing piece in my understanding of *how* consensus to free the river arrived. Thank you again.

Jim Unruh and Ron Davidson, that studio addition took shape through your skills. George and Kathy Joyner, your warm welcome to Mamba and me, your daily hospitality, and that fabulous tour soaked my research trip with friendship and visuals that found their way into the story. Dave Em, you can't imagine how delighted I was to find *salmon* at your boxofpuns.com. Thank you all for each and every insight.

Ruth Sebring, Avery Ullman, and my amazing agent, Cynthia Ruchti, thanks to your observations, I pulled weeds, thinned rows, and added compost to my early manuscript. I sure like gardening with you. And to extend the metaphor, Cynthia, Jan Stob, and Elizabeth Jackson, you read the book world weather and manuscript condition like no others; your literary rakes and shovels and soil testing are second to none. I'm blessed beyond measure to plant with you.

Editor Sarah Rische—airdrop me into any wilderness of words and I'd want you guiding me through it. Wow, you're good. From the big picture to the smallest details, your thoughtful questions and expert eye guided me into crucial edits that transformed the story. All of you on the stellar Tyndale teams shepherded this story with prayer, excellence, and care. Working with you is pure privilege, and I'm grateful.

Laura Buys, Connie Hardy, Maggie Rowe, Janet McHenry, Dana Vail, sisters in my small groups and cohorts, Redbud Writers Guild buds, and other precious friends and readers named and unnamed here, your rivers of prayers moved mountains, and your skills, creativity, letters, and camaraderie floated me. You share in this adventure. We're family, and I love you.

Jan Soto, month in, month out, you listened to each day's work. When I shredded pages, you taped them together, told me the story worked and was worth telling. The book's here because you did. How, *how* can I thank you enough?

Lower Elwha Tribal Chairwoman Frances Charles, I expect you and your Tribe will inspire me for the rest of my life—even as your uncle Ben Charles, Sr.'s lived-out faith will propel me. Your wisdom and your decades-long patience and perseverance carry Light. I'm humbled by and grateful for your example.

My Blake—my lifeline, lifeguard, lifeboat. My love. You went above and beyond on this one. Let's go camping. I'll cook.

And Creator? Dam-breaker, Lake-drainer, Sediment-dredger? Beloved Triune Healer of rivers and hearts? Thank you for your holy dynamite. I'm swimming your way.

Discussion Questions

1. Describe your first impression of Hildy Nybo. Was your perception accurate? How did your understanding of her change over the course of the story?

2. For more than fifteen years, Hildy lives a solitary life. How does her lack of community affect her self-concept and her understanding of truth? And how does her relationship with Luke and others begin to change her?

3. How has Luke been shaped by the suffering he's endured? Speaking of Luke and Miranda, June says, "If you live through what they have and still want to see mornin'? You've been *carried*." What does it mean to be carried through pain like theirs?

4. What makes Hildy keep such a meticulous record of her days, along with collecting physical reminders? By contrast, why do you think Miranda and Luke seem to easily accept the impermanence of her pottery studio?

5. Describe the ways Hildy has continued her family's generational pattern. What decisions does she ultimately make that free her? What would have kept her trapped?

6. Hildy perceives beings that Otis refers to as "lie-makers . . . hellhounds, accusers, fearmongers." What is the lie these shadows feed in her life? How do you imagine they contribute to her anxiety and difficulty moving forward? Do you believe such beings exist outside the story's narrative?

7. Knowing Violet's history, how much do you believe she should be held responsible for her decisions? How would you counsel Hildy as she grapples with the idea of forgiveness?

8. How does Hildy's story parallel that of the Elwha River? What does the river's history reveal about the Creator that Ben Charles, Sr. talks about? In what areas of your own life do you need encouragement to persevere and to hope that "you're just about there"?

About the Author

AUTHOR CHERYL GREY BOSTROM writes surprising fiction that reflects her keen interest in nature and human behavior. Combined, her critically acclaimed novels *Sugar Birds* and *Leaning on Air* have garnered more than two dozen literary awards, as well as international bestseller and Book of the Year honors. A columnist, photographer, and avid birder, Cheryl and her veterinarian husband live in the rural Pacific Northwest that inspires the settings for her stories. Connect with her at cherylbostrom.com or cherylgreybostrom.substack.com.

CONNECT WITH CHERYL ONLINE AT

cherylbostrom.com

OR FOLLOW HER ON

f cherylgreybostrom

◉ cherylgreybostrom

X cheryl_bostrom

▬ cherylgreybostrom.substack.com

crazy4fiction.com

TYNDALE HOUSE PUBLISHERS IS CRAZY4FICTION!

Become part of the Crazy4Fiction community and find fiction that entertains and inspires. Get exclusive content, free resources, and more!

JOIN IN ON THE FUN!

- crazy4fiction.com
- Crazy4Fiction
- crazy4fiction
- tyndale_crazy4fiction
- Sign up for our newsletter

FOR GREAT DEALS ON TYNDALE PRODUCTS, GO TO TYNDALE.COM/FICTION